Praise for *The* ~~...~~

"Frantz is a wor~~...~~ ~~ordinaire~~ who makes readers care about little-known episodes of history through her characters. This is one of her best novels yet."

Library Journal

"Frantz's atmospheric writing is easy to sink into, from the grimness of the disease-riddled voyage to the ethereal Acadian landscape. Frantz's fans won't be disappointed."

Publishers Weekly

"Frantz meticulously captures the violation of being forced from one's homeland in heartbreaking historical detail and crafts remarkable characters who are refined by trials and redeemed by choices."

Booklist

"Frantz deftly weaves themes of faith and renewal throughout this tale of profound loss."

WORLD magazine

Praise for *The Rose and the Thistle*

"A masterful achievement of historical complexity and scintillating romance sure to thrill readers with its saga of love under siege."

Booklist starred review

"Frantz explores how faith and love can triumph over most obstacles. Readers who love Celtic settings will rejoice over this offering featuring bonny Scotland."

Library Journal

"Frantz carefully unpacks a complicated period of religious persecution, lending this romance depth, fascinating moral stakes, and a palpable sense of suspense."

Publishers Weekly

"It is impossible to go wrong with a Laura Frantz book. Once again, the author delivers a tale filled with history, romance, intrigue, and danger."

Interviews & Reviews

THE
INDIGO
Heiress

Books by Laura Frantz

The Frontiersman's Daughter
Courting Morrow Little
The Colonel's Lady
The Mistress of Tall Acre
A Moonbow Night
The Lacemaker
A Bound Heart
An Uncommon Woman
Tidewater Bride
A Heart Adrift
The Rose and the Thistle
The Seamstress of Acadie
The Indigo Heiress

THE BALLANTYNE LEGACY

Love's Reckoning
Love's Awakening
Love's Fortune

THE
INDIGO
Heiress

LAURA FRANTZ

Revell
a division of Baker Publishing Group
Grand Rapids, Michigan

© 2025 by Laura Frantz

Published by Revell
a division of Baker Publishing Group
Grand Rapids, Michigan
RevellBooks.com

Printed in the United States of America

Library of Congress Cataloging-in-Publication Data
Names: Frantz, Laura, author.
Title: The indigo heiress / Laura Frantz.
Description: Grand Rapids, Michigan : Revell, a division of Baker Publishing
    Group, 2025.
Identifiers: LCCN 2024015308 | ISBN 9780800740696 (paper) | ISBN 9780800746759
    (casebound) | ISBN 9781493448654 (ebook)
Subjects: LCGFT: Christian fiction. | Novels.
Classification: LCC PS3606.R4226 I53 2025 | DDC 813/.6—dc23/eng/20240404
LC record available at https://lccn.loc.gov/2024015308

Scripture quotations, whether quoted or paraphrased by the characters, are from the King James Version of the Bible.

Cover image by Katya Evdokimova / Arcangel

Published in association with Books & Such Literary Management, BooksAndSuch
.com.

Baker Publishing Group publications use paper produced from sustainable forestry practices and postconsumer waste whenever possible.

25 26 27 28 29 30 31   7 6 5 4 3 2 1

To my mother,
Irene Sylvia Blanton

PROLOGUE

Doubtless the human face is the grandest of all mysteries.

Madame de Staël

ROYAL VALE PLANTATION, VIRGINIA
FEBRUARY 1774

Amid the timeless silence of the verdigris parlor, Juliet remained seated in her Chippendale chair . . . for the third hour. Resisting a twitch, she fisted her hands in the folds of her indigo silk gown. Beneath the artist's intense scrutiny, her back ached and her stays pinched. She nearly forgot to breathe. The once vibrant rose she clutched had surrendered its fragrance, its petals captured in delicate pink strokes. The portraitist, John Singleton Copley, stared at her boldly as no man save a husband would ever do. How long did a miniature, a tiny watercolor on ivory, take?

"You've an unusual look, Miss Catesby," he'd said to her after the first hour.

Unusual? She sensed his frustration. She did not doubt her beauty eluded his brush, for she was not that. *Striking*, some called her. Loveday was the beauty of the family. *Ravissante*, their former French dancing master had called her.

However had this commission come about? For being the son of a humble New England tobacconist, Copley had done well. Somehow Father had torn him away from his wealthy New England subjects to paint this far south, which was a mystery. They themselves could hardly afford it.

"'Tis my birthday gift," Father had insisted when the young artist appeared at their door days before. "Capturing my beloved daughters in miniature is overdue." He darted a fond look at an obliging Loveday. "Consider what you wish to wear and Copley will handle the rest."

Clasping her hands together, Loveday gave a graceful twirl in Royal Vale's hall. "I shall don my raspberry silk—or perhaps my duck egg–blue brocade."

Juliet smiled, not wanting to dampen her sister's high mood. "I shall wear my indigo taffeta and Mama's sable choker, then."

Father passed into his study with a mournful, "If only your mother were still with us."

A respectful hush followed as the sisters stopped at the study door.

Sitting down at his mahogany desk, Father began rummaging through the disorder. "I also want a lock of hair from you both—you know, housed in a gilt metal case. I'll have the date engraved upon it as well."

"Of course, Father," Loveday answered. "A lovely touch."

Juliet looked at him, confused. He wasn't usually so sentimental. In fact, he often scoffed at such. And what was he searching for amid the ledgers she kept for him? He'd all but abandoned his business interests of late.

As Juliet remembered the moment now, something failed to ring true. Then Copley's baritone voice returned her to the present.

"Lift your chin a bit, Miss Catesby." He held his brush

aloft, his caterpillar brows at odds with his small, close-set eyes. "There, that's better."

Across the chamber, Loveday watched from a window seat, her miniature finished and fussed over as a great likeness. She'd proved such a charming subject that Copley had asked to paint her in oils and Father relented. Since the artist liked to capture his subjects with what held significance for them, Hobbes, Loveday's tabby cat, lay regally on her lap. The creature hadn't lasted long before tripping away to other parts of the house, just long enough for the artist to capture the gist of his striped orange fur and long whiskers.

Copley hadn't asked Juliet for a second sitting. Did he sense her restlessness? Her disdain for repose when she'd rather be on her feet? After all the fuss, would her miniature please Father? Would it look anything like her? Some miniaturists flattered. She hoped Copley wasn't one of them.

On the other hand, how could a little flattery hurt?

1

I have the business of 3 plantations to transact which requires much writing and more business and fatigue of other sorts than you can imagine, but lest you should imagine it too burthensom to a girl at my early time of life, give me leave to answer you: I assure you I think myself happy.

Eliza Lucas Pinckney

JUNE 1774

*H*er favorite color would forever be indigo.

Never mind that it made a fine tea and medicine and ink, even an insect repellant when rubbed on horse harnesses. Or that its coveted leaves became the most extraordinary blue dye. A hundred acres of indigo took a hundred skilled hands to tend it. Blue gold, some called it. This year's hoped-for harvest of the plant was all that was keeping the Catesbys afloat.

As she rode amid blooms that stretched to the horizon on all sides of her, Juliet felt small and insignificant and adrift. Hardly the *indigo heiress*, as some called her. How she loathed the misleading sobriquet when she nearly owed her soul to its success.

She alighted from the chaise, her straw hat deflecting the noon sun, and faced Emmett Nash, one of Father's overseers hired from Montserrat. He approached, hat in hand, sweat spackling his dark, lined face. He eyed her dress, a frilly concoction that bespoke an afternoon outing, not standing idly in a sweltering field. Already her hem was dirty. Her gaze met the ground as she tried to stem her rising frustration at all that needed doing. Sometimes she felt like a weathervane, turned in so many directions.

"Have you time to inspect the newest vats, Miss Catesby?"

"The vats that cost us nearly the price of last year's rice crop?" she returned matter-of-factly.

He grimaced and returned his hat to his head. "And a few hogsheads of Royal Vale's tobacco to boot."

Swallowing down an epithet no lady would utter, she traipsed after him, holding her skirts nearly to her knees to not sully them further. Her morning bath mocked her as her armpits grew damp, her tightly laced stays more sweat than linen. But with Father away in Williamsburg again, who else was to manage plantation matters and be accountable?

Certainly not Loveday.

Her younger sister was likely waiting for her, holding tight to the promise they could honor their engagement at Forrest Bend. But first, the vats.

Housed under a wide, seemingly league-long roof, they were a fortune of pumps and pendulums and tubs awaiting the indigo. Once they were filled, the reek was such that they had to be placed a half a mile or more from the main house. Though it produced a beautiful product, indigo making was a putrid business.

"We need more indentures," she told him.

"What you need, Miss Catesby, are more seasoned indigo hands, and that's hard to come by with raw indentures." He pulled his hat lower. "We could bring up the best sugar slaves from further south. Exchange them for the least productive here."

She wanted to spit—and *that* was most unladylike. Belle Isle, their Carolina plantation, had been a thorn for years, the overseers there negligent because of distance, the marshlands breeding illness, the enslaved among the most miserable. "You know how I feel about Belle Isle."

Nash gave a terse nod. "As far as expense, new vats mean less repairs."

"The vats are the last thing on my mind," she admitted. "We can only hope that the damage done by grasshoppers during the last dry season doesn't recur."

"It reduced the crop by half, aye."

And our fortunes with it. The damage done to her and her fellow indigo planters was incalculable and sank them further in debt. But a successful yield this year . . .

Stemming a sigh, she turned back toward the chaise. "I must go."

The Catesby chariot raced down an avenue of oaks whose ancient branches brought blessed shade. Juliet felt the breeze brush her heated face as she drew her arms closer to her sides to hide the stained silk beneath. Beside her, Loveday chatted as if the summer heat was of little consequence. How was it that her sister didn't even perspire? *Dew*, Loveday teasingly called it. Was it because she was so tiny, so dainty? Juliet felt like an Amazon beside her.

Loveday took out a fan and waved it about in the windless

air. "Frances promised us ice cream at Forrest Bend. You know the receipt from Hannah Glasse's cookbook Mama gave Mrs. Ravenal that she was so fond of? When she used the pewter basins? I prefer raspberry but just remembered you have a penchant for peaches."

Nay, indigo, Juliet almost teased. With the first harvest bearing down upon them, her every thought was colored blue.

"I wonder if Judith and Lucy will be there. I regret we had that falling-out last month, but I can't stay silent when they speak of you as if you're a field hand with comments about your complexion—"

"Never mind that." Juliet sent her a sideways smile. "I am too often in the fields, and though I always wear a hat, the sun sneaks through."

"You must try my honey of roses masque. I've a fresh pot of it in the stillroom just for you." Loveday inhaled deeply as if savoring the scent. "Apply two drams honey of roses and oil of tartar overnight, then rinse clean with lemon juice in the morning."

"I do love roses, though it sounds a trifle astringent."

"Please try it, for my sake. Gentlemen aren't fond of be-freckled women."

"Oh? What are gentlemen fond of?" Juliet couldn't keep the mockery from her tone. "I've often wondered."

"Fortunes, to begin. One's connections." Loveday turned pensive. "A face and figure."

"You have the latter in spades, little sister."

"You are biased, of course. I'm not the belle I wish to be. I'm too . . . small."

"Petite is the better word."

"Petite, ah," Loveday said with a smile, arguably her best feature. Dimples dawned in both cheeks, drawing attention to full lips that never seemed to frown or scowl or be less than lovely.

"You make even the shortest gentleman seem tall, always a win for these proud Virginians. And you are voluptuous as velvet, not melting into thin air, as Shakespeare says."

"I shall never melt, as I like my victuals too well."

"And your stays tightly laced." Juliet chuckled. They'd snapped a few laces of late. Rather than have a maidservant, they relied on each other to dress—with varying shades of success.

Loveday looked up from beneath the brim of her bergère hat, its lavender ribbons fluttering. "I cannot wed before you. Even Scripture says it's not custom to marry the youngest before the eldest."

"Ancient custom hardly applies. Besides, there's not an eligible man in America I give a fig for. I'm too busy helping manage Father's affairs to think of courtship."

Another swish of her fan. "I suppose I'm a hopeless romantic at heart. I wish I was more like Aunt Damarus, content to be alone."

"I wonder if women have an easier time of singleness than men." Juliet worried her bottom lip. Should she spill what she'd heard from one of their neighbors? "Speaking of courtship, Mrs. Nisbet told me there's a widow in Williamsburg that Father is enamored with."

Loveday's fan waving stopped as her mouth made a perfect O. "You jest!"

"I don't know that it's true." Juliet felt another pinch of surprise herself. "Though our neighbor isn't given to gossip nor exaggeration."

"Details, Sister, details!"

"Precious few so far. I believe this particular widow is newly arrived from England, visiting some colonial relations in Virginia."

"So that's why Father is so oft in town of late." Loveday's

expression grew speculative. "Why do you think he hasn't told us but left us to find out secondhand?"

"Too soon, perhaps. I do hope he doesn't get hurt if he presses his suit and is rebuffed."

"Oh my." Loveday made a comical face. "How unsettling to think of Father as a suitor. He's not exactly a romantic sort. 'Tis sort of odd, is it not?"

Juliet nodded, wondering how best to confirm the matter. "Quite, though he seems increasingly lonely since Mama's passing and has entirely lost interest in Royal Vale."

They left the avenue and rolled to a stop before the brick mansion that was Forrest Bend, the James River a blue glimmer behind it. Up mosquito-ridden brick steps they trod, then entered an elegant hall that promised spirited conversation, music, and the much-anticipated ice cream.

Nathaniel Ravenal greeted them as he passed through the beeswax-scented hall. This man, the longtime master of Forrest Bend, had paid Juliet more singular attention than her own father all her six and twenty years. The admission pained her, but then, life in general pained her. She seemed to be losing her grasp on its pleasures.

Her godfather's gaze was steady. Astute. "All is well at Royal Vale?"

With an unchecked sigh, Juliet watched Loveday hurry into the parlor with Ravenal's garrulous wife and daughters. "'Out of difficulties grow miracles.'"

"Jean de La Bruyère?" He pulled on leather riding gloves. "'It is boorish to live ungraciously; the giving is the hardest part; what does it cost to add a smile?'"

"You always rise to the literary occasion," she told him, trying to smile. Their years-long game of exchanging quotes held sentimental satisfaction, at least. "'Tis that great library of yours."

"Always open to you," he said, gesturing to the door opposite the suddenly noisy parlor.

Slowly, Juliet removed her gloves, wishing to retreat. Today the girlish laughter chafed.

"I sense you could use a quiet corner." Ravenal looked concerned. "Or a book to borrow."

Was her weariness so transparent? The telltale shadows beneath her eyes?

Thanking him, she moved toward the library as he left the house, his horse's hoofbeats raising thick dust as he galloped down the long drive. Juliet could never resist a solitary space or a good book, especially at Forrest Bend.

2

There is an air of metropolitan dignity in Glasgow . . . which entitles it to a much greater share of the traveler's attention than even the capital of the country.

Novelist Mary Ann Hanway, 1775

GLASGOW, SCOTLAND
JULY 1774

Within the quiet confines of his oak study, Leith Buchanan perused the letter from Virginia Colony, lingering on one telling line.

It is as necessary to consult the pedigree of men and women as it is that of mules and horses. A good breed of either must be great riches.

How these Virginians amused. Great riches, aye. The advice held a stinging truth that seemed to sum up Leith's present predicament. He had not consulted any pedigree the first time. His late wife hadn't any. As for himself, he'd spent more time on his fleet of ships than on a suitable partner, and now there was Hades to pay. He took a quill pen from the inkstand on his desk, underlined those pithy lines, and let the ink dry, then handed the letter to his younger brother.

Euan looked from him to the paper in question. "Another one of Nathaniel Ravenal's instructive letters?"

"He heard about Havilah's death and read the scandal surrounding it."

"A far cry from his usual political rants and the price of tobacco."

"Lately things have taken a more personal turn." Leith wouldn't say he'd asked Ravenal's advice about women, specifically Virginia women. His gaze trailed to the velvet pouch half hidden by a stack of ledgers. He'd perused the twin miniatures by the artist Copley more frequently than he wanted to admit.

Euan read on, the dent in his brow becoming more pronounced. "What's this about you sailing to the colonies? Is Nathaniel Ravenal inviting you to be his guest at Forrest Bend?"

"Removing myself from the blether might be wise. At least till it dies down."

"If it ever does." Euan thrust the letter back at him. "You'll just trade one headline for the next—'Tobacco King of Lanarkshire Abandons Business and Flees to America.'"

"I suppose that sums up how you feel about the matter."

"I ken you're sick of the circumstances and observing the trappings of mourning." Euan reached for the whisky decanter on Leith's desk and poured himself a dram. "But is it wise to leave Scotland and let your interests here suffer in your absence? And what of your bairns?"

"Bella and Cole have their nurse. At almost three years of age, they dinna ken if their father is afoot or on horseback. Nor do they miss their mother."

"There was precious little to miss," Euan murmured, taking a lengthy sip. "God rest her troubled soul."

The relief Leith felt at Havilah's untimely death still held the burn of shame. Her troubled soul was finally at rest, free of her misery. But not his.

"Mayhap it's better that you remain a widower," Euan continued. "Or are you swayed by all the matchmakers who seem to abound when it comes to us Buchanans? Or rather, our assets?"

"I'll not let anyone play cupid. I'll choose my own bride with far more care than the first time. It might behoove me to look outside of Scotland."

"A colonial lass?" Euan shifted in his Windsor chair. "Surely you jest. And to be blunt, what sort of American would take you on?"

Leith folded up the letter and returned it to his desk. "I suppose if she truly cared for me, it wouldn't matter what came before."

"Then I wish you well finding her. Since a Scottish lass would undoubtedly be swayed or blinded by the name Buchanan, perhaps an American one wouldna be quite so beglamoured."

"All I want is a woman I can trust. A mother to my children. I dinna ken that feelings have anything to do with it. It was feelings that got me into my prior quandary." He sat down, his back to the window overlooking the Trongate. "It would help if the future Mrs. Buchanan was wellborn, and if fortune was familiar instead of foreign and a temptation and lure."

"Wise words." Euan's gaze swung to the paneled wall. "What are those blue lumps beneath the window?"

"Indigo."

"The new crop you're investing in?"

"Nae. The new heiress."

The next morning, Mrs. Baillie—Leith's Glasgow house-keeper, a well-upholstered woman from Lanark—saw him off. With the latest issues of the *Glasgow Courant* and the *Glasgow Journal* in hand, Leith descended the mansion's broad steps that emptied into Virginia Street. The closing thud of his front door was timed with the six o'clock gun that informed Glaswegians of the mail's arrival. A smirr of rain slicked the cobbles, his Malacca cane tapping a staccato tune in the dawn hush as he set off to join other scarlet-cloaked tobacco lords on the plainstanes by King Billy's statue.

His breathing was shallow since the River Clyde's stench was most pronounced in midsummer as it struck through the heart of Glasgow, mingling with the city's own distillation of wet moss and old stone—much like Scotland's capital some fifty miles distant. Edinburgh was the bigger bully, but it didn't hold a candle to Leith's birthplace with its renowned shipbuilding and fine linens, its seventeen snaking wynds and mastery of bridges.

A knot of bewigged men in scarlet capes brightened the damp bronze of the statue like the redbirds he remembered in colonial America. They all turned toward him as he approached. He'd long since shunned his fellow merchants' greeting of a kiss on both cheeks, refusing the courtesy to men who'd rather run him through. Nor could he abide the heat of a periwig. His own long hair was caught back with black silk ribbon in a queue.

He didn't smile at them. They weren't smiling at him, just looking at him with an oily regard as if anticipating his next move. He was a chess piece, always in play, privy to the schemes and moods of his fellow tobacco lords, forever trying to outmaneuver them. It was an endless, breathless, ruthless game that some said he had a genius for.

Francis Oswald's thin lips pushed slightly upward, though his expression appeared more grimace than grin. "A meridian with you this afternoon, Buchanan, to talk credit, aye?"

"Aye," Leith said, listening to the drone of voices around him. The mood was restless, even dour, no doubt owing to the rumblings coming across the Atlantic from discontented tobacco planters. Since Scotland's bank crisis of '72, business was again flourishing, and though he was sympathetic to his fellow merchants' losses, he was unstinting in secure loans with high interest rates.

Half a minute later he'd had enough society and started a brisk walk to the bank he owned, the usual minor merchants and tradesmen of Glasgow trailing him and peppering him with respectful if oft repeated questions as he called them by name.

"The *Glasgow Lass* seems frightful tardy, sir. Might she be lost at sea?"

"Any room for glass or calico in yer next Virginia-bound vessel?"

"When d'ye ken yer new pottery works will open, sir?"

"Is today the day yer going to advertise when yer ships are due to leave for the colonies?"

"I beg a meeting with ye at your countinghouse if ye please, Mr. Buchanan."

He answered them in terse snatches, passing the worn Ionic columns of the Merchants House with its carvings and inscriptions of its 1601 founding. He took a stair to reach the guildhall, then unlocked it with a heavy key. As Dean of Guild, the highest office among merchants, he was charged with opening the large building each day.

His habit was to walk the hall's long assembly room and

pause before a portrait of his father—one of many notable merchants of the past—on one paneled wall. Another wall bore the rules of trade, but he hardly had need of them, for he'd committed them to memory. If he sailed to Virginia, he'd miss this place most, the embodiment of his goals, small failures, and larger gains. The place pulsated with ink and specie, mercantilism and ambition.

The stuff of Glaswegian fortunes.

3

Gather the rose of love whilest yet is time.
Edmund Spenser, *The Faerie Queene*

ROYAL VALE PLANTATION

As the plantation bell tolled in the distance, columns of seeds sewn and crop yields swam before Juliet's bleary eyes. She looked up from the ledger to the open study window that overlooked Royal Vale's walled garden. An Apothecary rose pressed against the window glass as if begging to be cut and brought inside, its streaked petals infused with crimson, rose, and white, its fragrance heady, as midsummer roses seemed always to be. Was it truly named for fair Rosamund, the "Rose of the World," in the twelfth century?

Loveday preferred the English rose or wild rose for her stillroom uses. She'd recently turned rose petals into sugar, which held their fragrance even after drying. At the moment she was gathering herbs, a basket on one arm, her straw hat giving her away over the bricked wall of the herb garden.

Biding her four and twenty years till she had a beau, a matter that weighed more heavily on Juliet's mind of late.

If ever a sister was meant for marriage and motherhood, it was Loveday. Yet Father rejected most of her would-be suitors out of hand.

"I wouldn't part with a pittance for the lot of them," he'd exclaimed in exasperation after the latest, a fop addicted to gambling, was sent scurrying from the house a fortnight before. "I wish I could as easily banish your dimpled smile and those beguiling hyacinth eyes of yours," he'd continued, staring at his youngest as if trying to come to terms with her appeal. "The more comely a woman, the more addlepated her suitors, it seems."

On the other hand, no man wanted to press his suit with the elder, Juliet Catesby, for which she was eternally grateful. Like Loveday had noted, she aspired to be like their Philadelphia aunt, a happy spinster of independent means at forty. But for Loveday she wanted more. And she must carefully orchestrate her sister's courtship once she found a proper suitor before the truth of their financial straits became common knowledge.

Shrugging off her cares if only for a moment, Juliet left the study and went into the garden, her daybook in hand. Taking a shell-strewn path, she bypassed the herb garden with its fragrant rosemary and mint and entered the side lawn with its myriad trees and ornamental shrubs. At one end sat a foundation for a summerhouse. Flues underneath would heat the future brick structure in winter. But alas, this year's taxes had been high, and Loveday's dream was just that—a mere foundation, hardly the summerhouse of her dreams.

Juliet opened her daybook, having indulged her sister's vision. Even staring at her recent watercolor rendering brought a rush of longing. She was so engrossed she failed to hear the gardener approach.

"G'day, Miss Catesby."

She turned toward the unmistakable voice so richly inflected. Though nearly fifty, Hamish Hunter had braved the Atlantic two years before. Highly skilled and recommended by her father's many Scottish connections, he'd lent them *The Scots Gard'ner* by John Reid upon his arrival. A botanical feast.

"Good day to you, sir," Juliet returned with a smile. "How goes your earthy undertakings?"

"As well as expected for a Hades-like July." Taking a handkerchief from his pocket, he swiped his brow, but even the heat didn't dim his grin. "Watering takes most of my time."

"What's Scotland like in midsummer?"

"Cooler. Less thirsty. When the haar sweeps in from the sea, the gardens are veiled in mist, a sonsie sight."

"Sonsie." The word rolled off her tongue rather prettily. "What beguiling words you Scots have."

Chuckling, he focused on the daybook she held out to him. He perused the watercolor with a canny eye. "Reminds me of the princely orangery at Ardraigh Hall northeast of Glasgow, with its five-acre walled garden and serpentine walkways. Even a lake brimming with black swans."

Black swans? She tried to imagine it. He'd told them of grand estates where he'd worked. Dumfries House. Audley End. Bridlee Hall. She and Loveday hung on his words like children listening to a fairy tale. But Ardraigh Hall was new to her.

She moved into the shade of a dogwood tree. "Royalty, then."

"For the king of Lanarkshire, aye—one of the tobacco lords."

The magic vanished. Tobacco lords were synonymous with the vilest epithet, not only to the Catesbys but to all Virginia. These unscrupulous, voracious men across the water were enemies of the Tidewater like the French and Indians to the frontier.

Juliet was hard-pressed to keep the scorn from her tone. "I suppose this king of Lanarkshire has a name."

"That he does." Was it her imagination, or did his words hold sharp respect? "Mr. Leith Buchanan of Glasgow."

Forgetting herself, Juliet stared at him. Not *the* Buchanan of Inglis, Turnbull, and Buchanan, the foremost tobacco lords in Glasgow? The very men responsible for the Catesbys' misfortune.

Hunter continued as if oblivious to her disquiet. "Though Buchanan is all steel and whipcord, he has a prince's penchant for gardens."

She fell silent at this tribute to the villain in her mind—an old, wrinkled Glaswegian stacking coins in his counting-house from dawn till dusk, devising myriad ways to mire the Tidewater planters in more debt, even ruination.

"'Tis said a man is judged by his acreage and gardeners. Buchanan employed two and sixty gardeners in my tenure."

Juliet all but gasped. "At one time?" Two and sixty gardeners to their three. And they could hardly afford one, yet Father insisted they pretend otherwise.

"Our bedding plant list at Ardraigh Hall was nigh on sixty thousand plants from all o'er Britain and the continent, not including shrubs and trees and the like."

"I suppose this man has more than one orangery."

"Just one near the main house, but it's massive. These wealthy Scots merchants are fond of gardens. And kirks."

"Kirks?"

"Churches."

She turned speechless and breathless all at once. Did these tobacco lords mean to atone for their sins by erecting places of worship when they themselves worshiped mammon? She bit her lip to keep from saying so.

"Granted, these lords o'er the Atlantic commission such to display their wealth and power. But one can pray that in time their hearts turn to the One who alone is worthy of worship, aye?"

With a nod, Juliet bade him farewell and took her daybook back into the house, more troubled than when she'd first gone into the garden.

4

In a word, 'tis the cleanest and beautifullest, and best built city in Britain, London excepted.

Daniel Defoe

GLASGOW

Turning east, Leith left the heart of Glasgow by taking High Street up to the Drygate, which led to the steep, serpentine Carntyne Lone road. Eclipse, his newest stallion, was a bit flighty freed from the stable. Leith spoke slow and low to calm him, using less leg to lead him, and the horse soon rewarded him with a lowered head and huffed breath.

Niall rode alongside on a more placid mount, wanting to see the twins after a fortnight's business in their Edinburgh offices. Leith's youngest brother had been especially attentive since Havilah's passing, spending far more time with the twins than Leith did. So much time that Leith's pleasure in it turned to guilt. Somehow Niall managed to attend to business, acquire more art to adorn his new estate, and make time for family with a balance that eluded the rest of them.

"Did I tell you about my latest hoped-for acquisition?"

Leith slowed his gait. "Through your agent, James Christie?"

"Aye. Walpole's collection of the Old Masters. But alas, I may lose to the empress of Russia."

Leith stanched a chuckle, and talk turned to decidedly more banal matters.

"A fair day after so much rain," Niall mused. "I'd rather go twice the distance in such weather."

A few miles' ride was enough to clear one's head and earn the approach to Ardraigh Hall's gatehouse. With its dressed stone and arched Gothic windows, the structure was smothered in so many scarlet roses they obscured the tidy white door. Passing beyond the lushness that was sultry as a lass's embrace, Leith looked uphill to where Ardraigh Hall sat, August sunlight gilding it like a gemstone. Home, nay. This country house outside the chaos and competition of Glasgow held too many dark memories to be a haven.

Here the twins occupied a nursery on the second floor. He pinned his gaze on the bank of windows that were theirs, imagining wee noses pressed to the panes. Their white-haired nurse, Mrs. Davies, had a time of it trying to corral them. Walking before they were a year old, Cole and Bella tested the mettle of anyone who had charge of them.

Leith and Niall continued up and over the decade-old elliptical bridge that straddled a watercourse, the clatter of hooves atop stone loud enough to hear at the house. Their approach from the bridge soon gave way to an avenue of lime trees curving uphill past stone outbuildings.

Two grooms appeared to take their horses to the stables, and then Leith and Niall walked the short distance to the mansion's wide steps. The front door opened before they reached it, another example that this grand house of his ran as smoothly as the eight longcase clocks that graced the entrance hall, all chiming the hour at exactly the same time. A frightful racket, Euan always said. He had but one clock in Paisley's entrance hall.

"Messrs. Buchanan, welcome home." The senior footman gave a little bow and took their tricornes as Leith's gaze swept the space, the marble interior brightened by large south-facing windows.

They climbed the oak staircase, alert to childish voices. The second-floor east wing was a series of ancillary rooms, and they passed through open doors, first the children's dining area, then another room of cupboards and closets, even a future schoolroom. The nursery bedchamber was at the very end, a calm, spacious place presided over by the nurse, who was now dozing in her antechamber chair by a coalless hearth.

Walking past her, Leith found what he was looking for. Staring back at him warily was Cole, the gimlet-eyed image of Havilah. Asleep in the narrow bed opposite him was Bella, a toy unicorn clutched in one arm, Leith's stamp so strong in her she seemed his miniature except for her riotous hair. Both children had dimples in their impossibly plump cheeks as if they subsisted on marzipan and nothing else.

When Leith stopped in the room's center, Niall kept walking, holding out his arms. A smiling Cole began a clumsy climb down from the bed. Roused, Bella abandoned her toy and soon followed as if determined to be scooped up first, their childish babble amusing.

Putting a finger to his lips, Leith gestured to the slumped, half-snoring nurse. "Nae doubt you've both worn her out."

Niall caught up the twins in thickset arms, remarking on their sun-darkened faces and loose, linen clothes smelling of fresh air and line-drying. They were to have morning and afternoon airings barring the foulest weather, Leith had insisted from birth, and be fed as much meat as bread. He'd not rear the twins like hothouse flowers.

Bella nestled closer, resting her head on Niall's shoulder, while Cole ran a wee hand over his uncle's clean-shaven jaw, reminding Leith he hadn't shaved that morn.

"Soon you'll ken the aggravation of a razor," Leith murmured to the lad.

Bella looked up at Leith with a solemn regard as if chastening him for his latest absence. Tearing his gaze from her, he sought a chair as Niall started his usual tickling. With a shriek, Cole gave a kick to Niall's shins, which he answered by turning the lad upside down as if to silence him. At the outburst, Mrs. Davies awoke and dashed into the room with the fleet feet of a much younger lass.

"Sir, I beg yer pardon for a rare nap."

Leith regarded her without reply, wondering if so aged a woman was up to the task.

"Rare?" Niall answered. "I'd hope you take one every time they do lest they wear you to a nub."

She smiled despite looking shamefaced. "I've the best job in the world, sir, naps or nae."

Righting Cole, Niall took a chair near a window while Mrs. Davies began opening the shutters to emit daylight. Enthroned upon his uncle's lap, Cole seemed to settle while Bella crossed the Axminster carpet to a wooden castle complete with knights of the Round Table and even a princess or two.

"'Tis good to see ye both," Mrs. Davies continued, looking at Leith. "Are ye here for long, sir?"

Leith took a breath and leaned back in his chair. "I leave in a fortnight on the *Thistle*."

Never one to mind his bluntness, for she was a Scotswoman through and through, she said, "Where to, sir?"

"Maryland and Virginia. I need to see to my holdings

there . . . and other business." He wouldn't mention any matrimonial leanings, though she'd been remarkably outspoken since Havilah's death about the bairns needing a mother.

Done with the shutters, she faced him, hands on hips. "When will ye return, sir?"

"By Candlemas, likely." *With a bride.*

Though he omitted the latter, he read surprise in her eyes. He'd miss the twins' autumn birthday by his lengthy absence. But surely she could sense how weary he was of the scandal. The endless speculation. Since he didn't want them to grow up without a mother, or with a mother like his, he had to do something, even something rash.

"And ye'll be here till ye sail, sir?"

"I'll attend Euan's assembly tomorrow night at Paisley, then I'll return to Glasgow ahead of the sailing."

As if in protest of her father's words, Bella dashed a wooden knight over Cole's head, eliciting his howl of rage. Facing off like wee boxers, they made their uncle laugh, two tubby, defiant bairns who knew no better.

"Easy, lad and lassie," Leith said, warning in his tone.

They looked toward him, both pouting, their eyes bright with tears. Realizing his gruffness, Leith froze. *Comfort them, mon.* But he felt shackled, unable to break free of that terrible reserve that bound him. A better parent would ken how to soothe their fractured feelings, even if he didn't.

Niall proved the blessed balm for the moment. Leith watched him, rubbed raw with regret over all their circumstances. Niall remained unwed, and Euan and his wife of five years were childless.

The perfect distraction, Niall got down on all fours and gave a great growl, sending the twins shrieking with delight into the far corner, their former fracas forgotten.

35

When Leith entered Paisley's ballroom, all conversation stopped, if only for a trice. Heads turned and a great many sideways glances were given him. In that instant he wished himself anywhere else, even aboard a reeking, reeling ship. He felt certain these guests were reliving Havilah's death over in their minds, with all the accompanying scandal. Euan's wife, Lyrica, hastened to his side, while his brother looked at him from where he stood by the marble hearth at the far end of the room.

"I was afraid you wouldn't come." Lyrica kissed him on both cheeks, hasty pecks that conveyed a warm welcome nonetheless.

"What is Hector Cochrane doing here?" he asked, his mood souring.

"I'm merely trying to keep the peace, Leith."

"And sully your drawing room in the process."

Lyrica pouted prettily behind her extended fan. "I ken what's said about him, but he is one of your fellow tobacco lords, after all."

"I've cut all business ties with him, as you well know, based on his reputation alone."

"I understand. But Euan insists we maintain some semblance of cordiality."

Leith looked across the room, where his brother conversed with the man in question. Their shared laughter grated. Sailing to the colonies would save him from seeing Cochrane, at least. "I'll soon be done with society."

"Euan says your leaving is imminent."

"Aye." He hadn't had much time to dwell on it, settling his affairs with a finality akin to sealing his coffin instead. "My latest will and testament is in order, so if I perish at sea, let your last memory be of me here at Paisley."

"Nonsense." Tucking her arm in his, she smiled up at him, the worry in her eyes undimmed. "Thankfully, the voyage is far shorter to the colonies these days on your latest ship of the line, is it not?"

"Shorter, aye, with a passenger list of indentured convicts this time, not regiments of Highlanders meant for garrison duty in North America."

She frowned. "I've never seen anyone court risk and danger as you do even on a cruise. Perhaps that's what makes you the most envied man in the ballroom."

"Envied, nae. Gossiped about, aye."

"Well, I must say I'm glad you're not wearing mourning anymore. It just drew attention to the tragedy."

He took a cup of punch from a liveried footman, turning so that his back was to the paneled wall. Many of the guests he knew, a few he didn't. When the music started, he let out a relieved breath as everyone's sly staring ended and the dancing began. He hated dancing. He was not a man given to mincing steps or delicate maneuvers.

Lyrica studied him warily. "You look bored already."

He stifled a yawn till his jaw ached. "Who said dancing is a very trifling, silly thing but one of those established follies to which people of sense are sometimes obliged to conform, and then they should be able to do it well?"

"I believe that was Lord Chesterfield." She took a sip of punch. "Promise me you won't behave as a merchant tonight. I won't have this ball turned into a business meeting."

"You ken it's all I'm thinking about—business."

"I don't doubt it, but even you need a diversion. We shall miss you when you're gone. I've not been to America nor have any wish to go. Such heat and snakes!" Lyrica gave an exaggerated shudder. "I pray you don't succumb to some fever there. There seem to be as many maladies as mosquitoes."

"I'll land in the cool season where fevers aren't as virulent and wildlife is at a minimum."

"Ha! Hurricane season is no safer." She took another sip of punch. "Remember, pride goeth before destruction and a haughty spirit before a fall."

Leith smirked. "You are too often in kirk."

"Well, you commissioned it, after all, and would do well to darken its door more than an occasional Sabbath or two."

Euan joined them as their youngest brother entered the room at the far end, impeccably attired, a small sword at his side. "I must warn you. Niall's of a mind to journey with Leith."

Alarm scored Lyrica's heavily rouged face. "Why on earth would he?"

Euan shrugged, his expression resuming its hard lines. "He's not been to the colonies yet, remember, and wants to see the rebels firsthand."

"Perhaps they're not all puny Americans, their land a petty little province, as has been printed."

Euan shrugged. "Niall is interested in tobacco culture and why Virginia's planters are abandoning it and converting to more profitable endeavors."

"Don't be fooled." Lyrica rolled her eyes. "Niall is interested in Virginia belles, not business, the latter of which you both promised to not talk about tonight."

"I promised you nothing," Leith replied. "Every man in this room has been thinking of business from the moment I walked in, though I'd wager the ladies are only thinking of Havilah."

"Let's avoid both," Euan said as if to appease his wife.

"Lyrica has worked tirelessly on this assembly, and I'll not see it go awry."

She gestured to the chandelier, pleasure softening her worry of before. "Newly arrived last week. Not as grand as Ardraigh Hall's but stunning nonetheless."

"Tell me more," Leith said, pretending interest.

"'Tis Murano glass from the Venetian islands." She eyed her recent acquisition with undisguised delight. "Not quite eighteen arms nor as many flowers as yours but still exquisite."

"We're not having a competition," Leith said.

She laughed. "But of course we are! Everything you do is competition, right down to your brotherly rivalry over your various enterprises and investments."

"Nae business, remember," he murmured.

She dealt his forearm a stinging rap with her closed fan as Niall made his way about the crowded room, bowing over lasses' hands and exchanging greetings with the men. His presence slipped like a thistle under Leith's skin. He was the only one of them who'd done a Grand Tour of the continent after graduating university, accumulating a dash and polish his elder brothers lacked. Now he'd be primarily in Glasgow at the firm when not at his newly acquired property, Lamb Hill. Clearly there was no need to seek a colonial American belle. Niall had immense charm and set the lasses here agape.

"Good evening," he said once he stood before them, flashing a smile that reminded Leith of their mother though he bore their father's features. "A fine entertainment, which leaves me wondering what Virginia hospitality is like."

"I'll tell you all about it when I return," Leith said.

"Surely you need company on so long a voyage, Brother."

"What I need is for you to open the Wester Sugar House the day I depart, then oversee the new cooperage opposite

Castle Wynd. After that you're to mediate any further fracas at the ironworks and stand in for me at the guildhall meeting of tobacco workers."

"Stand in for you?" Niall shook his head in disgust. "All I'll do is field questions as to when you'll be back."

"So be it. Euan will assist you when the need arises, as will the half-dozen new clerks installed in your office trained in copperplate hand. All I have left to say is that you'd best devote as much time to business as your other . . . um, pursuits."

Niall stood between Leith and Euan, his shorter stature well compensated by his bulk, reminding all present of his ongoing obsession with pugilism. Whenever Lyrica confronted him about boxing as brutality, Niall replied it was simply the art of self-defense and reminded her that Leith resorted to his own fists on occasion.

As dancing continued up and down the long, shimmering chamber, Leith looked on stoically. Havilah had loved to dance when she'd first come to Ardraigh Hall. He'd even hired a dancing master for her, but she was such a natural she hardly needed one. Lithe on her feet, she'd entranced more than her husband.

The vivid memory lingered. Would it always?

"The best way to forget Havilah is to look to the future and dismiss the past," Lyrica had told him from the outset of mourning. "But I don't see you marrying again. I would tread cautiously given your last choice was such a disaster, though I won't deny Ardraigh Hall is a honeypot, made to lure a lass. But so full of ghosts!"

He didn't answer, as marrying again seemed as appealing as smallpox given her blunt words. Besides, he had his heirs . . . who would be hers and Euan's if he didn't return. For all his faults, Lyrica was fond of him and understood only the direst of circumstances could have led to his leaving Glasgow.

Eyeing his sister-in-law, Leith finished his punch. How long did she expect him to stay? He needed to pack his trunks since he lacked a manservant, unlike the gentry. Many of the nobility accused tobacco lords, mere merchants, of putting on airs. Some tobacco lords were even purchasing coats of arms, but he resisted. He'd not give the true aristocracy more cause to complain.

A lively reel began and couples galloped about, some of them none too gracefully. He swept the room with one haphazard, dismissive glance, aware of sumptuous Spitalfields silks and Bond Street jewels and even a tiara or two. He didn't see textiles, he saw investments. Specie.

Besides, nary a lass present held the appeal of the miniature in his waistcoat pocket.

5

I have given up the Article of Tea, but some are not quite so tractable; however if wee can convince the good folks on your side the Water of their Error, wee may hope to see happier times.

A Virginia woman in a letter to friends
in England, 1769

ROYAL VALE PLANTATION

T've crafted a balm and sage tea that would make even Aunt Damarus proud." Smiling so widely she dimpled, Loveday held up a glass jar as if it contained the elixir of immortality. "You really do take after her, you know, though at the moment you've lost all the bloom off your face from overseeing Father's affairs."

Bloom aside, Juliet took after her mother's Quaker sister not only in looks but in leanings. Though Aunt Damarus was in faraway Philadelphia, her convictions loomed large, of late her boycott of slave-grown sugar. She even refused to take sugar in her tea.

"No more hyson for us!" Loveday exclaimed with relish.

42

"I've just discovered another alternative—fennel seed and spicewood, a powerful remedy against agues and hysteric colics."

"Of which I have neither."

"Praise be for that."

"A tax should never have been levied against us tea drinkers," Juliet said as she examined the stillroom's tidy, well-stocked shelves. The very air seemed a salve, the mingling of dried herbs and simples astonishingly fragrant. "The British keep inventing new ways to control how America conducts business, right down to our very appetites."

"You're looking quite wan." Loveday's concern suffused her animated features. "'Tis that infernal pain in your head, I suppose."

Juliet didn't deny it. Headaches had become an almost daily occurrence.

"Nothing I've concocted has helped. I'm quite at a loss." Loveday's eyes turned teary. "If you would just put aside all your ledgers and correspondence, even briefly . . ."

"You know Father depends on me and I cannot."

"Well, let's plan a liberty tea party this afternoon, just us two. Or if you'd rather, we'll serve coffee or hot chocolate. I'll ask Mahala to make your favorite little cakes with currants and muscovado sugar."

"You're trying to puff me up when you well know I literally burst my stays last week."

"Losh! You simply need new stays as yours are so worn."

"What we need are new gowns for the coming holiday season."

Loveday returned the tea to the shelf. "We'll make do in remade ones, I suppose."

Juliet hated to disappoint her. "Remember Mama's trunk in the attic? I found some saffron silk from our silkworms that would work well for you, including some exquisite lace, though I'm happy to wear my green lustring."

"Green, not your usual blue? We shall walk about looking like lemons and limes, then." Sitting down on a stool, Loveday rolled her eyes. "I had in mind something softer like rose or even orchid, similar to the silk I saw at the mantua-maker's in Williamsburg."

"Last I heard, the mantua-maker was turning all away except those who can pay in advance in currency, not tobacco credit."

"So 'tis that bad, is it?" When Juliet paused, Loveday continued in quiet tones as if not wanting Father to overhear, as he'd just returned from town. "Are our dowries at risk?"

Juliet weighed her answer to the question she'd dreaded. "Yours is still intact."

A frown marred Loveday's face. "But not yours."

"Mine went to pay taxes, but given there's no suitor in sight, I'm not concerned. All that matters to me are your prospects."

"Prospects? Spoiled planters' sons, all, shirking work and giving themselves airs. Frightfully unattractive." Loveday surveyed a tray of drying marigolds and chrysanthemums. "Give me a virile man with callused hands, not an entitled pansy whose skin is fairer than mine."

"Perhaps your prospects would be brighter in Philadelphia. We could write Aunt Damarus about a social season there."

"I daresay she's too busy boycotting tea and sugar and the like to play matchmaker to her nieces."

"*Niece.*"

"We are in this together." Loveday pinned Juliet with her sternest look. "I'll not be the only one who walks down the aisle. It's long been a dream of mine for us both to wed and have families. My children playing with yours like we did with our cousins growing up. 'Tis no secret you adore children."

"And I shall dearly love yours when the time comes."

They paused as a door banged shut. Father's whistling could be heard as he left the house and skirted the kitchen garden on his way to the dependencies.

"My, he's in a mood." Loveday looked to the door, her voice a whisper. "Have you any further word about the Williamsburg widow?"

"Only a name—Zipporah Payne."

"Ah, rather lovely. How besotted is he, do you think?"

"Enough to spend nearly every waking hour in Williamsburg and whistle afterward." Juliet rubbed her thundering brow. "As for second courtships, they are usually of short duration, especially at midlife."

"You don't think he'd elope." Loveday looked perplexed. "I'm still trying to come to terms with his being in the arms of a woman other than Mama."

Juliet tried not to think of that. "Perhaps the widow Payne is the one Providence is providing for him at this stage in life."

"Why don't we plan a trip to Williamsburg on the morrow and drive by the lady's residence, at least."

"Under what pretense?"

"Fripperies at the millinery or mantua-maker. Ink and pounce at the store. A headache powder from the apothecary."

Pondering it, Juliet left her stool and walked to the stillroom's open door. "I must first go see about the indigo."

If the stench was any indication, this season's next harvest would be unmatched. Hope took hold as Juliet dismounted from her mare and held a handkerchief to her nose. The first harvest was well underway, the indigo flowers no longer showy, their stalks cut and fermenting in the costly yet critical vats. The exquisitely hued dye was eventually bound for textile mills in Britain.

"Miss Catesby." Nash pulled off his worn, blue-stained hat. He batted at a swarm of flies before leading her on the age-old ritual of inspecting the tubs.

A frenzy of motion was on all sides of them as fifty or so hands used wooden paddles to stir and beat the fermenting liquid. A few enslaved and indentured nodded to her, but most stayed intent on their work. Pushing her handkerchief into her pocket, she took the paddle Nash held out and all but attacked a vat, bespattering her oldest riding habit. She remained intent on the blue flecks that sank to the bottom and became coveted indigo mud. Next the mud was hung to dry. Packing it into barrels and shipping it across the Atlantic was weeks away.

"Matters look promising here," she told him, surrendering the stained paddle. "I'll check on the fields next to harvest tomorrow. Keep me apprised of any developments here."

Though this year's indigo seemed a success, neither fields nor field hands ever rested, forever preparing the soil for the next cycle. They fanned out for what seemed like miles, their bent backs a familiar sight as they worked beneath a merciless sun.

Again atop her mare, Juliet moved on to her next concern. Though beautiful, the carefully tended mulberry grove sent her spirits plummeting. Silk production was not a success in Virginia. After a decade of trying, she saw that they would never equal the perfection of Italian silk, a long-held dream. The white mulberry eggs they'd procured from Valencia hadn't survived shipboard conditions, and that debt made their pockets more threadbare. Mulberries were striking trees, at least, brightening in autumn and dropping leaves like gold coins onto the sunburned ground.

As the silk overseer walked toward her in a heat shimmer, she took out her handkerchief to dab her upper lip and brow. "I've news," she told him, remembering verbatim the latest letter in Father's study. "Our trunks of silk have arrived in London but were detained at the customhouse awaiting valuers and silk inspectors. We should have more details by the next ship."

"Fit for royalty, your factor said." His heavily accented words, so confident, boosted her. "Have you any word on the silk engravings from Italy?"

"They've arrived and are being translated in Williamsburg." She eyed her mare, as impatient to move on as she. "I'm also awaiting word from the managers of the Philadelphia Silk Filature on whether large-scale silk production is viable for us."

Next she went to the rice in the lower fields nearer the James River, their least profitable venture. She listened as the overseer droned on about manuring with mud and how much more favorable the Carolina marshlands were for rice, then she returned to the house.

In need of a bath and fresh garments, Juliet felt she was melting as fast as the remaining ice in the icehouse. Surely Loveday didn't expect her for tea. A hot beverage was not what she wanted, nor was the irritated voice coming from Father's study off the foyer. She paused at the bottom of the staircase.

"Colonel Catesby." The voice stopped her cold. The tobacco overseer, Riggs. "You need know that last night around ten o' the clock, Billy, Peter, Tom, Jacob, and Armistead ran away, taking one of my guns and a bag of bullets and powder."

"The youngest tobacco hands?" Father's voice was infuriatingly calm compared to Riggs's usual vehemence. "I'm sorry to hear it."

"The accursed thieves left in a scow on your very landing."

"I'm sure you've sent minutemen after them," Father continued calmly, though this was ever a concern. Runaway advertisements were thick in Virginia's newspapers. Would he now listen to Juliet's argument about employing only indentures instead?

"Indeed I have. There's some nonsense abroad that these runaways want to join the ranks of jacks crewing for privateers like Captain Sharp and other deluded fools."

I hardly blame them. She would certainly pray their brave getaway was a complete success.

Juliet came to stand in the doorway, ending their meeting. Seeing her, Riggs looked quite aggravated before withdrawing. Would Father comment on the runaways? Limping a bit, he began to search for the brandy decanter.

"I sent it to the kitchen for cleaning," Juliet told him apologetically. "Wouldn't a glass of cold lemonade do?"

"Nay, I need something to dull the pain. The gout has come upon me again, but perhaps a smoke will do as well." He gestured to a handsome, unfamiliar box. Cigars? "A gift from Glasgow. Buchanan."

Juliet regarded it with loathing. "The tobacco lord?"

"None other." He called for Hosea to bring a light and the missing decanter. His manservant, never far, soon appeared with both.

Juliet settled into the nearest chair. "Given I no longer have to roll tobacco into cigars for you like Mama did, I suppose I should thank him."

"I hope you do." Father sat with a wince, favoring his left leg. "The head of the firm, Leith Buchanan, will soon land in Virginia, or has promised to."

Leith. She swallowed, throat parched, lemonade now the farthest thing from her mind. "So this Buchanan would hazard a journey rife with risk to come here?" Her impression of a doddering old man as gouty as Father began to crumble.

"These Scottish merchants are all about risk, understand."

Tobacco smoke purled from the cigar's burnt end, its leathery, woodsy scent heightened in the heated room. Though Juliet preferred Father smoke a pipe, she favored cigars to snuff with its inelegant sneezing, spitting, and coughing. And at the moment she felt like spitting herself, trying to come to terms with this unwelcome news.

"Surely Mr. Buchanan shan't stay here," she said.

"Nay, Nathaniel Ravenal laid first claim to him. Buchanan's been invited to Forrest Bend."

"But Mr. Ravenal no longer deals in tobacco." Juliet felt slightly betrayed. Why would a man who shunned slave labor and its products entertain a man who dealt in both?

"Ravenal has a long-standing correspondence with the Buchanans, dating to the late father and founder of their firm. And you well know his reputation for being hospitable reaches far beyond Virginia."

This she couldn't deny. "Frances, Lucy, and Judith can keep him company, then," Juliet said of Ravenal's sociable daughters, excusing herself from any responsibility.

Father's smile was thin. "You'll be in charge of planning a ball in his honor, of course, here at Royal Vale."

"A ball?" *For the man who has us so wed to debt we are near collapse?* "You know there's no funds for it, Father." *And no heart for it either.*

"Tobacco credit should do."

She nearly ground her teeth at his quiet insistence. Did he not know the humiliation of going from store to store on credit? Of clerks and factors looking askance at them because they were so in arrears? She'd gladly eat hoecake and greens the rest of her life if it would help alleviate their humbling difficulty.

"Perhaps this would be a good time to tell Mr. Buchanan we're considering abandoning tobacco in favor of wheat and investing in indentures," she said firmly. "He needs to hear that we intend to begin repaying our debts once the indigo is shipped and settled."

"Oh? We're no longer in the position to tell Buchanan what we're going to do, Daughter." He leaned back in his chair till it groaned, cigar poised between thumb and forefinger. "He tells us."

6

Life often seems like a long shipwreck, of which the debris are friendship, glory, and love; the shores of existence are strewn with them.

Madame de Staël

GLASGOW

*L*eaving Glasgow on the *Thistle* in September, Leith took a last, hard look at the city of his birth. Sharp as pointed fingers, the spires and towers of the tolbooth, the university and hospital, and the Tron Church vied for attention against the sullen sky. Today the Merchants Hall failed to boast its gilded weathervane of a ship in full sail, for haar crept in like a ghostly invader, hiding it and mirroring Leith's mood.

He lingered longest on Glasgow Bridge, branded into memory ever since that racking November night Havilah fled their Virginia Street mansion. By then she'd moved far beyond his reach in her rapid descent from reality. It wasn't long after the twins' birth. She wasn't well, her pallor stark white against the blackness all around them, the streetlamps

51

illuminating her misery. He'd gone after her at a full run, but she'd been faster. Clad only in nightclothes, her feet bare, she'd fled their cocooned, coal-warmed home in an attempt to return to her Romany roots and the lass she'd once been.

If he'd hoped to set the clock forward as his ship left the Firth of Clyde and pulled away to the northwest, clear of the sea-lanes of French privateers, he'd been mistaken. Time seemed to tick backward, miring on that fatal moment. Havilah hovered like a specter on the windswept deck, her demise unrelenting. Haunting.

"Mr. Buchanan, sir."

Leith looked up to find a cabin boy on the quarterdeck.

"The captain has invited you to dine in his cabin, sir."

Glad for the distraction, Leith went below. Beef, pork, fowl, citrus, fruits, preserves, olives, capers, wines, and beer crowded the long table. Since it was his ship and the ill-named Captain Coffin and crew were first-rate, Leith was unstinting with provisions. He weathered an hour of conversation, a far cry from his last West Indies sailing when he'd kept mostly to his cabin, Caribbean rum his company.

"My swiftest cruise is five and twenty days," Captain Coffin said, forking a bite of beef. "Glasgow to the Virginia Capes."

Leith hoped this voyage bested that. He had no love for the sea and had never conquered seasickness. This journey was simply a miserable means to an end, revealing how desperate he was, a fact he hated. That he owned an entire fleet of ships hardly assuaged him, though it did earn him the respect of the crew instead of the ill-scrappit gossip of Glasgow. These sailors within their wooden world cared little about what happened on land.

"What was that book you mentioned bringing aboard?" Coffin asked him.

"*A General History of the Pyrates* by Captain Charles Johnson." Leith managed a tight smile. "Not the best reading on a cruise, mayhap."

"Hopefully not an omen." Coffin grimaced. "Reminds me of the pirate carcass in chains at the mouth of the harbor in Port Royal, Jamaica."

"The Pirates' Republic, aye," Leith replied, setting his knife and fork aside. "I remember those bleached bones."

"What brought you there?"

"My father sent me to clerk his mercantile firm in Port Royal—rum and sugar—when I graduated university in Glasgow."

"An ambitious undertaking. And you sailed home without incident?"

"You be the judge. On my return our brig was rammed by a whale then chased by French privateers." Leith could hardly believe it in hindsight. It rivaled the book he was reading. "I doubt this cruise will be as entertaining."

"I'd rather weather a gale than a whale," the captain said with a chuckle. "Though privateers are wretched enough."

In his cabin that night, Leith resumed reading Johnson's book, a whistle of wind riffling the pages through the open doorway. Sunk in the story, he'd failed to note the weather's shift till his stomach roiled with the ship's next heave. He eyed a water bucket near the cabin door, wondering if he'd soon be retching in it instead of drinking from it. Tossing the book aside, he rummaged for the vial of peppermint oil Lyrica had insisted he bring as the ship gave another lurch.

Hurricane season. What had he been thinking?

Storm sails were aboard, though they often took hours, even a day, to raise. At the very least, Coffin would furl the sails till the wind died down. The hold was full of convicts

as well as cargo—mostly Irish linens and portable goods—
that steadied the ship lest it toss upon the waves like a cork.

But rough weather was the least of his concerns. Hemmed
in like a convict aboard his own vessel, he found little to
distract him, and now the pirates on the page didn't hold
him. The darkness was edging in again, worse than the nausea, and no tonic could relieve it. He fixed his gaze on the
hanging lantern, willing the flame to hold as if his very soul
depended on it. Images of Havilah and the bridge and her
fear at his following amassed in the cabin's shadows with
cold, stark clarity. The darkness seemed to be widening, a
pit ready for him to fall into, capable of extinguishing the
sole flickering light—

God, help me.

The plea came unbidden, as did the sudden urge to retrieve
the miniature. He gave in to the impulse and pulled it from
his waistcoat pocket. Odd how the lantern light fell across
it, pushing back a fragment of the darkness. The woman
staring back at him was no conventional beauty—not the
pale, porcelain-featured kind he found dull. This lass, if
Copley's brush hadn't lied, was as ruddy-complected as a
Scotswoman, her hair black as Newgate's knocker though
she'd likely not favor that description. And her eyes? An
unquestionable gooseberry green. Mayhap she was tart as
one too.

Yet Nathaniel Ravenal had sung her praises in a letter.
And Colonel Catesby had sent him miniatures of both his
daughters.

Something in Leith stirred to life, some feeling he couldn't
define. Could he be half in love with the indigo heiress though
he'd not yet met her?

Mayhap she'd not want to be met.

7

Had my mistress been more kind to me,
I should have thought less of liberty.

Louis Hughes

ROYAL VALE PLANTATION

With Father's courting curtailed because of gout, and her and Loveday's own foray to town delayed, Juliet sat by her father's bedside as he barked commands as if he'd not left his military service in the French and Indian War behind him. Pain always sharpened his temper. Or was he worried that his absence might mean another gentleman would press his suit with the English widow?

Studying him with sympathy, Juliet still couldn't help but tease, "Please, Colonel Catesby, one order at a time."

"Zounds!" The epithet resounded through the room like buckshot. "Dr. Blair is overdue. Where can he be? Send Loveday to the stillroom for one of her remedies while I wait."

"I've already done so, Father."

"The sheriff should be here any minute. I've instructed Hosea to tell you immediately so you can oversee the matter.

Two of the tobacco hands have been caught—I don't know which two—and will be confined till Riggs confers with me about their punishment. Till then they'll be kept in irons in the bellhouse."

Schooling her reaction, she looked toward an open window, thinking she heard a wagon as the hall clock tolled seven. Dawn promised another sweltering day, and a final indigo harvest was underway. The year's previous harvests had been fair, a great many indigo cakes ready for export, and the bounty promised from shipping solely to England was forthcoming.

"After you manage the runaways, you'll need to accompany the slaves' physic, Dr. Cartwright, to the quarters. Last visit he dosed the sickest with draughts of aqua mirabilis and ginseng tea, which failed to ease them. Pay particular attention to Mercy, who is near her time and unable to attend to her spinning house duties. Once Cartwright leaves, go to the weaving house and ask the itinerant weaver how long he will take to make the needed coverlets before the cold sets in. Also inquire as to when he expects to depart, as I must settle accounts with him first."

"Of course, Father."

"Your remaining time must be given over to the ball we're hosting. Speaking of that, where is the guest list you promised?"

"I've not yet finished it."

"Bring it up as soon as possible." His attempt to shift his ailing leg led to a red-faced yelp.

Juliet hated to discuss such things when he was unwell. But she pressed on if only to forestall finishing the guest list. "What would you have me do about the stallion you sold to Mr. Lee, who says he wants it delivered as soon as possible?"

"I'll leave that for you to decide." Leaning back against

the bank of pillows, Father closed his eyes. "All I know is this misery delays me from important matters in Williamsburg."

Like courting?

Juliet leaned over and kissed his knotted brow. Loveday hurried in just then, carrying a cup and bottle and casting her a worried glance.

Excusing herself, Juliet went downstairs and waited just inside the entry hall for the sheriff to arrive. When the wagon pulled into sight, she noted the bound runaways. Shackled, Jacob and Armistead left the wagon. It took all Juliet's will to mask her feelings over the matter. She couldn't even summon a word for the sheriff other than to tell him to follow Hosea to the bellhouse as Father instructed.

She tried to catch the fettered men's eyes, to communicate some sort of assurance or hope, but their heads were bent as they were taken away. Only a few more hours and they'd be shackled no longer.

Lord, please let it be.

When Dr. Cartwright arrived, she accompanied him on his rounds to the quarters after he saw Father. She was glad when the noon bell rang, signaling a brief respite under cloudy skies for those who labored. She'd been hearing that bell all her life, but till now she'd not thought what it might be like to live without it. After returning to the house, she sat down in Father's study and took out the unfinished guest list for the ball, gravel in her belly.

Perhaps the Scot's ship would sink.

The uncharitable thought came with swift conviction. Resting her aching head atop her arms, she asked forgiveness. If ever she wished Mama back, it was now. Dear, hospitable Mama, who had so skillfully managed plantation life that Father suffered a greater, more grievous loss.

Taking up a quill, she combed through all of Williamsburg

in her mind before mentally scouring the James River on both sides for neighbors who'd expect an invitation. *Denbeigh. Carter's Grove. Richneck. Westover. Berkely* . . . Topping the guest list was Nathaniel Ravenal and family. Wounded pride was not to be dealt with. Offenses among the Tidewater gentry were never forgotten nor forgiven.

"You need me, Miss Juliet?" Rilla, their cook, stood in the doorway, her apron spotless, her turbaned head a vivid red.

"The menu for the ball needs discussing. Please, come in and sit down." Juliet motioned to a chair near the window. "I believe we should display an elegant cold supper in the Virginia tradition with punch, wines, and chocolate—but no tea."

A slight smile. "The forbidden herb."

"I've nearly forgotten what true tea tastes like, it's been so long."

"Your father will want oysters, Miss Juliet."

"Of course. Oysters. As many as you think will suffice." She couldn't abide them personally, but they were a Tide-water staple. "I'm thinking a hundred guests unless I can whittle down the list."

Rilla nodded. "Ahead of Christmas, then."

"Mid-November. I'll settle on an exact date once I hear Mr. Buchanan has docked." Again a broken ship's mast and wild waves flashed to mind, but for all she knew he'd already set foot safely in Virginia.

"Should I bake a queen's cake?"

"Perhaps several of them, sliced thinly with some late fruit from the orchard. A nice finish after a heavy meal."

"Very well. 'Twill be a fine gathering."

Rilla returned to the kitchen as the house settled into its afternoon routines. An early supper followed in the dining room with only her and Loveday at table. Without Father the usual dinner hour was halved, the fare a simple soup, veal olives, and raspberry fool.

"You've little appetite tonight," Loveday said, taking up her spoon for dessert.

"I've much on my mind."

"I'll be glad for winter, when the pace slackens."

"I'll rest easier when our last task is accomplished tonight."

"As much as I hate to say it, I'm glad Father is abed." Loveday set down her spoon, her voice a whisper. "But I do worry about Riggs in such a high temper of late. He's to return in the morning to mete out the punishment to Armistead and Jacob." She took up her spoon again while Juliet absently watched her own dessert melt in its tall glass. "With Riggs upriver tonight, the timing is right. Ten o'clock, is it?"

Juliet nodded. "I have the necessary shoes and garments . . . and passes."

"All is in order, then." Loveday darted a look at the open door. "Rilla has packed enough victuals. I stored them in the dairy till the time comes."

Juliet looked at the clock as it chimed the half hour, twilight encroaching in lavender hues. The melancholy twist inside her was like the turning of a rusty screw.

I wish I could run away too.

The distant quarters to the west were quiet save some singing, the rows of crude wooden cabins linked by dusty lanes. The indentures fared better—the free-willers, king's passengers, and redemptioners who rivaled the enslaved in number. Their brick lodgings were sturdier and better kept per the terms of their contracts. They lived nearer the overseers by the tobacco fields, both men and women, even a few children.

There was no light save the moon, but both sisters moved along stealthily and silently, as they'd walked this path since childhood. They were intent on the bellhouse, the small structure near the fields where an old bell hung that acted as a clock to divide the day, summoning hands to work or rest. Only there was no rest, in truth. Not for those who labored, and little more for those who managed them.

Inside the bellhouse were the hated iron collars Riggs sometimes used to keep track of returned runaways, and a vicious selection of whips. Here truant slaves were kept. Juliet could hear Armistead and Jacob moving about inside, as much as their chains allowed. Father's keys made a slight noise as the lock opened, and Juliet was first to enter the space smelling of sweat, fear, and worse.

She fought her own disquiet as she faced the two captured runaways in almost total blackness, one who'd been born at Royal Vale and one who'd come from Carolina at auction a year before. After several tense, fumbling moments, the chains fell from the men's thin wrists. With the practiced motions of repetition, she and Loveday distributed osnaburg garments and sturdy shoes, then stuffed victuals in haversacks that held passes for travel.

Juliet spoke softly to the startled men, alert to any outsiders. "Stay vigilant and off the main roads. Travel only by night when you can. You'll have safe passage on Ravenal lands. Once you make it to the York River, you'll see a sloop at anchor by an old pier and a warehouse marked with the sign of a dove." She paused, wondering how much would be remembered in the duress of the moment. "Captain Vaughn and his crew are expecting you. They'll sail you to Philadelphia, where you'll join Friends at Frankford Meeting House. That's all you need know for now."

Loveday stood at the door, her back to them as she kept

watch. Juliet pressed a few coins into Jacob's and Armistead's hands, then stood by as the men reached the door and slipped beyond it into the unknown. For a breathless trice, she sagged against a wall, her thoughts and emotions in a tangle. How she hated that doing right felt so wrong. That standing by one's convictions involved such deep secrets—and ultimately deceptions.

Yet Mama had begun the work, as had the Ravenals. Even Aunt Damarus. Though years had passed since she'd discovered Mama's part in it, Juliet remembered one whispered discussion in particular.

"Mama, what do you think Father would do if he found you out?" she'd asked one day when they'd been riding, just the two of them.

"I answer to the Almighty first, your father second. All of God's creatures should be free, even the smallest." Mama fixed her gaze on a butterfly that had alighted on the pommel of her saddle. "Sometimes I suspect your father knows yet says nothing. And so I quietly continue the work."

Did he?

Father seemed oblivious, but Juliet had begun to suspect others on the plantation were not so easily duped. Yet the risk seemed greater if these slaves stayed. In the morn, Riggs would unleash his fury, whip them till they bled, even punish their kin. At least tonight these men had a chance, a tendril of hope.

Lord, we're doing what we can.

Loveday squeezed her hand as they left the building, leaving the door ajar and the lock undone. Silently they made their way back to the house, slipped in a side door, and climbed a little-used back stair, which avoided Father and his chamber altogether.

8

Have had either Bacon or Chickens every meal since I came into this Country. If I still continue in this way shall be grown over with Bristles or Feathers.

Nicholas Cresswell's journal, 1774,
upon visiting Maryland

York Town, Virginia
October 1774

Twenty-six days after leaving Glasgow, Leith stood at the ship's rail as the *Thistle* sailed into Chesapeake Bay. What had transpired in his absence? The twins he wasn't worried about, as Lyrica was the best of caretakers. His business affairs were in his brothers' hands. But his colonial concerns were another matter. Virginia's sweet-scented tobacco was known for its quality, bore his mark, and fetched an unusually high price in London and elsewhere. Given that, why were so many planters abandoning tobacco?

As the ship neared port, the shoreline's jagged contours sharpened, autumn turning the town bright as a pumpkin. Scarlet oaks flamed amid golden maples behind a wall of warehouses and storefronts. An immense windmill he recalled from years before loomed on a cliff above a creek. Up the hill from Water Street a kirk spire pierced the leaden sky, but he was most interested in slaking his thirst and regaining his land legs. York Town boasted a staggering number of taverns within walking distance. He could practically smell the ale awash from Water Street.

"I recommend the Indian Queen or the Swan Tavern on Main Street, though the Black Thistle and Prince George on the outskirts will suffice," Captain Coffin told him. "But when in Williamsburg, only the Raleigh will do. You're headed for the James River if I recall."

"In time," Leith replied, his attention on the town unfolding before his eyes. He'd spend a night or two in York Town. Business called for it. He had a few matters to settle at the customhouse with the custom agent. "I'll see Williamsburg once I get my bearings. I'll meet with my factors and clerks here first."

"Your stores extend to Maryland, aye?"

"My father's stores foremost." Leith ignored the pained memory and forced a half smile. "I simply crack the whip on occasion."

"Since you've been here before, you needn't be told that Shaw's coffeehouse and chocolate shop are the finest establishments in York Town, especially for news in the Americas and abroad."

"Duly noted," Leith replied.

But first, pleasure.

The sharp crack of billiard balls was a satisfying, familiar sound. Leith didn't miss the looks of appreciation—nae, surprise—cast his way in the crowded game room. He rather liked the anonymity of York Town. Few knew who he was, just another Scotsman like so many who landed on Virginia's shores. He'd not told anyone his name save for signing the guest registry in an undecipherable scrawl upon his arrival at the Swan Tavern. He'd even shed his cocked hat and coat down to sark, waistcoat, breeches, and boots.

Now afternoon, the taproom and dining room were overflowing. He rather liked these forthright Americans, though something told him, from the conversations rumbling around him over tankards of ale and playing cards, that these colonials weren't content with the Crown but besotted with the notion of independence.

"I've not seen ye around these parts before," a man remarked near the bar. "Yer not an Englander, are ye?"

"Nae, a Scot," Leith said. "And as such, not overfond of German tyrants who claim to be king."

"Farmer George?" another jested. "Yer in good company here. Praise be a whole ocean's between us and them."

Joining the game, Leith chalked his cue stick with its leather tip as the tavern keeper returned the port to its starting position. His opponent, a burly, pockmarked Virginian named Farr, wasted no time telling Leith he was the undisputed Tidewater champion. Starting another round, Leith eyed the men circling the room who'd begun to place bets on the match.

Candlelight reflected off ivory balls and highly polished mahogany sticks. The cloth-covered green table, crafted by a Williamsburg cabinetmaker, was so exquisitely detailed it rivaled his own at Ardraigh Hall. Leith began the match with a single stroke, sending his ball within an inch of the target.

Farr circled the table like a hawk about to land on its prey. "Well done, Sannock."

The derogatory Scots name was not lost on Leith, who

made no comment as Farr placed his ball even closer to the king. Now the leader for their round, he quickly lost his edge when Leith sent his ball backward through the port.

"Crivens, Farr!" a man yelled. "He's bested ye!"

Spitting out an epithet, Farr selected a new stick. "I intend to hazard Sannock's ball."

He took a second turn, passing his ball through the port with a smoothness that sent another murmur through the room. Leith followed, pushing his ball through the port and Farr's into the king, thus bringing it down.

Another voice rang out among cheers and jeers. "The Scot's the winner!"

With an exaggerated move likely fueled by an abundance of ale, Farr aimed his stick like a javelin. It flew over the table toward Leith, who caught it in a lightning-quick move before it struck him. He stayed stoic though his pulse ratcheted. Drunken men made poor opponents and poorer enemies.

"Ho, there!" the tavern keeper cried as Leith handed him the stick. "That's five shillings, Farr, and ye forfeit the game!"

Coming round the table, Farr roared an unintelligible reply. Leith stood his ground, ducking too late as the man's ham hock of a fist found his eye. A searing pain momentarily blinded him before he lunged at Farr in a bid to knock him down. Farr grabbed another stick and swung it at Leith, whose raised arm broke the game piece in two before he sent Farr to the plank floor.

"Gentlemen, I beg ye!" The tavern keeper's voice was nearly lost in the fracas as Leith returned to where he'd been standing, the table between him and Farr.

A sudden, strained hush held the room still. Pulling himself to his feet, Farr fumbled inside his waistcoat. The flash of candlelight on metal was all the warning Leith needed. He reached for an ivory ball, reared back, and let it fly, hitting Farr between the eyes so soundly the thwack resounded around the room. Farr keeled over onto the floor, and Leith looked at the silver-mounted pistol atop the planks.

He kicked the weapon into a corner before handing the sweating tavern keeper a small sack of gold coins. "For any losses, ye ken."

Leith left the game room, the weight of his own pistol in a side pocket reassuring. But somewhere in the melee he'd lost a silver cuff link engraved with his initials.

Wheest.

These colonials needed a warmer welcome for their guests.

9

A variety of imployment gives my thoughts a relief from melloncholy subjects, tho' 'tis but a temporary one.

Eliza Lucas Pinckney

*J*uliet sat at her father's desk, having arranged the letter books and ledgers into manageable stacks, making a note that new ones were needed. At least the dog days of August and the lingering burn of September were now a memory. Today the house was even cool, the shutters open.

Inking her quill, she recorded the latest field work and other happenings.

27 October, Thursday

Began this day to sow wheat and another trial of French Indigo. Sowed ninety-six hills from seed in rich pastureland, three to four seeds per hill. Finished breaking up the tobacco ground with the plows. The smallest tobacco house was robbed. Advertisements have been

*posted offering rewards. A severe distemper has befallen
the livestock.*

As far as tobacco was concerned, theirs had sailed for Scotland, where it would be inspected from November through
the following August. Sometimes Royal Vale wouldn't learn
the profits from a particular crop for two years or better. Another reason to follow Nathaniel Ravenal's lead and switch
to farming grains instead. Corn and wheat depleted the soil
far less and, she firmly believed, were Virginia's future.

She refilled an inkpot and began hunting for the letter from their London factor that begged addressing. Her
reply to Aunt Damarus's latest post needed finishing too.
Father had invited Mama's sister to visit, but Juliet felt
certain her bluestocking relation would never venture
south. Still, letters flowed between her and her aunt like
the James River, thus Father failed to suspect the underly-
ing connection.

He'd said little when he learned the last returned runaways were again gone, despite Riggs's uproar. Did Father
not realize the pattern? Every few weeks, slaves went missing.
Trouble between slaves and overseers, or sales or auctions to
split a family or separate children from parents, were things
neither she nor Loveday could abide. They were willing to
risk exposure to keep that from happening. But what would
being found out entail?

It had all begun when Father had taken her south to the
Caribbean island of Nevis when she was sixteen. They'd
spent a year at Vasanti Hall, leaving Mama and Loveday
at Royal Vale. She'd learned much about agriculture there,
though Father had been flummoxed by her fascination with
farming instead of the fawning men from prominent families
who sought her company.

Her memories of the West Indies were raw and had little to do with romanticized trade winds, parrots, and bottomless blue waters. She'd never been able to conscience brutality toward animals, much less human beings. Yet the trade with all its complexities and tragedies and injustices continued.

As the plantation bell sounded to end the day's labor, she finished rifling through Father's letters. There, hidden beneath all the others, was a distinctive post, its broken scarlet seal of a ship bearing an ornate *B*. Was that for Buchanan? Would she always feel that breathless sinking in the pit of her at the thought of him?

When she opened it, a bond fell out. In a few terse words the matter was laid bare. Buchanan had obtained security on Royal Vale because they were so deeply in debt. The bond enabled them to pay interest on the amount owed. Common enough among indebted planters, it was nevertheless a stinging blow. All the air left her lungs, and she released the bond as if it burned her fingertips.

Dear Lord in heaven, can we not cancel the debt?

Numbers danced in her head, impossibly high, which no amount of tobacco—or indigo—could possibly repay for years on end. How had it come to this? Because the tobacco lords grew rich by making the planters poor.

To add insult to injury, word came just yesterday that Leith Buchanan had arrived in Virginia. His ship had not sunk.

Abandoning the desk, Juliet went out a side door, taking great gulps of air to offset the tightness in her chest. Clouds skittered overhead, thunder-dark, the wind bending the autumn-burnt foliage low. She smelled rain and saw lightning flash but didn't heed them as she walked about the walled garden, uncaring if the heavens burst above her. Only an unexpected summons to Father's chamber curtailed her pacing.

She always froze at his call. Would this be the hour he discovered her and Loveday? When their part in their mother's and aunt's mission became known? Granted, they didn't act alone. Ravenal was in the thick of it, as were others nearby who decried owning another human being.

She trod the staircase slowly, dread in her steps. No sooner had she darkened Father's doorway than her unease went another direction.

"Juliet, you'll have to represent me in Williamsburg at the annual tobacco meeting," Father announced from the edge of his bed, his attempt to take a few steps a failure. "I can't possibly arrive at a meeting with all the merchants and planters in such a condition."

"Of course," Juliet reassured him, helping him back into bed while Hosea put away the accursed cane, as Father called it.

"Which means you must leave posthaste, as the price setting is about to begin." Father grimaced as she arranged the pillows behind him.

"You know they don't want a woman present," she said. Though some planters, especially neighbors on the Upper James, were more obliging than others.

"Only because you have a better head for business than they do. Besides, they dare not deny or naysay you as my daughter. I must have a voice."

"Alas, I have far more on my mind than the annual meeting." She sat down on the bed steps, noting the discarded handbill on the floor. *Continuation of the Letters on the Pernicious Effects of Tea.* Below the article were a number of alternative teas to drink instead while the British boycott lasted. Would the controversy never end?

"What more can be on your mind, pray tell?" Father looked at her, his bald head covered by a silk negligé cap. When she hesitated, he added, "Ah, the ball, of course."

Across the room Hosea began powdering a new wig. For courting? Or their upcoming entertainment?

Juliet tried to muster some enthusiasm. "Now that you've approved the guest list and invitations have been sent, I've received confirmation from a French horn, harpsichordist, and two violinists for our gathering in a fortnight. Country dances are the order of entertainment."

"Why is no one smiling?" Father looked from her to Loveday, who'd entered the room with another tonic. "Need I remind you this fête isn't a funeral but a festivity?"

Loveday eyed his swollen leg. "I worry you won't be on your feet by then."

"I shall, even if I have to use a cane to do it. You're proving a better physician than the errant, harried Dr. Blair, at any rate. I hope you've struck him from the guest list."

"Unkind of you," Loveday chided gently. "He can't help it if he's been overly busy. A little entertainment might cheer him."

"I'll certainly be cheered meeting your lady love," Juliet said, thankful Father had finally confessed he was courting. "We're very excited to meet her since we know so little about her."

"What do you wish to learn that can't wait?"

"Well . . ." Juliet glanced at Loveday as she handed Father a glass of murky contents. "Her disposition, perhaps. Is she garrulous or quiet? Fair or dark? Plump or slight?"

He drank the tonic down, then leaned back against the pillow-flanked headboard. "She is a woman of many merits, second to your mother."

Juliet was glad to hear it yet sorry, too, the widow must henceforth live in Charlotte Catesby's shadow.

"Alas, my love life is none of your concern, though I am very concerned about yours." He skewered both Juliet and

Loveday with a look. "I have high hopes that this ball will bring about a change in your matrimonial fate as well as fête Buchanan."

"I don't suppose Mr. Buchanan's wife has come to Virginia with him?" Loveday asked.

Wife? Juliet hadn't thought of that in her estimation of him as a doddering old coot.

"Let the ball answer." For a trice Father's expression seemed more pleased than pained. "Ravenal has sent word Buchanan is to arrive at Forrest Bend by sennight's end."

10

There is nothing like tobacco. It's the passion of the virtuous man and whoever lives without tobacco isn't worthy of living.

Molière

*L*eith steered clear of the Raleigh's public rooms and went straight up the stairs, the black patch over his bloodshot, battered eye the only visible reminder of his bruising from the York Town fight. At least his nose wasn't broken. He'd wait here in Williamsburg till his injuries healed before venturing up the James River. But he had another, better reason to tarry.

The date for deciding tobacco prices was at hand, and he, by some stroke of fortune, had arrived one day ahead of the annual autumn meeting. The tavern was overfull, so he'd gotten the last available room, and a private one at that. Surprising what a little coin instead of tobacco credit could win.

His quarters were small, equivalent to the cabin aboard ship, but he wouldn't share a bed with snoring, unwashed strangers, at least. He'd asked for supper to be brought to his room—and an abundance of ale. It was the best remedy he knew for his aching body and would help him bide his time till the meeting on the morrow.

Juliet stepped from the Royal Vale landing into the bateau, the mist hovering over the James River like a veil. Sunlight skewered the cool dampness and added a fiery glint to the oaks and maples clinging to shore. The autumn dawn promised a fine day.

Their Jamaican waterman greeted her, pole in hand. She returned the greeting, sitting down at the boat's center, Lilith behind her. Father had insisted Lilith, Rilla's daughter and a housemaid, accompany her for propriety's sake. Juliet missed Loveday's company, but her sister remained home as Father was still abed.

Gathering her wits, Juliet pondered the long day ahead as the bateau reached midriver, safest from snags and shallows. Other water traffic floated both upriver and down, most burdened with cargo bound for Richmond and other landings. Plantations peeked from behind tree-lined banks anchored with newly erected tobacco warehouses and bateau sheds built since the great storm two years before. How that calamity had sunk them further, wiping out thousands of hogsheads of tobacco and seedlings in the fields and deepening the abyss of credit they'd fallen into.

Facing forward, she tried to distract herself with a bit of verse by Andrew Marvell, borrowed from the Ravenals' library. *Now therefore, while the youthful hue sits on thy skin like morning dew . . . let us roll all our strength and all our sweetness up into one ball, and tear our pleasures with rough strife through the iron gates of life.* She'd memorized the poem in its entirety save a few last lines.

Reaching up a hand, she slanted her hat forward against the rising sun, glad her unpowdered hair was pinned in a cascade of waves and curls at the back, not in the high poufs seen everywhere at present. Just like Mama's with its gloss and blackness, Loveday had said as she wielded the curling tongs. Juliet couldn't quite recall. Charlotte Catesby's presence, the way she'd moved across a room, and the gentle cadence of her voice were becoming increasingly hazy.

Juliet shut her eyes against the river's glare, the watery ride gliding by. A chariot would be bumped nearly to pieces on the rocky, rutted road to Williamsburg.

Once they reached the Lower James, a coach would be waiting to take them the rest of the way to Williamsburg. If only they still had their England Street townhouse. Though small, it was charming and comfortable and had been part of her mother's dowry years before. Thankfully, Mama had not seen it sold to settle a debt.

Instead Juliet would lodge at Christiana Campbell's, the town's finest, at least for ladies. Let the gentlemen frequent the Raleigh Tavern. She'd only set foot there for the meeting, though she did look forward to visiting the millinery farther down Duke of Gloucester Street and bringing Loveday a bit of lace or ribbon or some inexpensive trinket.

Juliet and Lilith reached the capital before noon and went to their lodgings, then made their way down the cobbled street on foot. Steeling herself against the Raleigh's smoke and spirits, Juliet stepped onto the tavern's wide front porch as Lilith left her side to wait on a bench around back near the kitchen house. Dread pooled in Juliet's middle as she entered, seeking the spot reserved for the meeting, a thick, ink-stained daybook clutched to her bodice. Several frock-coated gentlemen standing by the Apollo Room door greeted her and stepped aside, cocked hats doffed.

"Good day, Miss Catesby."

"Standing in for your father today, I presume?"

"How is the Upper James of late?"

The large chamber's new Prussian-blue paint was admirable, but her nerves were too taut to linger on it long. Planters and factors and agents stood cheek by jowl. A quick head count numbered nearly a hundred.

The Scottish merchants, those few tobacco lords who'd braved the Atlantic on various vessels to attend this autumnal meeting, stood in a line along the wainscoted back wall. Half a dozen in number, they were easily distinguished by their garments. Scarlet cloaks marked them, as did their ebony canes and silver wigs and cocked hats. These Scots looked proud. Entitled and imperious. Ruthless to a man.

Was Buchanan here?

A flicker of resentment kindled as Juliet moved to an open, fly-spackled window, her back to the chamber. Digging deep in her pocket, she found a vial of Loveday's. Bending her head discreetly, she breathed in the distillation of lavender, sage, marjoram, and mint. Suddenly her sister seemed close and the tightness around her temples eased, though her hand clutching the daybook stayed damp.

These meetings were notoriously long—and long-winded. Men loved dickering over the price of their premier crop, besting each other and calling out flaws and flummoxes. Today, freight expenses and custom duties ruled the day, voices already raised in varying degrees of aggravation. When a door clicked closed and the moderator made his way through the throng, Juliet let out a sigh of relief.

Leith rather enjoyed observing these garrulous Virginians. Their American accents varied, some with a detectable British influence, others indicating they were Virginia born and bred. Most were masters of backslapping and ale sipping, false bravado and coarse jesting. He kept quiet, a habit of his that gained far more than any jaw flapping. Tall as he was, he kept to the back of the room, where he had a wide view of the proceedings despite his eye patch.

What he hadn't expected was a woman amid so many men.

She stood by a window, her head bent, paging intently through a daybook. He couldn't see her features or tell if she was young or old. His gaze hung on her shawl with its blue ground and embroidered white flowers. The same blossoms adorned her wide-brimmed straw hat.

The indigo plant?

As he thought it, she shut her daybook and looked up and around, turning slightly forward so he could see her clearly beneath the brim of her hat. Dark hair crept past a lace cap that framed her pale oval face made up of pleasing if not perfect features. Young. Genteel. She stood out like a wildflower among weeds. Her gaze swept the room before she began talking with the elderly gentleman beside her.

Even at a distance she wore that tight, fatigued look he'd seen on his clerks who'd kept too long at their books. It was broken only by a flash of vitality now and then when she smiled or made conversation. Something oddly familiar about her tugged at him . . .

"Gentlemen—and one dear lady," the moderator began, with a sidelong look at her as chuckling rolled through the room. "As has been said, 'Life is a smoke! If this be true, tobacco will thy life renew; then fear not death, nor killing care whilst we have best Virginia here.'" Clearing his throat, he grew more serious. "We are gathered today to set our annual market price for tobacco this twenty-ninth day of October, the year of our Lord 1774 . . ."

Leith had never been here to witness price setting, though his father had on occasion. When they were absent, their factors stood in for them. On either side of him were three of his own agents—McCann, Innes, and Hendry—who managed his Virginia stores.

Planters began calling out numbers, much like an auction, to furious ayes and nays from both Virginians and Scots. It was one of the Glaswegian merchants' chief complaints that these planters established their own terms, though for tobacco growers, how could it be otherwise?

"Since those of us on the Upper James naval district surpass all others in terms of tobacco exports, we should have the first—or the most—say," one planter cried out amid the melee. "All here know our sweet-scented leaf is far preferred to the bitter Orinoco—"

"Only in France," another man countered. "The Danes and Northern Europe prefer the stronger, bright-leaf variety."

"That is neither here nor there. Let us return to the matter at hand." The moderator gestured to an assistant, who held a stack of what Leith guessed were accounts. "I shall call each planter by name, who'll then tell me by number their outbound cargoes for the Clyde and Glasgow—"

"We shall be here for a fortnight, then," another Virginian protested. "Surely there's a better way to agree upon a price without splitting hairs."

Frowning, the moderator consulted a ledger. "For this last season, a total of thirty-one thousand, ninety-six hogsheads of tobacco were landed there by a total of thirty-two firms in Scotland."

Another man's voice overrode the moderator's. "Yet our

debt to these merchants has only increased, dependent as we are on their stores here and the goods we require. Their markup along the Chesapeake is extreme and their profit exorbitant. I cower at the costs."

"Which must come to an end!" someone else all but shouted.

An aggrieved rumble swept the room even as several ayes crested above it from other Scots present. These colonists had a great many grievances that had to do with trade. The presence of the tobacco merchants simply put them in the midst of the storm.

As if to highlight the chasm, the planters faced the Scots, drawing a dividing line of sorts in the chamber. Would Leith's fellow merchants and their factors, few as they were, take a verbal pummeling and not speak?

"Well over a million pounds' sterling is owed by American planters— Virginians foremost—at the close of this season," one Glaswegian merchant said, his gaze fixed on the knot of York River planters complaining the loudest.

A stone-faced gentleman cleared his throat. "Fueling our debts are a number of unreasonable, arbitrary charges imposed by you tobacco lords that have somehow become law over time."

"Name them," Leith replied.

A bewigged, stout man removed his cocked hat, a puff of powder dusting his caped shoulders. "Among these aforementioned petty marketing charges are British duties, Virginia export duties, freight, primage, cooperage, porterage, brokerage, postage of letters, and the merchants' rising commissions, to list a few."

"Much of the duty is recovered on reexportation to European markets," Leith said matter-of-factly. To be less civil would earn him no allies in this simmering room.

"But in those markets, other heavy charges are again imposed."

"Yet you remain able to set tobacco's market price year after year," Leith countered.

"Mayhap you can speak to the market surplus that needs addressing too," another planter said.

An hour passed, then two. Leith consulted his watch. Half past four. Would these Virginians not come to the point? As he snapped his watch shut, a silken voice broke through the blether.

"We Virginians have set the annual price and tried our luck in all the principal tobacco markets for over a century, only to see Glasgow destroy London's supremacy in the trade. Shipments sent to Glasgow in 1773 were triple those sent to any other port." The young woman seemed to look straight at him. "Half the tobacco from the Upper James sailed under the Spiers and Buchanan mark. A handful of British merchants have complete control of the bulk of our tobacco exports, which is no longer tenable. I say we end Glasgow's monopoly and their ruthless policies, so different than traditional English trade."

Indignation turned to outright jubilation as her words fell away. Clapping reached a crescendo before she continued, her attention on the tobacco lords. Leith listened to her steady American cadence with only a hint of the mother country, a sort of linguistic independence.

"You Scots merchants have arrived at a remarkable time. No doubt you've heard our recent answer to your—rather, Parliament's—Intolerable Acts."

"Your Articles of Association," Leith replied.

She nodded, her thoughtful, calm words reaching across the room. "These articles propose a boycott on imports and exports from Britain, a ban on the slave trade, an improvement of American agriculture, and produce for colonists at reasonable prices."

"So you would cut us out," Spiers's factor said, steel in his tone. "Ship solely to continental markets."

"Such smacks of treason," another Scots merchant said. "An irreversible break with Britain."

"Perhaps, but the truth remains." Her voice stayed steadfast. "No civilized people on earth have been so badly paid for their labor as the planters of Virginia. You merchants have done more mischief to the tobacco trade by your outright corruption than anything in recent history. Treason or no, an accounting of some sort is long overdue."

Sweat broke across Leith's brow as the warm chamber erupted with huzzahs.

At last the moderator's aggressive pounding of his gavel quieted the room. "Let us return to the purpose of our meeting, one and all. Price setting for this season, I beg you."

11

Liberty, when it begins to take root, is a plant of rapid growth.

George Washington

Once a contentious price was set and the meeting adjourned, Leith accompanied his factors and clerks into the Raleigh's dining room, where they commandeered a large table. These men, all Scots, some of them kin who'd consented to live abroad and manage the colonial stores his father established, deserved a memorable supper at least. The bountiful menu was odd if impressive. Cheshire pork pie he knew, filled with tenderloin, autumn's apples, and Indies spices. But carrot puffs? Corn cakes? Salmagundi?

"A salat with vegetables and meat," McCann explained of the latter. "Quite tasty, though I prefer the onion pie."

"A trencher of chicken hash for me," Innes said as ale was set down in towering tankards.

But Leith hardly heard them. Positioned by a window, he had a view of the Raleigh's front porch, where a certain young woman stood on the top step, talking with several gentlemen young and old. They seemed rapt as she spoke, much as he'd been in the Apollo Room half an hour before.

"So," he began, taking his eyes off her, "tell me the name of the liberty-loving lass with the indigo shawl."

Grins commenced in the wake of chuckling on all sides of him. Hendry finally said, "Miss Catesby, you mean?"

Catesby. Leith felt a punch to his gut that rivaled the one to his still-sore eye. "Does she have a forename?"

"Indeed she does," Innes answered. "Miss *Juliet* Catesby."

Leith took a sip of ale, feigning a calm he didn't feel. "Daughter to Colonel Landon Catesby of Royal Vale."

"One of them. There's an even comelier Catesby, if you can believe that." Hendry couldn't stop grinning. "Younger. Quieter too."

This brought outright laughter from all but Leith. "So the eldest is a bit of a firebrand."

"Miss Juliet's generally polite but a bit of a firebrand when it suits her, aye," McCann explained, respect in his tone. "She has strong views, most of them having to do with tobacco and us factors and you merchant lords and the like."

Amid their continued amusement, Leith looked again toward the porch as Miss Catesby left it and headed east down the congested street. She drew her tasseled silk shawl about her shoulders, passing her daybook to the maid beside her. In seconds she'd disappeared from view if not from memory.

"She lodges at the widow Campbell's when she's in town and dines at the club there, a private room reserved for the best guests away from the gaming tables." Innes drew a sleeve across his upper lip, removing the ale's froth. "A bit more refined for genteel lasses."

"You ken an uncommon amount about her," Leith told him.

Flushing, Innes took another sip. "She comes to the Upper and Lower James stores oft enough on business for her father. Royal Vale sits betwixt the two. Sometimes she brings her sister, Miss Loveday."

Leith rolled this over in his mind, trying to come to terms with his new Virginia view. When he was behind his desk in Glasgow, American matters seemed more mundane, reduced to columns and sums, though their politics were fraught. Here, amid all the color and confusion of the colonies, his simplistic stance shifted. Much had changed in the decade he'd been away. He'd had no recollection of the Catesbys back then. Royal Vale had not been the force it was now.

"So, what is your plan, sir?" McCann asked as dinner was served atop shiny pewter platters. "Rather, how long will you be in Virginia?"

Long enough to avoid news print and let the curfuffle at home die down.

"Until business is done to my satisfaction." Leith cut into his tenderloin, his stomach rumbling. "I plan to visit each store, meet with the planters my Glasgow clerks correspond with and you deal with regularly. I may go to the northern neck—Maryland."

Innes looked up, knife and fork suspended. "I'll secure horses for when that time comes."

"First there's Forrest Bend."

"I'll arrange for a bateau upriver then. Due warning, though. The Ravenals will want to entertain you in true Virginia style till Twelfth Night."

"January?" Leith looked down at his burgeoning plate. He'd hardly put a dent in it. By January he'd be too heavy to mount a horse.

He wasn't here to eat or be entertained, though if he didn't take time for the latter, how would any courtship commence? Nay, courtship wasn't the right word. More business arrangement.

The miniature rested in his waistcoat pocket, hidden but never out of mind. And now that he'd just seen the object of his affection—his *scheme*—his determination doubled . . . though perhaps a more biddable lass would be best.

Juliet bade farewell to the pug-nosed Mrs. Campbell and left her lodgings to return to Royal Vale the next day, ruminating on the meeting all the way. The agreed-upon tobacco price was fair, and she'd felt a small triumph sparring with the tobacco lords and their minions. She knew none of them personally nor wanted to. Year to year their presence varied, though their finely tailored, flashy garments never did.

No sooner had Juliet and Lilith disembarked from the bateau on Royal Vale's landing than Loveday hastened down the hill from the house, her skirts ballooning in the cool wind. "You're just in time." She tucked her arm through Juliet's as they walked up the hill. "We'll enjoy some hot chocolate on the piazza as our days outside are numbered."

"I have much news and a few fripperies from town to help adorn your gown for the winter season." Juliet gestured to the portmanteau Lilith carried. "'Tis the loveliest shade of velvet seafoam, newly arrived from Three Angels millinery in London. Also a new lace cap for you—and Rilla and Lilith too."

"You are ever so mindful of us at home. I suppose you got Father some new daybooks at the printers?" At Juliet's nod, Loveday continued. "Well, he's roused himself in what seems a recovery and has ridden to Williamsburg. He could have gone to the bookbindery himself."

"When did he depart?"

"In the forenoon. He didn't say when he'd return."

"How I wish I'd tarried in town." Juliet gave a wry smile. "I did walk by the residence of the lady in question but saw nothing and no one."

Loveday gave a little laugh. "Well, we shall meet her at the ball, this mysterious Englishwoman with the poetic name."

"Don't remind me." Juliet nearly groaned. "The ball, I mean, not Widow Payne."

"But all is in order, is it not? You equal Mama in that regard. Her hospitality lives on in your impeccable planning."

"And in your hostessing. It takes the two of us, truly."

"I look forward to the festivities even if you don't." Loveday smiled brightly. "We've not entertained since we came out of mourning."

They sat down at the linen-clad table as Lilith went inside. Mahala brought the tray, the George I silver chocolate pot that had been their parents' wedding present foremost. It hadn't lost its luster after almost thirty years, reminding Juliet that Father hadn't either if he was courting again.

"So, tell me about the meeting at the Raleigh." Loveday poured the fragrant chocolate with such a practiced hand that nary a drop went awry. "I suppose it was frightfully crowded, as usual."

"More tobacco lords this time from Glasgow, including one wearing an enigmatic eye patch, though I didn't get a good look at him given the rumpus."

"Was our soon-to-be guest among them—Mr. Buchanan?"

"I don't know. The proceedings moved along with such fervor and confusion I didn't give it much thought. I heard the Glasgow merchants are a bit curious as to all the noise the colonies are making since Boston's tea debacle."

"Hard to believe three hundred forty-two chests were tossed overboard. A tidy tea party, though. Those masquerading as Indians even swept the decks clean before they left. Father said the stuff was old, hardly the quality of the smuggled Dutch tea many are drinking."

"'Tis a warning, that tea dumping." Juliet had spent the last evening reading copies of Virginia's papers in her tavern room. "A sign Americans won't take tyranny and taxes any longer. The Sons of Liberty, at least."

"Yet Colonel Washington condemned it and Mr. Franklin said he'd personally pay the tea back." Loveday sighed. "Most colonists still see themselves as British subjects. I do too. Though we're American born, we were schooled overseas, at least. I miss Bridelee Boarding School and the Siddons sisters."

"I've always hoped to return to England but doubt that will ever happen, especially if there's war." Juliet sipped her chocolate. At least Parliament couldn't levy a tax on cows and cream. "London is unlike any other place on earth, though Edinburgh is said to rival it."

They lapsed into a thoughtful silence before Loveday reached into her pocket and took out a letter, then slid it across the table to Juliet. "An express from Philadelphia. Our travelers have arrived there safely, Aunt Damarus writes."

Jacob and Armistead? Juliet pocketed the letter to pore over it later. "Truly, that is the best news I could have on my homecoming."

"Indeed." With a smile, Loveday took a second tea cake. "Now, let's talk seafoam ribbon and lace caps."

12

If you want something you never had, you must be willing to do something you have never done.

Unknown

Leith took his time dressing for the function in his honor. Farther down Forrest Bend's second floor came piping, feminine, American voices. His windows were open even in November—he found unaired rooms insufferable—and he had a view of the bateau that would carry them farther upriver to Royal Vale. Servants readied the boat even as he secured his cravat before his shaving mirror.

He'd arrived at Forrest Bend a sennight before. The Ravenals were exceptional hosts, though their young daughters seemed a frivolous trio. To have no sons seemed an outright calamity, reminding him of home. If he was gone too long, neither Bella nor Cole would ken who he was, another reason to accelerate his scheme if he could. But these indolent Virginians showed little regard for clocks or timetables, especially when it came to pleasurable pursuits.

As their guest, he'd ridden over Ravenal lands in all directions, won bets at horse racing, participated in a neighbor's fox hunt, endured an endless formal dinner or two, and was now dressing for the Catesbys' ball. An Irish indentured lad who'd been sent to act as manservant had just brought up shined shoes and was affixing his buckles. Leith took a long look in the mirror, his patch no longer needed, though a faint purplish mark lingered beneath one eye.

With a shrug he turned away from his unsmiling reflection and in a few moments had made it down the wide, curving staircase and out the door with his hosts. Ravenal's daughters walked slightly ahead with their mother while the men trailed behind.

"I nearly forgot to give you this." Ravenal reached into his waistcoat and withdrew an engraved silver cuff link. "From York Town."

Leith stanched his surprise. "From the fracas, you mean, upon my arrival."

"Your initials gave you away." Ravenal winked. "I did wonder the Scotsman who'd bested the billiard champion of York Town."

"'Twas I, but not exactly the welcome I'd anticipated."

"York Town has a rather rough reputation given the quantity of seamen coming in and out with the tide. On your next visit I'd advise you to proceed upriver as soon as possible."

Leith put the missing item into his pocket. He'd long since forgotten his tumultuous arrival. The task before him tonight crowded out any other thought.

"You're not uneasy, I hope." Assessing eyes turned on him, tempered with concern. Was Ravenal thinking of Havilah? The scandal Leith had left behind in Scotland?

Leith returned his gaze to the rocky path that led to the river. If his heart was involved, he might be. Why would he be nervous over a business venture when he failed in so few? "Nae."

"Good. The evening calls for a steady hand and a calm

head. Women can be somewhat"—Ravenal cleared his throat—"unpredictable."

With a slight smile, Leith followed him onto the landing. "Even the Misses Catesbys you praised so highly?"

"One never knows how these social occasions will go, nor have they entertained since Mrs. Catesby's passing, God rest her."

So he'd have no mother-in-law? Had she been as well-spoken as her daughter? "Now is probably not the best time to tell you I had a, um, verbal exchange with Miss Juliet Catesby in the Apollo Room the other day."

"At the tobacco meeting?" Ravenal stepped aboard the bateau and sat opposite him, away from the women at the bow. "She has a head for business that rivals many men. A true Proverbs 31 woman."

Leith regretted that intrigue now rivaled attraction. This was a business deal, nothing more, and he vowed to stop looking at the miniature in spare moments. How had a simple rendering woven such a spell? The affair, such as it was, was definitely one-sided. She didn't even know her father had sent it to him and asked him to make a choice.

He turned his attention to the river flowing beneath them without so much as a ripple, as the evening was so calm. Boatmen navigated the bateau away from the landing, the only sound the splash of water as the oars pulled against the current. The moon was up, riding the horizon facing him, while at his back the sinking sun seemed to melt into the water. Days were shorter in November, but he could still see the outlines of numerous plantations, each with a river view. The myriad docks and wharves were a calling card to the big houses, some scarcely seen through trees rapidly losing their leaves.

They neared the desired landing in a quarter of an hour, and he noticed a tall, elaborately wrought black-iron gate

onshore, open as if in welcome. He was unprepared for Royal
Vale's presence on the hill, a good quarter mile up from
the river. Colonials seemed besotted with red brick. It was
a handsome house, not nearly so grand as Scottish estates
but respectable with its three stories, tall chimneys, and slate
roof. Old poplar trees graced the sloping lawn, and an elaborate double doorway served as the mansion's entrance.

"There's a dry tunnel nearby leading from the river to
the main house, used in times of Indian attacks long ago,"
Ravenal told him, gesturing downriver. "Thankfully that's
a thing of the past."

"Do you hear the violins?" Mrs. Ravenal asked as they
disembarked.

"Aye," Leith answered. Remembering his younger brother's
gallantry, he offered his arm to the eldest Ravenal lass, only he
couldn't recall her name as the sisters looked so alike. Frances?

Flushing, she took his arm, stepping over the dry, leaf-
littered ground. He kept his eyes on the house and the front
doors, which suddenly opened as if bent by the force of his
gaze. From the sound of the music he guessed the ballroom
was in the west wing. He wasn't one for dancing, but if required, he'd dance till dawn.

Ignoring the sudden disquiet that bedeviled him, he prepared himself to join the Catesbys.

One in particular.

"Take a deep breath." Loveday put a hand to Juliet's lace
sleeve as they came down the staircase. "You're being a Martha when a Mary is needed. It pains me to see you troubled
about a great many unnecessary things, as our Lord said."

This Juliet couldn't deny. The syllabub had soured, only
half the oysters had been delivered, flowers were wilting in

their vases due to a touch of frost, five invited guests had refused to fête the tobacco lord, and Hosea had fallen down the cellar steps that morn, one of the queen's cakes with him. He was blessedly unhurt, but Rilla had to bake another cake.

Peace. Juliet craved peace, not the presence of a man she disdained who was sending them further into ruin with Father's elaborate insistence on this extravagant entertainment. And now Mr. Buchanan had arrived early, though she could hardly blame him for that. The Ravenals always arrived early.

Standing at Royal Vale's entrance, Juliet watched the six walking across the lawn, the women's colorful skirts swirling in a gentle wind along with the men's coattails. Frances Ravenal was laughing—dear, irrepressible Frances. Juliet would know that sound anywhere. Her lace-mitted hand was resting on the sleeve of a stranger she guessed was Buchanan, but Juliet refused to look closely at him as they began climbing the front steps.

Servants darted hither and yon, but all now seemed in order—a bountiful supper beautifully laid, the ballroom floor gleaming, endless candles flickering and perfuming the air. Father finally descended the staircase in back of her, Zipporah Payne on his arm. He'd been showing her the house. Juliet smiled at Zipporah, then turned back around to face the Ravenals and their houseguest.

The same man who'd been wearing an eye patch in the Apollo Room.

Surprise snatched all speech. Juliet stood to one side while Father managed introductions, trying to come to terms with what she'd said—and he'd said—at the Raleigh and if it would have any bearing on the present. And the present had him right in front of her, bowing like a seasoned courtier.

"Miss Catesby, I believe we've met." Leith Buchanan took her hand and brought it to his lips before standing tall again, his gaze lingering. "You argue tobacco so well I'm surprised it's not embroidered on the indigo shawl I saw you wearing."

"And you've since shed your enigmatic eye patch, Mr. Buchanan." Juliet managed a half smile as all her notions of this man being an aged, uncouth merchant collapsed completely. "I hardly recognize you."

Father was looking on bemusedly as if wondering why she hadn't told him about their prior meeting while Loveday was busy beaming at their guest with unfeigned interest. Few could resist her sister's dimpled smile.

"Welcome to Royal Vale," Father continued. "Allow me to introduce to you Mistress Payne, lately of Williamsburg from London."

London? Juliet's attention swiveled from Buchanan to the widow. Father had not mentioned it till now. A wealthy widow, perhaps. Her sumptuous claret-colored gown with its blond lace seemed to suggest so. Though past the first flush of youth, Zipporah was still a lovely woman and as warm and engaging as a spring day.

In moments they were moving as one toward the ballroom, Hosea lingering at the front doors to manage other arrivals. The noise of carriage wheels from neighbors who hadn't come by river mingled with the music as the clock crept toward six. Guests were overflowing both front and back doors on their way to the ballroom.

As hostess, wanting Loveday to enjoy herself, Juliet kept to the ballroom's shadows, intent on overseeing the evening. The ball opened with the French minuet—Lord Catlett partnering with the widowed Lady Norvell, their most prestigious guests—before moving to the more relaxed country dances. Mr. Buchanan partnered with the Ravenal sisters and, as the evening wore on, nearly every other woman present.

Except her.

Each time he came near, Juliet managed to slip into an alcove or weave between guests and disappear to the kitchen or pantry or hall. She was not in a dancing mood. Tonight she especially missed her mother, whose foremost gift had been hospitality. Royal Vale, even decorated and filled to the utmost, seemed empty without her.

Midnight found Juliet up in the cupola, blessedly alone, the moon's lucent light a stark white. Hobbes trailed her, purring round her petticoats as if asking where his mistress was. Loveday remained below, neither she nor the musicians nor other couples showing any signs of tiring. The jaunty notes of the violins crested clear to the rafters. Here atop the house in the solitude, Juliet wouldn't be missed.

Her crumpled thoughts seemed to iron out and a plan began to form. Once Father remarried and Loveday made a suitable match, she'd be free to make her own way, perhaps settle in Philadelphia with Aunt Damarus and continue the freedom work there. The thought was exciting, disconcerting, and something she'd not yet prayed about.

Hearing raised voices, Juliet hurried downstairs. There in the entrance hall were two inebriated burgesses, a Patriot and a Loyalist, calling for a duel at dawn over the former's suit sporting "No Stamp Act" buttons. Before she could intervene, Nathaniel Ravenal, bless him, escorted them outside. Tonight there'd been entirely too much talk of tea and taxes and tobacco.

Nerves frayed, Juliet entered the ballroom, watching the dancers whirl and the punch bowl empty. Mr. Buchanan had been standing with a group of planters to one side by an array of Palladian windows when she left. Where was their guest of honor now?

Despite her feelings, was it not her task as hostess to find out?

13

These are the times that try men's souls.

Thomas Paine

*L*eith left the ballroom, wanting to clear the color and confusion from his mind. Too many names and faces mixed with dancing, spirits, and incendiary politics were a potent combination. He stood in the cool silence by a boxwood hedge and noticed the skeletal outline of what appeared to be the beginning of a summerhouse.

All seemed a bit lacking, even threadbare, at Royal Vale. Though handsome, the place had peeling paint, cracked plasterwork, sagging floors, and crumbling brick. New World Virginia lacked the richness and grandeur of layered centuries of civilized Europe, but it didn't deserve the slur of *rustic* or *backcountry* either.

He walked a shell path away from the main house to what looked like a walled garden. Illuminated by hanging lanterns, the acre of space was of English design, the central fountain solid marble, its waterless basin strewn with leaves. Italian made, he guessed, the waterworks reduced to a single spout, or jet d'eau, as the French called it.

He sat down on the fountain's broad edge. Was no one else outside? As he thought it, into the lantern-lit darkness came a footfall. One of the Ravenals? He looked over his shoulder, surprised—and pleased.

Miss Juliet Catesby came to a stop a stone's throw away. "Are you in the habit of worrying your hostess with your absence, Mr. Buchanan?"

"Worrying?" he answered. "Not the term I'd use when you've fled like a fox before hounds since my arrival."

A startled hush ensued, and then she laughed—a low, rich, warmhearted sound. "Your Scots bluntness is, I must say, refreshingly welcome amid so much fawning and cringing going on inside."

He smiled—an unforced smile that felt retrieved from some dim, dusty part of himself. Fawning and cringing, aye. With her so close he was definitely guilty of the former. He watched her move to an ornamental copper spout along a brick wall, where a trickle of water splashed onto the ground. Taking something hanging beneath it—a cup?—she turned toward him again.

"The least I can do is offer you some pure, sweet Virginia spring water, though perhaps Scots whisky is more to your liking."

He took the cup she held out to him and downed the bracingly cold water in two swallows before handing it back to her. "Is this an olive branch of sorts after our rather contentious beginning in town?"

She refilled it as if in answer, her silvered features serious as the moon moved behind a cloud. Tall as Lyrica, she was, but comelier and dark. The miniaturist who'd painted her had not done her justice by half. What would she do if he withdrew her likeness from his pocket?

"As for my absence," he said, taking the cup again, "where were you half an hour ago?"

"We seem to be very aware of each other, Mr. Buchanan, which I'll blame on our rather tumultuous beginning in town, yes." Her gaze—and then his—turned toward the top of the house, where glass shimmered and a weathervane shifted slightly in the rising wind. "I escaped to the cupola."

He kept his eye on the cupola instead of her. It took Herculean effort. Whatever pulsed between them was business, he reminded himself, though attraction didn't hurt.

"I'm afraid the ball in your honor has become more a political debate, hardly what I had in mind when I planned it. Our American obsession with independence runs like treasonous fire through everything these days."

He stood. "Matters are nae less fiery over the water."

She turned toward him as the music crested. *Lady Ramsay's Strathspey?* "I do believe, given the furor all around, that George III will be the last king of America."

Treasonous, aye. Finished with the spring water, he replaced the cup. "If independence is given free rein, it will have irreversible consequences for us all."

"You're thinking of your Glaswegian dynasty."

"Dynasty? A grand word for a Scots merchant firm."

"You are too modest, sir."

"Modest? Nae, honest. We're not aristocracy."

"I do wonder what you make of us Virginians, being an outlander."

"And I wonder what you Virginians think of us Scots."

They faced each other as if at some sort of an impasse. In truth, his concerns about Glasgow shrank to pin-sized proportions in her presence. He'd not thought of Havilah or the bairns or business all evening. For a few hours, at least, the darkness seemed pushed back.

"Which side of the fight are you on?" he asked quietly.

"Am I a Patriot or a Loyalist, you mean? I'll let you decide." She gestured toward the ballroom. "By now my father might have gathered a search party for us both. Won't you accompany me back to the house?"

"Only if you'll promise me a dance." Her resistance was palpable, but the challenge didn't deter him. "Though it might be better to arrive inside separately lest we stir up another sort of storm."

"Wise, yes." She raised a hand to her unpowdered hair, where a curl hung loose. "But I must warn you, there's no hurry. The dancing will likely last till dawn."

He watched her go ahead of him up stone steps, her indigo skirts trailing.

A graceful ghost in the moonlight.

They stepped to the lively "Rakes of Rochester." Truly, the ballroom floor was no less empty now at a quarter past one than it was at the ball's beginning.

Smile undimmed, Loveday partnered with one of the Taliaferros in the longways set, and all the dancers wove in and out, Juliet and Mr. Buchanan the topmost couple. Though tired and thirsty, Juliet didn't miss how well the Scotsman performed, not with the exaggerated, theatrical movements of some gentlemen but with an easy grace that belied his stature—almost the equal of Colonel Washington, who'd once been their guest and referred to dancing as "the gentler conflict."

Juliet remembered it now with a half smile. Conflict, yes. That was how she felt dancing with the man whose presence turned her upside down. Though some pairs conversed amid all the sidestepping and circling, she and Mr. Buchanan did not exchange another word, only glances. And that, somehow, seemed a conversation in itself. A lingering, intent look not once but again, till she found herself watching for them—watching him—as if trying to decipher their meaning. But it was the touch of his hands that most startled her. Not womanish hands as many gentlemen had, not pale and thin and blue-veined and unremarkable, even repulsive.

"Give me a virile man with callused hands."

Was that what Loveday had recently said? Why had Juliet, the elder sister, not realized this heaven-sent situation sooner? Was this not her answer to prayer? To all their debt and misfortune? Loveday might make a match with the man right before her.

Loveday Catesby Buchanan.

It even sounded poetic.

14

If I be waspish, best beware my sting.

William Shakespeare

Royal Vale's stillroom embraced Juliet with a distillation of heady scents. Glazed crocks lined shelves and snipped plants adorned Loveday's homely worktable while aromatic bunches of rosemary, thyme, sage, and parsley hung above their heads, drying for winter's use.

"I was hoping you'd set aside Father's ledgers." Loveday looked up from harvesting her beloved herb garden before a hoarfrost. "I'm happy to have company."

"As am I." Juliet came to stand across from her, the burgeoning table between them. "Preserved marigold flowers?"

"For decorating porridge and cakes," Loveday replied with a wistful smile. "You know how fanciful I am in my little kingdom here."

How well she handled their lack of domestic help—and Mama's grievous loss, for this had once been Charlotte Catesby's domain. "Such becomes you. You'll make a fine wife and mother."

Loveday poured vinegar, nose wrinkling. "My success toward that end seems small, even after the ball."

"Nonsense." Juliet stifled a yawn. "We've not discussed it overmuch since we slept most of yesterday after staying up all night dancing."

"Which you did quite admirably with Mr. Buchanan."

"Me?" Juliet replied. "I danced with him but once whilst you partnered with him twice."

"Who's counting? Rather, what did you make of him? Father seems quite fond of this particular tobacco lord, even admiring."

"'Tis hard to form a fair opinion on such short acquaintance." Juliet took a seat on a stool, still entertaining the notion that Mr. Buchanan might become her brother-in-law. "I'm most interested in your first impressions."

With a little sigh, Loveday reached for a crock. "Mine are still forming."

Loveday seemed unusually restrained. Did she need prodding? "I forgot for a few hours how deeply we're indebted to him, as he can be rather charming, even erudite."

"Oh?" Loveday began sugaring a tray of lavender. "He seems rather steely at times."

"Steely? What means you?"

"Hard as marble. Even a tad melancholy. He seldom smiles."

"Well, he's a consummate businessman. I keep thinking how unfortunate it is he has no wife. No sweetheart."

"A solitary gentleman, yes."

"Given his many fine attributes, I doubt he'll remain a bachelor long."

"Indeed." Loveday paused, lips pursed. "Did you see all the ladies eyeing him openly at the ball? He seemed oblivious to the attention. I do find that rather remarkable."

Did she? Loveday seemed a step away from smitten. Juliet wanted nothing more than to see her sister happily settled in her own home, even in faraway Scotland if it came to that.

"As for love matches, we need to talk with Father about his own impending nuptials. He's wanting a small ceremony—a wedding breakfast."

A double wedding? Juliet bit her lip to keep from saying it aloud. "I wonder what Zipporah wants."

"We shall soon find out." Loveday consulted the watch that dangled from Mama's chatelaine at her waist. "We four are leaving later for an afternoon's entertainment at the Ravenals', remember."

Juliet had nearly forgotten. Surely her matchmaking would be more effective if she excused herself. "I shan't be joining you."

Loveday set the sugar scoop down. "Whyever not?"

"I need . . . a few hours' quiet." She eyed the shelves, feeling duplicitous. "And one of your headache remedies."

"Well, a little rest should do you good, though it shan't be the same without you." Loveday moved toward a closet, disappeared into it, and then returned with something in hand. "Dr. Blair always says drinking hot citron water is most beneficial, but I'm partial to the cucupha—here's one I've sewn with rosemary and lavender."

"Thank you, sweet sister." Taking the fragrant, quilted cap, Juliet made her way to the door that opened onto the kitchen garden. "Please excuse me to the Ravenals."

And Leith Buchanan.

Half an hour with the cucupha and a cup of tea had Juliet on her feet again, this time at Royal Vale's dyehouse. Situated near the bellhouse, it sat square like the other dependencies, with clapboard siding washed white, its gable roof and shutters green.

Loveday had harvested a great quantity of woad, and Juliet had been experimenting blending its blue dye with indigo. These trials were her favorite pastime—nay, obsession—but she'd not had much time for it of late given her other tasks. Leaving the door open, she moved toward the linen she'd dyed a fortnight ago, the hues astonishingly varied from violet to navy to sky blue.

The latest cakes of indigo, brought from the drying shed and laid out on her worktable, were from this year's fifth harvest. She'd not yet decided whether to continue using limewater for the process or pure water as the Europeans did. As for which indigo was her favorite, she favored the flora plant instead of the violet plant, or gorge de pigeon. It fetched the best price for dyeing linen and wool, at least in the current market.

Humming a hymn, she took up a hand grinder and ground a dried indigo cake into a fine blue powder before mixing it in limewater to form a paste. A barrel of cold water was on hand and she removed the cover, then added potash and other ingredients to form a dye in which to dip the clean linen cloth on hand. 'Twas her favorite part of the process—

"Where is your father?"

Whirling around, she faced an unsmiling Riggs. His bulk crowded the doorframe, and she realized anew why so many feared him. He was a bull of a man, his temperament the same. Never an observer of common courtesy, he'd not removed his hat or apologized for startling her.

"My father should return soon." Wiping her hands on her apron, she worked to keep her tone pleasant. "Why do you ask?"

"There's an outbreak of fever among the tobacco hands.

I need the doctor sent for—or at least your sister's stillroom remedies."

"I'll see to both, then." She replaced the cover on the barrel, abandoning her task. Outbreaks were common enough, especially after an exhaustive harvest. But the worrisome word *fever* might mean any number of maladies, including the dreaded pox. "Have you had the sick moved to the infirmary?"

"Nay."

"Then please do so at once while I summon Dr. Cartwright and send word to my father."

When he didn't move, her alarm spiked. She faced him, still wiping her hands on her indigo-stained apron though they were already dry. "Is that all, Mr. Riggs?"

"Nay, not all by half." His granite gaze held hers with sickening force. "I ken what you're doing in the dark. And I vow to see it end."

She groped for a reply, her long-simmering fury rivaled by fear. "You know nothing. And if you persist in this threat, I'll see you put off Royal Vale by the sheriff, your reputation so ruined no other planter in Virginia will employ you."

Bold words. Brazen words. She felt sick even saying them. To have countered a threat with a threat left her weak-kneed and wondering how he might retaliate.

He finally left, in no way cowed and seemingly more infuriated. She felt she'd stumbled into the wasp's nest she'd just discovered under the stillroom eaves.

What would a man like Riggs do? What was he capable of?

15

Born and educated in this country, I glory in the name
of Briton.

King George III

At Forrest Bend, Leith felt a bit out of his depth
in the midst of such civility. Here there was no
coarse talk or jesting. No swearing or drunken-
ness. Nary a misspoken word nor a foot put wrong. Everything was done in moderation with a sort of refined yet
unpretentious dignity. Other than the Ravenal daughters
paying him too much attention, he couldn't find any fault
with these particular Virginians. When he was with them,
he nearly forgot his other life. There was only the colorful
present with all its Americanisms and novelties.

Today was ninepins. These Americans improved upon it,
playing outside on a bowling green. Despite the competition, he emerged the winner after several rounds, enduring a
great deal of backslapping and handshaking. Far preferable
to billiards and a fistfight in a smoky tavern. Syllabub—
Virginians' version of the victor's drink—was served, but

what he craved was a drink of spring water in Royal Vale's garden at midnight.

The Catesbys were present, all but one, and cheered him on. When he finished the game he asked why Juliet was missing.

Loveday smiled, though the worried look in her eyes remained. "My sister is indisposed and sends her regrets."

Indisposed? She hadn't seemed sickly at Royal Vale. Nor was she fragile in spirit, given their forthright exchange at the Raleigh and then the ball. The tick of time was against him. He'd soon leave to visit Buchanan stores and settle business matters in various towns, a schedule hardly conducive to courting.

Only he wasn't courting.

"Are you missing Scotland, Mr. Buchanan?" Loveday was looking at him again as if still forming an impression. She had an engaging manner just shy of coy. "Or are our colonial diversions sufficient for the time being?"

He paused. He hardly missed Ardraigh Hall as he was seldom there. His heirs sprang to mind with the usual nick of guilt. Missing someone or something meant some sort of established bond, of which they had none other than that he'd sired them. Young as they were, Bella and Cole weren't giving him a single thought. Yet that odd longing he'd experienced since their birth washed through him again. To be a father. To have the tender tie he'd not had with his own father. And then, quick as it came, the desire vanished.

"Missing Scotland, nae, especially not on a blithe November day," he finally replied. "You colonials are sufficiently diverting, aye."

She flashed that easy smile of hers again, making him wonder if Juliet was dimpled and he'd overlooked it. "I've never been to your storied country, though my sister and I were schooled in England and learned your history there."

"You have nae trouble understanding my broad Scots?" he said, his Glaswegian dialect deepening with its rolling *r*'s and odd lilts. Americans sounded a bit flat in comparison, though colonial accents varied.

"I'm too used to Scotsmen here, particularly in your James River stores."

Was she hazarding a dig at the oft contentious relations between planters and the firm? His suspicions arose, though she showed no such guile. "The Catesbys are always welcome in Glasgow."

Her pleasantness turned probing but was nonetheless charming. "You have a great many business interests in the city, I understand."

"In the city and outside of it."

"Father mentioned a townhouse and a country house."

He gave a curt nod, looking toward the lawn. Another game of ninepins was beginning, but for now, he was content to talk. "Ardraigh Hall is a few miles southeast of Glasgow, but my townhouse is on Virginia Street."

Her brows arched. "You jest!"

"It seems fitting. This colony forms the foundation of the Buchanan firm. What about your own family history here? Virginia is not auld, so it should be brief."

She smiled and took a sip of syllabub, her gaze on her father as he took a turn at the game. "Best ask my sister that. She has a passion for the past and our humble Jamestown beginnings. Perhaps she'll even show you a portrait or two. They're nothing like your British long galleries, but we do try to honor those Catesbys who came before."

"Mayhap I should have done the same before leaving Scotland, though I find it as hard to sit still as my children."

"Children?" She looked shocked.

"Twins." He enjoyed righting her obvious misperceptions. "Bonny bairns, so tapsalteerie they're kept in the country."

"Does this mean there's a Mrs. Buchanan?"

So, she had a wee bit of her sister's forthrightness. Somehow it blunted the burn of his predicament. "There was once."

"My sincerest sympathies, sir." She turned mournful, only brightening when Widow Payne came toward them.

"I don't mean to interrupt," the middle-aged matron said with a smile. "But Mrs. Ravenal wishes to show Loveday and I her late-blooming roses."

Leith returned to the game, his thoughts anchored to the ailing Juliet.

16

What you seem to be, be really.

Benjamin Franklin

*H*e is not what he seems!"

Loveday burst into Juliet's bedchamber, bergère hat in hand, ribbons trailing on the pine floor. Seated at her escritoire, Juliet looked up from the letter she was writing Aunt Damarus.

She set her quill aside. "Whoever do you mean?"

"Mr. Buchanan." Loveday sank down upon an upholstered ottoman, out of breath and clearly aflutter. "He told me all manner of things about himself, but it was what he didn't say that has me most intrigued."

"Such as?"

"He's a widower, for one. His wife died and left twins. His Glasgow townhouse is on *Virginia Street*. Can you imagine? A street named after the fortune that founded him! And he has invited us to Scotland."

Juliet took a breath as she mulled these new facts. "Twins?" Her weakness had always been children. And motherless children were altogether another concern. "How old?"

A slight lift of her shoulders. "I know not."

"Their names?"

"He didn't tell me. He only said they're both tapsalteerie—whatever that means—and it didn't sound complimentary."

"Young, then." Juliet adjusted to this unexpected news. "Babies, perhaps."

"They live at his country house, Ardraigh Hall, likely with their nurse."

"I've heard of Ardraigh Hall. Hamish Hunter even worked there before coming here. He said the gardens rival royalty. What else did Mr. Buchanan tell you?"

"He has an interest in history. He asked about our Virginia ancestry, and I told him to talk to you since you know so much about our beginnings here."

Juliet felt a trill of delight. Could her much-prayed-for plan already be coming to fruition? "So you had a lovely afternoon together."

"Together? I'd hardly call it that. We spoke briefly over syllabub. He'd just quashed all the men present at ninepins, though he later lost to Judge Beverly at quoits."

"He's athletic, then."

"Quite. And he seemed rather concerned you weren't with us."

"A simple courtesy," Juliet said.

"I wonder." Loveday was worrying her bottom lip in that way that suggested deep thought. "Later he and Father spoke very seriously, just the two of them, for a noticeably long time."

"Speaking of Father, where is he?"

"He went out to the quarters with Dr. Cartwright."

"Very well." Juliet hid her disquiet with a smile. "Are you hungry? Should I have Rilla prepare us a small supper?"

"Yes, but let's dine right here, just the two of us, before

the hearth's fire. Though it was warm today in the sunlight, the evening is quite chill."

Supper was served, and they sat companionably by the circle of firelight in twin Windsor chairs, a tea table between them, partaking of peanut soup, cold ham, and wheaten bread.

Listening for Father, Juliet looked out the front window and saw Hosea lighting the lantern by the mounting block. "Speaking of the doctor, I supplied him with several still-room tonics."

"I pray they help. Father was quite alarmed when he received your message at the Ravenals'. I hope you didn't go to the quarters, as he's forbidden it."

"I try to respect him in that, though I'm always wanting to go where help is needed." Juliet set her spoon down, having little appetite. "I was in the dyehouse when Riggs found me. We had something of a confrontation there. I wasn't going to tell you, but now I feel I should if only to make you wary."

"He suspects, then." Loveday's face grew shadowed. "What exactly was said?"

Juliet told her in a whisper, eyes on the closed door. The memory, only hours old, still burned. "I suspect Riggs is behind Father's denial of indentures. They don't tolerate Riggs's mistreatment and come to Father to complain, so Riggs is against contracting more of them. And Father refuses to do what Ravenal has done by manumitting his enslaved since they're irreplaceable in the fields."

"And so we continue to do what we can, in even a small way." Loveday looked as worn as Juliet felt. "How many have passed by here since we took up Mama's work when she died?"

"Counting those who come to us across the river?" Juliet pondered her answer. "Twenty-three."

Not nearly enough.

17

He that would live in peace & at ease,
Must not speak all he knows or judge all he sees.

Benjamin Franklin

*L*eith sat in the Ravenals' parlor, eyes fixed on the mantel clock. Family devotions had begun half an hour ago with his host reading aloud from the Bible as he stood before the marble hearth. Occasionally, he chose to expound upon the text. Mrs. Ravenal and their daughters sat with their heads bowed in concentration, hardly moving or breathing, as if hanging on his carefully modulated words. Mayhap he'd missed his calling as a preacher. Ravenal rivaled John Knox.

Leith was only half listening. That darkness was drawing in again, cold as the rain-smeared Clyde in midwinter. It had begun shadowing him at Havilah's death, as if somehow, in the bewildering aftermath, her anguish had tainted him. Why the feeling would be stronger now when he sat in a peaceful colonial parlor was beyond him. His first inclination to counter it was to reach for a drink. Whisky was best, but here, a world away from the decanter on his Glasgow desk or a nearby tavern, he felt parched as well as shadowed. Shifting in his chair, he placed damp palms against the buckskin of his breeches and battled some unseen enemy.

Candlelight flickered in a draft as wind wrapped round the house. Earlier Mrs. Ravenal had said she felt a storm brewing—the first one of autumn—and the servants had taken precautions to clear the piazzas and lawn of anything that might scatter.

"As the scholar Matthew Henry said," Ravenal continued, "'The woman was made of a rib out of the side of Adam; not made out of his head to rule over him, nor out of his feet to be trampled upon by him, but out of his side to be equal with him, under his arm to be protected, and near his heart to be beloved . . .'"

Near his heart to be beloved.

The bruising words lingered. Ravenal spoke in low, thoughtful tones as Leith's darkness intensified. He had not loved Havilah well. With his head and hands full of business, he had left her to herself. Once he had thought he loved her, but when he wooed her, he had failed to keep her. Somehow his beloved had become the bane of his existence. She had changed into another lass entirely, and to this day he couldn't understand why. Her violent moods, her wish to harm herself at the end. He blamed himself foremost. He swallowed the bitter truth of it, something he'd not faced squarely before.

Ravenal lowered his head and began to pray. "Our Father, which art in heaven, hallowed be Thy name . . ."

Other voices joined, but Leith could not speak—or breathe. His hand shot to the stock around his throat. He pulled at it so savagely that it broke the back buckle. The silver piece skittered across the bare floor, but Ravenal continued his prayer. Leith took a deep, shuddering breath, fighting the impulse to bolt toward the door.

113

When Ravenal said "Amen," he looked straight at him. "All well, Buchanan?"

"Aye," Leith lied.

Dismounting in the parish churchyard the next morning, Leith and Ravenal waited for the coach carrying the ladies to arrive. Rain slicked the grass and the night's wind had torn down leaves and branches, but dawn arrived clement with only a light breeze riffling his coattails.

Once again he couldn't help but compare this small brick kirk in the middle of a field to the one he'd helped found in Glasgow. With its Spanish mahogany interior and immense spire, St. Mungo's was more cathedral. But this little building in the midst of a sunburned meadow seemed impossibly quaint.

Hobbling his horse, he looked west as the Catesbys' open carriage came into view. Juliet was easily spotted, wearing another indigo gown, her head topped with a jaunty, white-plumed hat. She'd been wearing blue in the miniature too.

Zipporah Payne left the carriage first, Juliet next. Leith waited to speak to her, but the Ravenal sisters moved in, linking arms with her and drawing her toward the kirk's open doorway, thereby sabotaging any chance he had for private conversation. Nor did she give him so much as a glance.

"Mr. Buchanan, have you quite recovered from your winnings at ninepins?" Loveday smiled prettily as she passed by him, following after her sister without waiting for an answer.

"Our pastor is more shepherd than orator, but we've no cause to complain," Ravenal said as they walked to the open doorway. "He's abandoned the Anglican tradition of reading sermons, which seems another move toward independence even within the established church. All the parish seems to have turned out today."

Was his host remembering what he'd said? In a rare moment of self-revelation, Leith had confessed he'd rather be a monk in a monastery than have to endure a throng. Parishioners were already eyeing him, the outlier in their midst. At home, Glaswegians often gawked at him. He didn't like it here nor there.

"We've been invited to Royal Vale for dinner after service," Ravenal told him as they passed into the shaded building smelling of dust and old wood and . . . jasmine?

Aye, jasmine. The scent wafted toward him on the storm's fading wind.

Leith sat with the Ravenals while Juliet sat directly in front of him between her father and sister. He looked toward the minister at the raised pulpit, then back at Juliet. Her head was bent, glossy coils draping her neck and the sheer lace fichu about her shoulders.

Had she recovered from whatever had kept her from the garden party?

An hour crawled by, and the minister droned on. "When our heads are fullest of care and our hands of business, yet we must not forget our religion, nor suffer ourselves to be indisposed for acts of devotion . . ."

Leith set his jaw, denying the urge to consult his watch. The crowded pews were stealing the very air he breathed. With the doors closed, the kirk air grew still and stale. No more jasmine wafted his way. He tried to keep his gaze from lingering on Juliet. To no avail.

He drew a deep, measured breath, the heave of his chest a bid to breathe. He pinned his gaze to the floor as if to anchor himself, feeling as fragile as the fly that whined about his head. He would do nearly anything to keep the darkness at bay. Anything to escape the shadows encroaching again despite broad daylight.

And then, when he thought he'd not weather another trice, a final prayer was said and parishioners hastened out of the building with greater zeal than when they'd come in. Dinner awaited. After a two-hour sermon, these congregants wouldn't be denied.

18

But you would have me say I am violently in love.

Mary Wortley Montagu

*B*ack in her bedchamber, Juliet returned her hat to its stand as she prayed for ample opportunities to sequester Loveday with Leith Buchanan. She'd seat them together at dinner. Send them out to the garden for a walk after. Corner the Ravenal sisters so they wouldn't be underfoot. Perhaps even make them co-conspirators in her plan—

"Juliet?" The frantic tap at the door preceded its opening. Loveday entered, her flaxen hair falling to her waist. "I wanted to wear my wig, but it's not freshly powdered. Please help with my hair."

Was she wanting to be seen at her best? Juliet's hopes soared.

"Betimes we need a maid, or at least a hairdresser." She began subduing her sister's unruly locks with pearl combs. "There, you look lovely. 'Tis a perfect color on you, that shade of rose."

Loveday darted a look toward the open door. "My, what a noise they're making downstairs."

"We've not had dinner guests in some time. Perhaps you could show Mr. Buchanan the dovecote afterward."

117

Loveday made no reply. She simply smiled and glanced in the looking glass a final time before they went downstairs together. Their noisy guests were gathered in the dining room—all but one. The Scot stood in the entry hall pondering a portrait. Loveday's steps quickened, and she slipped into the dining room, leaving Juliet alone with him.

Drawn in by the romance of the past and the particularly intent way he was studying the old portrait, Juliet said, "That is my great-great-grandfather on my mother's side. His is quite a story."

He glanced at her before returning to the oil painting. "Do you have time to tell it?"

"With pleasure." She pondered the gentleman who'd settled the very ground they stood upon. Handsome and dark, he wore the garments of a lost century. "Alexander Renick was among the first settlers who arrived in Jamestown in 1607 and survived. He went on to marry a Powhatan princess, who showed him the secrets of tobacco cultivation before she died young."

"Did he remarry?"

"In time, yes. Selah Hopewell was another colonist who helped bring the tobacco brides to Virginia. She became a stepmother to his son, Oceanus, who grew up to marry Watseka and live here at what was once Rose-n-Vale."

"Was Oceanus an only child?"

"The oldest of ten." She smiled, imagining it. "Six sons and three daughters followed. By that time King James had granted them more acreage for tobacco production, so Rose-n-Vale became Royal Vale and has remained so to this day."

He gestured to the painting beside it. "And this is Selah Hopewell Renick?"

"Yes, but if you look closely, you'll see Alexander's first wife in the portrait too, by the window."

"They're not wearing indigo like one descendant I ken."
He turned toward her. "Do you always wear that color?"

"I do, in all its varying hues."

"Did I mention I prefer blue?"

"Yet you wear mostly black."

"I've just come out of mourning."

"I understand." Suddenly missing Mama, she changed course. "Speaking of colors, is it true you have black swans at Ardraigh Hall?"

He paused as a burst of laughter came from the dining room. "Aye, black, not indigo."

She tried to suppress a smile. "Perhaps you could dye them a lovely shade of blue."

"A waterfowling feat." That steeliness Loveday had mentioned softened for the barest moment. "Better luck dyeing wool."

"So you have sheep?"

"You tell me. You seem to ken a great deal about Ardraigh Hall."

Guilty. She warmed all over. "Our gardener was your gardener once upon a time. Mr. Hamish Hunter. He often talks about British estates that have employed him. But," she added with a slight smile, "he said nothing about your sheep."

"Short-wool Blackface."

He was still regarding her much as she was regarding him, so keenly she completely lost the thread of conversation. His gaze seemed to travel about her face as if she were another painting. Such unusual eyes he had. The color of indigo—

"Juliet." Behind them, in the dining room's doorway, stood Father. "Are you regaling our guest with tales of Virginia's founding?"

With an apology, she started toward the scarlet-paneled chamber where a great many enticing aromas mingled.

Everyone else was seated, and Father returned to the head of the table, which left two empty places side by side. Alas, Loveday was safely ensconced between Mrs. Ravenal and Frances. Juliet had no other options. She looked at all the dishes spread upon the cloth and went from famished to flummoxed. Another lost opportunity for Loveday.

"A blessed day when ten are gathered round this table," Father was saying, clearly in the highest of spirits. Raising his wine glass, he looked toward Zipporah. "To new beginnings!"

Flushing, she raised her glass in turn. "Indeed, my love."

All followed suit, then fell upon the Sabbath feast as if there'd been no breakfast. Juliet passed platters and dishes, explaining the less obvious ones to the man on her left as conversation hummed on all sides of them.

"Succotash," she said. "Father's favorite. A medley of okra, tomatoes, corn, and bacon."

"Okra," he repeated as if perplexed.

"You have none in Scotland, then. Well, try these sweet potatoes, though I doubt you grow them either. They're my sister's choice."

"What is yours?"

"These yeast rolls." She passed him Rilla's specialty, their buttered tops golden.

"Bread I recognize," he replied wryly, adding it to his plate.

She handed him another steaming dish. "And lastly, the humble potato and turnip."

"Neeps and tatties. Fine fodder for livestock."

"I suppose your Scots fare resembles little here. I do wonder what you'd serve me if I were to sit down at your Glasgow table."

"Haggis."

"And what, pray tell, is that?"

"You're liable to cast up accounts if I tell you."

"Oh?" That odd amusement she'd begun to experience in his presence bubbled to the top again.

"I do enjoy your Virginia hams seasoned with brown sugar. Second to none," he said, taking plenty of that.

Over the next hour, Father steered them safely around all political talk. Their voices echoed in the large chamber and their laughter seemed deafening. Company was a refreshing change since it was often only Juliet and Loveday of late.

Toward the end of the meal, she tried to catch her sister's eye. To no avail.

"I'm hoping my sister shows you the dovecote," she said to Mr. Buchanan. "'Tis said to be the oldest structure here at Royal Vale and is quite charming. It even bears my great-great-grandparents' entwined initials."

"Your sister . . ." He took a drink of claret. "Why not you?"

She paused, fork halfway to her mouth. Mr. Buchanan was nothing if not forthright, though she'd found that to be true of many Scots. "You may be tiring of my company."

He turned toward her slightly as he set down his glass. "Mayhap you're tiring of mine."

Was she? *Nay.* The realization turned her pink. She felt a rush of heat from her head to her slippered feet. Thankfully, Rilla brought dessert, a French custard, while Mahala poured coffee. The strong, almost burnt scent braced her, and she took a sip without her usual sugar and cream, trying to clear her head.

This didn't fit into her scheme. She thought matchmaking would be simpler. Loveday was the prettiest, the most engaging. The most desirous of being wed. Yet not once had Loveday looked at Mr. Buchanan or directed a comment toward him during dinner. Obviously, Juliet must change her tactics.

But for now, she herself would show him the dovecote.

19

A plump widow needs no advertisement.

Scottish proverb

The Sabbath was followed by a tumultuous sennight. Two runaways arrived at the tunnel after dark, and Juliet and Loveday went below to meet them. Seldom did fugitives arrive in late fall or winter. The weather forbade it. There wasn't enough brush for cover as they traveled, not to mention scavenging in the woods. But somehow these two, a mother and daughter, had defied the odds.

Father never came near the tunnel. It led from the river's edge to the winter kitchen and cellar. This was the servants' domain, accessed by the servants' back stair leading to Juliet's and Loveday's chambers. The few house servants were closemouthed, respecting what the sisters did as they carried on their mother's work, knowing they could be in the runaways' shoes. Juliet never worried about a betrayal from within. Without was another matter.

Having become increasingly wary of Riggs and anything that might signal harm, she hardly slept. Thankfully, Father soon left for Williamsburg. With him away, all breathed easier.

It was rare to house any runaways for long. Usually they were equipped and sent on their way, but within moments of seeing these new arrivals, Juliet realized they required a longer stay. Exhausted and rail-thin, they were in desperate need of a haven till they grew stronger. Especially when the weather took a bitter turn and ice gathered at the river's edges.

Knowing their unexpected guests were hidden and in good hands, Juliet and Loveday accepted Zipporah Payne's invitation to her Williamsburg townhouse for tea. Bundled up in the coach, coal braziers at their feet, they traveled the distance, overshadowed by the memory of their mother.

"'Tis the anniversary of her death, which makes me less inclined to travel." Loveday's voice wavered, and she buried her hands deeper into her fur muff. "And that December day was much like this one."

"To think we almost went with her and then at the last caught colds that kept us home."

Juliet closed the window curtains more tightly against the gloom. She wanted to shut out the sight as they neared the bridge that had ended Charlotte Catesby's life. The carriage horses had bolted over it during a sudden storm, leading to their mother's death. Her maid had also died. In his grief, Father had even put down the injured horses so they wouldn't be a reminder.

"The one comfort I have is that it was no accident," Juliet said in reassuring tones. "Our day of birth and death are in the Lord's keeping, as Scripture says."

"Cold comfort." Loveday gave a little shudder as they passed over the bridge. "Why did she have to die so tragically and unexpectedly? She was even doing good at the very end, visiting a shut-in neighbor. I cannot make peace with her passing. Not yet. Perhaps not ever."

"A mother's loss is especially hard. Royal Vale seems empty without her—just a house, not a home."

At last they rolled up to the England Street townhouse during what seemed dusk, not midday. Cut holly and ivy adorned myriad windows amid bursts of yellow candlelight, a cheerful sight. A maid met them and took their wraps. Zipporah was waiting in the parlor, a cozy room painted a rich ocher, where a fire blazed in the hearth.

She held out her hands to them and kissed them on both cheeks. "Such a winter's day calls for hot chocolate. I sent for some at Shaw's in York just last week. They have a new master chocolate grinder who is the talk of town."

Demitasse cups shone white on a tray alongside a tall chocolate pot. Juliet detected vanilla and dried orange rind and cinnamon. "Your home is lovely."

"Not mine, dearest, though I am glad to have let it from a relative now in Maryland. Town suits me well. Everything is within reach, and I enjoy walking about to the shops close by." She darted a look at a window. "With the weather worsening, you'll stay the night, won't you? Your father shall join us for supper."

"Of course," Loveday assured her, though Juliet was already beset by the need to return to Royal Vale. Riggs and the tenuous situation there were a continual thorn. "Father said you wanted to talk with us about the twelve days of Christmas and your nuptials."

"Yes, we hope to begin the new year married and feel the holiday season is a lovely time to exchange our vows. But aside from that, I do hope you feel free to spend as much time here as you can, enjoying Williamsburg's festive parties and balls."

"I do miss our townhouse, especially during the holidays," Loveday said, taking a first sip. "So many of our neighbors along the James winter here, including the Ravenals."

Zipporah smiled, her crimson silk gown already proclaiming the season. "How convenient that the Ravenals are just two houses down from here. I find their Glasgow guest quite engaging."

"Mr. Buchanan has likely never celebrated a colonial Christmas," Loveday mused. "We must take pains to make it memorable for him."

Pains? Juliet stared at her sister with renewed hope as Zipporah continued. "Kind of you, my dear. A grieving widower needs such solicitations, surely. To be far from hearth and home at such a festive time must take a toll, especially given he has a large extended family."

Loveday seemed transfixed. "So the Buchanans are a large clan?"

"Quite. I have Glaswegian kin who know them. They're frequently in society and mentioned in the newspapers too."

Loveday leaned forward slightly in anticipation. "I'd love to hear more about his children, the twins."

"Ah, yes, where to begin . . ."

Juliet waited, equally curious. Mr. Buchanan had revealed little about himself so far, skillfully evading questions that didn't pertain to tobacco and other exports. Had anyone noticed but she?

"The twins are kept at Ardraigh Hall, Mr. Buchanan's country estate, though I've heard Paisley is even grander. That's the residence of his brother. Well, one of them. Mr. Euan Buchanan of Paisley is wed to a lovely lady from Edinburgh, while the younger brother, a renowned pugilist, is very much unmarried."

"A pugilist?" Loveday made a face. "I know little about bare-knuckle boxing. It sounds a bit . . . bloody."

Zipporah chuckled. "Only if you're on the receiving end, of which he is seldom. Sometimes the broadsheets print his exploits."

"But isn't boxing illegal?"

"When you're a Buchanan you make your own rules, my dear." Zipporah looked to the hearth as a footman added wood to the fire. "Though young, he's also a noted art collector, having toured Europe. He calls himself a dabbler in antiquities, but it's rumored his new estate—I forget its name—has an enviable array of Greek statuary in particular. He's a braw bruiser, as the Scots say."

"So there are three Buchanan brothers," Juliet observed, still stung by the fact the eldest wasn't as aged or as homely as she'd been hoping.

"All three form Buchanan and Company, a family enterprise begun by their great-grandfather. But you're already familiar with the firm, as they deal in your tobacco."

Loveday's brow tightened. "Tobacco aside, I do wonder what became of his first wife. And what he named his children. The sort of questions that are none of my business and I daren't ask."

With a nod, Zipporah poured more chocolate. "A person's past is best left for them to divulge in their own time."

"Yes, 'tis best," Loveday said. "I admire Mr. Buchanan's fortitude. Atlantic crossings, especially in autumn, are fraught with danger. I've only been to England and back, though Juliet braved a voyage with Father when she was but sixteen."

"Only to the West Indies, which is a much shorter sailing time." Juliet took another sip. "How long is Mr. Buchanan to be here?"

"Your father said he came to find a colonial bride." Zipporah passed a dish of small sugar-dusted cakes. "I don't know that he'll leave without one."

Juliet took a cake and could hardly contain a smile, delighted their conversation kept circling back to the Scot.

"Well, he certainly has a bevy of beauties to choose from, staying with the Ravenals," Loveday replied with a sudden nonchalance that pained Juliet.

"But aren't they a bit youthful and overly frivolous for a man like himself?" Juliet countered. "Besides, Frances is nearly affianced with one of the Byrds, and there's talk of Lucy aligning with the Lees. That leaves Judith, who is entirely too young. Surely a man of Mr. Buchanan's stature and sphere needs a more mature partner. Someone who has a fondness for small children and an understanding of estate management. Someone with a head and heart for entertaining."

Both Zipporah and Loveday stared at her, cups suspended.

"Think of all the possibilities with such a fortune," Juliet said with relish. "One could share the wealth, invest in the lives of others less fortunate, do all manner of good."

"Indeed," Zipporah replied, a mischievous light in her eyes. "We shall be considering all you've said most seriously."

Loveday gave an equally disconcerting wink. "And in the meantime we must hang some mistletoe."

20

A good conscience is a continual Christmas.
Benjamin Franklin

*L*eith returned to Williamsburg half frozen to the saddle, snow turning his matchcoat stark white. He'd made a circuit of half his Virginia stores on the coast and up the James River till rough weather had beaten him back. Visiting the southern colonies in summer was punishment enough, but mayhap winter was worse. His horse had thrown a shoe in the northern neck, and he'd had to cross a stream that seemed more river when a ferry failed. One tavern had no private room, so he'd shared a garret with one too many odiferous, snoring colonials. The next night, rather than repeat the travesty, he'd slept in the stables.

Now, frozen to the core, he'd never been so glad to see a kirk spire or smoke rising from countless brick and wood buildings. He turned onto England Street, the slush muting his horse's hooves. The borrowed stallion was smaller than he was used to and trained to a snaffle bridle yet tough as an Indian pony and of impeccable pedigree.

"Well done, Janus." He ran a gloved hand down the snow-white mane once he'd dismounted at the Ravenals'. Behind their townhouse, a small brazier burned at the stable door. "An extra measure of oats," he told the groom through numb lips.

After scraping his boots clean at the rear entrance, he went through the back door and up a back stair, finding the house empty. Had the Ravenals gone upriver again? His host had given him free rein of the townhouse during his stay, and the silence was welcome. Too exhausted to be good company, he passed down the second-floor hallway to his bedchamber, needing a bath and a meal but not necessarily in that order.

Within an hour he'd had both. The hearth's robust fire chased the chill from the room and cast orange light on the papered walls. Snow still swirled down and mounted against the windowsills. Finished with a hearty meal on a tray, he dozed in a Windsor chair beside the fire, chin to his chest. A deep, dreamless sleep was curbed by the sudden snap of the fire, returning him to the December dusk. Voices sounded from outside.

"The first noel the angel did say
     was to certain poor shepherds in fields as they lay;
     in fields where they lay keeping their sheep,
     on a cold winter's night that was so deep.
     Noel, Noel, Noel, Noel . . ."

He pulled himself to his feet, went to the nearest window, and looked down, finding a dozen or so carolers crowding the front steps below. Mumming and wassailing he was used to, but not caroling. They were a picturesque bunch in the snow, all wearing capes, the women's bonnets trimmed with bright ribbon, the men in beaver hats.

He'd nearly forgotten it was December. His parents, like many Scots, refused to celebrate Christmas or Yule.

When a knock sounded on his bedchamber door, a masculine voice invited him below. The footman? The last thing he wanted was to be sung to. He wasn't dressed for company. His hair hung lank and damp about his shoulders, and he was in a long sark, no breeches, feet bare.

"Nae," he half shouted to still the footman's knocking, then felt a sudden chiding. Why had he not simply ignored him instead?

The revelers were as exuberant as he was reluctant, their outright joy somewhat nettling. When had he felt that same sense of freedom? Of unguarded release?

To his dismay, they began another song. Yet he couldn't move from the window despite the chill reminding him to return to the fire's warmth.

"God rest ye merry, gentlemen,
   let nothing you dismay . . .
   O tidings of comfort and joy,
   comfort and joy."

Comfort and joy? He ken neither. His body felt cold and his soul colder still. It had been cold for a long time. Before Havilah's passing even. That coldness seemed akin to the shadow that encased him. A flat, joyless, comfortless cocoon he couldn't break free of.

The singing faded on a final note. Still he didn't move. The carolers were silent now, backtracking down the steps, all but one. A face turned up to him, framed by an odd mix of dusk and weather. *Snow light.* The white plume of her indigo bonnet danced in the wind. Juliet Catesby held his gaze in a way that reached down inside him and stirred something lost.

130

He couldn't give up that gaze. He returned it with a fervor that felt feverish. After several exquisite seconds, she was the one who turned away, hastening down the slick brick steps to catch up with the other carolers. Half wishing he'd gone below, he watched her cloaked figure disappear in faster-falling snow.

The tick of the mantel clock in the unfamiliar chintz bed-chamber was overloud. Juliet turned over in the canopied bed, facing away from the window, as charred logs settled in the grate. In this borrowed room on England Street she could hear all sorts of noises. The night watch. A dog barking. The clatter of coach wheels and horse hooves. The snow seemed to cushion yet magnify the world all at once. This, she told herself, was what now drew her to the window. Not the house across the street and slightly to the left, its hand-some lines dark save a light in a single window. The very window she'd spied Leith Buchanan looking down from as they'd been caroling.

Could he not sleep?

She'd heard he was traveling. Had it been a fortnight since he'd shared their Sabbath table? She and Loveday had been in Williamsburg nearly a sennight because of weather. In that time, Hosea had relayed the message that the runaway mother and daughter were improving but needed further refuge. Meanwhile, Father had secured a marriage license, and the wedding day was set for two days hence. The Rav-enals were to return from Forrest Bend in time to celebrate the nuptials in Zipporah's parlor.

Juliet wished they were Loveday's instead.

With the house asleep, Leith had free roam of Ravenal's residence. In his smallclothes, he ignored the possibility of causing tittle-tattle if found by a maidservant and went downstairs. Mayhap he needed something to read. Ravenal had a library adjoining the first-floor parlor. Snow light illuminated the windows and allowed him to kindle a candelabra from the hearth's dwindling fire.

Holding it high, he perused shelves that wrapped the room on all sides. A treasure trove of books was tidily grouped by subject. All the agricultural tomes, predominantly tobacco, bespoke Nathaniel Ravenal's former life. Once he'd been Virginia's most prolific planter. For years the Buchanan-Ravenal liaison was legendary on both sides of the Atlantic. Ravenal had enriched the Buchanans as much as they had enriched the Ravenals, dominating the market that some scathingly called a monopoly.

And then, all at once, Ravenal had a change of heart. It began simply enough. He declared himself done with tobacco trading. His depleted tobacco fields lay fallow, and he began to farm grains instead, selling vast amounts of acreage to settle his debts, both in Virginia and Maryland and in the Caribbean. He'd even talked lately of leaving the Anglican Church and becoming a dissenter instead.

Most shocking of all, he'd freed his Africans. Though some chose to remain as paid domestic staff, he'd contracted indentures instead. Ever since, boatloads of British immigrants had clamored to work for him because of his generous terms. Leith knew firsthand because they sailed on Buchanan ships.

But not once had Ravenal explained his extraordinary reversal. *Let my actions speak for themselves*, was his succinct explanation to Leith's father by letter. Leith had expected not only an end to their complex, lucrative business association but an end to their long-standing friendship as well. How many men—and there were few—who'd forsaken slaveholding and the tobacco trade and all that came with it would continue to befriend a man who'd forsaken none of it? Not only that, he'd even extended that hand of fellowship to Leith and his brothers.

Leith had accepted Ravenal's invitation to Virginia only because he'd wanted to avoid the scandal at home. He'd expected questioning about Havilah and his failed marriage, some form of judgment and condemnation. But there'd been no haranguing or lectures from Ravenal. No cleverly disguised counsel. Just a steady, thoughtful presence that didn't preach.

Leith left the agricultural shelves and moved toward novels and poetry. *Gulliver's Travels. The Vicar of Wakefield. The Castle of Otranto. Robinson Crusoe.* Those he'd read. He'd been traveling with Jonathan Swift's satire *A Tale of a Tub*, which he'd gotten from an Annapolis bookseller. An irreligious, profane work.

Much like himself.

As he moved toward the door, his candelabra cast light on a table. There lay a Bible, open to Proverbs. Proverbs 31, to be exact.

Who can find a virtuous woman?

21

Love does not dominate, it cultivates.

Johann Wolfgang von Goethe

"Tomorrow this townhouse will be full of guests and Father will wed." Loveday sounded both glad and sorrowful as she and Juliet sewed in the parlor. "Though I wish him every happiness, I am still sad that Mama is not with us and he's moved on without her."

"I feel the same, but life continues apace." Juliet looked up from her needlework. "And I'm much more concerned about you and your prospects here."

"Which are blessed few." Loveday looked distressed as she plied her own needle.

"All the more reason for you to widen your view beyond the colonies," Juliet said gently. "I've been pondering what Zipporah told us about Mr. Buchanan's reason for being here—seeking a colonial bride. If, by chance, you were to wed a Scotsman . . ."

Frowning, Loveday leaned back against the chintz cushions, her sewing in her lap. "Scotland seems a world away."

"I shall come visit you, and you, me." Juliet turned entreating. "Please, consider it."

"All snobbery aside, I've never considered marrying a merchant. Besides, Mr. Buchanan is part and parcel of all we stand against."

Juliet could not deny it, nor that she loathed it. "And are we not equally guilty with three plantations and nearly two hundred enslaved betwixt them?"

"We are doing what we can, even a small bit, to change that." Lowering her voice, Loveday looked more distressed. "At great risk."

"Aunt Damarus does far more." Juliet examined a tiny flower in rose silk. "Perhaps as Mrs. Buchanan you might influence him, do as Nathaniel has done and change course. I pray Father follows suit."

"But you know I've always, always wanted to marry for love."

"We've both entertained that rather childish notion for some time." Juliet hated to dash her sister's dreams, but reality stared them starkly in the face. "Father and Mama married by arrangement. Their parents broached the match. Let that be our example. We'll be femes covert, with few rights, and all that we have becomes our husband's, remember. Marriage is a contract foremost. A business arrangement that has little to do with love."

"Be that as it may, I don't feel the slightest nudge toward Mr. Buchanan. And unless I'm reading him wrongly, he feels nothing toward me in turn."

"*Feelings* again, Loveday, not facts. Besides, you've only just met."

"Is that why you bowed out of the Ravenals' entertainment, claiming a headache?" A sad light shone in Loveday's eyes. "So that I could be alone, as it were, with Mr. Buchanan?"

"Don't make it sound so dreary."

"He's hardly what I'd call dreary, but I still have absolutely no designs on him, nor will I ever. Given that, don't he and his children deserve more—a loving wife and mother?"

"Of course," Juliet replied, feeling chastised. "I wish that foremost."

Loveday looked relieved. "Then let us talk no more of such matters."

Yet the future had never loomed with such magnitude. Perhaps because Leith Buchanan was in their very midst, opening the door to a very different sort of life. A life free of crops and crop failures, tobacco credit and enslavement, weather patterns and the market.

Or . . . perchance he was a momentary distraction, a passing chapter. She and Loveday might stay on at Royal Vale. Continue the secret work their mother had begun. Become spinsters like Aunt Damarus. In all likelihood, Loveday would wed another colonial and leave, yet the very thought of living alone at Royal Vale left Juliet feeling bruised.

She, more than her sister, was deeply rooted to the land, the home of their family for generations. Selah and Alexander Renick's legacy lived on through them. But only if one of them married and their children continued the line. Surely that would be Loveday.

Her beautiful, sparkling sister.

22

They dream in courtship but in wedlock wake.

Alexander Pope

Upstairs in the guest bedchamber, Juliet readied her gown for the wedding, remembering Mr. Buchanan's remark as she pinned the elbow ruffles in place. *Do you always wear indigo?*

In light of blue being his favorite color, she chose a garish purple damask with silver lace. The only hint of blue about her was Mama's pearl choker with its center sapphire pendant. Wearing it brought a pinch of melancholy, though she'd felt melancholy ever since Loveday dismissed the notion of a Buchanan courtship.

But one mustn't lose hope. Time was short. If Loveday did not want to talk more of such matters, that didn't prevent Juliet from working behind the scenes. Matchmaking was not her forte, but Juliet sensed she must seize the opportunity when it presented itself.

Drawn to the window, she studied the icy street as coaches began to form a line in front of the townhouse. The large guest list included many planters in town for the holiday season that would last till Twelfth Night in January. Father and Zipporah would leave on their honeymoon the day after Christmas, when she and Loveday would return to Royal Vale.

A gust of wind rattled the glass and she stepped back, but not before she saw the Ravenals exit their townhouse.

With one tobacco lord.

Snow coated Williamsburg like sugar icing on a wedding cake. Bride's cake, to be exact. Leith had never tasted that confection, but Juliet explained its charms as they stood by the parlor hearth after the nuptials. He liked her timely explanations. When she shed her reserve, he'd begun to detect in her a keen enjoyment of life's little pleasures like confections. But first, the feast.

"We have an abundance of fish and chowder, and stewed oysters, which are Father's favorites. Mrs. Pay—*Catesby*—prefers venison and roasted pork. If you've a sweet tooth"—she gestured toward a window—"the bride's cake is the one surrounded by nutmeats and enriched with spices, Madeira, and brandy."

Aside from the bountiful table, the jollity and laughter in the room raised his spirits. Colonel Catesby was gazing at his new bride with all the adoration of a much younger man. The new Mrs. Catesby seemed equally besotted.

Unbidden, Havilah sprang to mind in her wedding garments at the front of the kirk. Had they been so devoted? At least at first?

"My sister has a seat open beside her if you'd like to sit down, Mr. Buchanan," Juliet continued, smiling up at him. "I've sampled so much in the kitchen beforehand that I've quite lost my appetite, though I confess I'm never too full for cake."

He continued standing, glad when someone took the seat she'd suggested. Juliet left his side, disappearing to what he guessed was the kitchen. Everyone else's attention was on the happy couple, who moved about the room talking with their many guests. Juliet returned in time for the cutting of the cakes, wielding silver knives, and helped the footmen serve.

When Loveday gave a delighted exclamation from the sofa she still sat upon, holding up a piece of nutmeg, all broke out into applause. Leith watched, mystified.

Juliet was again at his side, explaining, "The lady who receives the slice with nutmeg baked inside is said to be the next bride."

"A most curious custom." He forked a bite of cake. "How did you arrange it?"

She looked up at him, feigned innocence in her gooseberry-green eyes. "Whatever do you mean, Mr. Buchanan?"

"You seem unusually determined to foist me upon your sister, Miss Catesby. Do you deny it?"

At full flush, she stammered, "I—well, you are certainly . . ."

"Astute?" He waved his fork about. "Shrewd?"

"Inebriated and imagining things."

"I've had but one whisky with cream."

A tense lull ensued. She was clearly asimmer. Had he pressed her too far?

She sighed and sampled her slice of cake. "So, you've found me out."

"I'm always alert to any scheming." He looked past Loveday to a window filigreed with ice. "It doesn't become you. Have done with your matchmaking and apologize."

She fell into a sullen silence as myriad conversations swirled around them.

"Granted, you have a low opinion of tobacco traders, Miss Catesby. But it is clear you underestimate me."

She gave a curt nod. "You are nothing if not shrewd, in spades. Perhaps proud is the better word, Mr. Buchanan."

"Aye, proud, mayhap even arrogant." He pressed on, having given the matter some thought. "Your sister might make a better pairing with my youngest brother."

"The pugilist?" Derision laced her tone.

He shrugged. "Niall's as much a catch as your bonny sister."

"Hardly a catch, sir. Her dowry is in danger of being utterly null and void."

"Nae matter. He needs none."

Loveday was still making a delightful fuss over the nutmeg as if it was a divine revelation from above. Niall, the most swayed by exuberance and beauty, would capitulate in a breath. She could do worse. He was the brawest of the three Buchanans.

Wouldn't it be a wonder if he returned to Glasgow with a bride for his brother if not himself?

23

Distance lends enchantment to the view.

Thomas Campbell

efore Zipporah and I leave on our honeymoon, I
have something to discuss with you," Father said
to Juliet the next morning. He shut the parlor door
with grim finality, hemming them in.

"Me, not Loveday too?" Rarely did he single them out. It
portended something dire, truly.

"Only you." He gestured to a chair nearest the hearth.
"You look quite spent, poppet. At the wedding reception Dr.
Blair said there's a malady going round town. I don't want
you falling ill whilst we're away."

"I shan't, Father. Don't worry a tad about that."

"Rest all you can. This season is proving as hectic as it is
joyous. We'll be celebrating with the Ravenals day after tomorrow at their residence following church. They've invited
us for Christmas dinner."

The news left her more weary—and a bit vexed. How
could she continue facing Leith Buchanan?

"I must back up a bit." He took an iron poker and stabbed the fire. "'Tis been nearly a year since you and Loveday had your miniatures painted by Copley. What you don't know is that I sent both of them to Scotland with my London agent shortly thereafter."

What? She looked to her lap, her hands folded against her quilted indigo petticoat, steeling herself. His voice—that low, brook-no-argument tone—allowed for no interruption.

"He delivered the miniatures to Glasgow along with my proposition."

Proposition. Never had the word seemed so . . . alarming.

"I asked Buchanan to choose betwixt you and Loveday based on the miniatures." He paused to clear his throat. "He sent Loveday's back to me."

She tried to make sense of what he was saying. Copley's miniature, the debt, the impossible proposal. What else was he withholding? "He chose her?"

"Nay. After consulting with Ravenal, he chose you."

"He—what?" Panic raised her gaze and her voice. "Why?"

"I am done with debt. I offered your hand in exchange for his clearing accounts, at least where Royal Vale is concerned. My other plantations I shall sell in the new year. Belle Isle already has a buyer. Vasanti Hall is a leader in Caribbean sugar production, as you know, so it shan't take long to unload that either."

Her hand offered in exchange for clearing a debt? Leith Buchanan must think her family a scheming horde.

To make matters worse, she'd been bested by the very man she disdained. A rebuke to her presumed intelligence and pride. She should have handled matters with more finesse. All had misfired badly. Did he still have her miniature?

"I had hoped that by his coming here, you'd become amicable, at least—a fine precursor to marriage. He wanted to tell you how matters stand from the first, but I objected. I refrained from saying anything about our agreement until he'd had a chance to meet you and perhaps win you over."

"Which he has not." Her voice sounded strangled as she battled between composure and tears. The sudden beating at her temples promised a violent headache.

"You will honor my wishes as any dutiful daughter would do amid marriage negotiations." He cleared his throat again, a grating sound. "Regardless of how you feel about the matter, the arrangement stands."

Feelings. Hadn't she just lectured Loveday about marriage being first and foremost a contract? The irony lashed her with a vengeance.

"When is our"—Juliet swallowed past the painful ache in her throat—"marriage to take place?"

"I've left that decision to you and Buchanan."

"What of Loveday?"

"She'll go with you to Scotland, of course. Marriage prospects there are far better than here. I'm confident she'll make the same illustrious match as you. You'll lack for nothing in future."

"What of you and Zipporah?"

"We'll retire to her home in London . . . permanently."

Another blow. "You're leaving Virginia for good?"

"As soon as possible, before that liberty is denied us. All those loyal to the British Crown must return to the mother country or face the consequences of remaining here. There's even talk our estates will be seized by a new colonial government. If that happens I shall lose everything, so I must act quickly and secure my finances." His frown eased. "Surely it gives you some comfort to know we'll all be in Britain together henceforth."

"Does Loveday know of this?"

He paused as Zipporah's voice sounded in the foyer. More visitors were arriving with congratulations on their nuptials and a happy Christmas.

Reaching out, Father squeezed her cold hand before standing. "I want you to tell her. I'm sure she'll rejoice that you're not to be parted."

For that alone I can be thankful.

24

We steal if we touch tomorrow. It is God's.

Henry Ward Beecher

The townhouse was blessedly quiet. Father and Zipporah had gone to the governor's palace for some sort of seasonal fête. In the kitchen the servants were all abuzz with last-minute preparations for Christmas Day, and a hundred different fragrances threaded through the townhouse. But Juliet's usual joy in the season's details was benumbed.

Telling her sister about their change in fortune—and future—was not something she'd envisioned doing on Christmas Eve. To cushion the news, Juliet did what she could to help set the scene. A fire made brighter with pine knots. A dozen fragrant bayberry candles shining like starlight in each parlor window. Hot cocoa and biscuits. Even another light snow fell in windswept flakes beyond the windowpanes.

"A cozy evening for just us two. I could ask for nothing better," Loveday said with a smile as she sank down atop a

Chippendale chair. "Though I can't imagine why you look so glum."

Juliet tried to smile but couldn't. Time to be done with dissembling and subterfuge. "Actually, Father asked me to tell you his news . . . which has a direct bearing on us both."

A maid served the fragrant hot chocolate, setting the tray before the fire so that the silver pot and porcelain cups shone.

"Why, you're shaking. So unlike you." Loveday looked alarmed, taking the cup from Juliet's unsteady hand. "Please tell me everything at once."

Juliet tried to quiet her whirling thoughts. Where to begin? "First, Father is to sell everything."

"What?" Loveday's arched brows nearly reached her hairline.

"In his words, he is done with debt. He fears there's to be a war and Royal Vale will be confiscated by the new American government as loyalist property in the near future."

"Our home? The only home we've ever known?"

"To circumvent that, he's selling all his holdings in the colonies and the Caribbean. Royal Vale will become Mr. Buchanan's, and he has agreed to settle Father's vast debts on one condition." Despite her roiling insides, Juliet paused to take a steadying sip of chocolate. "That he marry me."

Loveday set her cup down so hard it rattled. "*You?*"

"Somewhat ironic, isn't it, given I've been foisting him upon you, as he so succinctly put it?"

For once, Loveday was speechless.

"Remember the miniatures painted by Copley and how odd we thought it that we never saw them again? I assumed Father carried them on his person, but instead he sent them to Scotland by way of his factor with a proposition to Mr. Buchanan."

"To marry one of us? To choose between us?" Loveday stared at her uncomprehendingly. "And he chose . . . you."

"Perhaps Father isn't telling us the entirety of it." Juliet lifted her shoulders in a shrug. "Perhaps he emphasized I am the eldest and that had some bearing on Mr. Buchanan's decision."

"You've always thought so little of yourself and been dismissive of your many merits."

"And you've always been so very gracious. We shan't be parted, thankfully. Father intends for us all to sail to Scotland and to make a marriage for you there."

"Scotland, a place we've never been."

"Mr. Buchanan's younger brother is in need of a wife, which makes me wonder if Father doesn't have that in mind too."

"The braw bruiser, Zipporah calls him. Ah, how the plot thickens very much upon us, as the duke of Buckingham once said." Loveday smiled, ever the optimist. "Surely there's a silver lining somewhere. Though I prefer the words of Saint Paul—in everything give thanks. Why not think of our sudden and precipitous situation in those terms?"

"We have no choice in the matter, it seems."

Loveday reached over and squeezed Juliet's hand. "So Father has arranged a Scottish marriage for you. You'll be mistress of Ardraigh Hall with its lovely gardens. More importantly, you'll be stepmother to the twins. Though we don't know their names and ages yet, that seems a delightful prospect."

"Delightful? More daunting."

"Perhaps a blend of both." Sympathy clouded her pale features. "But I shall be there to help you in any way possible. If we were to be separated, I couldn't bear it."

"Nor I." Expelling a sigh helped Juliet not at all. "But

there's tomorrow to get through first, when I must go to the Ravenals' for Christmas dinner and meet my intended, knowing all the facts and figures. How can I possibly face Mr. Buchanan when I feel such mortification over the matter?"

Her pride was wounded. Her independence. Though he'd seen through her own matchmaking, she'd not had a whiff of his—rather, her father's—scheme. The secrecy of it still stung. Amid the marriage negotiations, she felt a deep hurt. A betrayal.

"He wanted to tell you how matters stand from the first, but I objected."

At least Leith Buchanan had attempted to deal forthrightly. Father had likely objected because he knew she would refuse.

"I know 'tis difficult." Loveday's dulcet voice returned her to the present. "As for tomorrow, remember Christmas Day. Think of our sudden change of fortune as a gift."

25

Gestures in love are incomparably more attractive, effective, and valuable than words.

François Rabelais

*L*eaving their wraps in the Ravenals' foyer, a maid ushered the Catesbys toward the dining room on Christmas Day. With a wince, Juliet, in the rear, looked up to the generous bunch of mistletoe hanging by a red velvet ribbon from the chandelier. Unbidden, future intimacies leapt to mind. Though theirs was an arranged marriage, what sort of union would it be? In name only? Or did Mr. Buchanan want more children?

She smoothed her skirts, having chosen the indigo silk gown she'd worn for her portrait painting, with its tiers of lace ruffles falling nearly to her wrists. A sign of surrender? Nay. A statement that she was now well aware of his and her father's intentions.

Though Loveday had donned a wig for the occasion, like Father and Zipporah, Juliet chose unpowdered papillote curls, her one vanity. The tidy, tight spirals cascaded about her shoulders nearly to the small of her back, a velvet indigo ribbon threading through them. When she stepped into the dining room where all the Ravenals were gathered, her gaze found Mr. Buchanan by the hearth—and he was looking straight at her.

Did he know Father had told her all?

"A happy Christmas to you Catesbys!" Nathaniel greeted them with his usual high spirits. "Come, make yourselves at home. I'm sure I'm not the only one whose stomach is rumbling—but first some Christmas punch."

Tearing her gaze from Mr. Buchanan, Juliet looked to the sideboard, which held a cut crystal bowl afloat with limes and lemons atop the proverbial holiday punch. She took a cup and, in a few moments, moved to the dining room and her assigned place, unsurprised when the Scot sat to her left. Did the Ravenals know of their impending nuptials? Rattled, Juliet turned her attention to the spotless linen napkins folded like swans and the beautiful blue and white dreftware dishes.

She was very aware of the man beside her. His plain attire contrasted sharply with Father's gaudy green velvet dress suit. He regarded her with a tight smile as if gauging her reaction to being seated beside her future husband. Given that, how would she be able to choke down a morsel of food?

"A happy Christmas to you, Miss Catesby," he said, eyes on the ornate sugar sculpture atop a mirror at the table's center.

Her reply was a whisper. "And to you, Mr. Buchanan."

Across the table, Loveday sent her a reassuring look.

The next hour was a blur of dishes, dialogue, and dismay. Juliet felt the latter welling inside her as course after course was served. There was none of the banter like before when she'd explained any curious foods or customs. He seemed sunk in thought too, making no more attempts at conversation after his subdued Christmas greeting. Everyone else indulged in lively conversation and laughter.

When they rose from the table for the customary firing of the guns outside, Father took Juliet aside to tell her she was needed in the library. She froze, hands on the back of her chair, as Loveday and the Ravenal daughters moved to the music room across the hall.

"I'll leave you and Buchanan alone to discuss your future and all the particulars," Father said.

With that, he left and Juliet entered the book-lined room ahead of the Scot. Both of them passed beneath another giant knot of dangling mistletoe. Someone seemed intent on making kissing a requirement for every room.

She took a seat, feigning a calm she didn't feel, hands folded demurely in her lap. He sat in the chair opposite, feet to the fire, his engraved silver shoe buckles a work of art.

She focused on those, not his handsome face. There, she'd admitted it. He was handsome. Braw, didn't the Scots say? A trace of lime or mint lingered about his fine garments—or perhaps it was the punch. Desperate, she searched for something pleasing to murmur, feeling pushed into a corner.

"I sense this is as awkward for you as it is for me," he finally said.

She took a slow breath, saying on its release, "Yes."

"So I'm going to conduct this like the business venture it is."

"Very well."

"I'm leaving Virginia on Twelfth Night. I need to return to Scotland."

So soon? Twelfth Night was but a fortnight away.

"Upon the day of our marriage, you'll become my wife and Royal Vale will become my property, clearing any outstanding debts owed by your father."

Enormous debts, amassed over countless years. "You shall keep Royal Vale, not sell it?"

"Aye, for the time being," he replied, a bit too evasively for her comfort. "Once we land in Scotland, you'll reside at Ardraigh Hall and take possession of it as mistress and stepmother to my children."

"What are their names?"

"Cole and Isabella," he replied. She sensed a rare softening about him, and for a trice it softened her. "Rarely are they in Glasgow. They've recently turned three."

"Who cares for them?"

"Their aging nurse, who takes one too many naps."

She almost smiled, but he went on, as factually and formally as if they were hammering out a binding business contract. "I'll reside at the Virginia Street mansion in the city, only coming to Ardraigh Hall when time warrants."

"Not often, then."

His nay was so final, so dismissive, she envisioned a long, lonesome future. But aside from her, had he no more regard for his children than an occasional visit?

"If you should need something once there, send word to me by one of the servants."

"Ardraigh Hall is not far from Glasgow, then."

"A few miles."

The faint hope she'd brought into the room was now nearly extinguished. She loathed the arrangement more the longer she listened. "You don't need a wife, Mr. Buchanan. You need another nursemaid, and though I am rarely guilty of napping, I am not that woman."

"You would have otherwise, Miss Catesby?" His gaze swung to her instead of the leaping fire at their feet. "Then state your terms."

Beneath his sudden scrutiny she nearly squirmed. "As the

stepmother of your children, I would require your ongoing presence, not for my benefit but theirs. How else are they to know you as their father?"

"My ongoing presence?" He turned dark as a thunder-cloud. "I'll not be dictated to about my time or my relationships."

"You told me to state my terms. That is one of them."

"And I'm offering you marriage with honorable, contractual conditions."

"Contractual, yes. But marriage is foremost a covenant."

"I suppose that is some sort of biblical concept muddying the matter."

"*Muddying* the matter? Then I suggest you devote some time to it since it has existed since the foundation of the world."

"I need not ponder it. A covenant requires some sort of relationship. What I'm offering is a contract, in name only. I am a busy man with little time to expend. Many marriages are by arrangement under less suitable conditions, yet you balk. Given your father's finances, you have little to bemoan and less to demand."

"Yet I do have demands, namely my sister's dowry of five thousand pounds."

He shrugged as if she'd asked for fivepence. "Name whatever price you will."

"I ask that you forsake all trade built upon the backs of slaves."

His jaw hardened. She saw it and she hated it. His entire empire was built on rum and sugar, tobacco and misery.

"Yet you yourself are from a slave-owning family, Miss Catesby, while I own none."

A flash of white-hot fury swept through her. "My father owns slaves, Mr. Buchanan. I do not. And if we're to have any semblance of a relationship, you must find more noble ways of enriching yourself at the expense of others."

"Diversify, you mean."

"Let Nathaniel Ravenal be your example. Many inside and outside Virginia are doing the same. He's no longer in debt and has a clear conscience."

"I'm not here to discuss Ravenal, admirable as he is. Our marital arrangement is a way to cancel a debt with very generous terms." He leaned back in his chair, hands curving over its wooden scallop-shell arms. Confident. Unconcerned. The glint of his signet ring—of the very design that had sealed the bond owed, the one she'd found on Father's desk—caught her eye. Another reminder that she had little voice in the matter.

"I sense there is far more that needs discussing. What else would be required of me as your wife?"

"I would require your company on occasion," he said. "There are some society functions that demand my attendance—and yours."

On occasion. More a marital front, a mirage. Did he sense her continued resistance?

"I could augment the proposition. Take you to Bath." He ran a hand over his clean-shaven jaw. "A honeymoon by all appearances."

Bath? Did he know she'd always wanted to visit there? Father must have told him. Perhaps in Bath she could find relief from the headache that almost continually beat about her temples. Yet he was offering her Bath like a bauble on a silver plate. A sort of bribe. A faux honeymoon.

She nearly squirmed, her humiliation complete. She was livid not only with Father but at their circumstances, tobacco and all its ensuing wretchedness, and the powerful men who perpetuated it.

"I may be indebted, but I am genteel, Mr. Buchanan," she said breathlessly. "Never in my life did I imagine I would be reduced to discussing matrimony with a mere merchant."

Silence. Had she hurled one insult too many?

The gaze he turned on her was ice-blue. "I won't force you, Miss Catesby."

Shaken and needing air, she got up with what remained of her tattered dignity and fled the library, going in search of the music room. Leith Buchanan didn't follow.

26

The greater part of our happiness or misery depends upon our dispositions, and not upon our circumstances.

Martha Washington

*J*uliet felt trapped like a fox before hounds. A dozen different scenarios played out in her panicked thoughts, keeping her awake that night and bedeviling her on the return up the James River.

She could go to Philadelphia and live with Aunt Damarus. But if she did, Father would sell Royal Vale.

She could press Loveday to accept the Scot instead.

But he had, for unknown reasons, chosen her.

If she herself refused him, she might deprive Loveday of a suitable match, perhaps even a romantic one, in Britain.

What did Mr. Buchanan think of her now?

She'd seen no more of him since yesterday. Not another word had been exchanged between them after their fractious library meeting following Christmas dinner, when they'd all moved to the music room for further festivities. But the burn of it lingered.

Jostled about in the coach on the rutted road, Juliet swiped at her eyes with a gauze pocket handkerchief, glad Loveday was dozing. They'd stayed up till midnight at the Ravenals', and she'd been struck by how composed Mr. Buchanan remained the rest of Christmas Day, while she herself was a knotted thread.

She'd almost expected him to come bid her father and Zipporah goodbye this morning, but there'd been no sign of him. She'd overheard him say he had a few remaining stores to visit before his departure from York Town on one of his ships. Perhaps he'd already left. The Ravenals weren't expected to return to Forrest Bend until after Twelfth Night.

She looked out the coach window to get her bearings, but it gave her no joy that they were almost home. Home as she knew it had ceased to be a haven, a refuge. It was simply a structure and a piece of ground to be sold or given over to a husband.

As they passed beyond the wrought-iron gates that marked Royal Vale's entrance, it looked unutterably dreary, a stark landscape that simply reminded her of what had been lost and all that loomed.

Leith returned to the Ravenal townhouse after finishing his circuit of his Chesapeake stores. He'd stopped at the Williamsburg stationer's for a letter book to record the business he'd transacted in the colonies and what still needed addressing, including penning letters to various factors to be posted before he left for Scotland. Time ticked on, and he received word the *Glasgow Lass* had returned to Virginia from Barbados with a hold half full of cargo.

After supper that night, Ravenal invited him into his study to tell him of his travels and discuss the latest political news.

But their easy exchange eventually wound round to Juliet. Leith had made no secret of the circumstances from the first, at least with his host, who had been enlightened further by Colonel Catesby before he left on his honeymoon. Sore subject though it was, Ravenal dealt with it in his usual magnanimous way.

"So, how did you leave matters with Miss Juliet?" he asked, offering him the sweet leaf tobacco he once grew.

"On Christmas Day?" Leith lit his pipe absently. "Right before telling me she never imagined she'd be reduced to discussing matrimony with a mere merchant?"

Ravenal chuckled. "I don't mean to make light of it, but after having three daughters, I am not surprised by her, um . . ."

"Domestic gust?" Leith answered wryly.

With a nod, Ravenal sat down in a leather armchair and trellised his fingers. "Do you want me to talk to her?"

"I doubt it would do much good. Her pride is wounded. She sees me as the enemy, the ruination of her family's fortune, a lowly merchant." Leith drew on his pipe, remembering her unchecked horror. "She's also angry with her father, perhaps rightfully so."

"Being used to settle a debt wouldn't sit well with any woman, nay." Ravenal paused. "Colonel Catesby has treated her more like a son than a daughter, letting her help manage his plantations and make decisions most women would balk at. She's independent as a Patriot, besides."

"You ken her well."

"Being godparents, Catherine and I have known her since her christening twenty-six Septembers ago. She's as fine a woman as Virginia ever made, and you could do no better."

Leith studied the smoldering pipe in his hand, the bowl cherry red. "As it stands, I want to let her be."

"Sail to Scotland without her?"

"I'll not force her."

"Then she'll be left to face her father upon his return and all the consequences."

"I'll not have another tragedy on my hands," Leith replied, the darkness creeping in again like dusk. "Not when the former is still in the papers."

"Did you tell her of the first Mrs. Buchanan?"

"The timing didn't seem right, though I'm surprised she hasn't heard of it by now."

"She may have. To her credit, she's not a gossip and avoids those who are." Ravenal got up to add another log to the fire. "Despite her, um, domestic gust, I've never seen her speak or act unkindly."

"This is the second time she's put me in my place."

"The first being at the Raleigh Tavern?" At Leith's nod he continued. "She's not one to mince words when she stands in for her father, as you saw in the Apollo Room. Part of that has to do with the fact she feels he's too swayed by his overseers and factors. The truth is, he's long been bored with—even unsuited to—the planter's life and all its encumbrances."

"I gathered that. My fear is that if we wed, I'll not hear the end of it the rest of my life."

Ravenal seemed untroubled. "Perhaps she simply needs time alone to think matters through. She knows when you're leaving?"

"I told her, aye." Leith had relived the bitter exchange a hundred times in his memory. Usually he was better at scuttling unwanted thoughts, but worn down as he was of late, he'd entertained them instead. "I don't have any illusions about her deciding in my favor."

"I'll continue to pray about it," Ravenal said. "I'd advise you to do the same."

Pray? Leith couldn't recall the last time he'd gotten down on his knees. Not since childhood. But perhaps one's posture didn't matter. He'd rarely given that a thought either.

He stood, knocking the dottle out of his pipe in the hearth's ashes before excusing himself. He started toward the door, the headache he'd returned with tightening around his temples. Swallowing past the rasp in his throat, he reached into his waistcoat pocket and withdrew the miniature. Stifling the urge to open it and look at the likeness, he simply placed it on the table near the open Bible, bade his host good night, and climbed the stairs to his room.

27

My life had lost its relish when liberty was gone.

Olaudah Equiano

All thoughts of Leith Buchanan had flown from Juliet's mind when she'd arrived home, at least for the time being. Since she and Loveday had been in Williamsburg, the previous fugitives had been provisioned, then continued on their way as new arrivals reached the tunnel. They'd come from Carolina and for a time could go no farther than Royal Vale's winter kitchen and cellar. The couple's baby soon turned feverish and fretful, causing them all concern.

"They need thawing out," Rilla told Juliet and Loveday. "A warm fire and clean bedding and clothes. Rest and plentiful food."

"Tonics too." Mahala shared what she'd taken from Loveday's stillroom. "Your remedy for fever worked straightaway and relieved the babe. Didn't even use tincture of opium to help her sleep."

"Though it's hard to travel in winter, they came at a good

time, with your father away and the overseers busy with Christmas leave till now," Rilla said, returning to her cooking.

Ambrose and Grace and little Mary seemed safe for the time being, warm and well-fed near the kitchen hearth. Juliet found herself wishing they could stay longer, till spring, when the weather cleared. What brutalities had made them run? Were they about to be separated and sold? She daren't ask. She only concerned herself with the present, as it overwhelmed her to think about their past *and* their future.

She sat down to pen Aunt Damarus another carefully worded letter prior to the family's coming to Philadelphia, if they made it that far. For once her own personal woes were pushed from her thoughts.

Rilla watched over the new arrivals with the zealousness of a grandmother as the winter wind howled what seemed to be a warning. All of them seemed to share an unspoken thought. How could the family continue to freedom in such conditions?

"May I hold her?" Juliet asked tentatively, sitting on a stool beside the cellar's hearth, where they bedded down.

With the smile of a proud parent, Grace handed her Mary. Tiny and doll-like, the child seemed content to sit upon their makeshift bedding and play with a rag doll and teether. She turned wide eyes on Juliet, her dimpled hands suspended until she seized the necklace Juliet wore and brought it to her mouth.

"That's no play-pretty, child," Grace cautioned as Juliet smiled and exchanged it for the teether.

For some reason the Buchanan twins sprang to mind. Cole and Isabella. Though they tugged on her heart in a hazy, secondhand sort of way, she had little sympathy for them living in so elevated a place as Ardraigh Hall when the child on her lap had no home.

"How old is she?" Juliet asked.

"Born last year when the cotton bloomed," Grace answered without elaboration.

"She's of a calm temperament, seems like," Loveday observed, sitting down beside them.

"For that we're thankful," Ambrose said from the doorway. "Can't have her fretfulness give us away."

Loveday nodded, brow creased with concern. "I wish we could keep you here till the weather warms."

"How far is the coast on foot?" he asked.

"About twenty-five miles east of us," Juliet told him. "What do you know of the journey?"

He thought for a minute. "Needs be we go to salt water near a place called York. We've heard clear to Carolina that a ship's captain has a sloop there anchored on the river north of town."

"He flies a flag with a dove like the one painted on the warehouse where he docks." Juliet spoke slowly and softly. "He's Quaker and a well-respected seaman—one of the Friends who've pledged to help you gain your freedom. He'll carry you to Philadelphia, where you'll meet more Friends who'll help you there."

Lord, please let it be.

The next afternoon, Juliet met with the overseers in Father's stead. Of the four—Whalen who oversaw the corn, Kilgore who managed the grain, Nash who supervised the indigo, and Riggs—it was always Riggs who most worried her. Ringed around Father's desk, hats in hand, greatcoats in various stages of wear, they were an unsmiling, serious lot.

"My father will soon return, but in his absence I'm acting in his stead. He's requested your account books to review now that it's the start of a new year." Juliet chose her words carefully, crediting Father for leaving Hosea at Royal Vale. He stood behind her chair, an imposing presence, ready to assist in whatever needed doing. "Once Father returns, he'll meet with each of you separately regarding contracts."

Or would he, in lieu of further contracts, tell them he was leaving Virginia for good? She felt duplicitous in light of what she knew, and that alone stole whatever confidence she'd mustered for this meeting.

Taking a breath, she addressed plantation repairs that needed tending, as well as the overseers' sundry needs and complaints. Through it all she sensed Riggs's resistance. He even cracked his knuckles in a most maddening manner. He clearly resented her being a woman who deigned to tell him what to do. But his resistance went far deeper, she knew. Hosea had cautioned her this morning that Riggs likely had a spy in the quarters, privy to what she and Loveday were doing in the tunnel and elsewhere. That alone turned her to ice.

Riggs was cunning, resentful, and as unpredictable as the weathervane atop their cupola. Juliet had argued vehemently for his dismissal in the past, as had Mama, but Father refused. Never had Royal Vale boasted so competent a tobacco grower, and with their cavernous debts, the risk was too great to hazard the crop and production to a newcomer, no matter how well recommended. Or so Father said.

After an excruciating hour, Juliet ended the meeting abruptly if only to have Riggs out of her sight. The men filed out, and she sat, shaken, realizing she'd eaten nothing since yesterday.

"Would you like some breakfast, Miss Juliet?" Hosea's concerned voice reached out to her. She'd almost forgotten his presence.

She nodded, though she'd lost her appetite. "Gunpowder tea and toast, thank you. Then I'll return to Father's business."

28

No one will gain all without having lost all.

Madame Guyon

"Allow me to send for Dr. Blair," Mrs. Ravenal said to Leith from the doorway of his bedchamber. "Your cold has taken a turn for the worse and your cough is alarming. It could well become a pleurisy of the lungs."

"I've had worse." Leith tried to reassure her without sputtering. "If I keep to my room, I should be well by the time I sail."

But he was beginning to wonder. He couldn't actually recall a time he'd lain listless this long. Not in recent memory. Various fevers and maladies often laid his colonial factors and storekeepers low, but he shrugged such ailments aside, never thinking any would slow him.

His hostess went away and sent up a servant to bring him broth and toast. Nauseous, Leith told him to set it on the small table near the hearth. Ravenal had brought more books while he was sleeping. They were stacked on his bedside table beside a decanter of well water within easy reach. He

noticed Swift's satire was missing. Had his host removed
that blasphemous book? In its place were Thomas à Kempis,
Watts's hymns, and other edifying works. Leith's momentary
amusement veered to concern.

Did Ravenal think his illness mortal?

To prove otherwise, he pushed back the bedcovers, his
bare feet meeting the carpet whose intricate red pattern
swam before his eyes. The effort brought an instant sheen
of sweat. Dampness lined his brow and wet his nightshirt.
Another coughing fit seized him, ending with an unforgiv-
able curse. Fixing his eye on the unappetizing tray a few feet
away, he pushed himself up from the bed and grabbed for
the bedpost.

He missed the mark as another dizzying wave rolled
through him, and he fell headlong into blackness. His hearing was the last sense to fail him. The resulting thud shook
the room if not the townhouse, accompanied by a sharp
shattering of dishes.

Now early January, the snow melted and the weather
began to clear. Could this be the answer to their prayers?
The household made quiet preparations for their travelers,
and Juliet sought out Loveday.

When she found her in their dressing room among their
traveling chests, folding a gauze apron, she felt a flicker of
panic. "What are you doing?"

"Preparing for Scotland," Loveday answered brightly, as
if this was naught but a pleasure cruise up the Potomac.

Juliet withheld saying Hades would be more welcome. She
hadn't told Loveday about her last bitter conversation with
Mr. Buchanan. "I've not consented to Father's scheme. We
may not ever leave here."

She gave Juliet a slight smile. "We must be prepared, just in case."

"Do you truly want to forsake the only home we've ever known?"

"I want to make a fresh start somewhere." Loveday reached for a fichu. "I want you to be away from Father's business and all the things here that bedevil you. I want to see you free of headaches and the light returned to your eyes."

True, her headaches were always present now in varying degrees. She was either getting one, getting over one, or in the throes of one. But it hardly equaled the suffering of the trio in the cellar.

Loveday went about the dressing room plucking ribbons and lace ruffles from a drawer. "I feel in my spirit the liberty of travel will soon be denied us."

I feel in my spirit. It had been one of Mama's sayings. Rarely had it been proven wrong. Pondering it, Juliet leaned into the doorframe and crossed her arms.

"I shan't forget your favorite hat—the blue-flowered bergère with the Brussels lace." Loveday took it from a hat-stand and stowed it in a bandbox. "Never mind us. When will our guests be safely on their way?"

"Tomorrow, perhaps," Juliet said, her unrest rising. "All is in readiness if the weather holds."

At the sound of hoofbeats, Loveday paused her packing and looked toward the front lawn. Juliet stayed by the door. Father and Zipporah already?

"A post rider is turning up the drive." Loveday leaned into a sunlit window, hands pressed upon the sill. "Oh my, I pray nothing has happened to the honeymooners—or Aunt Damarus."

The very mention sent Juliet downstairs just as Hosea returned from outside, post in hand. She took the paper, thankful the wax seal wasn't an ominous black, and passed into the parlor, Loveday on her heels. There she opened the post, spilling something onto the carpet.

"Oh my!" Loveday bent to retrieve it. In her open palm lay the miniature Father had given Mr. Buchanan. She sent Juliet a beseeching look. "Please, read it aloud."

On tenterhooks, Juliet did so, the foolscap giving a crisp rustle.

> *Dear Juliet,*
>
> *I am writing this letter against the wishes of Leith Buchanan but feel it prudent to inform you he is gravely ill. He is now under the care of Dr. Blair, who is not hopeful of his recovery. Since you parted on uncertain terms, he left me this miniature he had carried on his person, which I now return to you.*
>
> *I trust you and your sister continue well at Royal Vale.*
>
> *Ever at your service,*
> *Nathaniel Ravenal*

"Uncertain terms?" Loveday's grieved look shamed Juliet. "You've kept something from me. Clearly I'm in the dark."

Juliet began brokenly, "'Tis complicated . . ."

Stepping back, Loveday passed the miniature to Juliet. She then burst into tears and fled the parlor, her hurried footsteps on the stairs carving deeper dismay into Juliet's heart. Her tenderhearted sister felt things deeply. Loveday's hopes were undeniably dashed. Had she truly wanted to sail to Scotland and make a new start, or was she just being brave to bolster the both of them?

Juliet sank down atop the carpet, the miniature before her. Never had she expected to hear such ill tidings. The letter had been written early this morn. "Gravely ill" meant a hundred haunting maladies. Malaria. Smallpox. Yellow fever. The flux. Leith Buchanan might now, hours later, be dead.

For all his faults, the man had seemed in the best of health. Robust . . . riveting.

The honest admission rebounded like a slap. She could no longer deny it. She'd expected revulsion, not attraction. Disgust, not desirability. He stood for all that she loathed.

Lord, please don't let him die.

"Are you well, Miss Juliet?" Hosea hovered at the parlor doorway, ever ready to help.

"I'm afraid Mr. Buchanan is gravely ill in Williamsburg."

"I'm sorry to hear it," he replied, raising his sleeves. "A most generous guest. Gave me the cuff links he wore that I admired upon his leaving."

Juliet blinked, feeling as if she was hearing about someone else. Had her prejudices blinded her to his finer qualities so completely? "Kind of Mr. Buchanan . . . good that you have that memory of him."

While she herself had last left the Scot with a scathing word.

"Should I have Lilith bring herbal tea up to Miss Loveday?" he asked.

"Yes, thank you. Perhaps that will help."

Juliet continued to sit atop the rug, the letter and miniature before her. She hardly heard Loveday come in a half hour later, tears dried, though her face was still blotched red.

Instead of taking a chair, Loveday sat down on the carpet across from Juliet, their skirts billowing about them. "Tell me everything," she said.

Juliet picked up the miniature, staring at her own reflection. "There's something I'm not even telling myself, mainly that my feelings for Mr. Buchanan override my good sense."

"Feelings? So you admit to them. And they aren't loathing."

"When I first saw him at the Raleigh Tavern for the tobacco meeting, I was . . . intrigued. He, being a stranger, of course, stood out, though it had little to do with the eye patch he's since shed. Then, the evening of the ball when I realized who he was, I was all the more enamored despite everything."

"And you feel it scandalous?"

"It defies explanation."

"Who can explain attraction? 'Mysterious love, uncertain treasure, hast thou more of pain or pleasure! Endless torments dwell about thee: yet who would live, and live without thee!'"

Torments, truly. "The late Joseph Addison." The poem only made Juliet more moody.

Loveday's luminous eyes turned piercing. "What are you going to do?"

"What is to be done?" Juliet looked at the discarded letter lying between them. "The fact remains, I abhor all that he stands for and can only pray my infatuation is fleeting. Meanwhile, Mr. Buchanan seems to be dying. That may well end the matter."

"And if it doesn't?"

Juliet returned the miniature to the letter and refolded it. "We have other pressing things to think about in the cellar with those who needs be on their way."

Bundling up in her warmest wraps, bonnet, and boots, Juliet cleared her head by taking a long walk about the grounds of Royal Vale. The frozen ground was slick, as slick as their circumstances. One wrong move could cost them dearly, both in terms of their cellar guests and her and Loveday's future.

Why had she been so caustic with Mr. Buchanan? Had her humiliation of him lent to his illness? Was she partly to blame for his current state? The possibility gave her no peace. She'd behaved abominably. Even Aunt Damarus would call her frightfully unladylike. Not to mention her outright rebellion against Father's wishes.

She continued on in silent melancholy, the wide river before her a shiny pewter beneath cannonball clouds. Even in midwinter the land held a deep, unshakable beauty. How blessed they'd been to walk where generations of Renicks and Catesbys had walked. Yet Father was willing to let it go to someone else entirely, a stranger with no ties whatsoever.

But Father wasn't a Renick. He'd merely assumed ownership of the land once he wed their mother. Juliet sighed. What would Mama think of this sudden turn of events? Would Father have dared to sell her family home in her lifetime?

Juliet turned round and looked hard at the house itself. A place was made of more than the bricks that built it. Those within were what mattered most. They loved and laughed, talked and dreamed, disagreed on occasion, and grieved. Though Royal Vale had lost its heart since Mama had died, it was still their home, the only home they'd ever known.

Was it wrong to be so attached to brick and mortar? Might she not make a home elsewhere, with other people, even on a distant shore? With the last man she'd ever consider?

Her earthly father had made his wishes plain. She looked skyward, more pensive than ever.

What would her Father in heaven have her do?

29

Our country is that spot to which our heart is bound.

Voltaire

With more determination than he'd ever mustered, Leith left the Williamsburg townhouse. Ravenal accompanied him in the coach, a gut-wrenching ride of thirteen miles that spilled them onto York Town's sunny, teeming harbor in sight of the ship that would take him home.

Home.

How little consideration he'd given to the word in the past. Now, with fierce longing, he craved the familiar plainstanes at the foot of King William's statue in the square . . . the sunrise over the Clyde . . . the blast of the six o'clock mail gun announcing the post-horse from Edinburgh with the newspapers. He needed to smell the ink and leather of his office and hear the tap of his Malacca cane across the marble floor of the exchange. He wanted to meet his fellow lords at the Saracen's Head and have a meridian while discussing market prices and cargo.

But a fathomless ocean lay between him and what he

wanted. He stood by, wishing he had his cane to help keep him upright in the bitter, gusting wind while Ravenal helped him manage his trunks and papers. For once Leith regretted he had no manservant to help him.

Ravenal clasped him firmly by the hand. "You'll write when you land."

Leith nodded, too worn for much speech. "I canna thank you enough for your many kindnesses."

"I'll pray for your continued recovery." Ravenal's eyes reflected serious concern. "I wouldn't agree to your going unless you'd convinced me a ship's surgeon was aboard."

"There's also a parson," Leith replied wryly. Ignoring the rattle in his chest, he kept his breathing shallow to refrain from coughing. "And a newly outfitted honeymoon suite."

Ravenal winced. "Let us get you aboard, then."

The next hour was a tumult of trunks and gangplanks and companionways till Leith was finally aboard the *Glasgow Lass*, more than ready to leave Virginia and its bitter memories behind.

Juliet had saturated the coming night in prayer. Surely that would protect them. The weather was clement if cold. Dawn would bring a hard frost. Staying away from the quarters was her goal, especially if Riggs had a spy there. She chose the little-used path from the side of the house that crossed the main road leading to Williamsburg and eventually York.

With Loveday standing watch in the unlit cupola for a half hour before their leaving, Juliet helped ready the fugitives, providing warm clothing and sturdy shoes for travel, the baby bundled securely to her mother in a linen, fur-lined sling.

Silent, Juliet led the way without a single light, letting the moon suffice. The wintry January ground seemed to seep past her thick leather soles and freeze her stockinged feet. Enveloped in her black mourning cape and hood, she blended in with the night and had taken pains to make sure the fugitives were darkly clad as well.

They reached the old oak that had stood since Rose-n-Vale's founding more than a century before and marked the farthest edge of the plantation. The trees were thicker here, providing cover as they crept forward, the stirring of an animal causing them to pause now and then. When they came to the road that led east, Juliet considered both directions as it snaked out of sight.

Few Virginians traveled by night in winter. Even the owls were silent, busy roosting in the coldest weather. When Mary gave a mewling cry, they all halted, and Juliet sensed the parents' panic.

Lord, have mercy. Please grant us safety.

They crossed the road and kept east, still on Catesby land. Mary cried again then quieted as they skirted an open meadow with a pond at its heart, shiny as a shilling in the moonlight. For a moment the beauty stilled the tumult inside Juliet as they pressed on toward the safety of Ravenal land. She wouldn't go beyond the boundary stone of Royal Vale. The fugitives must make their way alone. 'Twas always a moment brimming with hope yet blackened with dread. She'd get no sleep this night, nor would they.

She tripped over a root, righted herself, then looked behind to make sure they were following. When she turned back around, she saw not the empty path but the black, motionless silhouette of a horse and rider.

Lord, nay.

Her pulse, already adance, seemed to beat out of her chest. Not far behind her, Ambrose drew up short, Grace and the baby between them. Motioning for them to stay where they

LAURA FRANTZ

were, Juliet started toward the rider, who kneed his bay horse and moved around her swiftly, coming between her and the runaways.

Slave patrollers? Riggs?

The whip in his hand slashed like lightning, the snap of it magnified in the stillness. Ambrose's startled cry turned her to ice. Was he hurt? Riggs's horse whirled about with a distressed whinny as if struck too. Juliet rushed toward the uneasy animal, grabbed hold of Riggs's cape, and yanked the rough fabric with all her might. Unseating him, she tumbled him onto the frozen ground.

Ambrose flashed by her with Grace and the baby in the direction they'd been traveling. A few feet away, Riggs lay strangely still. Afraid to approach him, Juliet came near enough to snatch the whip from his lax hand. Roused like a wounded bear, he rolled over and pulled himself to his feet before lunging at her. The braided leather hung heavy in her fist, weighted with lead.

Backing away from him, she brought the whip down across his shoulder and chest in one forceful, catlike swipe. Riggs's scream of pain rent the woods. His nervy horse shied away with another whinny. Grabbing for the reins, Juliet hoisted herself into the unfamiliar saddle. She leaned forward, prodded the horse toward the main road, and galloped to Royal Vale.

It was the longest ride of her life. As she dismounted near the stables, her legs nearly gave way. Loveday suddenly appeared, her face bloodless in the lamplight. Her eyes fastened on the whip in her sister's hand.

Had she seen Riggs ride ahead of them from the cupola?

Shaking, Juliet started toward the house. "I struck Riggs with his own whip, then took his horse and left him where he ambushed us."

175

"Then the jig is up and we must be away," Loveday replied, sounding as calm as Juliet was rattled and riled. "I'll have Hosea ready the coach."

Juliet took a last look at Royal Vale in the darkness, its shadowed, lamplit lines more menacing than welcoming. Still, her throat knotted as she battled wanting to waste precious minutes by returning inside the house a final time. But they had no choice. Sensing their emergency, the house servants hurried to help, bringing trunks and baggage or whatever could be grabbed in haste.

At the last, Loveday caught Juliet's hand, hastening her toward the coach. As they piled into the conveyance, their baggage lashed on top, Juliet handed up the whip to Hosea. Who knew but they might need it yet?

"To the Ravenal townhouse—Williamsburg." Her words came out breathless and broken, just short of a sob.

"Wait!" Rilla's voice sounded as she pushed a small crate through the coach window.

A distressed meow followed as Loveday took her offering. Hobbes? At such a time as this? Did Rilla sense they were fleeing, perhaps for good?

The coach lurched forward, clearing the stables and turning east toward the main road. Juliet sank back against the upholstered seat by Loveday, hands clasped, Hobbes at their feet. Neither spoke. It was to be the second-longest ride of Juliet's life.

Just before midnight, Nathaniel Ravenal escorted Juliet and Loveday into his study. Still rattled, Juliet poured out her tale of woe behind closed doors, the coach out of view behind the townhouse.

"You're wise to leave Royal Vale." Nathaniel stood by the

hearth and studied them gravely. "With your father away, Riggs could have done you harm this very night, volatile as he is."

"I'm most concerned about the repercussions of all this," Juliet told him. "Legally and otherwise."

"If Riggs goes to the authorities, there'll likely be a warrant issued for your arrest," Nathaniel said, well acquainted with the law. "Not only for assault of Riggs but for helping harbor, conceal, and assist slaves to freedom. There's also a hefty fine."

Juliet stood by the hearth, more visibly composed if only because of Nathaniel's steady presence. "Go on."

"Unless your father can convince the law otherwise, a trial will follow, and then branding, imprisonment, or whatever punishment the court decides. Because you're a woman and a planter's daughter, the case—if it comes to that—will garner considerably more attention than it would ordinarily."

She had never delved into the consequences of her slave assisting lest it deter her. Knowing Riggs's vengeful nature would exact a frightful toll, she feared the Ravenals might be tainted by association. But for now, one thought gained the upper hand, and it had nothing to do with Riggs.

Her gaze rose to the ceiling. "How is Mr. Buchanan?" She had sent a note to inquire after his health just two days ago but as yet had received no answer.

"He recovered enough to travel to York Town yesterday. There he boarded his ship to return to Scotland."

Gone.

Though she set her jaw, the tears she'd kept in check began to trail to her chin in mute misery. They dripped onto her cloak and caused a fierce ache in her throat. Reaching into her pocket for a lavender-scented handkerchief, she touched the miniature instead. It held the sting of a hornet. Finally her fingers found the linen.

Drying her eyes, she could do nothing for the sinking in her spirit. "I assumed his illness would prevent him from sailing. I wronged him and hoped to . . . make amends, apologize."

Nathaniel studied her in the light of a sole candle. "I don't know that the *Glasgow Lass* has weighed anchor. There was some delay with cargo. He may yet be in York Town."

She stared at him. *He may yet*. But if not?

His gaze sharpened. "We could go to the harbor immediately and find out."

We. Such strength and reassurance in that word. But miles more in the wintry dark?

The clock chimed midnight. Bone weary, she felt she couldn't take another step, yet she mustn't let the past jeopardize the future.

"Then let us be away," she said with a last look at Loveday before starting toward the door.

30

In short I will part with anything for you but you.

Mary Wortley Montagu

*I*n his stern cabin aboard the *Glasgow Lass*, outfitted with all the luxuries his steward could provide—a bowl of citrus, nuts and sweetmeats, smoked fish, spirits, and a stack of more *Scots Magazine* and *Glasgow Mercury* than he could read before he made landfall—Leith examined the Philadelphia-made stove he'd had built for the supposed honeymoon suite.

Ships were uncommonly frigid in winter—all but the galley, where the cook held sway. Mounted on stone slabs and sanded to protect the deck, this stove was decoratively lined with blue and white delft tiles, its chimney snaking through the weather deck. The effect was a pleasing heat that extended to the room's corners, the astonishment and envy of the entire vessel.

He pulled up a chair and sat down beside the fire. Not quite the coal-red hearths of home, but it would suffice for a few weeks' passage. He'd meant it for the comfort of his bride, but all he'd left land with was a lung ailment and the assurance of war.

The darkness had also followed him, encroaching heavier and blacker than before. It hung about him like a sodden cloak. He hadn't the strength to push it back, and so it came on like an advancing army, withering his strength. His soul. Cold. So cold. The stove's warmth failed to reach him.

Mayhap he was dying after all.

"Mr. Buchanan." A sharp rap at the cabin door preceded the steward's entry. "There's been a commotion on deck. I don't rightly know how to describe it. Someone is requesting permission to come aboard. My apologies, sir."

At well past midnight?

Leith glanced beyond the six stern windows, where other ships lay at anchor in York Town's harbor, their flickering lights like stars in the blackness. Stifling a cough, he followed the steward up to the quarterdeck slowly, fighting for each step. The exertion of being on his feet taxed him abominably, but at last he was on deck, the wintry night biting his exposed skin.

The captain stood at the rail, looking down. He pivoted, a bemused expression on his lined face. Without a word, he handed Leith a letter.

Moving toward the glow of a stern lantern, Leith opened the paper to find it blank—save Juliet's miniature. It lay in his callused palm, bringing back their scorching confrontation.

"The lady is asking permission to board, sir," the captain said, gesturing to the water.

The lady?

Stunned, Leith went to the rail and looked down. There, in a lighter bobbing gently upon dark water, sat Juliet, her face turned up to him, much as it had been in the snowstorm when she'd been caroling. Tonight she was entreating, almost beseeching. Behind her sat her sister in a scarlet cape, and several trunks.

Was the returned miniature some sort of truce?

Leith coughed, his chest so sore he felt his ribs were cracked. For a long moment he did nothing but stare back at her. Dubious, even dreamlike. It wasn't a matter of pride. He had none left. He felt turned to stone as the unbelievable present tried to reconcile with the complicated past. Never in the furthest reaches of his thoughts had he considered this might happen. Was she willing to leave the land of her birth to go with him to his own, into the unknown?

Or did she simply seek passage on his vessel?

The yowl of a caged animal interrupted his musings. A cat? He slipped the miniature into his pocket and leaned farther toward her, hands on the rail. "Will you wed me, then, Miss Catesby?"

"I shall, Mr. Buchanan. This very night if you wish."

Leith turned to a near jack. "Bring her aboard—and all with her."

Once firmly on deck, Juliet looked to Loveday to see how she was faring. But her sister was only concerned with Hobbes, whose yowling had, for the moment, turned into a more manageable mewling. It was then that Leith Buchanan took her gloved hand. He bent over with a little bow and kissed the soft leather.

With the finesse of a man born to handling business, he led them below deck while issuing half a dozen different orders at once. He summoned the ship's chaplain. Ordered their luggage to stern quarters. Roused the cook to prepare a late wedding supper and asked that warm beverages be brought. Listening, Juliet stood on the threshold of the heated suite that banished the chill of York Town's harbor from her bones.

"Our humble quarters, Miss Catesby," he said, standing to one side while she entered, Loveday behind her. "Your sister will be in one of the adjoining quarter galleries, though she's welcome here in the great cabin, benefiting from the heat of the stove. There's also a stern gallery where you can walk about in private if you like."

"Thank you," Juliet said with a demure smile, relieved their ordeal was at an end.

Or was it only beginning?

As far as their humble quarters, Juliet took in the space that was sumptuous by any standard, ignoring the pain in her head and her terrible thirst. Another crew member entered with a tray of beverages, including hot tea. She and Loveday sat down while Leith stayed standing, talking in low tones with the captain near the open door.

"Well," Loveday whispered, "I hadn't expected a Viking vessel, but this is fitted out like a modern palace."

"You don't recall much about our voyage home from school in England, as you were so ill."

With a shudder, Loveday brought the fine porcelain cup to her lips. "That was years ago, and our quarters were much humbler. I pray this voyage is smoother even if it's the middle of winter. I do wonder why this ship is still in port."

"All the details will be revealed to us in time, on both sides." Juliet knew Leith had as many questions as he had answers. "We seem to have lived a lifetime in just one night."

Too tired to talk, they lapsed into a grateful silence, finishing their tea near the stern windows just as the ship's chaplain appeared. With Loveday and the captain as witnesses, the marital knot was soon tied, Leith's signet ring on Juliet's right hand, and their signatures inked on some sort of paperwork that she hoped was legal. Once and for all she put her vision of marrying at Royal Vale to rest, burying it beneath a wave of wonder that she stood here beside the tobacco lord she'd once loathed.

As for her groom, Leith looked a bit thinner than she remembered—his coloring noticeably less robust. Illness had carved a concerning line across his brow. But she was no better, clad in disheveled black, lightheaded and still out of breath at all that had happened.

A celebratory toast ensued, and then Loveday scurried to her cabin to set Hobbes free while Leith excused himself so that Juliet could ready herself for bed. Allowed some privacy, she drank in her surroundings like a second cup of tea, admiration overtaking weariness.

Paneled in mahogany, the room was dominated by a desk. Behind the desk was a treasure trove of books in glass-fronted cases, so many tomes it resembled a bookseller's. All the furnishings seemed to be lashed down with brass loops—including two elegant walnut armchairs with cabriole legs—giving her a premonition of gales to come. The carpet beneath her feet was a lovely, lush blue, akin to the delft stove tiles. Further proof of her new husband's favorite color.

Forward of the great cabin was Leith's sleeping cabin. It boasted a bed as well as a hammock suspended from the ceiling. Through yet another connecting door was a dining room, which led to the quarterdeck where they'd come aboard. A washstand near twin bureaus held a much-needed porcelain pitcher of warm water, a basin, French soap, and linen towels. Most astonishing of all was the flushing lavatory in the near gallery.

Juliet began donning her nightclothes and braiding her unpinned hair, trying to put down her trepidation. Would Leith honor what he'd told her originally? Would this be a marriage in name only?

A single candle atop a bureau burned brightly. Wanting to say good night to Loveday, Juliet backtracked to the quarter gallery and opened the door to her sister's room. Fast asleep. Hobbes curled atop the coverlet at her feet.

Juliet returned to her own bed, climbed between linen sheets redolent of lavender, laid her head upon the pillow, and listened for a particular footfall.

Leith.

Would they hold to formality or exchange forenames as easily as they'd exchanged vows half an hour before?

It took a different kind of courage for Leith to return to his cabin. Had he given his new bride enough time? Standing outside the door, he grappled with what they'd just done. He still didn't ken what had transpired to have her arrive in the middle of the night, and they were both too worn to discuss it. Several weeks aboard ship would see it all unraveled—and, he hoped, with few regrets.

After a light tap at the door, Leith opened it a crack. The sole candle, almost guttered now, cast light on a slight rise beneath the coverlet of what was, to his mind, a very small bed. Was she asleep? He snuffed the candle, undressed, and washed at the basin, noting she'd been there before him. Clad in a clean nightshirt, he took a last look out the bank of windows.

Weary and unwell as he was, he still willed himself not to cough and wake her. Whisky, lemon, and honey lingered on his tongue from the celebratory toddy he'd just drunk in the captain's cabin. It stole through him now as he lay down in the linen hammock like a common jack would do. Though he was hardly right beside her, he was close enough to catch a trace of her herbal scent and hear her faint, rhythmic breathing as she lay turned toward him.

31

There is no more lovely, friendly, and charming relationship, communion or company than a good marriage.

Martin Luther

When Juliet awoke, it wasn't to the twinkling midnight lights of York Town but infinite blue. Dawn had long departed, flinging them into the Atlantic, where the rising sun turned the sea to sapphire. How had she slept through their weighing anchor? She wasn't the only one. Pushing herself up on one elbow, she looked at Leith, clad in nightclothes and in the curve of a hammock. Wonder crowded out any regret. Sleep eased the lines about his eyes and brow and turned him years younger.

She lay back again, staring up at the canopied bedstead, her heart beating as hard as it had the night before when she'd come to the harbor, certain he'd already sailed. Her pulse doubled when his low voice rolled with a rumble across the cabin.

"What brought you to the ship last night?"

She shut her eyes briefly, trying to come to terms with what she'd done and where to start. "I had a, um, fracas with one of my father's overseers at Royal Vale, necessitating my leaving. Loveday and I took a coach to the Ravenal townhouse and found you were no longer there—"

"Back up—a fracas?"

She swallowed. "We were helping a family of escaped slaves to freedom when Riggs—one of Royal Vale's overseers—intervened. He used a whip on one of them, so I unseated him from his horse and gave him the same."

"You horsewhipped him?"

Had she? She'd merely acted out of a long-standing rage and revulsion. "'Tis hardly a blessed start to our union, I confess." Was he expecting something more romantic? "As for Riggs, I struck him but once, then left on his horse."

"After which you came to York Town."

"We arrived around midnight, yes. Mr. Ravenal woke the port's naval officer, who told us you'd not yet cleared the harbor, so he secured a lighter to take us out to you and the *Glasgow Lass*."

"I sense you're giving me the barest facts."

Truly, the past hours had been fraught with a valley and mountaintop of emotion too overwhelming for words. The port officer had been cross as a bear when roused from his bed. It had taken considerable time to consult the ship's log, which left them believing the *Glasgow Lass* had cleared port with its cargo of iron and lumber and Caribbean rum. Undeterred, Ravenal had paid the port officer to hasten his search and secure the lighter to deliver them and their baggage to the ship. It had been no small feat for the officer to row around the hulk of anchored ships in so small a vessel in the dark. And then for Juliet not to know what Leith's answer would be . . .

She darted a look at him. He was staring up at the cabin ceiling as she'd been doing, contemplative as a monk.

"At what point did you decide to become Mrs. Buchanan?"

She resumed staring heavenward, groping for answers. *The moment you returned the miniature. The moment I heard you were ill. The moment I heard you were gone.* "I don't know. Everything is still a tumult in my mind."

"I admire your American spirit."

Did he? His voice was wry, and her answer was half slurred with sleep. "Perhaps 'tis the same spirit that will win the war."

They lapsed into silence, and she surrendered to the warmth of the bed and the gentle shuddering of the ship under sail. Vivid dreams placed her on land again, her feet mired in sand, a desperate desire to escape overtaking her—

"Sister, please, wake up!" Loveday bent over her, dragging her from sleep. "I'm concerned as it's nearly noon, but Mr. Buchanan didn't want you disturbed before now."

Juliet opened her eyes and looked at the empty hammock. Where had Leith gone?

Behind Loveday was the bank of sunlit windows and the sea. "Didn't you sleep?" Juliet asked.

"I'm afraid Hobbes is a poor sailor and mewled half the night."

"He'll adjust in time . . . as will we." Juliet began to dress, exchanging her nightgown for a shift and stays and stockings already waiting near an open trunk.

"I've laid a gown out for you and will serve as your lady's maid, at least for the voyage." Loveday's words held wonderment. "Heaven knows what awaits us once we arrive in Glasgow. We're on the cusp of a new land, a new life."

Lacing her stays in front, Juliet eyed the chosen ensemble, the gown and petticoat different shades of indigo. "Did you pack any colored gowns but blue?"

"Nay. Blue suits you best, though I'm sure you're to have

a new British wardrobe soon. Think of it! You can go clear
to Three Angels millinery in London if you like."

"*We* can go." Juliet tried to imagine it. "Though after
living so long in debt, I don't want to be more beholden to
the Buchanans than I already am."

Loveday had finished pinning the gown in place when Juliet said in despair, "My hair. I can't leave it in a night braid,
and we've no hairdressing tools."

But Loveday was already at work, securing Juliet's waist-
length hair with antique aigrette hairpins studded with tiny
silver stars. Haphazard at best, but Juliet was grateful Loveday had packed them.

"Mama's favorites." Loveday smiled, passing her a hand
mirror. "They hold a special glitter in your midnight hair
whereas they are lost in my flaxen."

A steward appeared with both a tea tray and a bucket
of coal to replenish the stove. Juliet listened for Leith, who
seemed to have given them free rein of his suite. His own
chests were against a wall, but aside from that there was
little evidence he'd been there.

Except for his humble hammock.

Hardly the wedding night most imagined. Theirs was, she
reminded herself, no covenant.

"By now, Riggs may have gone to the authorities," Loveday
murmured, admiring her teacup's fleur-de-lis pattern. "Last
night seems a nightmare. I don't suppose you've told Mr.
Buchanan our departing woes?"

"Indeed, I did." Juliet poured tea, breathing in the bohea's
comforting scent and wondering if it was smuggled. "I'm
glad an ocean is between us and Riggs, though I rue what
Father will return home to."

"Let Nathaniel inform Father and let Father manage
Riggs. You're safe, and that is what most concerns me. I

pray our runaways are well away too." Loveday took a biscuit from a porcelain plate. "'Farewell, fair cruelty,' as Shakespeare said."

"I regret leaving so suddenly that we never had proper goodbyes. Rilla and Hosea and the house servants were quite alarmed."

"Perhaps we shall return someday," Loveday said softly. "But we can hardly dwell on the past when the future looms."

Looms. An ominous word Juliet didn't like.

They grew silent, adjusting to the shouts of jacks on deck above them and the odd careening motion of the ship. Leith's signet ring glinted as she curled her fingers around her cup's handle. She was truly and thoroughly wed, though she didn't feel married. She felt confused. And she hadn't any inkling of what awaited her.

32

Being in a ship is being in a jail, with the chance of being drowned.

Samuel Johnson

*L*eith watched the topmen climb the rigging to the mast's towering topsail. Working aloft in such windy weather was a marvel of fortitude and footwork. Standing on the yardarm, these monkey-like jacks stowed the sail amid the ship's careening. The ship was tacking, zigzagging in and out against the wind. The cold air that pushed against Leith braced him and likely weakened him all at once.

Months before, the Clyde-built twin to the *Glasgow Lass* had been lost at sea. In the spring he'd stood on the west quay of Port Glasgow and watched the *Ardent* leave, laden with manufactured goods, salt, and wine for the Americas. The pride of the Buchanan fleet boasted the best master of any merchantman he knew. But the ship never arrived in Philadelphia, the crew and cargo lost. The fortune of flesh and goods haunted him.

He went below, down the stairs to his—their—cabin. Was Juliet awake? The door to her sister's adjoining cabin was closed. He'd still not come to grips they were on his ship, these unexpected Virginia lasses.

Remembering to knock, he waited till Juliet bade him enter. She was standing at the windows, the sea streaming behind her, clad in a blue gown he'd not seen before. And they were alone.

She turned toward him, and he imagined her bedecked in gems, attending a fête at Ardraigh Hall or an assembly in Bath. He hadn't told her he'd invested in Bath's Royal Crescent, due to be finished any day. Best keep that close like a trump card in whist. He'd been invited to that very game in the captain's quarters after supper tonight if he didn't have other plans.

"You need to rest," she said when he began to cough. "You're still—"

He stopped making noise, his breathing labored. "Peely-wally."

"I haven't any idea what that means, but it seems to fit." Concern softened her and made her even more lovely. "I've no wish to arrive in Glasgow without you."

"The indigo widow rather than the indigo heiress."

"Imagine the explanations I'd have to give your relatives."

He imagined it with vicious humor, sitting down in the chair she seemed intent he occupy. "It would be a frightful shock since they dinna ken you're landing with or without me."

"So we're to create something of a tempest."

"I mean to replace the usual slanderous headlines with news of a bride, aye."

She took the chair opposite him in the circle of the tiled stove's warmth. "And what is the usual slander?"

He leaned back, stifling another cough. She was a forth-right woman with none of Havilah's subterfuge and secrecy, but it led to a familiarity he wasn't entirely comfortable with.

"My late wife was fleet of foot and prone to running away." He rarely spoke of it, but the lack of surprise on Juliet's face made it easier to continue. "She was Romany, known for their wandering. A Romany princess, if there is such a thing."

"Romantic."

"It was at first," he admitted, allowing a past door to crack open. "And then it wasn't."

She looked thoughtful but was too well bred to press him further, as if she sensed it was still a sore matter. When he coughed again, she got up and poured him a glass of water. "Well, if it's any consolation, I've never been good at running."

He gave her a half smile, taking the water and downing it in a few swallows. "I'd rather you ride. Ardraigh Hall has a fine stable. You'll have your pick of any mount you please."

"Generous of you." She sat down again, holding her hands out to the heated tiles, her sleeve ruffles cascading onto her lap. "I'm sure I'll be more than ready to canter about after being aboard ship. 'Twill feel like freedom itself."

He looked about their close quarters and wondered how they'd manage for weeks without tripping over each other. "The captain has invited us to dine with him tonight in the great cabin. Your sister too."

"Kind of him. Loveday isn't feeling well, though I hope she'll get her sea legs shortly."

"And Hobbes?"

She looked like she might laugh. "Fit as a fiddle."

"Then he's welcome at table too."

"Does the *Glasgow Lass* have a cat?"

"Aye, a half-feral feline by the name of Jezebel. Hobbes best take care."

33

The roaring seas and many a dark range of mountains
lie between us.

Homer

"*Y*ou may have heard the saying of English sailors,
Mrs. Buchanan," the captain said as the meal was
served. "That the only cure for seasickness is to sit
on the shady side of an old brick church in the country."

She smiled despite the poignant reminder of their parish
church and its age-old shade trees. "I shall share that with my
sister in hopes of her recovery—and pray I stay standing."

"If you've not succumbed yet, you'll likely make a fine
sailor."

Talk rumbled on about the price of tobacco, French privateers menacing shipping lanes, and the ongoing unrest in
America. Leith told her their ship's master, Captain Hicks,
had sailed on Captain Cook's secret voyage to the South
Pacific a few years before.

"When Australia was claimed for George III?" She looked
up from her plate. "My family followed accounts of it in the
newspapers."

"What with the naturalists, botanists, and artists aboard, it was a riveting cruise," Hicks replied with enthusiasm. "There's not a finer mariner alive than Captain James Cook."

"You yourself must be lauded since you were his lieutenant," Juliet told him with a smile. She turned to Leith. "And you no less for securing him as captain."

"We're exceptionally well paid and provisioned with the Buchanan fleet," Hicks said with a nod toward Leith. "And conditions are a wee bit better aboard the *Glasgow Lass* than aboard the *Endeavor* . . . with a remarkably shorter sailing time."

They laughed, and then she grew quiet, concerned. Though Leith acted hale and hearty, she saw through his bluster. His plate was hardly touched and his color was high. Had his fever returned? He was drinking an alarming amount of Madeira.

As for herself, she was having difficulty settling her nerves as they hurtled into the unknown. How she longed for the familiar contours of Royal Vale, the security of her hearth and downy feather bed, even her favorite Worcester teacup with its bright blue flowers on a sunny yellow ground.

Leith shifted in his seat, bumping elbows with her. The clumsy encounter left her atingle. Flushing, she realized this was the first time they'd shared a meal together as husband and wife. This cruise was to be a series of firsts.

"Are you available for divine service this evening, Mrs. Buchanan?" the ship's chaplain was saying to her right.

She nearly choked on a morsel of chicken. The Sabbath. Was her befuddlement so great that she'd lost track of time? "Of course. Where shall it be held?"

"Right here at eight of the clock."

Relief made her emotional. Even out in the midst of a vast ocean, God seemed suddenly near, not left on the shores of Virginia. "Perhaps my sister will feel well enough to join us."

Leith had never been able to pay attention to divine service. When he was a lad, his mother had threatened to sit on top of him to keep him still in the pew. Tonight it seemed he was beset by that same restlessness, hard-pressed to stay composed and rein in his thoughts. That they kept drifting to Juliet didn't help matters. She sat beside him, her sister on the other side of her, and seemed rapt, even a bit emotional. Her eyes glittered, and she reached for Loveday's hand.

Was she ruing leaving Virginia?

The possibility brought a swift ache, and he coughed as if to counter it. They'd just begun the cruise, a dangerous undertaking in any season but especially winter. In this close, congested cabin where his stock again felt more like a noose about his neck, he wondered not only how he'd weather it but if he would. His awe of the sea was equaled only by his dread of it. To leave his business affairs in Britain, along with the routines and comforts of home, and venture to the colonies and back had taken a toll he'd not reckoned with.

He pinned his gaze to a map on a far wall and took a careful breath. His lungs felt oddly heavy as if he'd run a race, his mouth dry. Instead of the bone-chilling shadow that often dogged him day and night, an odd warmth stole over him that felt just as menacing. If he could only have a bracing drink of water . . .

He needed sleep. The wine he'd drunk failed to still his coughing as he'd hoped. Bedtime was likely an hour away. And now there was the torment of sleeping near Juliet, making him half mad with intrigue and longing. She was his wife, yet she wasn't.

Usually he wasn't a man given to feelings. They were

195

always suspect, unlike facts. Yet there was no denying she was a winsome mix of all he found beguiling.

And he must fight against it with all his might.

As for Juliet, he fully realized she needed his name and position as a shield and a way to honor her father's debts. But as a husband—not at all.

Juliet readied for bed, aware of Leith in the small dressing room of their cabin. He'd drunk a glass of water that she'd poured for him upon returning from divine service, but he'd accepted it with cool courtesy. Did he not like her attentions? She pondered it as she braided her hair. He seemed to be taking a very long time doing whatever men did before retiring. Since he was nearly a complete stranger, she felt an awkward curiosity about his personal habits. When he didn't come out of the dressing room, she went in.

He lay sprawled in a chair at the back of the small space, still dressed save his stock, which lay on the floor at his feet. His eyes were closed. Her hand shot out to touch his fiery face. Feverish, just as she'd suspected. His breathing was alarmingly shallow, and he seemed oblivious to her presence. She rang the bell to alert the steward, then sent for the ship's surgeon, a man as stern as he was stout.

He frowned after a brief examination in the dressing room. "I recommend bleeding, blisters, and purging, in that order."

Juliet listened in dismay, images of widowhood gathering round her. "What medicines can be given?"

"A sleeping draught of diacodium would be best."

A wan Loveday appeared in the doorway. At Juliet's questioning glance, she said, "Derived from poppies. I prefer it to bloodletting or purging, which weakens the patient."

Leith's eyes opened. "I'm nae patient."

"You are—and a very feverish one," Juliet answered quietly.

"A lingering cough . . . chest pain," he murmured, closing his eyes again.

"Pneumonia, likely," replied the doctor. "The first order of treatment is to remove Mr. Buchanan to a proper bed."

Juliet already had the covers turned back and the pillows bunched to keep Leith upright and help his breathing. With a cabin boy's help, the doctor undressed him and put him to bed, something of an ordeal as Leith coughed throughout. When the miniature slipped out of his pocket, Juliet picked it up, tears in her eyes. Slipping it into her own pocket, she returned to the matter at hand.

"A tincture of opium might be more beneficial than diacodium," Loveday said, despite the doctor's obvious disapproval. "Four grains of laudanum, to be exact. Sleep is a great restorative, and he must be kept well watered."

"Have you a medical degree, Miss—?"

"Catesby. And I do not, as women are denied that privilege."

"Midwifery would be the best pursuit, then," he said briskly.

But Loveday was undeterred, staying by Leith's side opposite the doctor.

Despite an occasional protest, Leith gave them little trouble as the medicine was given, confirming how very ill he was. Juliet vowed to stay near, though the ship's surgeon would return as needed.

Left alone with Leith, Juliet tried to tamp down her alarm as she cooled his fevered face with a wet linen cloth. The rattle in his chest signaled danger, but what more could be done?

As the night deepened, she faced her greatest fear. Even if she arrived in Scotland without him, nothing must deter her. Loveday's future was her foremost concern. If Juliet couldn't find happiness, Loveday could. And Juliet would call upon the Buchanan name and fortune to help that happen if she could. Still . . .

Lord, I want to be a wife, not a widow.

The moment held a keen lonesomeness. It cast her back to the night her mother died and how grief had met them, frightful and irreversible. If Leith were to die, it would be a slower death, his grave the Atlantic.

A sennight passed, the longest of her life. Tending him nearly round the clock except to sleep in snatches, Juliet became heartily sick of the sea and the wicked insecurity of it all, though the Atlantic stayed blessedly calm.

Back on her feet, Loveday spelled her, though Juliet rarely left Leith's side. It begot a strange, one-sided intimacy.

She now knew by heart every angle and contour of his face. The slight scar on his left temple. The faint stubble on his jaw that grew into a beard, even more roguish black than his hair. The sweep of his lashes, as long as her own but still manly. And the slightly indented left cheek she'd not noticed before—but then, he seldom smiled, as Loveday had once said.

He was wasting away before her eyes, his robust frame diminishing day by day. But he remained one of those uncanny individuals who maintained a presence even in illness. She took off the too-large signet ring he'd placed on her finger the night they'd wed. Gently, she returned it to his own finger lest she lose it, as if it might restore him to the man of strength he'd been before.

Silently she pleaded for his life, snatches of Scripture threading her thoughts, though one seemed gilded. *Beloved,*

198

I wish above all things that thou mayest prosper and be in health, even as thy soul prospereth. This she prayed over him aloud, though it was naught but a recurring whisper. Sometimes she laid her head upon his chest when his lungs seemed especially labored and willed his heart to keep beating.

And then came the golden hour. As the mantel clock struck midnight, when it was just the two of them in the cabin, Leith rallied.

34

His descent was like nightfall.

Homer

*L*eith's indigo eyes shone with sudden clarity, though his voice seemed rusty with disuse. "Why is my signet ring back on my finger?"

Juliet sat beside him, stunned by his recovery, the water she'd been trickling down his throat a sheen upon his lips. "'Tis too large and I don't want to lose it," she said quickly, sensing he mistook her action as an affront, another rejection.

"Then I shall get you another bauble that fits if ever we land." He tried to sit up, but the effort was too much for him. "Get paper and ink."

"I beg your pardon?"

"Hurry," he told her, steel in his tone. "There's nae time to waste."

She set down the cup, then retrieved a lap desk, inkstand, and quill. The daybook she'd been writing in since they'd departed York Town still held plenty of blank pages. She returned for a half-guttered candelabra.

"Listen carefully and record all I tell you." He reached out and gripped her free hand with surprising strength before letting go. "I want you to defend my interests like you would your Royal Vale indigo."

"Of course." She inked the quill, willing her nerves to settle, as his intensity startled her so. "You have my word."

He grew quiet for a moment, eyes fixed on a far wall. "Once you arrive in Glasgow, your priority is to continue fitting out the Buchanan fleet, primarily the merchantmen, with arms for future Caribbean and European trade." He coughed, the sound so deep and thick it seemed all her prayers were for naught. "Don't let anyone deter you from the Carron cannonade, which doesn't slow a ship as markedly."

"You're talking defending and arming a fleet I know nothing about."

"You'll ken more in time. We already have privateers with a letter of marque and reprisal against the French freighting outwards from the Clyde. Sailing in convoy is recommended at all times, though it's nae guarantee."

The scratching of her quill seemed to steady him, and he continued.

"If there's to be a war with the colonies and ports close, the scarcity of tobacco will spike the price. Summon all the partners of Buchanan and Company to discuss selling their stock, then offer to buy each partner's share at a fair price. Few will refuse you. Keep a close eye on the market, then sell all of the accumulated stock before the price rises further, guaranteeing a sizable profit."

She kept up with his ragged voice, though her mind was reeling. "What if your brothers object to me, a stranger, handling your affairs?"

"They'll make peace with it in time." He paused, now hoarse. "In that vein, Niall has too much enthusiasm and Euan too much restraint. They're currently purchasing properties with mineral and mining rights throughout Britain, thereby investing in coal, ironstone, and other metals, having formed the Buchanan Coal Company."

"Land speculation," she murmured. A risky endeavor.

"Aye, with the added investment of turnpike roads and canals and such. Euan has in mind to be the foremost coal master in Britain, whereas Niall has begun an extensive planting of Scots firs, larches, pines, and other trees on acquired land." He stilled, allowing her to ink her quill again. "As for my fellow tobacco lords, beware of Cochrane and associates foremost. He's continually tried to undercut us in colonial trade. Engage in nae custom with them at any level. They're naught but a pack of liars and thieves."

She penned the Cochrane name with distaste, sensing an animosity years in the making.

"Look to my other commercial interests in almost every mercantile undertaking in Glasgow and elsewhere, including Edinburgh and London. There are numerous Buchanan sugar houses, rope and sailcloth industries, including bottleworks, printworks, and other staple textiles. Our main export markets remain France and the rest of Europe, not America."

"Have you diversified enough to form a buffer against bankruptcy?" she asked, so well acquainted with debt she couldn't shake loose from the notion no matter how vast one's fortune.

"I've learned a great deal from the financial crisis of '72, having watched some of the most spectacular fortunes in Glasgow collapse. The Ayr Bank and the Bogles of Daldowie come to mind. They've since had their estates put under trust."

"I read about it in the newspapers." She wouldn't say that at the time she hoped he'd follow suit. The remembrance shamed her.

"If you need an ally in the firm, consult my foremost factor in Glasgow, Leo Tate."

She penned the name then paused. "Do you truly believe you might die?"

"Wheest!" He closed his eyes briefly, his jaw clenched against a cough. "You're a braisant lass. But that boldness might stand you in good stead, given there's some abuse going on in the firm that I canna put my finger on."

"Abuse?"

"Aye. Missing ledgers and questionable accounts. Bank withdrawals that dinna make sense. Just a few instances of late, but they form a troublesome pattern."

Embezzlement within the firm? Fraud?

Aware he'd come to the end of the matter if she had not, she set aside the quill. "'Tis not your earthly affairs that weigh most on my mind. Not even suspect business dealings. Have you ever seen merchant princes depart this life fisting any funds?"

He regarded her with a cool detachment as he lay back against the pillows, his dark hair loose about his shoulders. "Och, a halie lass too, preaching to me on my deathbed."

Holy? She returned his hard stare, weary beyond words—and now entirely bereft of them. His eyes were clouding again as if the effort of speaking had worn him out. Or perhaps it was the emotion behind the words, entrenched as he was in Buchanan affairs.

"And lest you think I'm a complete heathen . . ." He took a labored breath, as earnest as she'd ever seen him. "I helped found the Literary Society of Glasgow, funded a new theater and an institute dedicated to sacred music as well as an almshouse for the poor."

She took up her quill again, adding these, though not at all assuaged given the blatant pride in his tone. When she looked up again, he was asleep.

Concern kept Juliet awake till she could not keep her eyes open, and she finally retired to the uncomfortable hammock. The next morning the ship's surgeon came to the cabin to assess their patient, turning on Juliet with a canny eye.

"You look nearly as ill as Mr. Buchanan," he rebuked her, "which will profit him nothing. Take yourself to the quarterdeck while I tend to your husband."

Juliet reluctantly obeyed. Rarely had she had time for fresh air or exercise since they'd embarked. Wrapped in her hooded wool cape, she traded the sickroom for the deck after taking a last look at Leith.

The January air was bracing, and sailors swarmed in every direction. The captain greeted her and, after inquiring about Leith, showed her the porpoise leaping alongside the ship in colorful abandon. Her joy vanished when several jacks set about trying to catch it for supper.

"I shan't eat any," she told Captain Hicks with a sad smile. "Let the beautiful creature alone."

"Porpoises are only beautiful in the water, where their colors are at play. Once caught, they fade to a dull gray."

Dismayed, she went below again to find Leith with Loveday, who sent her a concerned glance as the doctor prescribed yet another sleeping draught. He left abruptly, vowing to return soon, though several sailors were ill with some minor malady, demanding his attention elsewhere.

"No more sedatives," Loveday told her once the door was closed. "I believe if Mr. Buchanan could shake off his lethargy and move about, it would help clear his lungs. His pallor is concerning."

"He's very weak being abed so long." Juliet removed her cape and repinned her cap, half torn away by the wind. "I've asked Cook to prepare more broth. Perhaps between the two of us we can get some down him."

"We shall try." Loveday looked toward the stern windows. "I feel a change in the weather."

"The navigator feels a storm brewing. 'Mares' tails and mackerel scales make lofty ships carry low sails,' he said."

But the weather was the least of their concerns. Juliet went to Leith, who was so alarmingly still. Was he even breathing? She placed a hand on his chest, wanting to feel his heartbeat beneath the linen shirt, and bent low to feel his breath on her cheek. When it didn't come, she grasped his shoulders and shook him, her panic a living, breathing, clawing thing.

"Juliet!" Loveday was behind her at once, her hand on her shoulder.

Letting go of Leith, Juliet gave a little cry, her backside colliding with the bed and jarring him further. "Is he breathing? I cannot tell—"

"Be easy, Sister." With the calm resolve of a competent nurse, Loveday felt his wrist. "His pulse is faint but his fever seems to have lessened. I'm most troubled by the rattle in his chest. He has been too long on his back. Perhaps if we were to turn him over onto his side once he's fed . . ."

The cabin boy appeared with broth and the ship's biscuits no one was fond of. Little by little Juliet spooned the broth to Leith, following it with a healthy dose of water. He cooperated before sliding into sleep again, this time on his side.

"We'll continue with broth and water round the clock," Loveday said. "And look forward to trading ship's biscuits for Scottish bannocks in the near future."

Bannocks sounded no better to Juliet's thinking. "We've been at sea nearly a fortnight. I pray that's half the journey. I'm dreadfully homesick and long to be on land."

"As do I." Loveday took a seat by the stern windows, her sewing box in her lap. "I pray for calm seas. I don't want to be off my feet again. You're a far better sailor."

"I'm glad we have our handwork to help pass the time." Juliet felt a surge of thanks. Such offered a semblance of normality, at least. Loveday's needles were flying. "What are you knitting?"

"A blanket for your firstborn. I plan to adorn it with ribbon embroidery."

Firstborn?

"A fool's errand!" Juliet hissed, aghast. "I suggest you make mitts for yourself instead."

"Fiddle-faddle! Mitts are so mundane." Loveday gave a wistful sigh. "Need I remind you Mr. Buchanan is no monk."

What? "How you can have a virile thought about a dying man is beyond me." Weren't Leith's midnight rallying and the copious notes in her daybook proof he wasn't long for this world?

"Nor are you a nun," Loveday continued sweetly. "You yourself confessed you're attracted to him."

Stiffening, Juliet turned her back on Leith as if it could block Loveday's overloud words. "And I kindly invite you to forget it."

"Never. You've not said that about another man living save Colonel George Washington." Loveday's knitting continued apace. "I believe Mr. Buchanan shall overcome. He's not one given to defeat even in illness."

"Nae, I am not." The voice from the bed was hoarse but firm.

Juliet whirled to meet Leith's amused gaze. How much

had he heard? Somehow he had raised himself up to a half-sitting position. Hope smothered her shame, and with cheeks burning, she went to pour him more water as if nothing had been said.

He drank it down with reassuring gusto, expression still amused.

"So, you've risen from the dead." She plumped his pillows, unable to meet his gaze a second longer. "Please turn on your side again, and then later, if you can manage it, the steward and I will try to get you to your feet to walk about the cabin. Or perhaps sit in a chair by the hearth."

She wanted him to continue talking, but his eyes closed again, and in minutes he'd slipped away from her, her hopes with him. Meanwhile, Loveday's needles continued their maddening work, forcing Juliet to ponder any future Buchanans.

35

The heart of man is very much like the sea, it has its storms, it has its tides and in its depths, it has its pearls, too.

Vincent van Gogh

Juliet awoke from harried dreams to the pressing need of the chamber pot. How could it be, even when the sea heaved and the cabin slanted, that such mundane functions must be attended to? She climbed out of the hammock to first check on Leith. She'd not heard him cough all night. Her hand crossed the coverlet to lay upon his chest. It rose and fell with steadiness beneath his nightshirt and kept her former panic at bay.

Slowly she began a perilous journey to the gallery, ruing the chamber pot wasn't beneath the bed. Little, she was learning, made much sense aboard a ship, a wooden world with entirely different rules. Gripping the wall, she tried not to look toward the windows, where the usual unbroken blue ocean had become a wall of black, briny water. The roar of the wind was so loud she nearly lost her nerve to continue.

Was Loveday well and safe? Try as she might, she could not reach the corridor to check. In a breath, the ship rose then dropped so violently it seemed the floor beneath her gave way. Losing her bearings, she nearly fell against the tiled stove, her keening cry half drowned beneath the mounting scream of the storm.

The wind woke him. It cut through the fevered blur of untold days as only something as frightful as a storm could do. Leith pushed himself up on one elbow, aware of the cry that could only have come from Juliet.

Where was she?

A hanging lantern flickered, offering few clues. Though he sensed it was dawn, they seemed to be in a fierce struggle with the blackest gale he'd ever seen. Watching the Atlantic twist and foam beyond the cabin windows failed to steal his courage. He was done with being waited on. Done with dying.

Was she hurt?

Nothing else mattered. As the ship heeled leeward, he made his way none too easily to where she half lay upon the floor. Worn down as he was, his own steps were wobbly as a newborn lamb's. Sheer stubbornness drove him forward. Ignoring the roiling in his gut, he reached for her and brought her to her feet.

Another lurch pressed them back against the stern window. She fell against him as his arms went round her. With Juliet at the forefront of his mind, Havilah was pushed to the back of it. The realization stunned him and turned the tense moment more tender. He hardly knew her, but she was his wife, and he felt a protectiveness toward the woman who'd been by his side day and night.

Somehow they made their way back to the bed as the ship creaked and groaned and seemed about to break apart. Once they lay down atop the twisted linens he held her in his arms, savoring her softness and scent and the feel of her fine linen nightgown with its lace trim against his roughness.

Had he overheard correctly that she was . . . attracted to him? Or had he been imagining things in his stupor? She'd been so adamant in her initial refusal of him that he couldn't believe she was anything but repulsed. Aye, he must have misheard . . . or Loveday was teasing. What did it matter? He hardly felt whole, hardly had the wherewithal to attempt another tie after his colossal failure with Havilah.

Yet he still held his bonny bride despite the storm without and within. Tomorrow he'd return to his hammock. For now, he wanted her near.

Her back to Leith, Juliet lay curved against him, one of his arms draped over her as if safeguarding her from the ship's fretful rolling. Through the stern windows streamed broad daylight. A spent sea with only the barest ruffle of a wave met her eyes, not the briny watery wall of before. *Lord, thank You.* She'd not felt such elation since she'd climbed aboard the *Glasgow Lass* that fractious night.

"Time for a bath and a shave." The male voice near her ear was threaded with resolve and relief. "And breakfast."

Was he finally on the mend? Joy sang through her and she rolled over, their faces a handsbreadth apart. "I rather like you bearded."

His eyes sparked. "You might not if I kissed you."

Her first kiss. For a trice she forgot to breathe. Her eyes traced his sleepy features, and she found herself wishing his razor was afloat. He was savagely handsome, his rumpled

210

hair a different hue of ink than her own, the dark shadow along his jaw calling out the blue of his eyes and his patrician nose.

She brought a finger to her lips, all too aware of her disheveled state.

"Bethankit we'll live to see Glasgow." He coughed into his fist, but the sound had lost its racking depth. "If the gale didn't blow us off course, we're closer than we ken."

She closed her eyes, overcome with gratitude all over again.

He rolled onto his back and looked at the ceiling. "Where's your miniature?"

"Safely tucked away in your washstand."

He frowned but said nothing more, leaving her to wonder. The shadow she sometimes sensed about him seemed near again. What was the gist of his thoughts?

Not wanting to dwell on it, she turned away from him, missing the warm weight of his arm about her waist. "I'll fetch it."

She handed it to him, then went to the gallery lavatory, giving Loveday's closed cabin door a fretful glance. When Juliet came out, she knocked and, hearing nothing, opened her sister's door to find the cabin empty.

36

Did not strong connections draw me elsewhere, I believe Scotland would be the country I would choose to end my days in.

Benjamin Franklin

*L*oveday washed overboard?

Juliet dressed hurriedly, and her fanciful fear was discarded as she emerged from below to find her sister at the quarterdeck railing near the stairs, talking with an officer. Leith was not far behind, though he moved slowly as if still getting his bearings. Nothing short of a miracle there. To further allay Juliet's fears, Loveday turned toward her with the brightest smile she'd had since leaving Virginia.

"We survived what the captain is calling a near hurricane. I took a sleeping draught myself and missed most of it." Loveday gestured to the feline curled up with Jezebel atop a barrel. "Hobbes is none the worse for wear either. Nor is Mr. Buchanan, I see. Wonders never cease!"

Juliet's gaze shifted to Leith, who stood near the ship's wheel talking to the captain while sailors darted about the

212

decks, returning all to rights. Fully dressed but still unshaven, he brought to mind their light morning banter all over again.

"What's this?" Loveday's gaze sharpened. "Your neck is bruised."

"I fell during the height of the storm."

"Oh, Sister. Are you well?"

"Quite." For the first time in her life, she'd experienced something with someone else that she couldn't share with Loveday. Leith's words and actions remained a secret. Juliet faced the wind as her skirts whirled about her ankles and threatened to fling back her cape hood. "Were you flirting with the navigator a moment ago?"

"Ha! I admit he's rather dashing, but I was merely trying to orient myself and ask directions."

"What did you learn?"

"That the storm may have blown us closer to Britain rather than off course. Scotland's southern Hebrides should appear soon—the isles of Islay and Arran and Bute and all else."

Juliet nodded, amazement rivaling her happiness, and turned to look out at the sea.

In the coming days Leith's improvement was rapid, yet at the same time he seemed to distance himself. He spent more time on deck by day and returned to his hammock by night. Glad as she was he was recovering his health, Juliet felt a subtle sadness that he seemed to need her less, as if the crisis that had flung them together with all its odd intimacies was naught but a fluke or a dream.

Fair weather held and the seas continued smooth. Within days, land was sighted. Seagulls resembling white paper kites began their noisy careening overhead as if welcoming them in.

When they finally docked in Greenock for a few hours, Leith leapt overboard to swim around the ship and take an honest bath, so he said, astonishing both Juliet and Loveday if not the crew. His wordless joy at returning home was contagious, and when they left Greenock for Port Glasgow, the entire ship seemed to rejoice.

It took time for them to navigate the Lang Dyke in the River Clyde to Broomielaw, the heart of Glasgow. Tidesmen and naval officers boarded the vessel to manage the cargo before unloading. Arriving at high tide, they stepped onto a private jetty marked with the Buchanan name. Juliet tried hard to hide her curiosity lest she be a gaping fool amid the coal-streaked skies and sheer chaos of the city. Colonial Williamsburg seemed a homespun speck in comparison, and York Town a shabby relation.

Leith paid her and Loveday's bewilderment scant attention, busy with the details of luggage and acquiring a sedan that would take them to the Virginia Street mansion. Twilight fell, turning the waterfront and burgh ethereal, even ghostly, as fog snuck in from the sea and whitened the tangle of wynds and closes.

"A wee smirr of rain," Leith told them with his rolling Glaswegian *r*'s as they grew more damp. "Spring is not far off."

Candlemas had passed. Juliet had tried to keep track of time at sea, but the days blurred. Perhaps in spring the city wouldn't seem so many shades of silver but green.

Leith secured three sedan chairs, something they'd heard about but never seen.

"Never did I believe I'd ride in one," Loveday exclaimed as she stepped into the small, wheelless conveyance and sat down upon a plushly upholstered seat.

Hobbes was handed to her in his carrier, oddly quiet. It had taken some coercion to get the feline to forsake Jezebel and abandon ship.

Juliet climbed into her own sedan chair, as did Leith, their baggage coming by wagon. The chairmen—Highlanders— shut each door, then gripped poles and hoisted them aloft, hastening them to Virginia Street. When they turned down a lane and hurried toward a massive iron gate, Juliet gaped.

First to arrive at the residence ahead of Leith, Loveday emerged from the sedan with a gasp. "A townhouse? This is a palace!"

Juliet had no words.

The stone mansion seemed to sit atop a pillow of mist with its wide front portico and pillars. A double stair projected onto a pristine lawn. Feeling nearly as disoriented as she'd been aboard ship, Juliet moved toward endless steps to a broad, ornate front door. A footman in plainclothes material- ized, ushering them into the mansion's entrance hall inlaid with marble. The walls and ceiling were ornamented with a masterpiece of plasterwork, endless oil paintings on paneled walls. Grand as it was, it had the look of the British Museum.

A stout, spectacled woman descended a double staircase that seemed twin to the one outside the entrance. She eyed the Virginians with none of the stoicism of the footman, a surprised light in her eyes.

Before Juliet could untie her tongue and make introduc- tions, Leith appeared behind them, still looking a bit hag- gard, though he said with a robust courtesy, "Mrs. Baillie, this is my colonial bride, the new Mrs. Buchanan, and her sister, Miss Catesby, of Virginia."

With a bob of her mobcap, the housekeeper snapped to. "Welcome to Glasgow, ladies." Gesturing toward the stair- case after directions from Leith, Mrs. Baillie ushered them to their second-floor rooms.

Hand on a balustrade shone to a high polish, Juliet looked back over her shoulder.

"I'm going out," Leith told her from the middle of the echoing hall that held none of the homey warmth of Royal Vale. "Should you need anything, the servants will see to it."

She gave him a nod, glad he wasn't hovering yet at the same time wondering what would entice him out on a wintry night. A tiny tendril of suspicion took root, doubly shocking since she'd not considered it before. Had he . . . another woman? A mistress? Her stomach flipped as he shut the door behind him with a forbidding finality.

"Sister . . . oh my . . ." Loveday murmured as they went up the grand staircase. "Even the governor's palace in Williamsburg pales!"

Their upstairs bedchambers proved a pleasant distraction, the elegant canopied beds and Chippendale furnishings and papered walls looking new. A dressing room joined the bedchambers and left Juliet wondering where Leith's rooms were.

"Mr. Buchanan is on the west side of the house," Mrs. Baillie said. "Ye both must be tired after so long a journey. If ye like I can have Ruby ready a bath."

"Please," Juliet told her. "And supper in our rooms tonight since Mr. Buchanan is away."

With a deferential nod, the housekeeper disappeared, and Loveday gave a little twirl atop the thick floral carpet. "Have you ever? I feel caught up in a fairy tale!"

"One with a happy ending, I hope."

"I suppose the true question is—which chamber do you prefer?" Pointing to the ceiling, Loveday admired intricate festoons of plasterwork flowers and medallions that gave the impression of a hanging garden, a crystal chandelier at the center. "Notice this room is decorated and upholstered in shades of lavender while the other is lovely shades of rose."

"You choose," Juliet said, still pondering Leith.

"You're his Virginia bride, as he said," Loveday reminded her, passing through the dressing room with its enormous gilded looking glass. "'Tis only right that the choice be yours."

Juliet took a turn through both, then paused before a charming portrait between two windows of a lady at her writing desk. "The lavender, then."

"It suits you." Loveday seemed delighted. "'Twas Mama's favorite color."

Their luggage was brought, such as it was, and hot, scented baths were drawn in gleaming copper tubs. Situated side by side in their shared dressing room, they sank low into the fragrant water.

Loveday shut her eyes and breathed in the swirling steam. "Lavender with a hint of mint."

"No brine about it," Juliet said gratefully. "Even Parisian hair tonics and scented soaps."

"So many I hardly know which to choose." Loveday looked at the array of perfumed bottles and wash balls between them. The wrinkled sultanas they'd packed hung on hooks in shabby contrast to the sumptuous room.

Juliet made a mental list. "We must visit the milliner and mantua-maker as soon as possible."

Already she was envisioning what a tobacco lord's wife required. Leith had mentioned social occasions. Obligatory, perhaps. And nothing like Virginia's hospitality.

Once bathed and dressed, Juliet and Loveday sat down to a surprisingly simple supper of haddock chowder, cheese, and bread, then retired early to unfamiliar beds, leaving the doors of the dressing room open. Used to little noise but owls hooting and the passage of some night animal at Royal Vale, Juliet lay awake long after Loveday fell asleep, listening to all the unfamiliar sounds of the city. Clattering carriage wheels atop cobblestones. An occasional jarring shout. Barking dogs. The cry of the night watch. At midnight a clock struck from the bowels of the mansion somewhat mournfully.

Leith had not yet come home.

37

Among the active manufacturers of Glasgow are to be found men of prodigious wealth, and at the same time highly elevated and enlightened minds, who form a sort of nobility.

Robert Chambers

The next morning, Leith rose long before the mail gun shook the city. Mrs. Baillie, still a bit ruffled he'd returned with not one but two lassies, had his garments cleaned and pressed, his small sword and gold-knobbed Malacca cane in his dressing room.

He left the Virginia Street mansion on foot with an odd comingling of emotion. Dawn gilded the eastern horizon and the windows beyond where Juliet slept. He cast a look upward before rebuking himself to mind the day's business. He had much to catch up on and more than a little to enlighten his fellow lords.

"Buchanan!" George Spiers was the first to arrive at the foot of King Billy's statue, his excitement almost amusing since he was usually stoic. "I've been waiting for word of your return ever since you set sail last autumn. How I've missed your blunt, irreverent company. No one challenges the existing order of things like you do. By Jove, we've a lot to discuss!"

His echoing words seemed to summon every tobacco lord in Glasgow, including a few red-gowned magistrates. All were soon strutting over the plainstanes with more arrogance than Leith remembered. He endured their backslapping if not the customary kiss on each cheek, but it was Euan he was most glad to see.

"We must make time for the coffeehouse before the countinghouse," his brother told him as Leith found himself surrounded. "I canna wait for our usual meridian at the Sarry Heid this afternoon."

"Nor can I." Leith looked toward the Gallowgate, where their usual haunt, the Saracen Head, beckoned. "For now, coffee is what I need. I developed something of a taste for it in the colonies."

"Whiteford's, then," Euan said, looking about for a quick escape. They broke away from the crowd with difficulty, matching strides as they passed the tolbooth, the sun poking a wan finger through pewter clouds. "When I got your message that you'd arrived, I left Paisley immediately. Lyrica wanted to come with me given your glad news."

"My marriage, you mean."

"Aye, what else? We want to meet the newest Mrs. Buchanan once she's settled and welcome her to Scotland. But your note was terse. What's this mystery that she's arrived with company?"

"Her sister is with her. A verra marriageable lass with a dowry of five thousand pounds. Feel free to spread that abroad."

Euan chuckled as they approached the century-old coffeehouse at the corner of Trongate and Saltmarket, the aroma of the hot, bitter brew snaking out onto the street. The door groaned open, and they sought a corner table as other tobacco lords followed. Colonel Whiteford's was the place of many a political debate with an unrivaled collection of newspapers.

"So, tell me everything," Euan said, setting his cane aside and dangling his cocked hat atop it.

Leith did the same, then reached for a copy of the *Glasgow Journal*. "Virginia is as comely and contentious as ever."

Euan frowned as their coffee was served. "Details, Brother, details."

"I arrived in under a month. Got into a fistfight in York Town over billiards." Leith took a drink of the scalding, black brew as his brother rolled his eyes. "Made my way to the capital, Williamsburg, then Forrest Bend, where the Ravenals are in residence."

"You visited Buchanan stores amid all this."

"Aye, and warned our storekeepers and clerks at Farquair and Culpepper that they're becoming overly familiar with the planters and allowing them too much credit." Leith glanced at Edinburgh's *Caledonian Mercury*. One phrase caught his eye.

Familiar dialogue between Americus and Britannicus on the nature of human liberty.

"Let's get to the best part," Euan said impatiently, pushing the papers aside. "Virginia's renowned hospitality."

"I was fêted by the Catesbys at Royal Vale, then spent Christmas in Williamsburg, where I succumbed to a vile fever." At the mention, Leith stifled a stubborn cough. "Ravenal's doctor wrote me off as dead, but not before I'd stated my intentions, in a manner of speaking, to Juliet Catesby."

Euan looked smug. "Which were favorably received."

"Nae." The raw memory dogged him still. "She declared herself genteel if in debt and said she'd never imagined being so reduced as to become affianced to a tobacco merchant."

Euan leaned back in his seat, looking dazed. "Wheest!"

"Which only increased my determination to have her."

Euan's rare laugh took some of the sting away. "And then . . ."

"I returned her miniature through Ravenal, ending our fractious relationship . . . or so I thought." Leith took another drink of coffee. "Determined as I was to return home—or die—I made it to York Town and boarded the *Glasgow Lass*, but there was an unexpected delay with the cargo. The night before we sailed, I was called to the quarterdeck to find the lass and her sister in a lighter asking permission to board."

"And you let them."

"On the condition she marry me on the spot, aye."

Euan still looked astonished, his hard veneer cracking a bit. "Why on earth did she change her mind?"

"She said she wanted to honor her father's wishes that we marry and have the Catesby debt cleared. She also insisted on a generous dowry for her sister, believing her marital prospects brighter here in Scotia."

"She sounds like a competent businesswoman in her own right."

"She's a liberty-loving lass." Leith quashed the urge to show Euan the miniature in his pocket and tried to dismiss Juliet from his thoughts. She'd occupied them too much of late. "We met a gale on the return cruise, which helped move us here faster instead of blowing us off course. So there you have it—my American travails in short."

"I suspect there's a great deal more to them than that. You've dropped a stone since I last saw you. I'd caution you against your usual six o'clock start and nine o'clock finish."

"Five months I've been away." Leith reached into his pocket for his watch with its heavy gold chain. "There's much to be done with so much time lost."

"Lost? I say there's much you've gained." Euan motioned for more coffee. "Lyrica cannot wait to welcome her."

"Juliet wants to meet the twins."

"Fond of children, then? A fortuitous start."

Leith felt a pang he'd not asked about them sooner. "How are they?"

"Running everywhere. Cole took a nasty tumble on the bridge and blacked his eye while Bella has finally gotten over a severe cold. They spent half their time at Ardraigh Hall and half at Paisley."

"Bethankit," Leith murmured, his thoughts returning to Juliet.

"On a weightier note, what's happening with the American rebels?"

At the overloud question, every voice in the large room faded. Leith had an audience again, and though he wanted to get to the guildhall, he knew there needed to be an accounting with his fellow merchants first.

Looking out over the grim, familiar faces, he said, "Expect North American ports to close and all tobacco trading to cease."

38

When the heart is full the tongue will speak.

Scottish proverb

*L*eith definitely had a penchant for the color blue. In this case, Wedgwood blue. Tarrying on the staircase's landing, Juliet touched the blue and white wallpaper that framed an immense Palladian window overlooking the Virginia Street mansion's front lawn. Her lips parted before she reined herself in. Fawning and cringing didn't become her.

Her gaze returned to the street, and her heart gave a little leap. There came her husband walking toward her with fierce purpose, his expression as inscrutable as if he were at a masked ball. His scarlet cloak reminded her of Virginia's cardinals, and a dart of homesickness flashed through her.

Leith's entrance was quiet, that same purposeful tread across the foyer to what she guessed was his study. Down the stairs she crept, feeling an intruder, hardly a bride. His door was open, revealing a marvel of mahogany bookcases and high crown glass windows.

She stood in the doorway without speaking. Again she wondered where he'd been last night, his first night home. He'd shaved, further removing them from the ship. When he coughed, she felt a beat of alarm, biting her lip to keep from cautioning him to rest and recover completely.

"Mrs. Buchanan," he said, looking up from where he sorted through a stack of correspondence. "How goes your first hours in Glasgow?"

"Well enough," she said.

"Any concerns so far? I ken you have needs since you left Royal Vale so suddenly."

He gestured to the seat in front of his desk, a dark surface covered with more account books and ledgers than she'd ever seen in one place. Not even the Williamsburg printer boasted more. She sat, aware of a bewildering chasm between them. Gone were the ship's close quarters, the forced intimacy. Any vulnerability he'd shown in illness had vanished. The desk seemed a hefty barrier, a hallmark of their new life and relationship.

"I'll need a proper wardrobe," she began tentatively, looking over his shoulder to the globe in the windowsill, blue brocade drapes framing it.

"Of course. Have what you will." He uncorked a decanter and poured himself a drink. "Your custom will be welcome at any shop here, in Edinburgh, or London."

Juliet watched him. Whisky? So early in the morning?

"The other Mrs. Buchanan has loaned one of her French maids to show you the places she herself frequents here," he continued. "She arrives soon."

Lyrica, her new sister-in-law, wife of Euan Buchanan of Paisley. She'd wondered how they'd met. Probably not an arranged marriage like hers.

"Thoughtful of her." Juliet folded her hands in her lap,

225

her gaze trailing to an inkwell. "I was wondering where to purchase an escritoire. I'd like to resume my letter writing soon."

He nodded, setting down his empty glass. "Start your search at Mrs. Barclay's warehouse opposite the Tron Church. You'll find all manner of desks there, especially French made. For stationery supplies, Gardner's at the sign of the golden ball above Bell's Wynd should suffice."

She filed the details away, thinking she could spend a fortnight—and a fortune—just wandering the streets of Glasgow. Since he wasn't offering to go with her, she was doubly glad of Loveday's company and the maid on loan.

"I imagine you have all kinds of business awaiting you."

"Aye," he said.

She bit her tongue again lest she ask if he'd be home for dinner or supper. How did one navigate an arranged marriage? Did one build fences or bridges?

Leith heard Lyrica's maid delivered to the servants' side door as Juliet stood up to leave his study. He'd come home briefly to collect a particular ledger and then return to the countinghouse for a meeting with his clerks but had been waylaid at every turn. And now . . . his wife.

By all that was holy, did she have to wear that beguiling shade of blue?

She smiled at him, a tentative, almost shy smile that told him she was unsure of herself, of him, and their new relationship. He was hardly any better, overlooking the needed ledger in plain sight while raking his mind for the next sentence.

For the moment her attention turned to his bookcases. "Once I thought Nathaniel Ravenal's study boasted the most books I'd ever seen, but I'd not beheld yours."

"Mostly business tomes. Dry and dusty."

"Have you no novels? No classics?"

"Nae time for them."

"But you do have a library at Ardraigh Hall."

"Aye, which I hope you'll fill with the books I have nae time for."

"What I most want," Juliet said quietly, holding his gaze in that maddening way she had when she was intent on something, "is to meet your children."

Och, the bairns. Bella and Cole seemed to be more in her thoughts than his. "We'll see Ardraigh Hall soon enough."

She bit her lip as if about to naysay him, a frown in her eyes if not on her lips. She minded the wait, he warranted.

"My brother sends his regards and said they are eager to welcome you at Paisley. As for matters here, did Mrs. Baillie show you the house?"

"Yes, she's very thorough. I've been introduced to all the servants, including your French chef, and have been given the household's account books to peruse."

"You'll be well occupied, then," he said, retrieving the ledger. "As for shopping, the maid on loan has arrived."

"Then I shall leave you to your business, Mr. Buchanan."

39

These Virginians are a very gentle, well-dressed people—and look, perhaps, more at a man's outside than his inside. For these and other reasons, pray go very clean, neat, and handsomely dressed, to Virginia.

Peter Collinson, London merchant

Glasgow. What a wonder of a city! It rivaled London in Juliet's memory, though she'd been but a schoolgirl then and now looked through a woman's lens. Walking through the wynds and closes in her pattens, she was humbled and haunted by her old prejudices against Leith and his merchanting—and again felt at a disadvantage amid so many luxuries large and small.

Color and confusion abounded as street peddlers hawked their wares of fruit and fish and dairy along with printed sermons and political pamphlets. Colliers delivered coal from door to door, their ragged beasts of burdens tugging at Juliet's heart as much as the soot-faced chimney sweeps. The city's ragged edges were dark indeed.

She linked arms with Loveday, the loaned maid leading,

and moved toward the more genteel Gibson's Wynd near the city's center, where the air seemed perfumed by fruit and flowers. As the Tron's bells broke into song, they paused and looked up. At almost noon, the bells signified a break in the day when many Glaswegians sought the taverns.

"'Tis not Virginia, to be sure," Loveday whispered as they entered a millinery with the sign of the scarlet garter above the door. "I've not even seen a millinery this size in Philadelphia."

Minette, Lyrica Buchanan's diminutive maid, clucked her tongue as the sisters admired a fur muff on display. "'Tis time for American madams and mademoiselles to lay aside their furs for feathers."

"A French feather muff?" Juliet asked as a buxom woman appeared from behind a counter brimming with paste jewelry and rainbow-hued ribbons, gloves, and fichus.

Mrs. Betty Gibbons introduced herself as the millinery owner and wasted no time showing them about the well-stocked shop. "I have a number of goods suitable for the season, like this new Parisian ostrich feather muff lined with ermine, or perhaps a peacock feather muff lately arrived from London . . . even a tippet with macaw and canary feathers."

Silken stays and buckled shoes. Breast flowers worn on one's bodice that seemed more real than faux. Genteel pocketbooks. Colorful Indian chintzes and silks. Dimity riding habits. Barcelona handkerchiefs. Lace sleeve ruffles and clocked stockings.

"I've not had your ladies' custom before." Mrs. Gibbons took a lorgnette from her pocket to better look at them. "Americans, from your speech. Virginians, perhaps, from the plantations?"

Juliet was seized with a sudden awkwardness. To say she was now a Buchanan seemed a bold boast. At her reluctance,

Loveday took the lead. "I'm pleased to present the bride of Mr. Leith Buchanan of Virginia Street and Ardraigh Hall."

Another pause, this time on the part of the milliner. "Ah, so very pleased to make your acquaintance, Mrs. Buchanan." She gave a little curtsy then looked at Loveday. "And you are?"

"Simply her sister from Virginia, newly arrived in your fair city."

Mrs. Gibbons smiled. "If you tell me what's needed, I'll be happy to send a parcel of goods to Virginia Street, where you can make your selections in private at your leisure."

Accepting the courtesy, they moved on and by noon had acquired a Venetian writing desk from the warehouse Leith had named along with writing supplies to be delivered on the morrow. But it was the toy shop in Bell's Wynd that entranced them and took most of their time. Juliet left after purchasing a hobby horse and dollhouse, even a miniature tea set.

"I know the children are small and I haven't seen their nursery," she told Loveday. "But I can't arrive at Ardraigh Hall empty-handed."

In high spirits and with full hearts, they returned to Virginia Street in time for the four hours, as Glaswegians called it.

"Our first Scottish tea." Juliet looked with pleasure at the tea table situated by a parlor window overlooking the rear walled garden, a parterred space still asleep in winter.

A housemaid, Ruby, brought in a silver tray, her face rosy beneath a stark white cap. "Take a dish o' tea, Mrs. Buchanan and Miss Catesby. 'Tis unco refreshing." She set down her burden. "Scones, marmalade made with Seville oranges, and a wee bit of Scots whisky. If ye like, I can bring toast with Tay salmon and kippered herrings. Minette and I are having that in the kitchen before she returns to Paisley."

A far cry from their James River fare. Juliet thanked her and asked for a small sample, delighting the maid, while Loveday admired the engraved silver teapot with its matching hot milk jug and sugar bowl and a tall hot water urn.

"I must confess I miss Virginia not at all." Loveday smiled so widely her dimples all but disappeared. "Though I do wonder how Father and Zipporah are faring."

"Ah yes, and dear Aunt Damarus." Juliet could only imagine her aunt's shock at receiving all the Catesbys' news. "I shall write to her as soon as my writing desk is delivered. 'Twill be a verra lang letter, as the Scots say."

Chuckling, Loveday watched as Juliet poured the fragrant tea. "I'd rather talk about one Scot in particular. How is he?"

"Busy . . . preoccupied." Juliet tried to banish the princely picture he'd made behind his desk. It tugged at her in ways she couldn't fathom. "We'll travel to Ardraigh Hall soon, he said."

"Then I shan't go with you."

Juliet set the teapot down with a little thud. "Whyever not?"

"I'll not have this be a marriage of three, which it has been ever since we set sail from Virginia. The two of you need to meet his children—a momentous occasion—alone."

The prospect of a carriage ride from Glasgow to Ardraigh Hall—of unknown mileage, close marital proximity, and decidedly stilted conversation—filled Juliet with dread. "While I do see the wisdom in it, I always rely on you to . . . lighten things."

Loveday hadn't a care. Sampling a still-warm scone slathered with marmalade, she rolled her eyes in a sort of culinary ecstasy. "As I said, I miss Virginia not at all."

Juliet took in their surroundings, still awed. "'Tis like

night and day, truly, as if we've stepped not only onto a different shore but a different world. I'm very thankful we've arrived safely but still feel more guest. I'm headed to a country house I've never seen to mother two children who don't know me and may not care for me—"

"Posh! The twins will love you, as all children do." Reaching down, Loveday stroked Hobbes, who wound round her skirts. "I'm more mindful of your being a wife. You need to proceed carefully with Mr. Buchanan. And wisely."

"Well, I shan't ever horsewhip him."

"Ha! You make yourself sound a tawdry jade!" Loveday's laugh resounded around the elegant room. "I simply mean you don't want to set a pattern you can't recover from."

"Clearly you've given this much thought."

"I want what's best for you both." Loveday added more milk to her tea. "I see a driven, grieving, brilliant man of business and a loving, astute woman who is capable of doing much good—or much harm, depending on how you approach these sensitive matters. You want to grow together, not apart."

"I hardly know where to begin."

"Remember what Mama used to quote? 'Strength and honour are her clothing; and she shall rejoice in time to come. She openeth her mouth with wisdom; and in her tongue is the law of kindness.'"

"Proverbs 31, yes." The comparison left Juliet feeling more overwhelmed. "Mama rarely put a foot wrong."

40

You will never know a man until you do business with him.

Scottish proverb

*L*eith came downstairs and went into the small dining room for breakfast, the papers arrayed atop the table for his perusal. Edinburgh's *Caledonian Mercury*, its front page dominated by foreign affairs, didn't seem to care much about him, but Glasgow certainly did. News of his return was featured prominently, though one particular boldface line caught his eye.

TOBACCO KING OF LANARKSHIRE WEDS AMERICAN INDIGO HEIRESS

The *Glasgow Courant* waxed on about the extraordinarily beautiful Juliet Catesby, who had been seen stepping out around the city, her custom coveted at the most desirable city shops.

Flaxen-haired and fair of face, the queen of Lanarkshire has been seen with a retinue of servants.

233

He sat down, mildly amused but more aggravated. They were describing Loveday. As for a retinue of servants, Minette hardly qualified, and Juliet didn't look the part.

Mrs. Baillie swept in, armed with both a coffeepot and a teapot. "Coffee this morning, sir?"

"Aye," he replied. "Is Mrs. Buchanan awake yet?"

"Yes, sir, since dawn, and at her new desk. Miss Catesby remains abed."

He looked at his large breakfast absently, wanting company. Should he go up and ask Juliet to join him? Send Mrs. Baillie instead? The awkwardness of it had him stabbing a sausage and ignoring the impulse. He'd been dining alone for a long time. Why should today be any different? Besides, she'd be residing at Ardraigh Hall soon while he'd remain here.

Their time aboard ship brought a strange nostalgia. Sick unto death he'd been but salved by her continual presence. And now an entire city and mansion divided them. He sensed a dismay in her that bordered on awe at her new surroundings. Virginia Street was a far cry from Virginia. He'd not considered the impression it would have on her.

Before breakfast was done, he heard faint music coming from the drawing room across the hall. An oddity. Lyrica played the harpsichord, and it had been her suggestion he have one for entertaining. As Mrs. Baillie poured him a second cup of coffee, he wondered who the musician was. He knew so little about either Juliet or her sister he couldn't decide. Nor would he investigate.

Finishing his coffee, he got up to grab his cane and cape before heading to the plainstanes in the square.

Juliet heard Leith leave and traded the harpsichord for the drawing room's window that fronted the street. She'd hoped by coming downstairs she might bump into him or pique his curiosity about her playing, but both had come to naught. Leaning into the sill, she traced his fading silhouette with her eyes. The brisk stride. The silky queued hair beneath his cocked hat that trailed between his shoulder blades. The swirl of his crimson coat in the wind. The grip on his cane.

Have a profitable day, Husband.

Bending her head, she uttered a little prayer for him. And for herself. She had no heart for more playing so decided to take another tour of the rooms, including his own, which she'd not yet seen. Up the stairs she went nearly on tiptoe, wanting to evade the servants, even Loveday, should she be awake.

Her heart beat fast as she came to his door. She turned the knob and stepped inside, leaving the door cracked open. At once the essence of Leith enfolded her as her eyes adjusted to the darkness and the room's details. A four-poster bed crowned with a canopy was hung with blue and tan damask. Window shutters were closed against the cold, but she saw well enough that this was a masculine, spartan place. While no expense had been spared on her bedchamber or any of the other rooms, his was surprisingly austere.

A desk sat beneath one window, inkwell, sealing wax, and several quills in perfect order. A letter lay unfinished. To Nathaniel Ravenal? She looked down at the bold, decisive strokes, struck by a qualm at trespassing.

We have arrived safely in Glasgow as of 16th February. All are in good health and spirits. I cannot thank you enough for your Virginia hospitality and your help with the former Miss Catesby. She proved a fine sailor and cared for me unfailingly on the cruise. We hit a gale—or rather a gale hit us—near Ireland, but instead of limping into port it pushed us along.

She read on, captivated, finding him more open and engaging in prose than he allowed himself to be in person.

I trust in time my matrimonial endeavors will prove me a faithful, caring husband in every respect. But I am yet unsure if my new bride will ever

Her heart caught at the words as a lump knotted her throat. Such a poignant half sentence. What had he been thinking? Was it too hard for him to finish?

She moved to the bed, leaned over, and placed her cheek against his pillow, the linen smooth against her skin. This, too, held his scent. The few paintings on the wall, the globes—one terrestrial and the other celestial—the rugs and fire screen, all bespoke a world she had no part of. The only nod to embellishment in the entire room was the marble fireplace. It reminded her of one in the governor's palace in Williamsburg and invited her to stay. She sank down in a leather armchair within its scarlet, heat-drenched circle. Above the mantel was a seascape featuring a ship at sail remarkably like the *Glasgow Lass*.

She sighed and yawned all at once. Thought longingly of home. The chiming of a longcase clock brought her to her senses. As did the sight of a small black chest to the right of the hearth. It bore painted flowers in vibrant hues, the only adornment in the thoroughly masculine room. She went to it, knelt, and ran a hand over its lovely lines. Curiosity prompted her to lift the lid. Firelight flickered over a tasseled red shawl and a number of newspaper clippings within.

She hesitated, not wanting to disturb anything. Had this been his late wife's trunk? She took out the papers and held them nearer the light. Leith's name was printed, as was Havilah's. *Havilah*. Such a lovely, biblical forename.

Details about her death consumed the front page. Juliet read a few lines, nearly forgetting she trespassed. What would borrowing the papers hurt if once she read them she put them back?

She left Leith's room reluctantly, pockets full of the papers, then checked on Loveday to find her dressing before she went below to a meeting with Mrs. Baillie and a few of the upper servants. All the while she wondered . . .

How did they take to their unexpected American mistress?

She entered the austere servants' hall. Half a dozen servants were gathered round the long table, the latest account book open and waiting. Juliet greeted them, trying to remember names and stations. She'd written them down, but the list remained on her desk upstairs.

She took a seat at the table's head, smiling past her skittishness. "Perhaps it would be best if we start by my hearing any of your needs and grievances about running a townhouse such as this."

The next hour had her penning their responses and making note of needed changes or what was working well and needed continuing.

"I believe Ardraigh Hall is to be my principal concern," Juliet told them. "But Mr. Buchanan asked me to oversee the workings here too, with your assistance."

"Will ye be needing a lady's maid, Mrs. Buchanan?" Ruby asked a bit overloudly. "Minette was telling me she's available, as the other Mrs. Buchanan has one too many and is willing to let her go."

"But we realize Americans might do things differently," Mrs. Baillie added quickly, darting a look at Ruby as if to quiet her.

"We thought ye might bring yer own maid, ma'am," said Haskins, the footman.

"Indeed, every genteel lady here has one," Ruby said with renewed enthusiasm.

Juliet smiled. "Minette would be a great help as I alternate between both houses. If Mrs. Buchanan is willing to part with her, I'll gladly employ her."

"I'll send word right away to Paisley, then." Mrs. Baillie took off her spectacles and cleaned them with the hem of her apron. "Mr. Buchanan spoke of hosting a ball soon for Miss Catesby in the formal drawing room here or one of the assembly rooms in Glasgow. Yer choice, ma'am."

"I shall be glad of it," Juliet said, imagining Loveday's reaction. "My sister too. I'm guessing the drawing room here would be more suitable for a smaller gathering while the assembly rooms you mention are for larger functions?"

"Och, to be sure." Mrs. Baillie nodded so vigorously her mobcap seemed in peril. "I ken all of Glasgow and beyond is wanting a look at ye both, so the assembly room might suit. But 'tis entirely yer pleasure. Mr. Buchanan told us to do whatever ye wish."

Though they were all obliging, Juliet felt another qualm. Must she and Leith communicate with each other through the servants in future? "I'll confer with my sister, then, to see what might suit her best."

"I've a list of what was required at the last function Mr. Buchanan hosted to give ye some idea of the outlay." Opening a daybook, Mrs. Baillie adjusted her spectacles. "My handwriting isn't what it once was due to rheumatism. Might I read it to ye, ma'am?"

"Of course," Juliet replied.

"The bill of fare was as follows." She cleared her throat. "One hundred sirloins of beef. One hundred tongues. One hundred baked pies. One hundred geese roasted. One hundred turkeys, ducks, and pullets. Fifty hams. One thousand

French loaves. Two thousand large pints of butter. One hundredweight of Gloucester cheese. Tea, coffee, and chocolate in abundance. Two thousand saffron cakes. Two thousand, five hundred bottles of wine. A most splendid and large pyramid of sweetmeats in the middle of the dessert in the center of the room, along with a great number of stands of jelly and a curious fountain playing, handsomely ornamented with ivy, etc."

Juliet tried to keep the astonishment off her face. "Was this just one occasion?"

"Oh, aye, ma'am," Haskins told her. "The breakfast following the twins' christening."

"Such a sonsie time everyone had," Ruby said, eyes alight. "I'll ne'er forget it."

Juliet tried to imagine the expense and extravagance. And failed.

"There's another matter, ma'am." Mrs. Baillie took something from her pocket. "The keys to the sugar and tea chest are to be yers when yer in residence here."

"And I've the keys to the medicine chest." Haskins got up to show her the delight of any apothecary, Loveday included. "If ye have any questions or needs, we're ready to assist ye at any time of the day or night."

"Just one final question," Juliet said. "There's a locked room I haven't seen on the second floor."

The servants threw each other wary glances. Had she trespassed on a tender topic?

Finally Mrs. Baillie said, "'Tis the former Mrs. Buchanan's bedchamber and dressing room, ma'am. The ones she kept till the night of her death. The master said 'tis not to be opened nor touched."

Unwilling to keep the newspaper clippings a moment longer, Juliet shut her bedchamber and perused them. Seven in all, they marked the progression from Havilah's death to the private funeral afterward. The public loved a printed scandal, and they'd had it in spades. But could the papers be trusted? There was mention of poison . . . foul play. One of two maids was named. But no mention was made of where Havilah had been buried. Leith's sealing of Havilah's rooms suggested he wasn't finished with the matter.

When Mama had died, Father wanted no remembrance of her save her portrait on the wall. Juliet and Loveday had taken from her possessions what they wanted to keep, then given the rest away to the servants. But grief, she supposed, was as unique as its personal pain and was handled differently by different people.

She returned the papers to the chest just as she'd found them. Somehow they helped her understand this new husband of hers and all that had transpired before he'd sailed to the colonies and become a part of her life. Yet Havilah also seemed to pose a complication she didn't know how to grapple with and made her all the more curious to meet their children.

41

As for myself, I am now with Mr. Glassford and shall continue there for about four years. I have been very close confined there from 6 o'clock in the morning till after 9 at night.

William Scott, Glasgow clerk

"I do have another question," Juliet said after greeting Mrs. Baillie the next morning. "Is it common for Glasgow merchants to work such long hours?"

"Indeed, ma'am, though their clerks have the worst of it, from six o'clock in the morn till after nine at night." She began clearing the breakfast dishes away. "There's plenty of leisure time for these tobacco lords, though, when they wish to be idle. Horse races and the pleasures of the bottle and gaming table get the best of some o' them. But not the Messrs. Buchanan."

She went out, carrying a tray of dishes, as Loveday rose from the table and looked out the nearest rain-streaked window. "We mustn't forget the milliner and seamstress will be arriving right after breakfast, if I'm not mistaken."

241

"How could I possibly forget?" Juliet answered, following her into the entrance hall. "Your illustrious debut here in the drawing room is days away."

Loveday looked delighted. "To be immediately followed by an assembly to appease those not on the debut guest list, where *you'll* be presented as Mrs. Buchanan."

Juliet said nothing. Years of indebtedness at Royal Vale had made her cautious and uncomfortable. Nor did she want to create another divide between her and Leith with such expenditures. Had he really told the staff to do whatever she wished? Rather, had he meant what he said?

"I'm especially excited about the new violet taffeta for the ball," Loveday was saying. "The lace detail is exquisite!"

Pondering the occasions to come, Juliet started up the stairs to meet with Minette, who was busy in their dressing room putting away the purchases that had arrived yesterday from the glover. At nine o'clock, a footman let in the seamstress and milliner accompanied by an apprentice laden with more goods. Loveday led them into the parlor while Juliet sought the dressing room.

Minette stood by a hatstand, arranging faux roses and ribbon on a bergère. "Madame Buchanan," she said with a charming curtsy.

"Good morning, Minette. 'Tis a squally day, Mrs. Baillie said, but I've decided to take a carriage nevertheless if you'll accompany me around town."

"Alors! What shall you wear?"

Juliet considered several gowns draped over a sofa. "Something warm, perhaps the quilted petticoat and my new blue velvet redingote with matching feather muff." Fingering the lovely fabric, she added, "And some butterfly curls?"

"Oui! Papillote curls are my specialty." Minette began taking out curling tongs and brushes. "And perhaps your new French hat with the Italian flowers? The silk lilacs are a lovely foil to the blue velvet."

An hour later they were confined in the carriage and beyond the mansion's iron gates, moving past other homes and tenements that led to Glasgow Green and the Bridgegait. Ahead was the towering steeple of the Merchants House with its gilded ship weathervane. Soon their coach rolled to a stop in front of a century-old stone building, and Juliet and Minette stepped out onto the street in pattens that held them above muddy cobbles.

This was the heartbeat of the tobacco lords, a place she'd only heard about, the driving force behind Glasgow's trade. Ignoring any qualms, she went through the door framed by tall columns and stone carvings into a foyer where a staircase beckoned upward into the guildhall.

"Shall we take the stairs?" she asked Minette, who smiled and followed her lead.

A bit breathless, she ignored the blatant stares of several men in black satin suits and scarlet capes as they conducted their affairs. Leith wasn't among them. Nary another woman did she see. Juliet prepared her response in case they were stopped.

We've come to see the assembly room where balls and banquets are held. Being from the colonies, I am anxious to learn all I can about your great city.

The staircase led to an imposing rectangular hall that reminded her of a drawing room, oil portraits of former merchants on the walls. Was Leith's father among them? Suspended from the ceiling was a fully rigged ship twin to the one atop the steeple. Juliet paused before a framed, painted board whose words surprised her.

Scripture Rules to Be Observed in Buying and Selling

Minette turned in a slow circle. "Will it suit, Madame Buchanan, for the assembly?"

"I believe so," Juliet answered with a final misgiving. *But will I?*

Somewhere here lurked the magistrates made up of to-bacco lords. Mrs. Baillie remarked they had a fearsome reputation. Something told her these men might not take kindly to women encroaching upon their territory. She was surprised they'd not been confronted so far.

"We must be away," Juliet said, a beat of excitement over-riding her skittishness. "To the Buchanan countinghouse."

Sensing something amiss, Leith looked up from the letter he was writing to a Virginia factor. The sudden hush among his clerks in the large chamber beyond his office door was telling. He pulled his watch from his pocket. Half past eleven. Not yet the dinner hour when they bolted like a herd of wild horses. Next he heard the scraping of chairs that suggested a great many of them had come to their feet.

Returning his quill to the inkpot, he stood, glad to ease the cramp in his hand from working on correspondence since dawn. He rounded his desk, went to his office doorway, and came to a halt. There, in the main entrance to the Buchanan firm, stood Juliet. She was exquisitely attired in shades of blue, her hat at an angle he could only describe as alluring, its flowered brim drawing attention to her hair and her pale, expectant features. He wasn't the only one spellbound.

She smiled at the clerks and moved past them while her maid waited by the door, her back to their gawking. When Juliet came nearer she said, "So, Mr. Buchanan, is this your lair?"

"Aye," he replied, extending a hand to invite her into his private sanctum before shutting the door. She was, he real-ized, the first woman to ever set foot in his domain.

Her gaze, alive with curiosity, trailed round the room, lingering on the glass-fronted bookcases that stood floor to ceiling and covered all the walls before returning to him. He held her gaze as emotion washed through him. Admiration . . . aggravation . . . amusement.

"You're flying your American colors," he said.

She smiled up at him from beneath that beguiling flower-brimmed hat. "Nice to blame any untoward behavior on that."

He sat on the edge of his desk as she settled in a cane chair, her skirts a perfect half circle about her.

Gesturing to the bank notes on his desk, he asked, "Are you in need of any funds?"

"Nay, just seeing how the land lies."

"So, where have you been?"

"Far enough to know to avoid the horse ford and slaughterhouse near the river and keep to the Bridgegait, the safe, respectable part of town."

"Briggait, as we Glaswegians say."

"Where exactly is Ardraigh Hall?"

"Are you bored with the city already?" He crossed his arms, remembering his promise about the twins. At her continued study of him, he yielded. "A few miles southeast of Glasgow, on the right bank of the River Clyde in the county of Lanark."

She seemed relieved.

"I've sent word ahead of our arrival," he added.

"Meaning all the house servants will be on tenterhooks."

"All seven of them."

"So few?"

"You'll need to hire more. There's already a veritable army for the gardens, park, stables, and the like."

"Meaning you are more out of doors than in."

"Aye."

Reaching out, she fingered his waistcoat, pulled on the gold chain attached to his watch, and lifted it out of his pocket.

"Should I send for tea?" he queried, only half joking.

"Tea?" Her face flashed amusement. "Something tells me you prefer something stronger." She let go of his watch and it returned to his pocket with a small plop. Her gaze rested on the bottle atop a small silver tray at the edge of his desk.

"I've more refined brandy if you'd rather." He reached for the whisky and poured a dram. "You've ne'er tasted Scots whisky?"

"Having it flavor my marmalade is plenty."

He swallowed it down, along with a lick of guilt. Confound it, but she trod on his temper. Did she mind his drinking?

With the door closed, she was driving out the scent of ink and paper and all his ironclad intentions with it. Rosewater, he guessed. She was so close, his right shoe buckle was hidden beneath the hem of her petticoat.

"Where do you take your midday dinner if not Virginia Street?" Her curious question was absent of blame or rebuke.

"Most days I go to the Saracen's Head on the Gallowgate, renowned for its mutton." He omitted the cockfighting and Jamaican punch. "Nobles and judges and the like gather there."

"Then I shall leave you to that."

She went out as gracefully as she'd come in, rosewater trailing in her wake, every clerk standing and looking after her. Nearly forgetting common courtesy, he watched her leave, then followed her to the front of the building and escorted her to her coach. When he returned, the office was again at a standstill.

"Return to your work!" he all but roared. "This isna a garden party."

"But, sir, will there be nae introduction?" asked his senior clerk, the boldest of the bunch and a third cousin.

Introductions? He'd completely forgotten. Rarely did he mix business with pleasure. Further proof of the effect she had on him.

"That, lads, is Mrs. Leith Buchanan of colonial Virginia," he said, hardly believing his good fortune.

Another lull ensued, no less astonished.

"With all due respect, sir . . ." Another clerk worked to conceal a red-faced grin. "I wouldna be wasting time here in the countinghouse with a lass like that at home."

42

Give a little love to a child and you get a great deal back.

John Ruskin

That night Leith came home before midnight. Glasgow law was more lax now, no longer keeping to the ten o'clock curfew he remembered from his university days. The house was dark, and he felt a tick of regret for keeping anyone awake, but the servants were well compensated so it seemed a slight grievance.

"Good evening, sir."

"All is well?"

"Verra weel, sir. Still snowing, I take it?"

"The ground is covered, aye, and my cloak and hat." Leith gave them over to the footman's outstretched hands, then climbed the stairs. The cold in his bones would only be countered by a coal fire. He reached his room by the light of hall sconces but then backtracked. Was Juliet's door ajar?

The memory she'd made at the countinghouse refused to budge. Though he'd had shipping notices to post and cargo inventories to check, he'd gotten little done since her visit.

Midafternoon, a note had come round from the guildhall saying a lady thought to be Mrs. Buchanan had been seen in the assembly room at the Merchants House. Bold of her.

His hand on the knob of her door, he debated the wisdom of what he was about to do.

Wise, nay. Needy, aye.

The door was so new it didn't creak when opened, nor did the floorboards when trod upon. They were further muffled by the thickest carpets he could find during construction. Though she'd only been here a few days, her presence was palpable. But she'd soon be gone to the country once her trousseau was finished, no longer a temptation or a distraction. He'd allow himself this one last concession.

He saw that the shutters were open as if she'd been watching the change of weather. He recalled her delight while she'd caroled in the Williamsburg snowstorm, when he'd been watching her from the upstairs window at Ravenal's. The hearth's fire was blazing as if recently resupplied with coal, and her bed curtains were as open as the shutters, illuminating her form beneath the covers. Her cheek lay upon her hand atop the pillow. A nearly forgotten line from *Romeo and Juliet* leapt to mind.

See, how she leans her cheek upon her hand! O, that I were a glove upon that hand, that I might touch that cheek!

He stopped, willed himself to leave . . . and lost. It didn't help that her hair—that extravagance of black that had been all curls earlier—was now subdued and braided like he remembered from the ship. The beribboned end of it draped over the coverlet nearly to the floor.

Drawing closer, he reached out and fingered the silken plait, wanting to unravel it. But the stubborn shadows crept in again, intruding on the moment and destroying the small intimacy before he turned away.

Confined in the coach-and-four the next morn, Juliet and Leith left Glasgow. Feeling that unwelcome beat at her temples, she prayed she wouldn't be coach sick. She wanted to be her best for the children. For Leith.

He seemed intent on showing her Jamaica Street before crossing New Bridge and the Clyde. "Lyrica and Euan live there in the townhouse my father built. They're not often in residence, preferring the countryside, though Euan travels to London and Edinburgh oft enough on Buchanan business."

"I see the Buchanan initial on the gate." Juliet looked at the shuttered stone building much like theirs, her curiosity about her in-laws growing. She missed Loveday, even Minette, and sat somewhat rigid in the coach, a brazier of hot coals beneath her feet, her hands fisted in her feather muff.

"You're looking . . . colorful," Leith said. Did she fancy she heard admiration along with amusement in his voice?

"Children like color." She studied her silk cape with its whimsical embroidery of flowers and animals, even tiny mint-green grasshoppers. "I don't want to frighten them, being a stranger."

"Have you been around children much?"

"At church, mostly. Once Loveday and I taught the enslaved children at Royal Vale like the Bray School in Williamsburg, but Father was against it so we stopped."

He said nothing to this, just leaned back on the upholstered seat opposite and lowered his eyes. Though she didn't dare say it, he looked more like an undertaker in unrelieved black save the white stock about his neck. Was it a reflection of how he felt about this visit?

Stifling a sigh, she lifted the curtain and looked out on a snowy landscape and what resembled a small, smoke-hazed village. "What are those quaint tents and wagons beside those twin towers?"

"The Romany."

"We have none in the colonies that I know of."

"This band—the Ruthvens and Lindseys—make camp at those two auld towers on Buchanan lands. They're granted leases and pay a small sum yearly. A quitrent of sorts. But the younger of the Romany tend to roam."

Like his wife. What had he said? *A Romany princess, if there is such a thing.*

"Many work as tinkers. A few are horse traders, even thieves. One tells fortunes for the nobility and bonnet lairds in these parts. They're not to trespass near Ardraigh Hall."

"But what of Isabella and Cole's kin? Should they not see the twins?"

"Bella, I call her. As for kin, they've since dispersed. Where to, I ken not." His terse tone told her to delve no further.

She closed the curtain, only to open it again when he said they were nearing Ardraigh Hall. A Palladian bridge took them over the River Clyde, and then the drive wended uphill through towering trees before reaching level ground. She'd expected his country house to be no grander than the Virginia Street residence. She'd woefully misjudged. Three-storied, the mansion was infinitely sprawling and grand, a front garden at the foot of a wide double staircase leading to double front doors. Countless chimneys sat atop the main roof and the wings flanking it. Brushed with snow, the magnificent house looked austere, though gardens and parks on all sides promised a lush spring.

"Welcome to Ardraigh Hall," Leith said, helping her alight from the coach.

"'Tis . . . wondrous" came her awed reply.

Before they had trod the first stairstep, a liveried man

came out the front doors. Hand on her elbow, Leith tried to shield her from a bullying wind as her cape blew sideways.

"I nearly forgot—" She paused as another gust yanked her hood back and threatened to tumble her carefully coiffed hair. "The toys."

Leith turned and reminded the postillion to fetch them and bring them inside before the coachman drove on to the stables.

Once in the gleaming entrance hall with its herringbone parquet floor, Juliet noted a frightful number of clocks, so many she lost count. Was Leith obsessed with timekeeping? Bewildered, she faced a housekeeper, several maids, and footmen. Leith made quiet introductions, but overwhelmed as she was, the servants' names turned to mush in her mind.

Was her thudding heart loud enough for all to hear?

Next came a labyrinth of lamplit, wainscoted corridors that became an impossible maze, far more complex than Virginia Street. The twins were in a separate wing entirely.

Leith stopped just shy of the nursery door. "Are you well?"

"Nay." The unfamiliarity of everything flooded her. Juliet missed Royal Vale and the cupola and the smallness and sameness of Virginia like never before.

Concern tightened his brow. "Mayhap you need something to drink—and smelling salts."

"Both." She smiled, but it took all her composure to do so. "But first, the children."

Hearing the postillion and a footman following with the toys, she took hold of the knob before he did. With a desperate prayer, Juliet pushed open the nursery door.

43

Hush ye, hush ye, dinna fret ye,
The black Tinkler winna get ye.
                    Scottish nursery rhyme

*L*eith let Juliet lead. The door opened on the white-haired nursemaid, Mrs. Davies, who had been expecting them. She bobbed her capped head in deference, then excused herself as he'd hoped. The unusually tidy nursery lay before them—just the four of them—and despite Juliet's obvious skittishness, she stepped into it as if she was coming home. There was no other way to describe what left him feeling an outsider. A spectator. His twins had grown tall as milk thistle in his lengthy absence.

With admirable grace, Juliet sank down onto the carpet in the middle of the room, her skirts billowing about her. At once, Bella stopped her babbling and Cole dropped his wooden soldier as if to say, *Who is this colorful creature?*

Both children regarded her openly without a hint of

shyness. Bella trundled straight toward her, stepping onto her cape, plump arms outstretched. Juliet opened her arms in turn, gathering her up and kissing her disheveled wisps of hair.

"Mam," Bella said with a little sigh.

Mam. Leith turned to stone in the doorway. Havilah had long been buried. He thought his daughter would have forgotten the word if not her. Was it Juliet's dark hair? Her same height?

Cole took a more cautious approach, picking up his soldier again and offering it to Juliet just beyond the hem of her petticoat.

"Thank you." Juliet smiled and took the toy, beckoning for him to come closer.

He obliged and she gathered him up too, giving him a peck of a kiss on his forehead, both of them on her lap. Memories of his own mother gutted Leith in stark contrast. He'd never been in her arms. Didn't recall any affection from her, just a severe, haughty indifference bordering on distaste that never altered.

Gruffly greeting the twins from a distance, he turned to bring in the toys left at the door, though the bairns were more interested in the lass before them. Changing course, he took a chair by the hearth, realizing his children hardly knew him while a complete stranger claimed their undivided attention. His throat grew so tight he couldn't swallow. In Juliet they had found what had been lost . . . and what he himself could not give.

"Mam," Bella said again, stroking Juliet's curls with a clumsy hand. Cole, on his stomach now, was absorbed with a tiny fox embroidered on her cape, tracing it with his finger as if to feel its fur.

Juliet was talking to them now in such low, musical tones

he couldn't make out the words. The knot in his throat nearly choked him. Ravenal hadn't been wrong.

She is equaled by few and excelled by none.

Her headache and homesickness fled. Juliet sat with her back to the fire, the children in her arms, their linen and soap scent a balm to her heart. There was something so near the divine in little ones. An unsullied freshness and purity. Cole gave her a wet kiss on her ear and proceeded to examine a pearl earring she wore, while Bella turned her attention to an embroidered ladybug. Juliet was very aware of Leith behind her in a chair near the fire and could only guess his thoughts. This seemed a good beginning, but how would it all end?

"Bonny," Bella said, playing with her other earring.

Juliet endured her tickling ears as she took in all their little details. They were rosy and stout, even double chinned, and had their father's vivid ice-blue eyes. Dressed alike in linen frocks that fell to their ankles, they were bare of foot, their dimpled feet white as milk. The Buchanan imprint was strong, and she succumbed to a steady fascination as she stared at them, trying to pinpoint where else their father lurked.

Cole looked at her, then over her shoulder at Leith. "Da."

'Twas the twins' name for him, Mrs. Baillie had told her. Her heart gave a little leap.

"Would you like to see your new playthings?" she asked. They were now looking at the pile of presents Leith had just brought in. "Can you bring your father—Da—your new hobby horse?"

They hurried over to the toys. But when Juliet looked back at Leith, he had gone.

Upon Juliet and Leith's leaving at visit's end, the twins commenced such a howling as to bring the house down, summoning every servant to the nursery. The benefit was that he and Juliet were quite alone in Ardraigh Hall's foyer to discuss the matter.

"Surely you have an extra coach in the stables to bring their nurse and what's needed to Virginia Street." She was looking at him so sweetly, so beseechingly, his resistance began to crumble. "*Please.*"

"Meaning the twins will travel with us." That noisy possibility was enough to have him walking back to Glasgow.

"Of course, 'tis best."

"I say they bide here a while longer."

Her hand rested on his sleeve. "They've endured enough separations and losses."

He held fast. "You ken I keep them here for their health and safety."

"Wise to consider, but I know of no contagion at present in the city."

"There's always something vile going round."

"'Twill only be for a short time. After Loveday's debut I'll return here with them."

He avoided her gaze. Sweetly beseeching, aye. And undeniably stubborn. Ravenal hadn't mentioned that. "You'll have your hands full caring for them even with a nurse."

"So be it." She smiled, starting up the stairs. "You're rarely at home, so any fuss shan't bother you."

In another hour they were off, two coaches lumbering over the road to Glasgow with its ruts and pockets of snow. Nurse and baggage followed in the second coach, where she was likely stealing a second nap. Leith held Bella, while across from him Cole sat enthroned upon Juliet's lap. Both bairns were asleep, worn out from their howling at the house.

"I'm sorry you weren't able to walk in the gardens and enjoy the park," he told Juliet as Bella shifted in his arms, her head on his shoulder. "There's an orangery you might like in particular."

"Something to look forward to," she replied, looking triumphant. "I've heard spring in Scotland is altogether different than Virginia."

Did she miss America? He wouldn't ask if she was homesick because it would add to the burden that he'd somehow tricked or coerced her into marrying him against her will. Lately that sat as heavy as a bad case of indigestion.

"Spring at Royal Vale is a wondrous season." She seemed wistful, though her smile offset it. "The blooming redbud and dogwood are so exquisite, words fail."

He tried to think of something equally bonny about a Scots spring other than the infernal damp but came up empty.

She opened the curtain and looked out upon a landscape he could only describe as bleak, one arm about Cole. On the seat beside him lay the hobby horse.

Leith voiced what he'd been thinking ever since he'd first seen the toy. "In a few months they'll be able to ride a Shetland pony on a lead rein."

She turned back to him. "I've never heard of such. Are they a small breed?"

"Aye, from the Shetland Islands. No more than eleven hands high. Small but strong, intelligent, and docile. My grandfather saw to it that I had three before I was twelve."

"Oh? What were their names?"

"Mungo, Burra, and Bressay."

"Let me guess." She looked at him intently. "Scottish names, all."

"Aye."

She turned pensive. "I know little about your childhood."

"I survived it."

She gave a little laugh. "As did I, obviously. I pray Bella and Cole do the same."

He looked down at Bella, now drooling on his frock coat, before returning his gaze to Juliet. "Are you content to have nae children of your own?"

Her rosy expression told him the question was too bold. But it didn't slow her response. "Rather, are *you* content that I not?"

He didn't answer. How could he without vexing them both further? He reached for the window and opened it. The rush of winter's air did him good. But it didn't settle the question, nor did it temper his suddenly perplexed mood.

They rode in silence the rest of the way to Glasgow.

44

I could bend you with my finger and my thumb . . . But whatever I do with this cage, I cannot get at you, and it is your soul that I want.

Charlotte Brontë

The house was in a state of high excitement. Loveday's debut was at hand, and sixteen new servants joined with Mrs. Baillie, Haskins, Ruby, and the other Virginia Street staff to make the occasion a shining success. Upstairs, Juliet heard the musical clock on her escritoire play eight bells as she adjusted Bella's sash on her satin dress.

Minette moved to a window, her French accent heightened when she was delighted. "Coaches have lined up clear around the corner. I've never seen so many!"

Loveday swept in, as unpowdered and hoopless as Juliet, her violet taffeta skirts rustling. "We shall start a new American fashion, you and I."

Cole abandoned the musical clock he was winding and raced over to his aunt Lovey, as he called her, raising his arms. She picked him up promptly despite Minette exclaiming about his crushing her gown. Finally Minette took him

259

from Loveday and balanced him on a hip as Juliet finished with Bella and turned to her brother.

"Does Mr. Buchanan ken the bairns are to make an appearance?" Nurse asked, standing by the hearth.

Her distressed tone didn't dim Juliet's high mood. "I thought I might surprise him, Mrs. Davies. Make him proud."

"And if they misbehave, Mrs. Buchanan? What then?"

"I shall take all the blame." Juliet smiled to reassure her. Nurse had as many worries as wrinkles. "They shall only make a brief appearance, mostly to see their relatives."

"Bonny." Bella pointed to her tiny shoes embroidered with forget-me-nots.

"So very bonny," Loveday agreed. "Très belle, as the French say."

Not to be outdone, Cole pointed to the small toy sword at his waist, a gift from Niall.

Nurse tsked. "Next the younger Mr. Buchanan will be giving him boxing lessons."

"Surely not," Loveday replied with a touch of dismay. "I've not met him, but . . ."

"'Tis time to go down," Juliet said, holding out her hands to the children. "Remember your manners. Smile at our guests, and practice saying sir and ma'am and please and thank you."

"Mind yer stepmother, aye," Nurse said, patting her pockets. "There'll be a sweetmeat for ye if ye do."

Juliet drew a steadying breath as the door opened and they passed into the corridor. No reason for nerves. Her own debut at the assembly hall was yet to come. This was Loveday's hour, and she prayed it wouldn't disappoint.

Below, the flower-festooned chamber was filling, the chandelier spilling light on the first arrivals. Loveday went ahead of her, and Juliet was careful the children didn't step on the trailing hem of her dress.

Leith stood near the drawing room door, greeting guests as the footman announced them.

Was she tardy?

The qualm dissolved as he came into sharp focus. *Oh, my heart.* She'd hardly seen him since that day they'd fetched the twins from Ardraigh Hall. Tonight he was remarkably braw.

And he was looking up at her.

Well played, Juliet.

He'd not expected to see the twins by her side, but there they were, navigating the staircase with surprising ease, the harmless sword swinging from the sash at Cole's waist. Bella was beaming at him, and in the shifting light he caught a glimpse of what she might look like as a young woman in fancy dress. Years from now, would he remember this shining moment?

Delighted guests turned toward the children as they stepped into the entrance hall. If Juliet was nervous, her attention given the twins surely relieved it. She was clad in a new gown of blue damask. On purpose? It seemed arrogant to think she dressed to please him.

Glasgow seamstresses didn't disappoint. No other woman was her rival. But he had no eye for any other.

"Da," Cole said with a little bow when they stood before him.

Leith knelt down as Bella curtsied, and everyone watching gave a collective "ahh." He took her hand and kissed it, wanting to take Juliet's as well. When he stood up, he met her eyes, which were smiling. She was never happier than when with the children. Would she never light up that way with him?

"Shall we?" he asked, extending his arm.

She accepted and kept hold of Bella, while Cole, spying his uncles and aunt already in the drawing room, took off at a cumbersome run. Leith's brothers turned toward them, and Lyrica began laughing behind her fan at the amusing spectacle.

"Allow me to present Mrs. Juliet Buchanan, lately of Virginia." Leith felt more than a beat of pride.

His normally taciturn brothers wore a look of unmistakable admiration as introductions were made.

Lyrica embraced Juliet, kissing both her cheeks. "Welcome to the family. I'm thrilled to not be the only Mrs. Buchanan!"

Juliet warmed to Lyrica at once. She exuded a candor Juliet found refreshing among all the pomp and powder here. Euan looked a tad like Leith but wasn't so tall, his attire boasting a hint of a dandy with his embroidered claret suit of gold and silver thread with a lace jabot about his neck. But that was the only softening thing about him. He bore the Buchanan stoniness Juliet found disturbing, the jut of his jaw and the arrogant slant of his brows distancing, even daunting.

Euan regarded her with cool calculation, reminding her she was a foreigner. But she couldn't blame him when she'd arrived without warning and hadn't brought much to the marriage except a dowry of colonial debt.

Niall was a youthful Leith but a more engaging one with his ready smiles and teasing of the twins. He had an honest, boyish vulnerability entirely absent in his older brothers.

Loveday approached, so lovely and gracious that tears came to Juliet's eyes. Her little sister seemed more mature, and she sensed this night would be a turning point not only for Loveday but for their relationship.

Euan bowed stiffly and Lyrica greeted Loveday promptly, but it became obvious that Niall looked the longest, seemingly at a loss for words. Loveday met the youngest Buchanan's eyes with a spark that hinted at an instantaneous, unspoken attraction. Leith appeared amused, as if remembering his words of weeks ago.

"Your sister might make a better pairing with my youngest brother."

"May I have a dance, Miss Catesby?" Niall said, recovering himself.

Loveday rewarded him with a dimpled smile, acceptance written in her every feature. "The first of many, I hope."

The music hadn't yet begun, and more guests were pouring through the drawing room doors. Excusing herself, Juliet led the children up a hidden back stair to pacify Nurse, who was waiting with their sweetmeats and would soon tuck them into bed. By the time she returned, the dancing had begun, the first lilting notes of the violins enchanting.

Loveday was still talking with the Buchanans, but Leith was giving a woman his undivided attention on the other side of them. The stab of dismay Juliet felt was surely a reflection of her own insecurities. If only the woman wasn't quite so lovely—or quite so riveted, turned toward him in a too familiar way. The flash of diamonds about her ears and throat and her coiffure of curls would tempt the most pious parson. And pious parson Leith was not.

Juliet loathed the woman on sight. And immediately repented.

As she did so, Leith turned toward her, and the woman slipped away into the crowd, disappearing from view if not from mind.

45

So agreeable and innocent an amusement.
George Washington on dancing

*L*oveday opened the ball with Leith, foregoing the usual minuet and dancing a country dance before partnering with Euan then Niall. Juliet watched breathlessly as her sister performed admirably, for that was what this was—a performance by an American, an outlander. Loveday's new chalked shoes prevented her from slipping on the polished floor, her steps faultless even with every eye upon her. Niall seemed the perfect partner.

"Your brother is accomplished," Juliet said to Leith behind her extended fan.

"He had an Aberdeen-born dancing master." His wince had her anticipating his next words. "I didna."

"You slight yourself. I think you even enjoy it."

His mocking half smile told her otherwise, but when the music changed, he gave a little bow that not only disarmed but charmed her. "Will you step a quadrille, Mrs. Buchanan?"

Her brow lifted. Her duty as hostess was to look after her

guests and make sure the ladies had partners, or so she'd recently read in *The Art of British Society*. "'Tis not customary for a married couple to dance together, only courting couples."

"Court etiquette, mayhap. Not Glaswegian society." He took her gloved left hand in his right. "Besides, when you wed hurriedly, you court after."

His low words, the look he gave her, sent a little thrill through her. Who was she to argue? It was his house. His rules. But courting?

"It's a foregone conclusion, ye ken," he said during the set. "My brother and your sister."

She spied Loveday again, clearly enjoying herself. Niall had yet to leave her side. "But it seems so sudden."

"I'll wager they'll be married by Michaelmas."

She spun away from him, then stepped close again. "Is he worthy of her?"

He seemed to give this some thought, waiting till the next turn to say, "Of the three of us, Niall is the most amiable. And the most malleable."

Their hands joined as they came together in a carefully orchestrated turn. When his shoe buckle caught on the embroidered rose of her slipper and left her shoeless, laughter rippled over the ballroom. At least it hadn't happened to Loveday. Mortified, Juliet watched as Leith deftly retrieved the missing item and returned it to her foot, much to the amusement of all watching, themselves included. A little humor never hurt, she decided.

Loveday sent her a joyous glance as she promenaded with Niall before he handed her to another gentlemen, albeit reluctantly, Juliet thought.

"Would you care for refreshments?" Leith asked over the music. "Far safer. You'll likely lose nae shoes."

Still flushing, she let him lead her to the adjoining room that seemed more garden, overflowing with flowers from city hothouses. Just beyond was an endlessly long table set for a midnight supper, after which dancing would resume till dawn.

"Is anything the matter?" he asked her quietly as footmen buzzed about them carrying silver trays.

"This extravagance . . ."

He met her eyes. "There's nae end to it."

"Your pockets?"

"Aye."

"Then let's do something different. Something that out-lasts this night."

"Meaning our guests will go home, forget about what they ate and drank or who they danced with, then move on to the next fête, where they'll do it all over again without a single thought for anyone else."

"Yes." She took the punch he gave her, the glass chill in her hand. Though she'd not been here long, the city's dark wynds and closes heaped with refuse and misery blackened her thoughts.

He said nothing more, just looked over the fragrant, candlelit chamber as if seeing it with new eyes. Or so she hoped.

She took a breath. "I shall do this for Loveday tonight, but I shan't do it for myself or anyone else."

46

We live in deeds, not years; in thoughts, not
     breaths.
In feelings, not in figures on a dial.
We should count time by heart throbs.
He most lives who thinks most, feels the noblest,
     acts the best.

                                        Philip James Bailey

*L*eith looked up from where he stood discussing a matter with the Buchanan bank manager to see his brothers come into the lobby from the street. Though the party for Loveday had passed a few days ago, Euan and Niall had stayed on in the city.

Leith didn't miss the ream of newspapers beneath Euan's arm. Lately they'd been poring over them to try to come to some agreement about how to proceed with trading and shipping given the expected revolution. But the Americans were hard to read. Many remained loyal to England, while others, especially Virginians, were outright rebels.

"We'll wait for you in your office," Euan told him, backtracking out the bank door, Niall in his wake.

Leith excused himself and caught up to them, the wind coming off the Broomielaw sleety and raw. They climbed steep steps to the countinghouse's third floor, which had a territorial view of ships coming into port from the colonies and elsewhere.

"I suppose you've come to discuss the American problem," Leith said, leading them up the stairs.

"Nae," Niall said. "My business is more personal."

"Anything personal can wait," Euan murmured with a scowl. "We have transatlantic troubles to discuss."

"A look at the papers confirms nothing new is worth printing of late," Niall replied. "The colonies have been quiet since their first Continental Congress."

"Quietly gathering ammunition," Leith said. "And tarring and feathering a few factors in the Chesapeake."

"What?" Euan exclaimed overloudly. He muttered an oath as they passed by numerous clerks and factors at work in an anteroom.

Leith unlocked his office door and stood back as his brothers entered. "I'm considering recalling every man in our employ and shutting down the stores there. Nae matter which Glasgow firm, factors have never been in good standing with the colonists, particularly planters, even in the best political and economic climate. If they're not recalled now, they'll likely be expelled or even arrested by colonial authorities."

Euan and Niall took the two chairs fronting his desk while he went to the window, restless, eyes on the Broomielaw. "I've another meeting with fellow merchants at the guildhall on the morrow."

"Speaking of the hall, what's this about the assembly for the new Mrs. Buchanan being canceled?" Euan asked, setting the newspapers on Leith's desk. "I don't like the sound of it."

"'Tis owing to her American mindset, if you will," Leith replied. "In her words, 'Let society call on Virginia Street or Ardraigh Hall if they wish to make my acquaintance.'"

"American mindset, indeed." Euan all but spat the words. "She sounds every bit as rebellious as those Patriots."

"Careful. She's my wife." Leith poured them all a dram of whisky. Not the watered-down spirits Juliet insisted on serving at home. She was causing him to reconsider his habits, drinking included. "My American bride has made a great many charitable contributions instead. She tallied the outlying expenses for the fête and decided they could be better spent elsewhere."

"What?" his brothers said in unison.

Setting the bottle down, Leith gestured toward a new ledger labeled *Juliet Catesby Buchanan*. "Have a look if you like."

Euan was the first to open the ledger and peruse it. "She's given over a substantial amount to every guild in addition to our Buchanan Society charity and hospital? The trades' accounts show a number of gifts paid to orphans, widows, needy students, those displaced by fire and flood, and the infirm." He expelled an aggravated breath. "Those are funds that could be reinvested in land, mining rights, and whatnot."

Niall gave a tight half smile. "Her benevolence is unprecedented and long overdue, in my opinion."

Euan dropped the ledger onto the desk. "You'll both attend the Spierses' coming ball here in the city, surely. More than one business affair hinges upon it."

Leith perused another ledger, distracted. "I shall see what she says."

Setting aside his empty glass, Euan leaned forward in his chair. "You're letting *her* decide?"

Leith shrugged. "With a looming war, I've nae time to consider it."

"You'd best pay attention. She sounds twin to the Blue-stockings Society overseen by Elizabeth Montagu, encroaching on and undermining men's affairs."

"Juliet is simply following biblical commands to show mercy, generosity, and all the rest. I canna fault that."

Euan snorted. "Rather than bankrupt us with extravagances and luxuries as many a lass would, she may well do the same draining the Buchanan coffers."

"She's quite amiable about having her way," Leith said.

Niall expelled a tense breath. "At least you've won her. I beg you both to consider my predicament at present." Finished with his whisky, he returned his empty glass to the desk. "I am at an impasse in my courtship of Miss Catesby and need you to put in a favorable word for me."

His youngest brother looked so dejected Leith almost felt sorry for him. "I am rarely home." The admission came with a nick of guilt. "I thought it went well enough at the fête."

"As did I." Niall rubbed his jaw in agitation. "But there've been so many suitors at Virginia Street I'm surprised you're not stumbling over them when you return home at night."

"What means ye?"

"Yesterday I waited in line an hour and a half."

"When you could have been attending to business," Leith said, near scathing in his tone. "Why didn't you get out of line and come back at a better time?"

"There were more suitors behind me than ahead of me." Niall shook his head. "It's that ruinous five thousand pounds. That and the fact she said she wants to choose carefully and pray about her future first."

"Wise beyond her years," Euan said, his tone mocking. "Or perhaps utterly glaikit."

Niall sent him a warning look. "She asked how I felt about spiritual matters."

"You go to kirk," Leith said, sitting down.

"Apparently she's looking for more than that, though she doesna elaborate. The right gentleman would need nae elaboration, she gently explained."

"Then she should marry clergy," Leith said. "Not a Buchanan."

"I told her I would give up sporting if she would consider me a serious suitor."

"Take her to Lamb Hill," Leith told him. "That's better leverage."

Euan yawned. "You both make me doubly glad Lyrica and I are well past these theatrics."

"Theatrics?" Leith said wryly. "If I recall, you were her second choice."

"Her first suitor had the audacity to die, aye." Euan lifted broad shoulders in a shrug. "He was her father's preference, being the son of an earl. But I cared enough for her that in the end a title didna matter." Euan looked hard at Niall. "Are you willing to persist?"

"She's the loveliest lass I've ever seen." Vulnerability eased Niall's tense features. "But there's more to her than that."

Aye, more. Far more, Leith didn't say. And he wasn't thinking of Loveday. He pulled at his watch chain and noted the time. With a wink at Niall, he said, "Then I advise you to go stand in line."

47

A lofty cane, a sword with silver hilt, a ring, two watches,
and a snuff-box gilt.

Holbeach

W e've a letter from Father!" Loveday burst into
the yellow damask parlor, waving a sealed paper
about.

A letter, at long last?

Juliet looked up from her embroidery as the children
stopped playing with Hobbes and a tangle of yarn at her
feet. Securing her needle in the tambour frame, she turned
toward Loveday, who all but collapsed onto a sofa, already
immersed in the post.

"Read it aloud, please," Juliet said with a bite of aggravation brought on by a near sleepless night. Leith hadn't come
home, and she'd worn herself down worrying.

"Father is coming! In fact, he and Zipporah are already
on their way as of this letter!"

Juliet sat back and took Bella onto her lap. "I wonder if
they'll weigh anchor here or elsewhere?"

272

"'We should arrive in spring, a shorter sailing since we dock at Port Glasgow. Once we've visited with you, we will then go on to London as Zipporah is anxious to return home. After suffering a bout of ill health, I would like to continue on to Bath. The waters should do me good.'" Loveday put the letter down to produce a tiny pocket calendar. "A month? They should arrive any minute! Such glad news. And they'll stay here with us before moving on to England."

Bath. Juliet remembered Leith discussing some investment he had there. The Royal Crescent, he'd called it. "Perhaps you should make a Bath debut too, though Father's health concerns me." To say nothing of his pocketbook.

"Poor Father." Loveday's elation faded. "I do wonder if his gout has returned. Bath is said to be the best curative anywhere, and I've no remedy to help. Perhaps a visit to the Glasgow apothecary is in order. I confess to feeling at sixes and sevens without my stillroom."

She picked up the letter and read more, though Father was notoriously short-winded by post. Their honeymoon, he penned, had been fine. They were increasingly concerned about the political situation and that radicals like Patrick Henry would plunge them into a world war. Both of them had decided Britain was their true home.

Loveday passed the letter to Juliet, but Bella grabbed it with one fat fist. They laughed as Cole came to investigate, never wanting to be deprived of anything his sister might have.

"'Tis a letter, not a toy or sweetmeat," Juliet told them, taking the letter back and pocketing it. "Shall we have tea?"

Both children nodded, and soon the four of them were seated by the window, where sunlight streamed in like yellow ribbons. Ruby brought a miniature tea service, made to fit small hands, and Juliet presided.

"When you're a little older you shall pour your own tea. For now, 'tis too hot," she cautioned as Loveday passed sugar and milk. "Cook has fashioned some tiny biscuits for you with lemon cheese too. We must remember to thank her. But first, your bibs and a 'please.'"

"Peas," Bella said prettily while Cole just stared at the tray as if debating whether to grab it like Bella had the letter.

"Master Cole, can you say 'please,' please?" Loveday cajoled.

"Nae," he replied as firmly as his father might have done.

"Let's say grace and thank our heavenly Father." Juliet folded her hands and bowed her head, touched as the twins did the same. Had someone taught them prior to this? "Lord, we give Thee endless thanks for all Thy bounty. Bless especially these little hands and hearts. Amen."

Bibs aside, soon Bella had more lemon cheese on the tablecloth than in her mouth, and Cole seemed more interested in his shiny silver spoon than anything else. While Bella chewed her biscuit carefully with wee white teeth, Cole snuck more sugar from the sugar bowl, toppling the lid and sending it to the carpet, and Hobbes leapt to the sofa to avoid a collision. Both sisters worked hard to hide their amusement.

At a masculine voice outside, Loveday's attention strayed to the window and the sunny street. "I've nearly forgotten 'tis time for callers."

"And I'm to meet with the servants while the twins take a nap." Juliet looked to the mantel clock as it chimed two o'clock, in time with the grander timepiece that resounded like cannon fire in the echoing entrance hall. "Then I may take a walk, as the weather is fair."

"We shall both be busy, then." Loveday put a hand to her hair. "I suppose I must change."

274

"You look lovely—and your suitors will no doubt think the same."

Flushing, she made a face. "I do confess I'm surprised at the number. Some come out of curiosity, I'm sure. I'm an American, after all. And then there's Mr. Buchanan's generous dowry, which is partly your doing, of course. And while I'm thankful, I do wonder if these gentlemen are seeing bank notes all the while as they converse with me."

"Then marry a man who doesn't need them," Juliet said.

Loveday laughed. "That narrows the field considerably, Sister."

"Once I thought debt a cruel gaoler, but now I'm beginning to see money might be the harsher taskmaster."

"Peas," Bella said, reaching for another biscuit while Cole swallowed a spoonful of sugar meant for his cup.

"Oh my, you are one for sweets," Juliet said, pouring him more tea and pushing the sugar bowl toward Loveday. "Did you know your father is going to get you a pony?"

"Da?" Cole looked up at her with the same intent expression Leith wore. "Ride a pony?"

Juliet smiled and nodded. "A handsome Shetland pony from the islands. You'll need to name him, and then he will come when you call to him."

Bella stopped licking her fingers. "Pony for me too?"

"A pony for you both," Juliet said. "You're almost big enough to go riding, but we'll have to return to Ardraigh Hall first for lessons."

Yet Leith hadn't made arrangements to return them to the country. She waited, though not impatiently, since to be beyond Virginia Street was to see him not at all, or so she feared. Then she remembered the Spierses' ball invitation. And now Father was due any day . . .

The Spiers mansion seemed lit by a thousand candles. Nerves high, Juliet wished Minette hadn't laced her so tightly. Or perhaps her breathlessness was simply the thought of facing so many Glaswegians for the first time, all who would undoubtedly be curious about Leith Buchanan's American bride. Loveday, her constant support, remained at home with a miserable cold.

Footmen announced them at the front door and then again at the entrance to the drawing room. Being so new to marriage, Juliet always felt a little start at her new name. The man beside her was impeccably attired but markedly reserved as if he didn't want to be here any more than she did. He'd said little in the coach when she'd craved a reassuring word, but she'd been equally tight-lipped, and now her faux smile seemed pinned in place.

Amid the dazzling candlelight, gowns and jewels were aglitter, a veritable rainbow of gemstones flashing about the huge, gilded room. Her pearls, always her preference, seemed out of place. She'd worn a blue gown to please Leith, but he seemed not to have noticed, hardly giving her a glance. Introductions began, but try as she might, she could not keep up with the flood of names and faces. Yet she did overhear a knot of older women pass by behind her who seemed distinct as a trumpet blast.

"She dresses regally despite being from a rebel backwater like Virginia."

"I suppose she'll soon be called the queen of Lanarkshire since he's the king of it."

"Given she prefers to associate with Glasgow's poorest, even tolbooth prisoners, Mr. Buchanan must have forced her hand to appear here tonight."

Stung, Juliet moved as far away from them as she could, though she sensed their eyes boring into her back. Leith had fallen into conversation with a group of men while Lyrica led her to the punch, her saffron silk skirts flowing about her as she walked gracefully.

The music and dancing moved from the opening minuet to country dances, and Juliet's hopes of partnering with Leith were dashed. He'd not disregard protocol and dance with her here like he had at home, she guessed. Envy colored her dismay when a lovely young woman was the first he partnered with. Was Leith a faithful husband? She was certainly an insecure wife.

Before she could ponder the matter further, Euan intervened, bowing and proving himself as adept a dancer as Leith. But it was Leith she wanted, as this ball had a decidedly different feel from the warm, winsome one at the Virginia Street mansion, where the guests had been close relations and friends. Here they were simply business associates, as if the function was little more than another shrewd business transaction, lacking genuine feeling.

"So, what do you make of our society, Mrs. Buchanan?" Euan asked.

"I'm too bedazzled to form an opinion," she replied from behind her fluttering fan.

"I hope your former indebtedness doesn't keep you from appreciating our elevated entertainments. You wouldn't want to jeopardize the Buchanan name or business interests by appearing less than grateful as an American."

His harsh words were cloaked in a smooth tone. For a moment she lost her footing.

"I've never been accused of being ungrateful," she said evenly.

"As a foreigner you must tread carefully. First impressions are everything."

At which you are utterly failing. She bit her tongue lest she let that slip, relieved when the music waned. Her initial impression of the middle Buchanan, far from high, plummeted to her feet.

When Euan departed, Niall seemed to appear from nowhere, his obvious concern touching. Did he sense her disquiet?

"I hope you're weathering this long evening well. Please don't think me guilty of flattery when I say you Virginians could teach us Glaswegians a thing or two about dancing."

She thanked him, assuaged by his gracious words. He had none of the stoniness of his older brothers. And truly, Virginians were some of the finest dancers on earth.

She gained a measure of confidence as she moved through the familiar steps across the polished wood with other partners. The *Lady's Magazine* had kept her abreast of what was happening on the dance floor here.

Niall waited his turn. Being the topmost couple, they chose a longways dance she had stepped countless times in colonial ballrooms.

Afterward, slightly breathless, Niall led her to a corner, brought her punch, and wasted no time inquiring about Loveday. "How fares your dear sister?"

"She regrets her absence."

"Not as much as I do." He brought a handsomely tailored sleeve instead of a silken handkerchief to his damp upper lip.

Juliet felt a beat of amusement. These Buchanans, despite their lofty business standing, were callused, practical men who would never be guilty of taking snuff from a tortoiseshell box or sporting pink powdered hair like Parisians.

"Her sincere hope is that she soon mends and enjoys your company again," she said, sensing his uncertainty.

"I suppose her illness gives her a blessed rest from her hurricane of suitors."

She nearly laughed. "I don't think she'd mind my telling you that there is only one gentleman she's given a second thought to."

"I'm glad to hear it." Hope ignited in his eyes. "Courting is riskier than the tobacco market. I'll be glad to see it done."

"I hope you shan't wait much longer."

"Are you playing matchmaker, Mrs. Buchanan?"

"More overly zealous sister, perhaps."

"I suppose she had a crush of Virginia suitors."

"Despite her lack of a fortune, yes. Her good name stood her in good stead."

"'A good name is rather to be chosen than great riches, and loving favour rather than silver and gold.'" He frowned as if the Scripture came with a bitter memory.

"Spoken like a pulpit preacher," she said.

"Our father didn't practice what he preached but insisted we learn it just the same." His gaze veered to Leith walking their way. "And your good name is why my brother chose you. Or mayhap coerced you."

"Coerced?" She smiled, feeling suddenly lighthearted. "'Twas I who all but begged to be put aboard his departing ship."

He grinned, his boyishness charming. "I can only hope my and your sister's story ends half as well."

48

The superiority of chocolate [hot chocolate], both for health and nourishment, will soon give it the same preference over tea and coffee here in America.

Thomas Jefferson

The youngest Mr. Buchanan sends his best wishes for your recovery," Juliet told Loveday upon returning home from the fête.

"How I hated to miss it." Loveday sneezed into a handkerchief, looking pleased to hear it nevertheless. "How did the evening go?"

"Well enough, except I missed you terribly. These tobacco lords aren't nobility, but they do enjoy a flash of jewels and finery."

"I've heard some of them are procuring titles to go with their fortunes, though the Buchanans might not be among them."

Juliet sat down on the edge of Loveday's mattress, wondering if Leith had gone straight to bed. The midnight hour had passed, and she stifled a yawn herself.

"You look lovely. That indigo silk with the silver thread is exquisite." Loveday touched a lace sleeve ruffle in admiration. "So what's next on our social calendar?"

"Tea with Lyrica day after tomorrow."

"Lyrica?" Loveday's expression clouded. "There's something about her . . ."

Juliet's weariness vanished. "What do you mean?"

"Remember when Mama would tell us to take caution with this one or that? Rare though it was, her admonishment never failed to prove true in time."

"And you feel chary of Lyrica."

Loveday looked pained. "I saw her berating a servant most harshly behind the scenes at my debut. Perhaps it was a one-time occurrence. I've noticed these Scots are very different than Americans. The Buchanans are especially worldly. But I certainly don't want to naysay your new family."

"You rarely naysay anyone." Juliet staunched the impulse to confess her low opinion of Euan. "You're always gracious."

Loveday took her hand and gave it a gentle squeeze. "Lyrica Buchanan's behavior is not my concern. But at the same time, I'd rather not go visit her myself. Let the new sisters-in-law have time together first."

The March day chosen for meeting with Lyrica Buchanan was dry with a hint of spring. Juliet walked along with Minette, wishing for more plainstanes underfoot like those the tobacco lords stood upon beneath King William's statue. Would summer's dust be as thick as winter's mud? Today it seemed everyone in Glasgow had spilled out of their homes and shops to stand in the fragile sunshine.

"Watch for pickpockets," Minette cautioned, looking

about with a wary eye. "They often work in pairs, these thieves, and have a particular fondness for silk handkerchiefs and gold watches."

Juliet avoided the press of people when she could but nearly came to a stop once they rounded a corner. Among all the faces before her, one leapt out. A man, hat lowered to shade his features, seemed to be staring right at her from across the street. As she met his eyes, he slipped into the crowd and vanished from view.

Riggs. He resembled Riggs.

Juliet fought the urge to flee and stood her ground. He'd only reminded her of Riggs. Nothing more. But that last night at Royal Vale still haunted her. Or perhaps it was Loveday's rare word of caution about Lyrica that shadowed her.

The alarm of the moment soon faded as she and Minette moved into a lane of birdsong and sunlight, the crowds lessening.

"The Buchanan Street residence, where the other Mr. and Mrs. Buchanan reside, is smaller than the Virginia Street townhouse. 'Tis older, for one, and seldom used," Minette told her as they passed beneath an avenue of shade trees. "My sister was in service there once . . . until she ran away."

Juliet looked at her in surprise. "Ran away?"

"I know not where, Madame Buchanan."

To not know where one's sister was? Loveday sprang to mind, their bond as close as two sisters could be. "I'm so sorry. 'Tis saddening."

"Oui, très difficile." Minette's features crumpled. "She was all I had in the world. Édith was sent to attend to Madame Havilah on Virginia Street until her death, then returned to serve Madame Lyrica briefly. Much like I have been sent to you."

"She was one of the two maids in service to them both?"

Juliet recalled one name from the newspaper clearly. "The other was a Mary Andrews."

"Two maids were needed to attend Madame Havilah as she was so ill." Minette looked more distressed. "How did you know about the details?"

"I read some old newspapers about it. Mention was made of poisoning, which I find alarming, to say the least."

"Oui. Poisonous powders. Calomel, perhaps."

Juliet mulled this as they continued on. "What became of Mary?"

"Mary died soon after Madame Havilah. And then my sister left Buchanan Street."

Juliet slowed her steps. "Was Édith unhappy in service, Minette?"

"Servants are not expected to be happy or unhappy, no?" Minette's tone turned resigned. "It is all about pleasing one's employer, in this case the powerful Buchanans."

Juliet sensed Minette had finished discussing the matter, for her sudden shift in demeanor seemed a closed door. Her heart was understandably sore about her sister. The entire matter turned Juliet more skittish.

They walked on in silence for several minutes. "Paisley is nearly as grand as Ardraigh Hall, and I'm sure you'll visit soon, madame." Minette brightened as they turned a corner. "And then there is Lamb Hill."

"The younger Mr. Buchanan's country house?"

"Oui. It is newer and *très belle*. Not so far from Ardraigh Hall. And true to its name, the mansion is built on a hill surrounded by sheep."

Once they were inside the Buchanan Street townhouse, Lyrica greeted them, ushering Juliet into a small parlor while Minette went to the servants' hall. "Brave of you to walk about with our changeable weather. I'm so glad you've come.

We didn't have a chance to exchange anything but pleasantries at the last *fête*."

"Which you've recovered from, I hope."

Lyrica laughed. "Being up late is something I rarely choose to do, though a fête of any kind is invariably entertaining. But enough of that. How are you adjusting to Scottish life? I hope you're not homesick."

"I'm so occupied I scarcely think of it." Juliet looked toward the door as a footman brought hot chocolate rather than tea in a tall pot. Cinnamon and chiles laced the chill air. "You're a Glaswegian?"

"Born and bred, yes. I've never been beyond Britain. I hear America is indeed a brave new world."

"Full of heat and insects and fevers," Juliet admitted, Leith's malady in mind. "But there is beauty, too, in the wild newness of it all. I stand amazed at how many centuries of history are here. It makes one feel small. Glasgow is enormous."

"Compared to London, Glasgow is almost a hamlet. Leith will have to take you to his townhouse in Mayfair, my favorite of all the Buchanan residences. And then there's his Edinburgh tenement on High Street."

"Does he often travel there?"

"Not since Havilah died. He told you about her, I suppose?"

"Only that she was Romany and they made an unusual match."

"It all started quite harmlessly, as things often do." Taking a drink of her cocoa, Lyrica seemed at a loss for words. "'Tis tradition here for Romany babies to be presented for baptism. Ladies of the parish give these infants and their families gifts when they are. On the Sunday that Havilah's clan took a newborn to the Buchanans' parish kirk, Leith's

284

elderly aunt—his mother had passed by then—was recovering from a fall, so she asked him to accompany her. You can guess what happened."

Juliet envisioned it. A newborn. The parish kirk. A cartload of gifts. A bewitching beauty with an unusual name. And a very marriageable Buchanan.

"It all happened so very fast. Soon Leith was taking great interest in Havilah's family as tenants when he'd not done so before. He courted her, she accepted, then it all came apart."

"It wasn't a happy union from the first, then."

"For a time, perhaps. He did seem to care for her deeply early on. But she was so very . . . common. Refreshingly different and without guile, Leith said." Lyrica shook her head. "There was talk of his being unfaithful to her in the papers, but that was a lie. Leith had a great deal going on business-wise, and she fell ill with a difficult pregnancy. She nearly died at the birth, though the twins were healthy and thriving."

Juliet all but held her breath as Lyrica continued.

"She seemed to almost lose her mind for periods of time. Violent mood swings and the like. A wet nurse was hired in the hopes Havilah would recover her strength. I've played it over in my mind dozens of times and believe the final straw had to do with her family moving on without her and not letting her know. She went to the tower encampment to see them and they'd left without a word. The few Romany who remained couldn't say where they'd gone or when they'd be back."

Juliet felt a surge of pity, not only for Havilah but for Leith. And she couldn't help but note the disdain with which Lyrica spoke of her.

"That last night in Glasgow . . ." Lyrica paused, her features haunted. "Havilah left after midnight and went toward the Jamaica Street bridge without so much as a cape or a hat or even shoes. Leith followed in a hard, driving rain, intent on giving her her freedom if she wanted to return to her people. She saw him and shouted for him to go away as she climbed up on the bridge's side. And then she jumped. The fall was far and the water icy, and Leith jumped after her, but she was swept away by the current. If he wasn't a strong swimmer he'd likely have perished with her."

Juliet wondered at the depths of Havilah's despair and Leith's horror at watching her take her own life. Was it any wonder he was emotionally reserved? Afraid to risk his heart again?

"Of course, Leith's critics blamed him. The newspapers continued to print it as the worst sort of scandal. He hadn't a moment's peace for months. He went into mourning and shut himself away."

"Where is she buried?"

"In the park at Ardraigh Hall. She always loved swans, so Leith made her final resting place near the lake."

A touching consideration given their last haunting moments. Juliet wondered if he ever went there or would show the twins one day.

"For a time, I feared he would forsake the bairns completely and leave them solely to the servants. They seemed to remind him of Havilah, of his personal failings regarding her."

"Cole and Bella . . . I sense they miss their mother."

"Perhaps. We spent all the time we could with them when Leith was away in the colonies. There's nothing like children to enliven a house. Yet he sees so little of them." Tears shone in Lyrica's eyes, and suddenly Juliet realized what she'd overlooked before. Lyrica and Euan were childless. While Leith spent little time at home with his twins, they were denied the privilege of having any.

"Yet they seem to care for him despite his frequent absences. They even prepared a surprise for him last night before bedtime—some drawings they made—but he didn't come home." Swallowing, Juliet pressed on. "I always listen for him . . ."

There, she said it. Clumsily and inelegantly but honestly. The young women he'd partnered with at dances still haunted her. And there was mention of infidelity in the newspaper printings she'd found about Havilah, though Lyrica denied it. Had Leith been faithful to Havilah? Had he been faithful to *her*?

"Leith spent the night here," Lyrica told her. "After tearing up the second floor of the Saracen's Head in your defense."

Juliet recoiled. *What?*

"He's a bit of a brawler when he feels maligned—or when someone maligns you, in this case." Lyrica chuckled. "He didn't want to hazard seeing you after the fight."

"Is he hurt?"

"The offending party got the worst of it, though Leith does have a few bruises. Not enough to keep him from business as usual today, though it may have cost him his standing as city councillor."

City councillor? How much she still had to learn about this man whose name she shared, if nothing else. "And pray tell, what was the offending remark?"

"A fellow tobacco lord, Cochrane"—Lyrica looked pained—"called you a saucy minx on account of your canceling the assembly. He felt slighted, it seems, to have been second to the city's poor."

"Humble of him," Juliet murmured, taking another sip of the now lukewarm chocolate. Leith had warned her about Cochrane aboard ship, had he not? "I've never been called a saucy minx before, at least to my knowledge."

"You shan't ever again, I assure you." Lyrica smiled knowingly. "Perhaps you should think of it as a token of Leith's affection."

"His defense of me?"

Lyrica nodded. "He is more than fond of you. He even told me you prefer hot chocolate to tea." She lifted the pot to refill their cups. "Remember, it is thought déclassé to show much outward affection toward one's spouse, at least here. Though I must say your graciousness is a perfect foil to his gruffness."

"You understand him well."

"As well as Leith can be understood." Lyrica gave an enigmatic little smile. "Don't let his reserve fool you. Behind it lies a vitally beating heart. Flashes of it come out at uncertain times—like the fight with Cochrane."

"I wish he'd come home to Virginia Street instead. I want no secrets between us. It pains me to know so little about him, including his past life and upbringing."

"When the lads were small they rarely saw their father, he was so immersed in the firm. Their mother, Sybella, was often unwell. Neither of them cared for children, and so nursemaids and housekeepers managed them. On the rare occasions they were together, it proved frightening and formal, even loveless."

Even hearing it secondhand made Juliet ache. A stark contrast to her happy childhood. "And when they came of age?"

"Leith and Euan were educated at university here while Niall trained at a London firm after doing a Grand Tour of the continent. Leith spent considerable time in the Indies and America prior to becoming principal in the firm. At one point, their father had a penchant for gambling and nearly lost a considerable part of their fortune. If not for Leith, they'd not have the standing they do today."

"Their parents have been buried some years now?"

"They both died of smallpox in the last epidemic and are buried in Ramshorn cemetery. All of the brothers survived it, but only Euan bears scars." Lyrica set her empty cup on the table. "And you? What is your upbringing?"

"As an American rebel?" Juliet replied, leading to Lyrica's obvious amusement. "I'm Virginia born and bred, though schooled with Loveday in London for a time. When my mother couldn't bear being apart from us any longer, we returned to Virginia when I was fourteen and my sister twelve. We resided up the James River on a plantation called Royal Vale, inherited from my great-great-grandparents. My mother died in a carriage accident a few years ago. My father continues well and has recently remarried and is on his way here."

"To Glasgow? How delightful! We must welcome him, then. Show him a wee bit of Scots hospitality."

Juliet smiled, wishing she could ask about the maid Édith. Though all seemed peaceful and still, there seemed an echo of warning in the refined, papered parlor.

49

When my mother died I was very young,
And my father sold me while yet my tongue,
Could scarcely cry "'weep! 'weep! 'weep! 'weep!"
So your chimneys I sweep and in soot I sleep.

William Blake

*L*eith climbed the mansion's stairs and stopped at the second-floor landing, hearing voices down the corridor.

"He's a climbing boy, ma'am," Mrs. Baillie was saying in her no-nonsense way. She stood with her back to him in the doorway of the guest bedchamber being readied for Juliet's father and stepmother.

"But he's scarcely bigger than Bella and Cole," Juliet replied in a sort of anguish as he heard a scuttling that signified the lad had disappeared up the chimney.

"Only the wee ones can get up and down in such tight places, Mrs. Buchanan. Ofttimes their impoverished parents sell them into the trade or they're workhouse orphans, lads and lassies both. The master sweeps keep them plenty busy in the city."

"And they start them so young?"

"Four years old ofttimes," Mrs. Baillie confessed. "Ye've nae coal fires in yer country?"

"Just an abundance of wood, at least in Virginia."

"Nae chimney sweeps either, I take it."

Silence.

Though he couldn't see Juliet from where he stood in the corridor, Leith could imagine her looking up the chimney, ready to get soot-faced for a child she'd never seen and had little control over. And his own chest ached.

He moved toward the bedchamber door and motioned for Mrs. Baillie to go elsewhere. Standing where the housekeeper had stood, he saw Juliet doing just as he'd suspected, on her knees before the cold hearth, which had been covered by a sheet from mantel to marble tile to protect the chamber.

In a trice, a cascade of coal came whooshing down the chimney, followed by the thud of an iron ball as it pushed the brush down. The sheet ballooned but held, catching the storm of soot. A fascinated if dismayed Juliet waited, her back to Leith and still unaware of him. In time the small sweep emerged, his beleaguered blue eyes huge in his coal-blackened face, the tools of his trade in hand.

"Enough climbing for now, Arthur," Juliet said in that soft, deferential way she had. "Are you well? What is that growling I hear?"

The lad darted a look at Leith, then returned his gaze to her. "My belly's empty, ma'am."

"Then please put aside your brushes and tools." Taking him by the hand, she turned and drew up short when she saw Leith standing in the doorway. Flushing scarlet, she seemed almost alarmed. Had he that effect on her? Or was it just the shock of seeing him home in broad daylight?

"There's plenty to be had in the larder," he said as if to reassure her. His eyes fell to her soot-smeared hand as it clasped the lad's grimy fingers.

Some strong, unidentifiable emotion reared up in him again. He looked at the sweep anew, seeing him through Juliet's eyes and realizing the soul of the matter. Swallowing, he stepped back and let them pass, breathing in coal dust and rosewater in their wake.

Juliet didn't take the servants' stair but led Arthur down the central staircase, unmindful of his black footprints and Mrs. Baillie's potential displeasure. Still startled by Leith's appearing, she kept on toward the kitchen, sure her husband would slip out again as stealthily as he'd come in. Seeing him during daylight hours turned her more than a wee bit tapsalteerie.

"Madame Buchanan." The French cook gave a little bow when she appeared.

"What do you have ready to eat, monsieur?" she asked. Her gaze roamed the cavernous kitchen, which was nothing like Royal Vale's save the pots and pans and hearth.

"Ah, a small feast for a small boy? Chicken pie, a delicate white soup, wheaten bread, Stilton cheese, potatoes, potted pigs' cheeks, even a steamed pudding with custard."

"Everything but the potted pigs' cheeks," she said, afraid too much rich fare might turn his stomach. "And please pack him some things to take away, including nuts and several oranges."

She asked a kitchen maid to bring water and a towel for washing, then pulled out a chair for Arthur. The lad sat, surveying the leaping fire and mutton turning on a spit, its fat sizzling, with a kind of famished bewilderment.

"Can I take a bite o' bread for Sadie?" he asked, a hopeful cast to his lean face.

"Sadie? Such a pretty name." Juliet took a chair next to him. "Is she your sister? She shall have more than bread."

He nodded, plunging his hands into the water to wash. An uncut pineapple sat upon the table, and at his curiosity, Juliet asked another maid for a knife. The fragrance as she cut into it reminded her of home. Father had ordered pine-apples from the Caribbean, but for some reason she'd not thought to see one here.

The maid whisked the washbasin and blackened towel away, then returned with a cup of cider, her face showing shock as she looked toward the kitchen door. Leith stood there, stoic, arms crossed.

Juliet excused herself to let Arthur eat in privacy. "Are you needing anything, Mr. Buchanan?"

He gave a half smile. "My wife."

With a little sigh, she followed him away from the servants' wing to his study. He shut the door, pulled a handkerchief out of his pocket, and took one of her hands. With a few gentle motions he began removing the soot from her skin—or tried to. His face was so earnest, so intent, the years fell away and she saw the boy he might have been in a strangely loveless household, trying to do his best.

For now, she wanted to smooth away the faint purple bruise riding his left cheekbone and the split lower lip that nearly made her wince. Had Cochrane done that? All on account of Leith's defense of her?

"Have you come to chastise me?" she whispered.

"Nae more than you do me my late hours and incessant trading and eccentric clock collection."

"I'm ruining your handkerchief," she lamented. The monogrammed *B* was hidden now in a swirl of black against white linen that would never come clean.

"Soiled handkerchiefs are of little consequence when a

starving lad is in my kitchen." He turned her hand over, his callused fingers gentle, and wiped the soot from her palm.

"Then we are of one mind."

He let go of her hand. "Which reminds me . . ." He reached into his weskit and withdrew a small velvet box. "The bauble I promised you aboard ship."

Bauble? She'd nearly forgotten the signet ring she'd returned. She took the box and opened it, stifling a gasp at the contents. When she hesitated to remove the jewelry, he did so for her.

"For my American bride," he said, his voice more gruff than usual.

He slid the gift onto her finger, as snug as the other aboard ship had been loose. A gold signet ring, the intaglio a rich, deep blue and carved with an indigo blossom. The pairing of blue and gold was especially beautiful, but all that paled beside the thought behind it.

This was a glimpse of the vitally beating heart Lyrica had mentioned. *"Flashes of it come out at uncertain times."* Without a doubt, this was Leith Buchanan at his best.

"I don't know what to say." She looked up at him, her eyes damp. "Thank you, Leith."

She said his forename so rarely that even he looked startled.

"If you're wondering why I'm home so early, my barber is due. 'Tis nearly the Sabbath and I canna go to kirk bewhiskered . . . even if you prefer it." His gaze canted to the window as if searching for the tradesman in question. "And while I'm waiting, there's another matter that needs discussing."

"Oh?" Was it time to return to Ardraigh Hall with the twins?

He sat down on the edge of his desk while she took a chair facing him. "My brother is besotted with your sister."

She almost laughed at the absurdity of his words. "I knew that from the moment they met."

"Aye, but things are not progressing as well as Niall had hoped."

"And you want me to help move any fine feeling along."

"In truth, I ken little about romantic matters, including my own." His stoicism faded to perplexity as he passed a hand over his bewhiskered jaw. "So I ask your help, aye."

"Then you shall have it."

"Is she holding out for a title? I heard Lord Talisker's heir has been by."

"Loveday cares nothing for titles," she said quickly. "But my sister does have a mind of her own."

"A family trait." He winked—or did she only imagine it? "Niall doesna want to press her if she's not so inclined, but at the same time he doesna want to lose his place in line, quite literally."

"She's been besieged by suitors, truly, and he's been very patient. I will do what I can, though these matters are some-what . . . delicate."

"Delicate is the word, aye. I hardly ken where to begin."

Was he implying more than Loveday and Niall? There seemed a sudden ruddy cast to his tanned features, or perhaps it was just a play of the light through the tall windows. Heat tingled about her neck and reached her ears and left her wishing for a hand fan.

"Lastly . . ." He looked at her as if keeping secrets. "Your father and stepmother are here, along with the domestic servants from Royal Vale."

"What?" She stood, elated. "When?"

"Their ship has docked at Greenock, and once their baggage is dealt with they should arrive here shortly."

She stared at him, coming to terms with the magnitude

of what he'd done. He, as the new owner of Royal Vale, had arranged for the servants to come to Britain. "You're aware that as soon as any enslaved man—or woman—sets foot on English soil, they are free."

"Aye." He met her damp eyes, and the steel in his softened. "I ken."

50

A flower cannot blossom without sunshine nor a garden without love.

Chinese proverb

I hope you don't think me a meddling sister," Juliet began as she and Loveday dressed for church the next Sabbath. "But I do hope you give special consideration to Niall Buchanan."

Loveday paused before the looking glass to adjust her garnet necklace. "And why would I?"

Juliet warmed to the teasing in her tone. "Because we would not only be sisters but sisters-in-law?"

Laughing, Loveday turned to face her. "What does he have to recommend him in your eyes?"

"'Tis not my eyes but yours that matter."

"Very well." Loveday sat down on the dressing table stool and trellised her fingers in her lap. "On the face of it, he is remarkably handsome. Braw, rather. He seems kind. Kinder than his brothers—or at least less hardened by business. He's promised to give up pugilism."

"Has he?" Juliet said as Minette brought her cape. "Go on."

"We have more than a few things in common. A love of gardens, art, travel . . . children."

"He is indeed a devoted uncle. Bella and Cole adore him."

"I was doubly smitten when I saw him playing with them."

"Does anyone else compare?"

"No one." Loveday's smile faded. "But am I being too forward or foolish to give my heart away so quickly?"

"One can lose one's heart at first meeting—even against one's will." Juliet was thinking more of herself and Leith, a mystery that still confounded her. "You have no reservations, do you?"

"Nary a one, but . . ."

"Who can define such a mysterious feeling? There is often an undeniable attraction, an inexplicable infatuation, which strikes like a lightning bolt out of the blue."

"I won't deny it."

"I also know that hope deferred maketh the heart sick. But when the desire cometh, it is a tree of life."

"You sound much like Mama."

"If Mama was here, she might tell you the same. Sometimes 'tis best not to mull matters too much. Just pray about them and see where the Lord leads."

"In your case, to York Town and a lighter." Loveday's wistfulness turned to relief. "And if you hadn't done that, where would we now be?"

"We'd be at Royal Vale, facing charges brought by Riggs, still yoked to a system I abhor, including insurmountable debt."

"You rescued us both."

"Not me, Loveday. The Lord made a way forward despite

my foibles and missteps. Yet despite being grateful, there's much here that needs help and nettles me—" Juliet left off as Minette reappeared with Loveday's cape.

From somewhere in the heart of Glasgow, church bells began pealing, reminding them it was the Sabbath. With a last look at each other, they linked arms and went below to the waiting coach.

Sitting side by side with Leith for the first time in St. Andrews-by-the-Green gave rise to all sorts of new feelings. Around them in the Buchanan pew were her family and his, a magnet for curious onlookers. Juliet kept her eyes down, moved by the music and a bit awed at hearing a pipe organ for the first time.

"'Tis known as the kist o' whistles, or the whistling kirk," Leith told her at its first soaring notes. "Some say the devil himself helped build it."

Being here amid all the mahogany and crimson velvet and a towering pulpit adorned with a canopy and miter made her feel very small, the memory of their parish church smaller still. But the order of the Episcopalian service was similar to that of their Virginia parish, including the *Book of Common Prayer*, if the music was not.

The minister greeted them cordially after the service despite Euan commenting wryly that their seat rents were in arrears. Moving toward the green that bordered the kirk, where their carriages waited, Juliet spied Niall and Loveday bringing up the rear. He'd touchingly brought her a gift that had charmed her completely—Robert Sayer's *The Florist*, a book of engraved flower illustrations from London. And even a set of paints to color them by.

"I must say, I'm relieved to be back in Britain," Father

was saying, walking somewhat slowly with a cane. "I despaired of setting sail, given the colonial threats of closing ports."

Zipporah laid a gloved hand on his arm. "I believe it was worry more than gout that upended you. Bath should see you completely restored."

Ah, Bath. Juliet felt a keen ache to go there. Though her headaches had lessened since coming to Scotland, she felt Bath would do her good too. But for now, Leith seemed intent on returning her and the twins to Ardraigh Hall. Royal Vale's servants were already there.

She wrestled with disappointment at being separated from Leith, momentarily distracted by the sight of Loveday getting into another coach with Euan and Lyrica and Niall.

"I see that we've arrived in time to witness your sister's courtship commence," Father said with a smile.

"Indeed!" Zipporah settled back on the upholstered seat beside him with a satisfied smile. "How fortunate we've arrived in spring with everything beginning to bloom."

"You should see the garden in back of the Virginia Street house," Juliet said. She'd taken the twins there nearly every day, rain or shine. They were particularly fond of the little stone-rimmed pond with its ducklings. "'Tis quite charming."

"Wait till you see Ardraigh Hall's," Leith told her, shutting the door. "The wilderness there is remote, but the park should suit you and the children."

"Wilderness?"

"The acreage between the formal gardens and the deer park. I'll show you myself."

"So, you're coming with us?" she asked, nearly holding her breath till he answered.

"Aye," he said.

300

Their return to Ardraigh Hall was exactly in reverse—Nurse riding with the baggage in a lead coach while Juliet and Leith accompanied the children in the rear. This time, however, Cole sat upon his father's lap while Bella sat on hers, safe from the coach's swaying and dipping. Juliet felt a bit anxious as the spring wind whipped the conveyance, threatening to topple them. Closing her eyes, she sent a prayer heavenward for safety, then gave thanks it was only a few miles more.

"Are you well?" Leith asked, concern tightening his features.

"I am now." She smiled at him and braced herself as another gust of wind shoved them. The brazier at her feet had never been more welcome. Would she ever adjust to Scotland's weather? At his continued regard of her, she added, "I was just remembering my mother, who died on a windy winter's day."

He held her eyes for a second longer, and she wondered his thoughts. Would small revelations like these build some sort of bridge between them? Soon Father would leave. Loveday also. Juliet despaired of being alone with this man unless she knew him better.

When Bella held out her arms to her father, he raised his brow, but he took her from Juliet and passed her Cole, who held tight to his hobby horse. Bella locked her arms about Leith, standing in his lap and kissing him with enough vigor to dislodge his cocked hat.

"Who's been teaching them such tricks?" he half growled at Juliet.

"By tricks, if you mean a show of affection, then I am guilty," she said, retrieving the hat.

"I even caught them kissing the cat."

"Have you never kissed a cat?" She caught the barest glimmer of a smile in his eyes as she said, "Then your education is quite lacking."

"Kitty?" Bella asked, looking about.

"Kitty is coming with Aunt Loveday in a special carrier," Juliet told her. "Hobbes would be meowing quite loudly by now if he were here."

"Da?" Bella said, bringing his hand to the leather shutter to raise it so she could see out.

He obliged, looking at the windswept landscape pulsating with new life. Juliet did the same, her eyes drawn to the twin towers that were let to the Romany. Smoke spiraled upward, hazing the green fields about them.

She thought of Havilah. Did he?

Rather, did he think of her often?

"I'm excited for Father to join us," she said. Loveday had decided to stay in the city on account of Niall. Perhaps Juliet's talk with her about him had done some good. "Will your brothers and Lyrica be joining us at Ardraigh Hall?"

He cleared his throat. "All three estates border each other, so we often go back and forth."

"Are we there yet?" Bella chirped as she began kicking her legs against the seat in a flurry of quilted petticoats. Cole began squirming beside Juliet, clearly done with riding, so she dug in her pocket for some marzipan fruit Cook had made.

Raising his cane to tap on the ceiling, Leith instructed the coachman to use the west entrance. "You'll get a better view of the park and gardens that way," he said to Juliet.

"Go over the bridge?" Cole asked, chewing on the marzipan.

"Not today," Leith answered as they left the main road for the back of Buchanan land.

Raising the window shade higher, Juliet took in the rolling landscape as her mind stretched beyond the James River to make room for her new view. An Eden-like park soon to be awash with bluebells bordered the house on two sides. Black swans floated on a vast lake that rippled in the wind. From the back, the house looked more castle on the rise, and she felt she'd stepped into a fairy tale.

"Home, Da?" Bella asked, looking back at Leith as he held her up to the window.

"Aye, home," he answered. "And glad of it."

Ardraigh Hall seemed more home to Juliet too with Royal Vale's servants about her. She embraced them, realizing Hosea had grown taller and Rilla more lean while the others seemed unchanged—all but Sage, their former coachman, whose remaining hair was now snow white. All were anxious to share their experiences aboard ship.

"When Colonel Catesby told us Royal Vale was now Mr. Buchanan's, he gave us the choice of staying in Virginia, where we might see war, or braving a land we've never seen." Sage took a breath as if worn out by the words, given he was a taciturn man. "We held a meeting, even talked with Reverend Moses, and decided to come together by ship."

"I never did see such a sight as all that water," Rilla said with a shake of her head. "I was sick afore I set foot on the boat and all the days in between till I landed. I aim to die right here, as I'm never going to cross back over to Virginia again."

"I watched those jacks on board and wanted to join them." Hosea looked proud. "Captain Walker let me take the great wheel a time or two and even explained celestial navigation."

Lilith and Marion showed her the lacework they'd done

while Vestal remarked about the dolphins and sighting a whale. They were anxious to know their places in the household, and Juliet sensed their concern about how the other domestics would accept them.

"You understand that by your coming here, the laws of America, especially colonial Virginia, no longer apply." She marveled that when one simply changed shores, their standing and future changed with it. "British law states that as soon as you set foot on English ground, you became free. Free to leave here and seek employment elsewhere if you choose— something I support you in wholeheartedly—though if you desire to remain in our employ, I'll do all that I can to see that you're well rewarded."

They fell into a thoughtful silence. Such a realization would take time, though she wondered, having been born into slavery like they'd been, if they'd ever feel truly free.

"Miss Jul—Mrs. Buchanan, since you're the new mistress, will you be managing the household here like at Royal Vale?" Vestal asked.

"I shall, so please come to me with any questions or concerns like before. Father will be arriving shortly, and I know Loveday will be overjoyed to see you again."

51

What of soul was left, I wonder, when the
kissing had to stop?

Robert Browning

he sublime lime announces spring," Father said as
he and Juliet strolled along Ardraigh Hall's lime-
tree avenue the next day. "Imagine the scent of the
summer blossoms."

As the wind tugged at her hat, Juliet looked up at the rustling branches in their first flush of leaves. Light shot through
them in a play of sunshine and shadow, spackling the figures
ahead. Leith and Euan flanked Lyrica, while Loveday and
Niall were in the front, their talk and laughter floating back
like dandelion down in the wind. At the end of the avenue
was an iron gate leading down to the Palladian bridge, an
arched masterpiece as it spanned the burn beneath. Cole had
an enduring fascination for the bridge.

Nurse had put the twins down for a nap after Juliet promised to take them for their daily airing when they woke up.
With hundreds of acres to explore, there was no end of ad-
ventures at Ardraigh Hall. Her soul sang with the possibilities, at least those involving Bella and Cole.

"So, Daughter," Father said. "I see that lovely ring on your finger. Are you to be a content mistress here? 'Tis a far grander place than Royal Vale."

"I'm home wherever the children are."

"And your husband?" he asked, hands knotted behind his back and head bent in thought. "I had hoped . . ."

Heat filled her face. "Hope for Loveday, then."

He looked aggrieved, even pained. Was he regretting the whole debacle with the miniatures? Her marriage canceling his debt?

Her own hopes, so high on the coach ride here, had quickly dwindled when Leith had all but disappeared since their arrival, busy with estate business, meeting with his foresters and farm managers. Though he had joined them for supper last night and this present walk.

Father slowed his steps. "'Twould be good if you and Loveday were neighbors and your future children could be cousins in the very best sense. London is so far, and I'm sorry I'll be there more than here."

"You're welcome to Scotland anytime, and I'm sure we'll visit you in England too. The Buchanans have a London townhouse, I've been told."

She looked ahead to Leith, who was intent on whatever Lyrica was saying. When he laughed, the sound shook her. She'd never heard him laugh. It was a little grief to realize she'd never seen him so amused, nor had she been the one to amuse him.

"As for myself," Father said, "'tis rather odd to be selling my plantations and starting anew at my advanced age."

"You're hardly ancient, Father. Eight and fifty?"

"Aye, on my next birthday." He coughed, coming to a halt. "I suppose as absentee Leith has told you what's to be done with Royal Vale."

She felt a little start that he had not, and she had just enough pride to refuse to admit it as Father continued on.

"I'm thankful to be done with plantation life. Enslavement and crop failure and ruinous overseers like Riggs are not to be borne."

"What of Riggs, Father?"

"He left an angry letter on my desk before he sailed for Antigua. It was waiting for me when I returned from my honeymoon. Royal Vale's house servants told me what happened between you that last night. 'Twas something your aunt Damarus would have done. And frankly, I wanted to take a whip to Riggs long before, insolent and prideful as he was."

Riggs had sailed? To save himself the shame of being humiliated by a woman, perhaps, the owner's very daughter. He was a proud man and an unforgiving one.

"I'm sorry, Father. In the tumult of our leaving, there was no time to pen you a note. I assumed you would find out from the servants, but it still must have been a shock."

"What's done is done, my dear. We shall all have a fresh start here."

A fresh start. *Please, Lord, let it be a fortuitous one.* "How long shall you stay with us before you move on to London or Bath?"

"I'll let Zipporah answer. She's not yet recovered from the cruise and didn't feel like walking about with us today. But I suspect she'll join us for dinner."

There was something wondrous about living in a newly built house. In hindsight, Royal Vale had been lined with dust no matter the beeswax and vinegar, worn down by more than a century of living. But Ardraigh Hall seemed to be warm

307

wax, waiting for their personal imprint like a seal on pristine paper. What would their mark be?

Coming down the hall in her nightclothes, Juliet reveled in the quiet house. A quarter of an hour earlier she'd gone to the nursery to kiss the twins good night, then tiptoed past her father's closed door long enough to hear him snoring. Poor Zipporah.

She continued her tiptoeing to the very end of the hall, where her and Leith's bedchambers connected through a dressing room and water closet. She'd not seen his side as it had been locked. Hers was open and had been designed in a way that bespoke beauty and peace. A haven of color and calm. She felt a little rush of appreciation as she returned to it, her candle casting light on lemon chinoiserie walls and large sash and fan windows open to the moonlight. A coal fire burned brightly enough to last the night, and she moved toward the hearth, the fireside chair inviting.

She was not the least bit tired, though it had been a full day. After breakfast they'd all paid a visit to Lamb Hill, where Loveday had fallen in love with the stillroom and gardens. They'd dined at Paisley at two o'clock, a sumptuous meal ending with blancmange and fresh hothouse berries. Once they'd returned to Ardraigh Hall, Leith had gone riding with Father, then they'd all gathered for supper. Afterward Leith had disappeared again into his study, which adjoined a library shelving more books than she could count.

Pondering it now, she looked toward an open window. All the night sounds of Glasgow were missing. No cry of the night watch. No ribald laughter of latecomers. No carriages on cobblestones. Just the sigh of wind and the subtle call of a nightbird.

Sitting down, she listened for Leith to come upstairs. Or

was he already abed? Perhaps he'd retired when she was in the nursery.

Guided by her candle, Juliet entered the dressing room leading to Leith's bedchamber. Now his door was ajar as if inviting her in. Surprise overcame reluctance. They were married, were they not? A quick look would quell her curiosity.

One glance at the smooth counterpane told her he was not in the four-poster bed. While her room was more airy and bright, his was heavy and dark blue. If not for the firelight, the darkness would have been profound. She longed to open all four shutters and better see the design of the drapes and the patterned rug beneath her feet.

Setting down the candlestand, she ran a hand over his shaving stand, then, on a whim, hid his razor in a bottom drawer. The looking glass reflected a pale woman with luminous eyes, a loosely tied braid draping over one shoulder of her nightgown.

She opened a shuttered window as quietly as she could. Below was the forecourt with its stone lions and the mile-long driveway that unspooled like silver thread. He'd graciously given her the more colorful garden view.

Hearing a footfall in the corridor, she started toward the dressing room just as the door to the hall clicked open. Caught!

Leith stood there, his gaze canted toward her candle. He himself was backlit by a wall sconce in the corridor. Surprise washed his features. She summoned a breathless apology as he shut the door, and the ensuing draft snuffed her candle.

"Are you waiting up for me, Juliet?"

How rarely he used her given name. "In Glasgow it became my habit to not sleep till I heard you come in."

He draped his frock coat over a nearby chair. There was a

hint of tobacco about him . . . and brandy. The peach brandy
Father had brought from Virginia?

"So, what do you think of my bedchamber?"

"I confess I like mine better."

"Too dark for your taste, I'd wager. A blunder of mahogany and brocade."

She almost smiled at his wording, except he was entirely too
near and her feelings began to get the better of her thoughts.
If he was striking by day, he was doubly so by night. The
shadows erased his hard lines and daunting stoniness, and he
seemed altogether more approachable out of his black coat.

"You're welcome here as my wife." He reached out and
took hold of her left hand where her signet ring rested. It
returned her to the moment on the *Glasgow Lass* when
they'd made their vows, binding them irrevocably. "I confess to coming into your bedchamber once when you were
asleep in Glasgow."

"Why would you?" she whispered.

"Mayhap the same reason you stand here tonight."

He let go of her hand, his fingers grazing her braided hair.
At his touch, the ribbon that bound it slipped free and fell
between them. Rather than retrieve it, he lay a cool hand
against her cheek so gently it seemed to hold a question.
She simply looked back at him, rimmed in firelight, as his
fingers moved to her braid and unraveled it.

She stepped nearer, the satin of his waistcoat smooth beneath her palms as he entwined his hands in her loosened hair.
She'd never been kissed, but now she was being kissed so thoroughly and completely she tingled. Lost in the rich newness
of him, his rare openness and obvious need of her, she kissed
him back. Together they plunged headlong into a wellspring of
pleasure made up of murmurs and caresses that had no end—

Until his hands fell away. When he took an abrupt step

back, she looked at him, stomach plummeting. Through the haze of her tears he seemed equally stricken as he stared at her. Their honest, tender moment ended.

Forgetting her ribbon, she turned and all but fled to the loneliness of her room. Had he mistaken her tears for unwillingness? Revulsion?

There was no sleep to be had that night.

At dawn, Leith rode into Glasgow on the fastest mount in Ardraigh Hall's stables as if he could outrun last night's memory. A dozen excuses flailed his conscience. He'd had too much Virginia brandy, and then as he was faced with a Virginia beauty, his ironclad defenses had scattered like billiard balls. The tears in Juliet's eyes had told him his attentions pained her, and she'd fled like he was doing this morning after a long, tormented night. Absenting himself, he'd give her room to collect herself and reestablish the hedge between them.

God, forgive me.

The plea was nearly as jarring. He had no recent memory of asking forgiveness, yet he owed her and the Almighty that. For some uncanny reason she made him want to be better than he was. Different than he'd been. But the truth remained. She'd never wanted this marriage, and he had no right to expect more than a contract as he'd once stated. The best, most sincere apology he could give her was to remove himself from her presence.

52

He whom love touches not walks in darkness.

Plato

*S*ister, you seem unusually preoccupied this morning.
I hope you're not worried about Minette's malady."
Loveday's query nearly made Juliet miss a stitch as
she worked her embroidery. "The leading Glasgow physic
is attending her, remember."

Juliet was worried that Minette's ailment seemed to have
worsened. Her sister, Édith, was never far from her thoughts
of late. Though Minette had said no more about her, the
puzzle of her disappearance haunted.

But far more than this beat about her beleaguered brain.
She could hardly share her concerns about last night and
Leith. The very memory made her lightheaded if not light-
hearted.

When she hesitated, Loveday pressed, "You're not skittish
about the Paisley ball, are you?"

Juliet looked up from her tambour frame to the window
she sat beside. On a clear day she could see Paisley's chim-

neys across a vast expanse of parkland. "I've not much time left to worry about it, you mean."

"Time enough for the mantua-maker to finish our gowns. A spring engagement is lovely to look forward to." Loveday turned coquettish. "As is a spring proposal."

For a moment Juliet forgot her misery. "Has Niall asked you?"

"I expect he might declare himself after the ball."

"And judging from your rapturous expression, I don't have to wonder at your answer." Juliet's eyes narrowed. "This doesn't have to do with a certain stillroom and garden, does it?"

"Such doesn't hurt, but in truth he's always been first in my affections. I just wanted to be sure it was best for us both." Loveday leaned over and lifted a meowing Hobbes onto her lap. "There's only one thing the matter. He's not fond of cats. They make him sneeze."

"Poor fellow," Juliet replied. *If only my situation were as simple.*

"I'd like to wed before Father leaves for England." Loveday ran a hand over the cat's silky back. "Speaking of gardens, let's go out and walk in yours. 'Tis much too pretty to stay indoors."

A quarter of an hour later, they did just that. Bella and Cole were gamboling down gravel paths ahead of them while a small army of gardeners sheared and rolled and cultivated the lawn and flora all around them.

"Look." Loveday gestured to a bench where Father and Zipporah sat watching the swans upon the lake. "Lovebirds abound."

With a small smile, Juliet returned her attention to Bella, who stood beneath a flowering cherry tree, reaching for a blossom on her tiptoes, while Cole made a clumsy effort to climb its trunk.

"Nay, Master Cole." Loveday removed him from the danger as Juliet plucked some blossoms for Bella and tucked one into her dark hair.

They walked toward the central fountain, then paused when a footman appeared, announcing Loveday had a caller. Soon Niall arrived as her escort, leaving Juliet and the children alone. Might Loveday receive a proposal before the ball and not after?

Juliet looked toward the wilderness and deer park. Where exactly had Havilah been laid to rest? The twins were too young yet to visit with any understanding. But when they were older, she hoped to take them there and bring flowers, honoring their mother's resting place.

Hand in hand with the twins, Juliet walked toward the summerhouse, lush foliage and blooms pressed against the glass. This was the very place the Royal Vale gardener had told her about months before. Never had she imagined she'd stand here and literally see it for herself.

"'Tis summer inside," she told the wide-eyed twins as they entered the glassed-in space perfumed with oleander and camellias and exotic blooms she had no name for. Cole found the pineapples fruiting in large clay pots, returning Juliet's thoughts to Arthur, the chimney sweep. Such a tragic chasm between him and her stepchildren.

"Mrs. Buchanan." The summerhouse gardener gave a courtly little bow. "'Twould seem your hands are a wee bit full at present." He chuckled good-naturedly as Cole began playing with a daisy grubber, while Bella only had eyes for stone lambs beneath an orange tree.

"Let's go see the live lambs," Juliet said with a smile, steering the twins outside again. "And leave Mr. McFee to his fine work."

"Take care not to fall into the ha-ha trenches," he cautioned. "They're mostly hidden."

314

Father and Zipporah were still overlooking the lake, while Loveday and Niall were playing croquet on a far lawn. Glad as she was for Loveday, the thought of her marrying and leaving, even to move across the park, left Juliet at sixes and sevens.

Lord, why must all these leave-takings happen at once?

The hammering at her temples began again, and she thought longingly of Royal Vale's stillroom remedies. She'd not yet ventured to the stillroom here, as it was overseen by the head housekeeper. Like the servants from Royal Vale, she had yet to find her place.

Bella yawned and held up her arms. "Mam."

The tender word turned Juliet's heart over. 'Twas a marvel she'd become Mam to them both at first meeting. Picking Bella up, Juliet kissed her cheek, then smiled down at Cole as he kissed her hand with childish fervency. She led them the rest of the way to where the sheep grazed beyond a ha-ha. Watching the wobbly-legged creatures leap and run made them all laugh.

The joyful moment banished the worry of before, and with a full heart she said to the twins, "You are my beloved lambs."

How good and necessary it was to belong to someone.

Leith finished his perusal of all business done in his absence, a study that required long hours and more than a few headaches. He kept returning to the name Sinclair, the newest limited partner in the Buchanan firm. Who was Sinclair? Someone had signed him on but had left no paperwork or contractual documents. Odd.

Leith summoned his foremost clerk, Leo Tate, and waited until he appeared and shut the door.

"What do you ken of Malcolm Sinclair?" Leith asked.

Tate took a seat, his wary expression perplexed. "Never heard of him, sir."

"Nor have I. But he's now a limited partner with considerable shares." Leith handed him a ledger. "Go to the bank and ask the attending clerk what transpired the day Sinclair became a partner in my absence. We're missing needed paperwork."

"An apprentice clerk—Thompson—also recently reported missing papers that I've not been able to track down. Ledgers involving recent transactions about mining rights in Berwick and beyond."

"Then find out all you can about that matter too."

"Of course, sir. Anything else?"

"Nae, for the moment." Leith cleared his throat. "Actually, now seems a good time to tell you that I've decided to conduct most of my business from Virginia Street in future."

"From home, sir?" Understanding dawned in Tate's eyes. "Many merchants do, aye."

Tate left his office, and Leith looked at the clock as it struck seven. Supper was at hand. If he left now he could return to Virginia Street for the meal, but without Juliet and the children the past sennight, the mansion seemed especially hollow. Yet his offices, in his current agitation, seemed unbearable too. Restless, he reached for his coat against the smirr of rain darkening the streets. And his mood.

As he left the countinghouse and began to walk down Ingram Street, that uneasy feeling overtook him again. Unlike a shadow on a sunny day, this felt cold. Dark. Darker than before. Fisting his cane, he wanted to beat away that unwelcome presence like he would a pickpocket or ne'er-do-well.

He walked faster, his cocked hat lowered against the damp, the sheen of his scarlet cape aglow in the lamplight. The doors of Ramshorn kirk stood open for evening service.

Rarely did he give the place a glance, though his parents were buried in the large graveyard.

As he sought a back pew, some congregants turned to look at him. Few knew him here, though they knew who he was. Wasn't that the mark of his entire life? To be unknown. To keep himself apart. To let his head rule, not his heart.

Here, in the kirk's light, the shadows seemed to recede. He'd come in late, mid-service, he guessed. He wasn't particularly interested in the sermon. He just needed a refuge from the rain that didn't hold the absence of Juliet. Yet the very thought of her cut him, and with that laceration rushed in fresh despair. It seemed an ocean lay between them, the way together too deep. Had his losing his wits with her in his midnight bedchamber done irreparable harm?

"A new heart also will I give you, and a new spirit will I put within you: and I will take away the stony heart out of your flesh, and I will give you an heart of flesh."

Weighted, Leith wasn't listening, yet somehow the preacher reached him. It seemed he sat alone in the kirk and the words resounded to no other. He stared down at his clenched hands and imagined other roughened, invisible places. His very soul seemed callused. Encased in granite.

He had become his father all over again. Frozen with arrogance. Caustic of tongue. An intimidating presence.

His base nature blinded Leith to the good around him. To those nearest him. The deeper into the shadows he descended, the more life's beauty was blunted. He seemed to see no color. All was hues of gray, darkened by his own smallness and selfishness. And yet into his darkness had come a glimmer of light. Someone warm. Gracious. A welcoming presence.

He felt for the miniature in his pocket, never far away. Beside it curled a blue satin ribbon.

How did one exchange a heart of stone for one of flesh?

53

The greatest happiness of life is the conviction that we are loved; loved for ourselves, or rather, loved in spite of ourselves.

Victor Hugo

As the Buchanan coach rattled over the road to Paisley, Juliet could see lights from the glittering house shining from a distance. Across from her sat Leith, newly arrived from Glasgow. They'd barely had time to give a greeting, though she'd heard him rumbling around their shared dressing room upon his arrival. When he emerged, she'd felt her heart give a little leap. *Resplendent.* That was the only word for how tailored he appeared tonight, his jaw smooth. Had he found the razor she'd hidden in his washstand?

His navy suit paired perfectly with her pale blue silk, as if they'd conspired. But he'd barely glanced at her tonight, only murmured something complimentary about her gown as he accompanied her downstairs then helped her into the waiting coach. Settling her skirts around her so as not to crowd his legs opposite, she felt at a complete loss for words, though her feelings seemed to fill the conveyance to bursting.

She'd not seen him in a sennight. Long enough to let the romantic memory they'd made in his bedchamber fade. Was that his hope? To remove them from the embarrassing blunder? For her, the delay had given her time to ponder and conclude she'd rather risk her heart than hide it. She must explain to him her tears, her fleeing, rather than endure another clumsy separation and uneasy reunion.

Was now the time? The beat of her heart seemed as loud as the coach wheels bumping along the rutted road.

Into the stilted silence they spoke at once.

"Forgive me, Jul—"

"Pardon me, Lei—"

Awkwardness ensued as they left off. A feverish heat engulfed Juliet, tying her tongue and sending her digging for her feather fan.

"We obviously need to continue this conversation in future," Leith said as the coach slowed and joined the line delivering guests to the front door. "For now, please accept my apology for my conduct the other night."

There was a note of regret in his voice she'd not heard before. Instead of his usual cool courtesy, there was just . . . courtesy. A contrite courtesy. Mystified, she mulled it.

"No apology needed." Her voice came soft but insistent. "'Twas I who trespassed—"

The coach door opened, halting her words, and she was handed out, her husband following.

As footmen announced them at Paisley's front door and then at the opening of the drawing room, Leith was hard-pressed to keep from staring at Juliet as she made her entrance.

Every eye in the suddenly hushed room was upon her. She was Mrs. Leith Buchanan and she wore it well, though what she deserved was a tiara and a title.

He led her forward, her gloved hand resting on his forearm. Lyrica greeted them, Euan not far behind. Since the guests were mostly neighbors and kin, this gathering lacked the heavy presence of the city's assembly room. Loveday followed with Colonel Catesby and Zipporah, adding a pleasing Virginia air to the Glaswegian gathering.

"Your gown is exquisite," Lyrica said, voicing Leith's thoughts and kissing Juliet on both cheeks, "as are your pearls."

"They were my mother's." Juliet smiled, touching the necklace with a gloved hand.

Was she nervous? Or still thinking, as he was, of their honest exchange in the coach?

Leith took stock of who was in attendance, watching Niall extricate himself from his present company in favor of Loveday. A wedding was in the offing. Lamb Hill needed a mistress too. Having Juliet's sister near would be as beneficial as having his brothers near him. Family was always a bulwark for a more secure future.

When the country dances began, Leith partnered with Lyrica while Euan escorted Juliet and Niall accompanied Loveday. Round and round they went until Leith broke protocol by choosing Juliet for a reel, avoiding the men and the usual cliques of political talk along the room's edges. He'd had enough of America's cry for liberty, at least for now.

"You're breaking all the rules," Lyrica teased as the reel ended. "First, you partner with your wife, and second, your affection for her is evident to all."

"All but the lass in question. I've not seen her for some time."

"You've been in Glasgow?"

He nodded, regretful, holding fast to his change of heart. "There's much that needs deciding regarding the colonies and our interests there."

"Have a care . . ." Her gaze pivoted across the room. "We've enough trouble at home. Cochrane is here."

Even the name raised his hackles. "Why did you invite him?"

"Because I didn't want to snub his poor, long-suffering wife."

"Better that than offend mine."

"Come now, Leith. Juliet doesn't even ken who he is. Besides, any lass who took a horsewhip to an overseer can take care of herself."

"He was a brute."

"I dinna doubt it. And now 'tis the clipeing going round town. You ken how Glaswegians adore colonial gossip."

He felt unusually protective of Juliet, aware in that moment that he always had been. "Mayhap I should have schooled my ire with Cochrane. Walked away from our fight at the Saracen's Head."

Lyrica studied him in bewilderment, then flicked her fan open. "Since when do you take blame for any Cochrane-related offense? You've always settled matters with your fists since you were a wee lad."

"It hardly becomes a grown man. A husband and father."

"Speaking of children, how are they?"

How would he ken, absent as he was? Yet he felt a growing need to know. "Ask Juliet."

"Remember what you told me about Ardraigh Hall when the foundation was laid? That you wanted it built big so it could hold half a dozen bairns."

Such plain speaking resurrected thoughts of Havilah and

his high hopes before everything had come crashing down. But it also kindled his desire that he and Juliet might build a different sort of life.

"If you have plenty," Lyrica said a bit more lightheartedly, "then we can continue to borrow yours."

The music ebbed, and she began talking with another guest while he sought Juliet, who was in a high flush after dancing several sets. Catching his eye, she looked toward open double doors as if signaling she wanted to go outside. He fixed his gaze on a footman lighting a globe lamp on the terrace and ushered her out into the cool, damp dark where lanterns flared along walkways, illuminating the first blooms of spring. Together they walked to the farthest edge of the terrace overlooking the formal knot gardens edged in boxwood.

She gave him a tentative smile. "The ballroom is so warm that this is welcome. Thank you."

He swallowed, more tapsalteerie. He'd been absent long enough that it seemed almost as if they were starting over, trying clumsily to accommodate each other. Would they continue the conversation interrupted in the coach?

He raked his mind for a start, then took a safer approach. "How are the twins?"

"They ask after you. They approached one of your horses the other day thinking you were near."

His chest tightened. So they associated him with coming and going. Such had never occurred to him before or troubled him much. Till lately. He'd always thought children should be reared by servants if one had them. Juliet obviously protested the notion.

She continued quietly. "They are doing well, taking an interest in everything outdoors, especially the lambs, now that warm weather has come."

"I've arranged for the Shetland ponies I told you about

to be delivered to the stables next week." Heat crawled up his stock to his ears. He had the uncomfortable sense he was talking to someone in his hire. A governess or domestic servant. Hardly a wife.

"They'll be so delighted, as will I. We've been discussing ponies, and they're eager to try riding."

"I'll be in Edinburgh, but the head groom kens they're coming."

"When do you leave?"

"Daybreak." When she didn't reply, he asked, "Have you had time to choose a mount and go riding?"

"Not yet. I've been occupied with merging households and looking over accounts. I'm still recovering from the fact that your candle count runs into the thousands."

His smile was rueful. "Would you return us to rushlights, Mrs. Buchanan?"

"I'm not complaining, mind you, just recovering. On a lighter note, the children get the best of my time, including taking our meals together, all but breakfast."

"An American custom, mayhap."

"At Royal Vale, yes. But not in Britain, I take it."

Uneasy, he reached back into the vault of memory he kept locked. "I rarely saw my parents. The few memories I have of them are ones I'd rather forget." The admission, never voiced till now, seemed more lesson. "Aside from the day of their burial, I've ne'er returned to their graves."

"I understand," she said softly. "It was hard to return to my mother's."

Was it? He didn't even know when Charlotte Catesby had died. A husband should. The right husband would take pains to offset its melancholy. God help him. He didn't know how to be a husband, how to share a life. All he knew were market prices and tons burden and profit and loss.

323

Emotion thickened his next words. "If matters had been different between us, I would have asked you to take me to your mother's grave."

"A gracious gesture."

Gracious. Few would accuse him of that.

Light flickered across her lovely profile, her expression poignant. "I have regrets of my own in regard to us, including the night I surprised you in your bedchamber."

"When I behaved badly."

Her voice was so low it was nearly lost beneath the music. "I thought you behaved very well indeed."

He leaned in to hear her and caught the teasing lilt in her voice.

"I'd never been kissed before," she said, looking up at him. "And I enjoyed every moment of kissing you back."

"But your response—"

"My reaction was far from a refusal—or distaste. In those moments we seemed to have found a way forward, and then . . ."

"And then I ended the matter because I misread you."

"Which I deeply regret at so tender a time," she said, making him want to kiss her all over again.

He stared into the darkness. Regrets, so many of them, on both sides. But she admitted she enjoyed his kisses? He'd never been so lost for words.

As if sensing his struggle, she turned toward him slightly and placed a hand over his as it gripped the stone terrace railing. "Perhaps—together—we can right any wrongs done."

He swallowed past the thickness in his throat. "How so?"

"By not being strangers. By taking time for each other—for the children, at least."

Could it be? Would she rejoice that he'd made the decision to be more at home? "You want to see more of me?"

"I do. 'Let the wife make the husband glad to come home, and let him make her sorry to see him leave.'"

"Clever, Juliet."

She squeezed his hand. "I didn't say it. Martin Luther did."

"The monk turned preacher who married a nun."

"He had many things to say about marriage. 'There is no more lovely, friendly, and charming relationship, communion, or company than a good marriage.' But I like this best—'The Christian is supposed to love his neighbor, and since his wife is his nearest neighbor, she should be his deepest love.'"

His deepest love. He swallowed hard. "A high standard."

She faced him, as resolute as she was romantic. "Then we shall start small."

We. His gladness in the word was tempered by *small.* His feelings for her weren't small. They were staggering. Did she not suspect it? In that light, might he mean more to her than he realized? Mightn't it spur him past his fears and move him forward?

At midnight they opened the door of the nursery and entered, the only sound the silken swish of Juliet's skirts. Leith held a candle, and they looked into the miniature beds that held the twins. Fast asleep. Both wore linen nightgowns and caps, the sound of their easy, relaxed breathing reassuring. Bending low, she kissed them both. Though Leith didn't follow, at least he'd come.

"I missed saying bedtime prayers with them," she whispered, lifting a blanket over Bella.

He looked down at Cole, whose boyish features reminded him increasingly of Niall. In the hall outside, he heard Juliet's father and stepmother make their way to their bedchamber, followed by Loveday. Paisley's parties were especially agreeable given they ended early.

They left the nursery and traveled the length of the long corridor, past portraits and mirrors and wall sconces and then the main landing with the central stair to their rooms. Leith paused at Juliet's closed door. Behind it he could hear a recovered Minette moving about, waiting to help her undress and ready for bed.

"I suppose this is not only good night but goodbye," she said softly but matter-of-factly. "May Edinburgh treat you well."

"I should return by sennight's end." Even to him the forty-six miles loomed long, and he was already wondering how he could curtail his business there.

"Is it safe traveling that road? Safe from highwaymen and such?"

"With a pistol and fast horse, aye."

"And my prayers," she added with a fleeting smile. She reached for his hand as if about to shake it and seal some sort of business arrangement.

We shall start small.

He brought her gloved fingers to his lips, wanting something more. Wanting even to remove the glove—or take it with him. Though he did have the miniature and her blue ribbon and the now blissful memory of their midnight kiss.

"In the spirit of Luther, you are making me sorry to see you leave." She gave him a last, lingering look before she entered her bedchamber and shut the door.

54

My heart is like a singing bird.

Christina Rossetti

A few days later, Juliet returned to Ardraigh Hall with Loveday after spending several hours at Lamb Hill. Niall had proved a consummate host, and they'd begun talking of the coming wedding. Since the ball, Niall had approached Father with his intentions, and a settlement was underway with the Buchanan lawyers. In lieu of the banns being read, a license would be signed.

"A contract! When will these matters rest on love alone?" Loveday exclaimed as they emerged from the carriage onto the gravel drive. "'Tis silly when your very dowry comes from the Buchanans themselves!"

"Well, these protocols must be observed, however illogical," Juliet said, looking past the carriage and horses to a sunlit meadow behind the stables.

Leith? Home already? Her heart gave a little leap. She pulled her hat lower to block the sun and better see him.

There, on lead reins, were the twins atop two Shetland ponies with flowing manes and tales. Bella's was black and cream and Cole's dun colored. Forgetting herself, Juliet hurried across the forecourt toward the meadow, leaving Loveday to enter the house alone.

Amid an expanse of green, Leith led Bella while a groom led Cole. But in truth, Juliet had eyes only for Leith. Out of his frock coat and weskit, stripped down to his shirt, breeches, and boots, he walked the pony backward and forward across the velvety grass, oblivious to her approach, his attention on his daughter.

"Mam!" Bella shouted with a little laugh, waving a hand.

Leith turned round and nearly brought Juliet to a halt. Caught up in the moment of the spring day—the warm breeze that bent the grass, the joy of his children—he seemed altogether altered. Nay, not altered. Better. His higher self. She wanted to throw her arms about him in gratitude, and only with the utmost effort did she temper her response in front of the stable hand.

She came to a stop along the edge of the meadow. "Such bonny ponies! What are their names?"

Cole looked at his father in question while Bella shouted, "Flora!"

After leaning down to whisper to Cole, Leith stood straight again while the lad yelled, "Charlie!"

Amused at the history lesson therein, Juliet continued watching them till Leith brought them to a stop, promising more on the morrow. They continued on to the stables with the groom, leaving Juliet and Leith following behind.

"When did you arrive home?" she asked, already wondering when he'd leave again.

"Soon after you left for Lamb Hill in the forenoon."

"We just missed each other, then. How was Edinburgh?"

"Auld and reeking," he said with a grin as she fell into step with him. "What happened while I was away?"

"Glad news—there's to be a wedding Wednesday after next at Lamb Hill."

"Och, I'm neither surprised nor disappointed."

Elated, she tried to remember all the details. "You're to stand up with them, as am I. Then after a wedding breakfast, the couple will leave on a wedding trip to Bath in the company of Father and Zipporah."

"A reasonable plan. Needs be we join them at some point."

Her discarded hopes revived. "I've always longed to see Bath."

He looked at her in that intent way he had. "And eat Bath Oliver biscuits and visit the shops on Pulteney Bridge over the River Avon, likely."

She smiled, trying to imagine it. "All of it, yes."

"I suppose we didn't have a proper honeymoon." His brow creased, and he looked down at his boots. "The *Glasgow Lass* hardly suffices."

"I sometimes wonder what I would have done had you sailed away without me."

"Fate is a fickle thing."

"Fate, yes," she said. "But not Providence."

"Meaning the divinely delayed cargo allowed you to overtake me and ask for my hand."

She almost laughed. His teasing was not far afield. "Do you regret it?"

"Nae." He came to a stop behind the stables in a patch of shade where ivy climbed to the gambrel roof. "Do you?"

"Do I?" She stepped nearer him into the shade of the building. "Let this be my answer."

Mindful of her hat, she pulled it free and let it drop into the grass at her feet. Standing on tiptoe, she kissed him, so quickly and lightly it was more a brush of her lips. When he reached for her she eluded him, snatching up her hat.

"Let the wife make the husband glad to come home, Luther said. Or as a wise Scotsman recently told me, 'When you wed hurriedly, you court after.'" She turned away with a last look over her shoulder. "For now, 'tis the four hours, as you Glaswegians call it. Time for tea."

That night, Leith joined them for supper in the smaller of the two dining rooms off Ardraigh Hall's entrance. This one was Juliet's favorite, with its sculpture niches and stucco panels of the four seasons. Niall arrived from Lamb Hill and sat beside Loveday, their hands intertwined beneath the table, while Father and Zipporah sat across from them, leaving Leith and Juliet at opposite ends. The twins, worn out from their time in the saddle, had an early supper followed by a bath and bed, overseen by Nurse.

"So, I'm pleased to hear you'll soon join the Buchanan clan," Leith said to Loveday, raising a glass of Madeira at meal's end.

Juliet lifted her glass, as they all did, toasting the coming nuptials.

"With pleasure," the would-be bride replied, beaming. "To live out my days at Lamb Hill beside my sister and yourself gives me the greatest happiness."

"Praise be that we're all on this side of the Atlantic." Father set his glass down, and a footman refilled it. "Have you seen the latest papers?"

"Full of American news, aye." Niall sat back in his chair. "All the colonies continue to ban the use of British goods, and there's now rumor of a second Continental Congress to come."

"Moreover, there's talk that the soldier and surveyor, George Washington, may be appointed commander in chief if there's to be a war." Father heaved a sigh. "He's a formidable foe if it comes to that."

"I met his lovely wife, Martha, whilst in Williamsburg. A lively, engaging woman," Zipporah added. "But all this war talk seems nonsense. How would these Americans fight us? They have no military, just ragtag militia."

"They're said to be amassing an army and have begun building their own armed ships." Leith took another drink. "My guess is they'll strike British warships near colonial ports. There's even talk that they're soliciting aid from foreign nations. France will likely be paid in tobacco for arms and ammunition."

"Our avowed enemy." Father muttered an oath. "But closer to home, how does it affect you tobacco merchants?"

"Mayhap the ladies best retire to the drawing room while we continue that conversation," Leith said, looking to Juliet.

"Thank you kindly." She stood and gave him an appreciative glance. "I shall always prefer wedding to war talk."

Chuckling, the men resumed their conversation before the women had cleared the chamber. Juliet closed the door to allow both sides privacy.

Zipporah stood by the hearth, drawing her shawl closer about her shoulders. "I'm so glad your father and I will be here to attend your wedding. You'll be a beautiful bride."

"Nine more days," Loveday said with a smile, sitting down on a sofa facing the fireplace. "Loveday Catesby Buchanan sounds almost poetic."

"Indeed it does." Juliet took a cup of hot chocolate from Rilla with a smile. "If only Aunt Damarus were here. You've written her of your plans?"

"Just yesterday I posted a letter telling her all the little details."

Zipporah raised a brow. "Do tell!"

"Well, to begin, I shall wear my lilac silk taffeta, and my bouquet will be lily of the valley from the orangery at Lamb Hill." Loveday took a sip from her own cup. "Our wedding cake shall be decorated with royal icing and candied violets, though I suppose Aunt wouldn't care for our use of sugar."

"Well, perhaps one might make an allowance for so special an occasion," Zipporah said. "I'm very happy to have all the tea we want at our disposal on this side of the Atlantic too."

In the next room the men's voices seemed to rumble. Tobacco smoke snuck beneath the door. Fragrant Tidewater tobacco. Yet this room was a far cry from Royal Vale's parlor. Would she ever be at home here? She didn't miss the steady hum of the city, but at least there she could be alert to the needs about her and do good. Here she felt like a plant in the orangery, all foliage and little fruit.

After a game of whist, the women sought the staircase amid yawns and murmuring about plans for the morrow while the men talked on in the dining room till well after midnight.

55

For there is no friend like a sister
In calm or stormy weather;
To cheer one on the tedious way,
To fetch one if one goes astray,
To lift one if one totters down,
To strengthen whilst one stands.

Christina Rossetti

There's never been a more beautiful bride," Juliet said, passing Loveday her bouquet once Minette finished her coiffure. "Your groom has sent word all is ready at Lamb Hill for your arrival."

Loveday took a last look at her reflection. "Do you regret having so hasty a shipboard wedding?"

"Not a bit," Juliet said with a smile. "Yours is all the fuss and bother I need."

Their easy, mingled laughter was something Juliet would miss. But no melancholy thoughts should mar this memorable day. Even the weather was glorious.

Nurse appeared at the door, ushering in the twins wearing frocks and new shoes, their hair shining with a just-washed luster.

"Mam!" they chorused, running to her and hanging on her

petticoats. They regarded Loveday with admiring eyes but seemed to know better than to ruffle her wedding finery. She gathered them close despite it, even taking two blossoms from her bouquet to give them. They took them proudly, and then Cole uttered the one word that sent Juliet's heart reeling again.

"Da?" He looked about as if expecting Leith to be hiding in a corner.

"Da is on his way." Juliet went to a window that overlooked the long drive and, seeing no one, turned away.

"D'you have a biscuit?" Bella asked coyly, examining Loveday's bouquet.

"Nary a biscuit, but we shall soon have wedding cake."

"Come along." Juliet ushered them out of the room and downstairs to the waiting coach. "Time to go see the lambs at Uncle Niall's."

The few miles to Lamb Hill was awash with bluebells. Loveday sang a song with the twins while Juliet pondered all that had come to pass. Though she had no remorse about her own hasty nuptials, she did sometimes wish for a more romantic beginning. But what did it matter if there was to be a romantic end?

"Wee lambie, lambie, lambie," Bella sang.

Lambing season was in evidence on both sides of the coach as shepherds and sheep roamed beyond the borders of Lamb Hill. The newer mansion seemed miniature compared to Ardraigh Hall, more a fairy-tale castle with its turrets and dry moat filled with wildflowers. Both children were bouncing excitedly on the primrose silk seats since Uncle Niall was a favorite. The Paisley coach had already arrived, but Lyrica and Euan seemed to have gone inside.

Niall was waiting on the steps, having dispensed with the usual footman. "What? You didn't ride your ponies. Flora and Charlie, is it?"

LAURA FRANTZ

"Aye," Cole replied with the gravity of a three-year-old. "They're napping."

"Nae, they're eating oats!" Bella said, running up the steps past him.

Loveday smiled at her groom as she emerged from the coach. Leaving them alone for so private a moment, Juliet followed the twins into the house, where Father and Zipporah were waiting, dressed in their best just inside the open doorway.

"I spy another Buchanan." Father pointed over Juliet's head toward the driveway.

Relief flooded her as she turned around and looked through the open door. Leith was coming down the driveway at a canter, raising both the dust and her admiration. No finer horseman in green frock coat, leather breeches, and spurred boots existed, at least in her eyes.

Back out the door she went just as Loveday and Niall came in, leaving her alone with Leith in the forecourt as the coach rolled away. He dismounted, handed Eclipse to a stable hand, and reached for her hand, bringing it to his lips. Her heart turned over. He met her eyes and held her gaze for another heart-halting moment.

"Am I late?"

"You're more gallant than tardy," she said, smoothing his collar.

"A few matters needed finishing in Glasgow. Euan has agreed to manage Buchanan affairs while we're away on a proper honeymoon."

"Away . . . as in Bath?" At his nod, she felt childishly emotional, like she might burst into tears as Bella and Cole sometimes did.

"You might enjoy Bath more if you were in the company of your family."

Was that what he thought? Did the taint of her onetime re-fusal of him still trouble him? "Leith, all that I require is you."

Still, a shadow seemed to cross his face. "Can you be away from the children for a time?"

"'Tis best. A long journey would tire them so."

"And not only them," he said with a chuckle as a sudden commotion behind them ended their intimacy.

Bella and Cole hopped down the steps and cavorted about them like leaping lambs. "Da! Da!"

With a last look at Juliet, he took them both by the hand and started up the stairs. "Let us waste nae time and see your uncle wed, aye?"

The parlor's cool interior was hushed, but the moment's pleasure and anticipation were palpable. Only a few family and friends had gathered, the parish clergy present too. A Scottish wedding required sprigs of white heather, worn by the groom and tucked into the bride's bouquet. If Juliet had any reservations about Loveday's feelings for Niall, they were put to rest simply by the adoring way she looked at him.

Did she herself regard Leith that way?

She stole a look at him as he stood by the groom, only to find his eyes on her. Heat bloomed in her neck and face, and she felt as much a bride as Loveday, so much so she forgot to listen to the hallowed vows or watch the fidgeting twins or pay attention to the time.

Suddenly the stirring ceremony ended. The joyful couple turned round as man and wife and led the way into the din-ing room for the wedding feast.

On the next clement day, Juliet and Leith slipped away to ride through Lanarkshire to the ruins of Kairthmere Castle. Juliet had chosen a young mare from Ardraigh Hall's stables named America while Leith rode his favorite, Eclipse. Summer seemed to reign instead of spring, the sun gilding the rolling hills with a special sheen.

Atop a rise sat the old pile with its commanding views, retaining its medieval essence. Entirely alone, they dismounted and turned the horses loose to graze on wildflower-colored grasses.

"I grew up playing here as a lad, pretending I was a knight in armor." Leith led her past gnarled trees toward a tower house. "Some of these yews have been here for hundreds of years."

"Does Kairthmere have a colorful past?"

"Treason, torture, and trysts, aye." He took her gloved hand to help her over the uneven ground. "But such is Scotland's turbulent history."

She lifted her gaze from the ground to the blue sky. Walls of arched windows were still standing, as well as a worn turnpike stair that spiraled left.

Leith let go of her and began to walk up the narrow steps backward, wielding an imaginary sword. "These stairs are made for a car-handit, or left-handed, swordsman to fight his way up and down against mostly right-handed foes."

"Foes who would be at a decided disadvantage," she said, imagining it with a slight shudder.

He climbed higher till one wall gave way and he could have stepped into open air.

"I feel a bit like a damsel in distress watching you." She held her breath till he came down again and stood on solid ground, the rush of the wind rustling the ancient trees around them.

"I suppose you'd like for me to live to see Bath," he jested.

"I overheard you and Niall talking wills, which seems to have shadowed me."

"Nae worries. When you wed, a will becomes null and void and a new one is made, hence the morose conversation."

She smiled up at him, wishing he'd take her hand again. "I'd prefer to talk weddings . . . honeymoons."

"Niall and Loveday seem content to go nae further than Lamb Hill."

"You can't blame them for wanting to spend their first days and nights of married life at home instead of aboard ship. Loveday is a poor sailor and often sick."

"I don't blame them. I'm just impatient."

"You're fond of Bath, then?"

"Nae." He took her in his arms slowly as if they were about to dance. "My impatience has nothing to do with Bath."

She leaned into him, woozy again. Being alone atop the hill, with no servants or family near, led to a dizzying intimacy they'd never known. Would he kiss her a second time? She wanted nothing more than to be close to him. When he held her, she felt whole. Wholly his.

"You ken how I feel about you, Juliet?"

His tender tone turned her heart over. "We've never spoken of our feelings."

"Mayhap we should, though mine are plain enough."

"You care for me enough to have risked coming to Virginia—and my refusal."

"All a bit hazy in hindsight. It began with your miniature and Ravenal's letters. At first, I was in love with the idea of you." His lips brushed her hair. "I actually penned you a love letter of sorts before I sailed to Virginia, then burned it. Once I met you, you had me heart and soul."

Heart and soul. It seemed she'd waited all her life to hear those very words. "You're a true romantic underneath it all."

"I'm wholeheartedly yours. You're my first thought at break of day and my last thought at night, and all the times between. I carry your miniature everywhere."

338

"And it thrills me to hear it. I love you, Leith. I've loved you longer than you think."

He grew still as if trying to take it in. "But when you look at me, you surely see all the things you stand against. Trade and tobacco and a brutal monopoly that ties you in knots."

"I see a man who is trying to do better, who is willing to risk a great deal, including his heart."

"You think me better than I am."

"We are all of us fallen. By God's grace we rise and are made new—together."

"So you have cast your lot with a man who adores you but has a long road ahead."

"All we have is this moment. And before we leave this place, I want to mark it by removing all doubt from your mind about my devotion." She stood on tiptoe and slipped her arms around his neck, their foreheads touching. "You were the first man who kissed me, and you will surely be the last."

Her steadfast words seemed to unlock something inside him. Yet another thawing, she sensed, a step closer to whatever united them and a step away from whatever had bound him before. His hands spanned her waist and he drew her even closer, his faint beard chafing her skin as his mouth met hers. She tasted need and relief and unmet longing in his kiss. Her own breathless desire swirled amid it all, filling her to the brim with a delight she'd never known.

When a circling hawk shrilled a cry, they came to their senses but only for a trice. They looked down and laughed, as they had trampled her hat. Uncaring, she threaded her hands into his hair, wanting more of him, her rising heartbeat like a rush of wings. Twining the black, silken strands between her fingers, she stole his queue ribbon as a reminder of this heaven-sent day, mischievousness rivaling her pleasure.

56

Love must be as much a light as it is a flame.
Henry David Thoreau

Birdsong and the sound of childish, hushed voices in the corridor woke Juliet. She sat upright, momentarily dazed to find herself in Leith's chamber. Then the ardor and intimacy of the night before came rushing back. Pushing aside the bed linens gingerly, she tried not to wake the man beside her. Silently, she stole across the carpet and passed through the dressing room to her bedchamber in time to meet Nurse opening the door and admitting Bella and Cole, as was their morning custom once the twins had dressed and breakfasted.

"Mam!" They ran to her, showing surprise to find her still in her nightclothes, her feet bare and her unbound hair hanging about her shoulders. Usually she was fully dressed and seated at her escritoire by the window, having her morning Bible reading and cup of tea or writing a letter.

Shutting the door behind her, Nurse went on her way to break her fast in the servants' hall. Putting a finger to her lips,

Juliet led the twins through the dressing room into Leith's bedchamber, where she returned to her cocoon of bed linens beside him and patted the mattress in invitation.

Smiling and mounting the bed steps like they were playing a grand game, the twins eyed their father as if he was some sort of hibernating bear. Their glee at finding him asleep was plain, and when he rolled over at Bella's tentative poke, his deep growl nearly sent them leaping off the bed in terrified titters.

"Wheest!" Leith sat up, grabbing Cole by the ankle and pulling him across the coverlet. "Twa faeries?"

Bella jumped into Juliet's arms as Cole tried to escape his father's grasp, their shrieking surely raising the servants' brows elsewhere. But Juliet's heart was full, her own laughter bubbling over at the morning melee.

"I've ne'er awakened to fairy folk." Leith growled again, tickling Cole as Juliet kissed Bella and smoothed her petticoats.

Dressed alike, the twins were nearly indistinguishable save for the tiny freckle on Bella's left cheek. She pressed into Juliet, smelling of herbal soap and the dried lavender sewn into her hem.

Cole's lilting voice held a lisp. "I want my sword, Da."

Leith stopped his tickling. "The toy sword Uncle Niall gave you?"

"Then I could fight you."

"Where is it?"

"Nurse took it away."

"Then ask Nurse to bring it back."

Cole kicked at the covers. "Scairt ol' woman."

Bella nodded gravely. "She hid in a closet."

"Shall we go outside this morning and give Nurse a rest?" Juliet pointed to a window where light crept past the shutters. "Look how lovely the day!"

Cole cast an adoring look Juliet's way, finally squirming free of his father's hold. "I want to ride Charlie!"

Bella jumped off the bed to run to the window. "I want to ride Flora!"

The twins climbed onto the large windowsill to better see outside, parting the shutters with clumsy if careful hands. Sunlight drenched them, highlighting the red glints in their hair. Again, like Leith. His mark was all over them. Surely Havilah was there too.

Turning toward her, Leith kissed Juliet's fingers, concern in his eyes.

"You're leaving after breakfast," she said before he did.

"Against my will. But soon there's Bath."

She took a breath, hardly believing they were to have a true honeymoon. "Praise be we're not traveling four hundred miles by coach."

"Depending on weather, it's considerably shorter by sea from Glasgow to Bristol, and far more comfortable."

She looked toward the children still by the window. "I'll miss them." Turning back to Leith, she leaned in and kissed him. "But if you were to go without me, I'd miss you more."

"And I you. For the first time in my life, business is my last thought."

"All you needed to do was be here. Be near."

She thought of all they'd done since Loveday's wedding. Riding to the castle ruins. Roaming the gardens and what seemed like every ell of the wilderness area. Leisurely meals together. Lengthy conversations about Buchanan business and his concern over missing accounts. Reading news of the American colonies. Quiet evenings reading by the fire or playing whist.

A tumult of recent intimacies rushed in, including Leith quoting lines of poetry she loved by Mary Wortley Montagu.

Could you see my heart, how fond, how true, how free from fraudful art, the warmest glances poorly do explain the eager wish, the melting throbbing pain which through my very blood and soul I feel, which you cannot explain nor I reveal.

Their honeymoon had already blessedly begun.

They'd gathered at the Virginia Street townhouse—Father and Zipporah, Loveday, and even Minette, who would accompany them when they sailed tomorrow. If clement weather continued, the voyage would be short and uneventful, leaving them a fortnight in Bath. The twins remained behind at Ardraigh Hall, too young to understand the coming separation, though Juliet did. Suddenly four hundred miles seemed far indeed. She'd gotten down on her knees and prayed with them before she left. Absence could bring many things, the least of them homesickness.

"I'm counting the minutes till we depart," Loveday told them at dinner. "Though I never thought I'd be saying that after the ocean voyage we had coming here."

Father chuckled. "Thankfully, a cruise around the west coast of Scotland and England has plenty of places to shelter should the weather turn surly."

"I shudder at how often voyages go awry," Zipporah said. "I cannot wait to see Bath now that it's spring."

"If we could only get the Buchanans in line." Father had begun making jokes about their frequent absences. "Though I must say, Niall already feels like a son-in-law, and Leith has been home more than in the countinghouse of late."

"All three shall join us for supper," Juliet told them. "Lyrica is on her way too. For now, the men are taking care of last-minute business since Euan will be in charge while we're away."

"How expedient to have three male heirs." Father was studying her and Loveday as if imagining the future.

"Perhaps you shall have grandchildren in time." Loveday patted his hand. "Even a lad or two."

Juliet looked at her across the table. It was too soon to think she or Loveday might be expecting—but one could hope.

Father lifted his glass in a sort of toast. "A grandson or granddaughter from either of you would be a fine thing, though Cole and Bella are more than sufficient in the meantime."

"Truly," Zipporah echoed, smiling at Juliet. "You have a lovely way with them, my dear. One couldn't tell they weren't yours to begin with."

Thanking her, Juliet turned her attention to the sound of footsteps in the foyer and a footman's voice giving a greeting. Leith? She rose from the table, giddy as a girl at his homecoming. But it was Euan who appeared in the dining room doorway with no one in his wake, the stricken look on his face bringing Father to his feet. Everyone else froze.

Euan swallowed, visibly struggling for words. "Leith has been taken into custody at the tolbooth for the murder of Havilah."

57

Whatsoever is done in charity, however small and of no reputation it be, bringeth forth good fruit.

Thomas à Kempis

"Arrested?" Father spoke first. "There must be some mistake."

Juliet thought she might be sick. Nausea was followed by a jolt of disbelief so strong it made her light-headed. The tolbooth with its daunting steeple at Glasgow Cross flashed to mind. Its harrowing Gallowgate had held countless executions over the centuries, many of them unjust. Though she'd made a few visits, she'd never imagined having someone she knew or loved imprisoned there. The very sight of it wrenched her heart.

Euan entered the room, crossed to a chair, and gripped the upholstered back. "It seems Cochrane brought the charge. He claims a servant he employs saw Leith push Havilah from the bridge that night."

"How convenient given it's his servant," Zipporah said icily.

"I must go to him at once." Juliet started for the foyer, but Euan stopped her.

"Once in the tolbooth, none can see him but clergy—though Niall is still there trying to challenge that."

Loveday came round the table to take Juliet by the arm. "Please sit down lest you faint. We must try to make sense of the matter together, all of us."

But Juliet was hardly listening. She sat stupefied, knowing little of British law. Leith *arrested*. And why did the charge come so long after Havilah's death? She looked at her father as if pleading with him to do something.

Euan's frown deepened. "Cochrane says his servant—a coachman—was too frightened to report it till now but upon Leith's second marriage decided to declare it."

A commotion in the foyer halted the conversation, and then Lyrica swept in, her face pale as linen. Niall was on her heels, his own features florid and irate. At Euan's urging, they all passed into the smallest drawing room, where a coal fire burned and threw light about the shuttered chamber.

"We must act quickly," Niall told them. "Under the Murder Act here in Britain, trials are held swiftly by Crown Courts. I've already sent to Edinburgh for the best defense counsel available."

"Might this false charge have to do with Cochrane coveting being Lord Provost of Glasgow, which the other tobacco merchants mean for Leith?" Lyrica asked, obviously well versed on city matters. "Even if he's not found guilty of murder, it certainly ruins his reputation."

"Ruins?" Niall shook his head in disgust. "Only by those who believe Cochrane's lies—or his coercion of his coachman to testify against Leith."

"I'm very sorry he can't claim benefit of peerage since he has no title." Lyrica took a seat by Juliet on a sofa, reaching for her hand. "Murder is a capital crime that has all kinds of implications."

"None of which I feel at liberty discussing just yet," Euan replied. "I don't want to frighten nor raise false hopes. Suffice it to say, Scots law is oft brutal, but we have more on our hands than this false charge. There's been new news regarding the colonies. We must quickly take action now that America is in open revolt or run the risk of ruining the Buchanan firm in future."

Lying awake in Leith's bedchamber without him gave rise to all sorts of speculations and frets. What sort of lodging did he have in gaol? Was there adequate food? Warmth? Though it was April, the Scottish weather still chilled Juliet to the bone. She tried not to think of the blooming redbud and dogwood of home and how the sun shone upon the James River like molten gold, warming everything it touched.

Leith had yet, in her eyes, to fully recover from his Virginia illness. Such harsh conditions could return him to that frightening state of before, the fever and coughing and far worse. He might even be denied a doctor.

Turning over, she laid her head upon his pillow, his beloved masculine scent a part of the smooth linen casing. Was he lying awake thinking of her? Stunned by this turn of events? After she had shared his bed as his wife in more than name, his absence cut deep, the recent memories they'd made deeper still.

Woven into her scattered, weary thoughts was a psalm. *They compassed me about also with words of hatred; and fought against me without a cause . . . But I give myself unto prayer.*

She must give herself to prayer. And she would go to the tolbooth to determine if she could gain entry herself or persuade Leith's gaolers to take him a letter.

The tolbooth was unlike anything Leith had imagined from the outside. A peculiar odor hung about it, of stale sweat and urine and boiled neeps and tatties and worse. His gaolers were respectful of him simply because they feared him and his position, knowing he might be exonerated and turn on them in time.

"Mr. Buchanan, sir." The head warden walked him back to a cell at the very end of the hall, past the deranged and thieves and suspected witches and other destitute men and women, who shook the bars as if to rattle him as he passed. "Your wife has been here thrice now."

What? Leith nearly stopped walking. He missed Juliet with a physical ache. She was his every waking thought.

"Before ye yerself came to be here, sir. Mrs. Buchanan visited the women inmates and even arranged for regular deliveries to be made to provision the poorest. A few other well-placed ladies are now following her example."

Throat knotted, Leith said nothing, unwilling to admit he'd not known, though his reaction surely told the warden plenty as they walked through the labyrinth of suffering all around him. He'd never given much thought to the misery within these walls, nor a second glance at those whose ears had been nailed to the Tron outside. His hard-heartedness assured him these vermin-ridden prisoners had simply gotten what they deserved. Juliet had come here and seen things he could not.

His thoughts swung to the warm coal hearths of Virginia Street and the climbing boy she'd taken to the kitchen and fed. Arthur? Had she continued to help him too? The lad had left Leith's mind the moment he'd departed the kitchen.

Surrounded by society's outcasts within four walls, Leith

wondered why he'd never truly seen them before. He'd only seen through them.

His gaoler unlocked his cell. It was no different from any other inmate's. Cold. Spare. Reeking. It chased all benevolence from his thoughts.

58

The only true wisdom is in knowing you know nothing.

Socrates

Juliet sat in Leith's Jamaica Street office as she had every day since his arrest five days before. The Buchanan factors and clerks still seemed uneasy with her presence, but she felt a pressing need to be about his business in his absence—and it proved a formidable task. His clear instructions to her aboard ship when he thought he was dying returned to her now with greater urgency. As principal in the Buchanan firm, he had his steady hand in everything, though his brothers had their own considerable share of the business.

Across Leith's immense desktop, newsprint swam before her eyes from both sides of the Atlantic.

King George III to issue royal proclamation closing American colonies to all commerce and trade.

Provincial Congress in Massachusetts orders 13,600 American soldiers to be mobilized.

Governor Gage secretly ordered by the British to enforce

the Coercive Acts and suppress open rebellion among colonists by using all necessary force.

Second Continental Congress convenes in Philadelphia.

Virginians state they will surrender their liberties only at the expense of their lives.

She called the nearest clerk, who hurried in to do her bidding. Forcing a smile, she said with far more confidence than she was feeling, "I need to summon the Buchanan board for a meeting. Can you arrange that?"

"Of course, Mrs. Buchanan. Right away, aye."

He left and Juliet shut the door after him. She returned to the desk and sank down into Leith's chair. Thunder beat behind her temples, and she closed her eyes, a short, desperate prayer rising.

Lord, please help me.

The next morning she faced the board members in the boardroom, some of them the leading tobacco lords of Glasgow, Euan and Niall among them. Most regarded her with a wary suspicion, but she didn't blame them. She was a Virginian, not a Glaswegian, and she was a woman, neither of which were welcome in this male-dominated sphere. With Leith's future hanging in the balance, the situation was even more tense.

She took her husband's place at the head of the table, several carefully prepared papers before her. "Gentlemen, I'd like to pray before we call this meeting to order."

Euan frowned, his thoughts plain. Did they not pray before they conducted business? Yet Niall's head was already bent, his eyes closed. Juliet bowed her own head, hardly knowing what she said, only that without the Lord's guidance she'd be utterly lost.

She launched into the matter at hand immediately lest she lose courage. "I've not seen my husband since his arrest, but aboard ship he authorized me to act in his stead, having prepared for such a time as this, whether it be from illness, accident, or death—and now incarceration."

The last word was hard to utter. It held a taint she hated since the charge was a lie. She swallowed and continued after glancing at the wall clock behind Euan's head.

"The first matter is obvious. America is soon to declare her independence and sever all ties to Great Britain. Merchanting as you've known it for a century or more is coming to an end. As it stands, there are now no outward-bound cargoes for the colonies, bringing Buchanan enterprises to a halt there. Glasgow will go from importing seventy-five percent of all Virginia tobacco production to nothing at all this season."

Silence. An onerous one.

"I, for one, doubt it will come to war." Euan folded his arms across his chest. "An olive branch petition to the king is said to be forthcoming from the colonies, which I'm sure will bring an end to this nonsense."

"My contacts in America say otherwise," Mr. Cameron said with a decisive shake of his head. "The tide has turned, and George Washington has been appointed to lead an American army. There will be nae olive branch, nae truce."

"They're all traitors sure to hang, the upstart Washington foremost," Mr. Turnbull uttered with such vehemence that spittle landed on the papers before him. "The war, even one of brief duration, will spell the ruin of us all."

Ruin. That was what she must avoid. Aunt Damarus's latest letter had arrived at an opportune time, full of news since Philadelphia was nothing less than the pulse of the Revolution. "I've just received word from a trusted source that the colonies are preparing to pay France in tobacco for arms and ammunition even as they're investing in nonto-bacco crops to fund colonial militias."

"France? Our avowed enemy?" Mr. Inglis said in disgust.

She continued calmly. "I'm going one step further and selling the Royal Vale estate in Virginia before it is seized and confiscated and of no benefit to us."

Murmurs of assent went round the table, heartening her even as it hurt to part with her ancestral home.

A flash of exasperation lit Euan's face. "It seems you're being decidedly foolhardy, as rash as my brother with his decision to recall our store factors and shutter operations there."

Juliet hesitated, his harsh tone daunting. Instead of being the ally she'd hoped for, Euan was proving a formidable opponent. Niall even regarded him with a show of perplexity as Juliet forged ahead.

"The true purpose of this meeting," she said, firming her voice, "is to tell you the time has come to sell all Buchanan tobacco stock."

Any assent she'd hoped to muster died with those bold words. Their complicity soured, all but Niall's.

She continued, feeling Leith's absent approval. "We must invest those profits in calico printing and dyeing industries. Found the Buchanan Calico Printing Company—"

"I beg to differ." Euan made an abrupt shift in his chair. "Indies rum and sugar are our second-best resource after Orinoco—and the most lucrative. If we canna be tobacco lords, we will be sugar lords instead."

Juliet met his gaze with a steadiness she didn't feel. "I suggest—nay, dictate—buying more acreage to use as bleaching fields here in Glasgow's east end instead. There's also a robust trade with Ireland of Buchanan manufactures, namely woolens, cordage, and glass, which must not lag."

"I take it you're against Caribbean trade and anything related to it," Mr. Inglis said. "Yet I concur with your brother-in-law that sugar and rum are sure to save us."

Everything in her rebelled at the notion. "I maintain that all Caribbean trade be forsaken and we concentrate our efforts and resources elsewhere. My husband spoke of investing in Turkish and Egyptian suppliers, which I advocate for as well."

"You've certainly studied Buchanan enterprises thoroughly." Euan was regarding her closely, his knuckles rapping the tabletop in a tight cadence. "I do wonder what your husband would say about all this were he here and had a voice."

"For now, I am his voice," she replied, holding his mulish gaze.

Oh, Leith, I am trying to defend your interests as best I can.

She was at sea here acting in a man's stead. That gaping emptiness took hold again, drawing her nearer helplessness, even hopelessness, in the face of the men's rising antagonism. These were some of the most powerful men in Scotland, two of them reputed to be among the wealthiest in all Europe.

Niall leaned forward, the sudden set of his jaw reminding her of Leith. "I stand behind selling all Buchanan tobacco stock and removing our presence in North America from this day forward."

A tense pause and Juliet's hopes revived. Combined with Leith's, Niall's vote and shares in the firm were all that were needed to override the other partners.

59

But come what may, I do adore thee so
That danger shall seem sport, and I will go.
                    William Shakespeare

*B*ella climbed into Juliet's lap, a welcome distraction. "Where's Da?"

Juliet hugged her close, glad she'd had the twins removed from Ardraigh Hall to Virginia Street for the time being. "He's away at present, but I pray he shall be home soon."

On the carpet at their feet, Cole played with his toy soldiers, a veritable wooden army replete with cannons and cavalry. Juliet gave silent thanks he wasn't old enough to join the military in the escalating colonial conflict. Around them the parlor clock chimed a familiar cadence, and supper smells permeated the small chamber on Virginia Street. None of them had left Glasgow since Leith's arrest a fortnight before.

Father set aside his paper. "I'm rather cross-eyed with all the news of late. I've begun to believe it is more fiction than fact, as there are so many conflicting reports about the colonies and what is happening there."

Juliet eyed him sympathetically. "I do think you and Zipporah should go on to Bath. Though I treasure your presence here, there is really nothing you can do."

"Nonsense," he replied.

"We shan't leave you till this is finished," Loveday told her. "What sort of holiday would it be with us forever wondering how you're faring here?"

"Indeed, Bath can wait." Zipporah looked up from her embroidery. "All the rain of late makes for frightful travel anyway. With the assizes ready to begin, I'm confident this matter will be resolved soon, and then we shall all be on our way. A delightful prospect!"

The assizes, the formal time when court proceedings got underway, were but four days hence. Zipporah's cheerfulness in the face of such a calamity encouraged them all, though Juliet worked to mask her own growing dismay.

Zipporah smiled, eyes alight. "I'm particularly excited to take you to Prior Park Gardens overlooking Bath and walk those serpentine paths amidst an astonishing wealth of trees, grottoes, and exotic plants like the passionflower."

Loveday was at full attention. "I've never beheld Passiflora before. How I'd love to meet Mr. Lancelot Brown, who helped design the gardens."

"Ah, *Capability* Brown, indeed." Zipporah shared her love of botany. "For a man appointed master gardener at Hampton Court Palace for His Majesty, he's done well for himself, though he's quite aged."

The conversation continued, but Juliet moved beyond it, dwelling on the window where a late afternoon rain streaked the panes. How often she'd looked for Leith out this very glass, her heart quickening at the sight of him returning from the countinghouse or bank.

For now, only Euan and Niall appeared at the closing of

356

front door. Abandoning their toys, the twins rushed at Niall, nearly sending him off balance.

laughter put a dent in her dark thoughts. But Euan seemed a trifle annoyed at their noise, and Juliet was struck by something she'd not given much thought to before. The children always shied away from Leith's other brother. They seemed fond of Lyrica but not Euan. Why?

ripple of alarm passed through her. Euan was looking at her now in that dogged way he had, as if admonishing her for trumping him in their last meeting when she'd won the shareholders' critical vote. Then, in a flash, that coldness melted as he turned to Lyrica. But Juliet's startling realization remained. Somehow their relationship, never warm, had become a sort of frigid competition that chilled her to the bone.

brothers took seats by their wives, and a servant brought refreshments. Euan sipped his brandy and once again began to inform them of the legalities as they unfolded. "Given the charge of murder, the trial will be before the High Court. The lord advocate has appointed the prosecutors. Leith has just been served the indictment and the list of witnesses against him, as court protocol requires. One witness is Cochrane's coachman and another is a disreputable trollop who claims to have found Havilah's body."

there no witnesses in his favor, like the magistrate on night watch the eve of Havilah's death?" Lyrica sounded as indignant as Juliet felt. "Leith went to the authorities immediately after and explained all that had occurred. An investigation ensued and no stone was left unturned."

looked equally dubious. "I don't recall mention of any trollop before now."

I." Euan looked at his empty glass. "The courts are going to have a devil of a time silencing the newspapers ahead of the trial. Surely the drivel they print will sway the jury."

"How many jurors are there?" Zipporah asked.

"Since it's a criminal trial, there are five special jurors and ten common jurors according to the property they own."

"Sounds complicated." Father set aside the book he'd been reading and looked at Juliet. "And very unlike colonial American legalities."

60

This house doth hate all wickedness,
Loves peace, but faults corrects,
Observes all laws of righteousness,
And good men it erects.

Frontispiece on the
Glasgow Tolbooth

The next morning before first light, Juliet took a carriage to the tolbooth. Minette accompanied her, a basket in hand full of carefully gathered items for Leith. Foodstuffs, soap, artwork by the twins, a pipe and tobacco. Juliet also brought a pipe and tobacco for the tolbooth governor, a surly man she was slowly becoming acquainted with but remained chary of. He lived alongside the prison in a tenement while the keepers and custodians resided inside to maintain order and security, their keys a harsh jangle in the cold, unwholesome air.

As Juliet stepped over the threshold in time to see a rat darting into a corner hole, she said another silent, hasty prayer. This formidable place dashed any and all expectations.

"G'day, ma'am." The greeting was hardly hospitable, but

359

what could she expect from a man who seemed encrusted in calluses? The grimy, iron-grated window behind him let in scant light, just enough to see how the pox had ravaged his heavy features and a hump bowed his back. "Yer husband's been moved to another cell after a fracas. Seems another inmate wished him ill, so he's been taken to solitary on the third story."

Alarm clawed at her once again. "Is Mr. Buchanan well?"

"Och, weel enough." He took a key hanging from the wall, raising both her curiosity and her hopes. "I suppose we've ye to thank for the wagonloads of goods here lately. I'd suspect yer trying to bribe me, but yer too barrie a lass for that."

Barrie? Better than a saucy minx, she guessed. Nay, a bribe was not what she'd had in mind. Her only thought had been for the poorest inmates she'd heard were starving, some of whom had died for lack of bread and water. It pained her that she had no way to see if the goods were being distributed as she hoped.

She took the pipe and tobacco from the basket and held it out to him without a word. His eyes lit up and he muttered, "Weel, one good deed deserves another."

Motioning her to a turnpike stair, he told Minette to stay behind while he took her basket. Juliet fought tears as she climbed the steep, winding stair that reminded her of Kairthmere Castle's ruins. Oh, to return to that blessed day when they'd not known what was round the bend.

Minding her steps, she wanted to cover her ears when the massive tower's bells chimed and left her half deafened. Finally they arrived at the top floor, where a large apartment housed Leith away from the debtors and criminals.

"Ye've a quarter of an hour," the keeper said before handing her the basket. He shut the door behind him and, Juliet guessed, descended the stair.

Leith stared at her from behind the iron bars as if seeing a

LAURA FRANTZ

ghost. And then he turned away, broad shoulders shaking. Was he . . . weeping? Without a sound, but undeniably weeping. The realization so tore at her that she was nearly weeping too.

"Leith . . . please . . ." She stood still, groping for what to say. How did one comfort a proud—but broken—man?

"You shouldn't be here. I never intended you harm, to demean you like this." He spoke the words over his shoulder in winded snatches as if wrestling with control of his emotions.

"I don't care, Leith. Wherever you are is where I'll be. Where I want to be."

"You're far better than I deserve. I expected condemnation . . ." His head came up but he didn't turn around. "But what I see in you is Christ."

She crossed the empty, echoing room. Setting down the basket, she wished away the barrier that stood between them. "Look at me, Leith. I couldn't love you more than I do right now. God is here with us. We mustn't lose heart."

He turned around slowly and swallowed so hard she saw his throat constrict. "What miracle did you perform to gain entry?"

It was hardly the greeting she'd imagined after a fortnight apart. With a half smile, she reached for his hands that fisted the bars. His clasp was cold, but his eyes were tender.

"I'd rather be locked in with you than be away from you another minute." The admission brought a new footing. Their circumstances had tumbled the last stronghold between them, leaving only raw vulnerability and honesty in its wake.

"How are you?" His gaze roamed her face as if discerning the answer before she gave it. "The bairns?"

"Missing you. But the only question that matters is, how are you?"

"Weel enough for a criminal." He rolled his eyes heavenward, an echo of the old insolence. "I've retained the best

361

barristers in Britain as legal counsel, who agree we're dealing with liars and slanderers as far as the charges."

"Then I pray their evil will call them out." She took a breath, trying to steady her own emotions at seeing him again. "There's so much to tell you. I hardly know where to begin." She didn't want to waste their precious time with business, but what else could they do? "All the tobacco shares have sold, every one. Euan tried to dissuade me, but Niall was unwavering in his support. The sale has reaped a great profit to be reinvested when you're free."

"If I'm free." His voice held nothing but a brisk acceptance of matters. "If not, it's to be handled by you."

"There are other, more pressing things you should know. Things I've found out while going through accounts and bills of lading and such in your offices."

"Speak freely, then."

"There are several missing account books and ledgers, more than you told me about prior, including a new investor—a silent partner named Malcolm Sinclair—who is unknown to your clerks. I don't know what to make of it. I suspect Sinclair is a front. A false name used to cover illegal activities."

"I'm aware of Sinclair." He looked down at the flagstone floor, clearly perplexed. "Have you told anyone about this?"

"None but you."

"Confide in Leo Tate, my foremost factor. He's also aware of Sinclair and can be trusted. Ask for his help in future. Swear him to secrecy. Before my arrest Tate found two of our engravers forging note plates at our bank, and they're now in custody. Something nefarious is afoot, someone internal working against us who took advantage of my lengthy absence in America and my absence now. Someone who kens the business with all its complexities and can profit from that knowledge."

"I'll confide in your factor, then. Not your brothers?"

"Nae. All are guilty till proven innocent." He paused, his alarm palpable. "I want you to send a note to the criminal officer named John Tennant at Session House in the Trongate. You'll need protection."

"Protection?" Her whispered word held resistance. She'd not felt in any danger, though the alarm that scored his half-bearded face made her reconsider. Who would wish her ill?

"Promise me you'll not do anything else till you settle your protection with Tennant."

"Of course."

His tone turned gentle. "How are you spending your days?"

In a whirlwind of disbelief and grief.

She forged ahead, aware of the clock and dreading their parting. "I'm often at the countinghouse in your office, keeping apprised of what is happening in your absence. Betimes I attend meetings. A woman's presence is not always welcome, but I do what I can."

"And I commend you for it. Stay the course, but comply with Tennant as far as your safety is concerned. How is your family handling all this?"

"They are very concerned but continue to support us and pray. We're all of us certain you'll soon be free, this debacle over."

"Aye, debacle. That's the word for it." He kissed her fingers. "You're the first person I've been allowed to see—"

The scraping of a key in the lock signaled the end of their time. Juliet felt that unwelcome, heavy breathlessness weighing her like sodden wool. Not knowing when she'd see him again—if she'd see him again.

"Mrs. Buchanan, this way, please."

Turning back to Leith, she mouthed, *I love you,* unwilling to trust her wavering voice.

61

Love all, trust a few, do wrong to none.
William Shakespeare

At noon the next day, John Tennant stood before her in Leith's Virginia Street study. Juliet received him there as it was absent of doors and alcoves, unlike the mansion's other rooms where servants might over-hear or even spy. Everyone had now become suspect save Loveday, Father, and Zipporah.

"I hardly know what to say, Mr. Tennant." Another head-ache building, Juliet felt a touch of madness as events un-folded. "My husband has expressed concern for my safety and asked me to meet with you. Please, take a seat. Would you like refreshments?"

"A dram of whisky, aye." He took a tufted armchair by the window, allowing her a stark view of his taciturn features once she'd summoned a maid. Gray about the temples, he was no older than forty, she guessed. Finely tailored garments made him look less gaunt, tempting her to offer more than libations. Only whisky was brought, ending the matter.

He downed the drink quickly and set aside the glass.

"Since you have no idea who I am, let me say I'm a former Bow Street Runner in London. Since coming to Glasgow a decade ago, I've acted as auxiliary to the bailies and magistrates who police the city. I also have a cadre of men who serve as private guards. Mr. Buchanan no doubt wants one of them assigned to you."

"An escort charged with my protection when I venture out," she said quietly, still wondering if it was even necessary. "But I've felt no danger . . . not yet."

"A preventive measure, then."

"Perhaps your time would be better spent investigating the ludicrous charge brought against my husband."

His small, tight smile was so telling she knew at once he was already doing so. She also knew better than to press him. Mr. Tennant was an enigma. But she could certainly talk.

"I want you to know my suspicions now that I've acted in my husband's stead since his arrest. Someone close to him seems determined to undermine him both professionally and personally." She went on to explain the unaccounted-for business matters, the missing maid, and anything she felt would help Leith, however small.

When she'd finished he asked her a few simple questions rife with meaning. Had she ever noticed anyone following her? Had she ever felt afraid? Was she aware of any out-of-the-ordinary activity? Did she trust the servants?

"Thank you for taking care of my welfare in Mr. Buchanan's absence." She stood when he got ready to leave. "But more than that, thank you for whatever you're doing on my husband's behalf."

How was it even possible that one continued to take tea, have meals, sleep, and converse when such a life-shattering event played out in unseen courts with strange jurors and judges deciding one's future and fate? Juliet went through the motions, eating little and sleeping less. Almost everyone seemed suspect to her now—not only Cochrane, who'd leveled the charge, but even the Buchanans themselves.

As the weather changed from a wee smirr of rain to a goselet, she spent more time in Leith's study, seldom leaving Virginia Street lest she draw notice. She could almost hear the whispering of "the murderer's American bride" wherever she went. The news had leaked to the newspapers, at first a trickle, then a deluge. She avoided any print but heard Niall, Euan, and Father discussing details of the case from as far away as the *London Gazette*.

Even now, through the downpour, she detected her guard's silhouette on the corner across from the mansion's gates. She'd met him briefly one evening but knew nothing about him. Tennant hadn't even told her his name, only not to be alarmed at his continual presence.

"Sister . . ." Loveday pushed open the door after a light rap. The toll was telling on her too. Her face seemed almost haggard, the window's light calling out fine lines not visible before. She shut the door and gestured to the sofa before the coal fire. "I've been missing you and have asked that tea be brought. Herbal is quite calming with a touch of honey."

Juliet joined her, stomach uneasy at the mere suggestion. Holding her hands out to the hearth's heat, she tried to think of something lighthearted to say.

"You haven't tried to visit Leith again, have you?"

Juliet still felt the cold finality of having the door literally shut in her face. "I was denied twice and told not to return." Not only that, the man who'd let her see Leith the first time was absent. Where had he gone and why?

"The trial begins soon. I suppose it's best you stay home,

LAURA FRANTZ

though I do wish there was no need for a guard to be lurking, always reminding you of what is at hand."

"I need no reminding since I think of nothing else."

Loveday squeezed her hand reassuringly. "England's mineral baths sound especially soothing right now."

Dear Lord, let it be.

Tea was brought, medicinal mint threading the chill parlor. Juliet looked at the closed door as her sister handed her a cup and said softly, "There's something I cannot keep to myself any longer."

Loveday held her cup aloft, gaze fixed on Juliet. "Then by all means tell me, and I shall keep it a secret."

"Though I haven't been to the countinghouse and bank in a few days, I've discovered during the long hours I spent there that there are records and funds that can't be accounted for, dating to Leith's absence when he sailed to Virginia."

"Are you sure? Or is it being unfamiliar with the business that has led you to believe such?"

"I've gone over what's missing countless times, and it forms a sort of pattern. Leith's most trusted factor, Leo Tate, agrees with me regarding our findings. And it points to the person who would benefit most from Leith's absence and arrest."

Loveday set her cup aside. "Then you must tell me."

This time it was Juliet's turn to squeeze her sister's cold hand. "I hope and pray I am wrong, but the guilty party in league with Cochrane may well be someone close to us."

Horror leached the color from Loveday's face. She simply stared at Juliet as if hoping this was all a jest or she'd misheard, or Juliet had misunderstood.

"I'm going to meet with Leo Tate again this afternoon. He sent a note round this morning that said he has new evidence that points to who is aligned with Cochrane. After that I'll meet with Mr. Tennant again to reveal our latest findings."

"Then I must go with you."

"Nay, only Minette." She looked toward the windows fronting the street.

"Can Minette be trusted?"

"I believe so, though I've not forgotten Lyrica sent her to me. I don't confide in her and am careful in front of all the servants. Minette simply accompanies me along with my guard."

"You don't believe the guilty party is Niall, do you?" Tears shone in Loveday's eyes. "It can't be. He's too selfless. Too honest."

Juliet had never suspected Niall. "Euan."

Loveday gasped. "What about Lyrica?"

"Lyrica may well know."

Horror returned to Loveday's face. "They may be complicit?"

Juliet looked toward the closed door again, her voice a scant whisper. "Since I last spoke with Mr. Tennant, we've uncovered extensive gambling debts. Payments to properties and mining rights that don't actually exist, which we believe are simply a front for Cochrane's involvement. To complicate matters, Lyrica and Euan have no heirs. Before my arrival, Leith's will specified they were to become the twins' guardians with his demise. I am now in the way of that." Juliet took a sip of tea to quiet her roiling stomach. "I'm in the way of everything, showing up on their doorstep like I did, married to the principal in the firm, and standing to benefit when it was solely them before."

"Then you're in danger too."

Juliet nodded. "It may be that Euan or Lyrica was pressuring or misleading Havilah's lady's maid to poison her under the pretense of medicinal powders. I found a doctor's report of her symptoms in Leith's safe here, and they're synonymous with calomel. That maid—who happened to be attending Havilah alongside Minette's sister—died after Havilah's death. Minette said her sister, Édith, then ran away. She denies knowing where Édith is."

"Did Leith do nothing about his suspicions at the time?"

"He attempted to locate Édith as well, to no avail. The attending physician, an elderly man, has since passed away. Leith's legal defense is now aware of all this, but there are still missing pieces."

"Be chary, then, until the whole truth is known."

They drank their tea in silence until Juliet excused herself and said, "Please pray for me. I am especially skittish today."

A blast of wind buffeted the carriage as it made its way slowly from Virginia Street to the Buchanan firm. Juliet held on to her hat as she and Minette stepped out of the coach's damp confines and hurried through the door held open by a fellow merchant. Up the stairs they went to Leith's offices, past the clerks' chambers and rooms full of ledgers and an enormous vault. The scent of leather, paper, and ink hung about them, and today Juliet felt particularly unwelcome.

It was two o'clock. Leo Tate would join her at half past the hour. She was early, but she'd meant to be ahead of schedule.

Juliet closed the door behind her and went to a window while Minette sat in the chair outside in the corridor. Below on the street stood her guard. She was used to his movements by now, the slow swivel of his head as he surveyed everything coming and going, including everyone in and out of the bank and countinghouse.

Had she been wrong to confide in Loveday?

Bending her head, she shut out the rain-smeared panes

and prayed. Or tried to. Since Leith's arrest she'd barely been able to string together a coherent plea.

Father, forgive me for being so . . . tapsalteerie.

Should she not instead be thanking Him for a victory won, truth to prevail? She did just that, listening for Leo's familiar footfall, grateful for his intelligent insights and unswerving belief in Leith's innocence. What had the factor found out? Could it be the key to Leith's release?

She chafed as the minutes seemed to lengthen. A quarter till three. Leo was never late.

Something ominous stole over her as she looked out the window again. In his note, he'd said he would be coming from the bank. She scoured the street, but it was remarkably empty on so dreich a day. She crossed the room, opened the door, and shot a questioning glance at Minette, who raised her shoulders in answer.

And then the terrible truth dawned.

Leo Tate was not coming.

62

The only thing necessary for the triumph of evil is for good men to do nothing.

Unknown

At midnight in Leith's candlelit Virginia Street study stood John Tennant once again.

He spoke slowly as if wanting Juliet to remember details. "We now have one death accounted for. Havilah Buchanan's supposed suicide was in fact brought on by madness caused by calomel poisoning. There will be expert testimony at your husband's trial, based on the residue tested by a renowned physician admitted to Havilah's chambers at Virginia Street."

Juliet put a hand to her suddenly aching head. So many frightening details.

"We have also located the missing maid—rather, she came forward when she heard that your husband was being charged for a crime he did not commit."

Tennant turned as the door opened and Niall entered without knocking. Juliet felt another beat of alarm. What was her brother-in-law doing here at such a late hour? Was Loveday with him?

Nay, not Loveday, but a petite woman who resembled Minette. Édith?

Introductions confirmed it was she.

"Does Minette know of your return?" Juliet asked her in concern.

"Not yet, madame. I am being safeguarded until the trial. I have information that may help your husband. Afterward my sister and I shall be reunited."

Thanking her, Juliet looked to Niall.

"Loveday is safely asleep at our townhouse," he said quickly, the flickering light showing shadows beneath his eyes. "I came under cover of darkness to avoid notice. I'm not wanting to rouse Euan's suspicions. Given that, it might behoove us to work together instead of separately."

"So, you suspect him like I do." Though Juliet hadn't asked a question, he gave a nod. "And you're working with private investigators like Mr. Tennant here."

"I can't determine yet the depth of his and Cochrane's involvement, though embezzling is just one concern."

"Murder is another," she said without pause.

Niall looked more grim. "Leo Tate, you mean, not only Havilah."

"I feel certain he met his demise resisting them or uncovering more about their schemes. But I don't want the search for him ended till you know for sure."

Tennant nodded, relieving her somewhat, only to raise her concerns with his next utterance. "The trial is expected to turn ugly. There's concern, given Cochrane's unpopularity, that there may be mob activity, and it's thought you and the twins should move to the safety of Lamb Hill till the verdict is announced."

Lamb Hill, not Ardraigh Hall. She needn't ask why. The latter wasn't any safer than Virginia Street. "Will my sister go with us?"

"Of course," Niall said. "I'll have my coach sent round after breakfast if you and the children will be ready. Loveday already knows and is fully agreeable to the plan."

"What about Lyrica?" Her mind kept circling back to her sister-in-law with more urgency. How much did Lyrica know of Euan and Cochrane? She hated to think ill of her, but . . .

"She's being watched," Tennant said when Niall seemed to grapple for an answer. "She continues on at Buchanan Street with Euan and has no plans that we know of to leave Glasgow."

"Any news of Leith?" How she ached to know his state of mind, his surroundings. The strength of the case against him.

"He's been moved to an undisclosed location," Tennant said. "As for the coming trial, I believe the entire debacle may hang on the expert witness regarding the poison. There is a veritable army of character witnesses in the wings waiting to testify on your husband's behalf, the maid Édith foremost."

"But servants are rarely considered valid testimony," Niall said. "And Leith has his enemies, namely Cochrane's many associates. We've nae idea what they've prepared for the courtroom."

"Whatever it is, Mr. Buchanan's legal counsel has mounting evidence against Cochrane," Tennant told them.

Relief crossed Niall's tense features. "Which I hope pressures Cochrane to turn from accomplice to testifying against Euan so that he's granted protection from prosecution."

A sudden lull had Juliet saying, "I'll prepare to leave for Lamb Hill in the morning." She thanked them both, though their meeting set off another alarm inside her. She'd get little rest tonight.

Leith shifted on the bench beneath the barred window. An isolated cell gave a man plenty of time to think. Here there were no ledgers, no clerks or clocks, no frantic, profit-induced pace. Just a cold, damp corner that was only slightly preferable to a public hanging. Amazing how one's focus crystallized and sharpened when life's least extravagances fell away. He'd been allowed nothing but a Bible, which he'd not taken much interest in before.

Wilt thou set thine eyes upon that which is not? For riches certainly make themselves wings; they fly away as an eagle toward heaven.

He'd read entire passages to pass the time, Proverbs in particular. He held the Bible, yet it seemed to grab hold of him.

The way of the LORD *is strength to the upright, but destruction shall be to the workers of iniquity.*

And today of all days he was four and thirty. Celebrating a birthday in gaol was doubly sobering, especially when he'd spent his last at the Sarry Heid playing billiards and consuming so much whisky he could barely walk.

Now, a year later, the Leith Buchanan of before had lost a stone from humility and degradation, love and desperation, a potent combination. He felt the need to better explain himself, apologize to all who knew him, Juliet especially. She'd been here only two days ago, but it seemed two years. Ever since, his heart hung so heavily it seemed too large for his chest. Had she tried to see him again but been turned away? Was she well? Were the twins safe?

If he stood convicted of murder, would the authorities even allow Juliet a final visit before his execution? If he was exonerated, he had in mind to consider more pressing needs than imports and exports, starting with the tolbooth and other prisons. The continuous cries of the children kept with gaoled adults were like a sort of Hades on earth, as were the cries of all those charged for petty crimes with no counsel. He wanted to do things differently, build a life with a more lasting legacy than a street named after him and the colony he'd exploited.

Simply put, he would give all that he had to gain all that he did not.

A vibrant double rainbow arched over Lamb Hill. The twins exclaimed over it as the carriage turned off the main road onto the mansion's driveway. Juliet blinked, hardly believing her eyes.

"A double blessing!" Loveday leaned toward the window to better see the sight. "Such a promise then and now."

Gloriously hued, the rainbow arched like shimmery ribbons over a deep green meadow. Juliet's eyes filled at the sight, then she clenched her jaw lest she lose her wits altogether. Lack of sleep was taking a toll. Was Leith feeling the same?

"I like the blue part," Bella said, reminding Juliet she'd been teaching them their colors with some success.

Cole pointed to the pond they were passing. "Uncle Niall has white swans, not black ones."

"Black as burnt sausages," his sister replied nonsensically.

"Swans aren't burnt!" Cole grew more indignant. "Your hair is black too." He tugged hard at one of her ringlets as if to verify the accusation, and Bella burst into tears.

"Come now," Juliet admonished softly if sternly. "That's hardly the behavior of a gentleman, even a wee one."

"Sorry, Mam." He looked penitently at Juliet and then at Bella. "Sorry, Sister."

"I do believe a nap is in order," Loveday said. "But first a nursery tea."

In a half hour they'd washed and gathered at the low table assigned for the task. The windows of the makeshift nursery were open wide, and the sun seemed to have melted the rainbow, for it had vanished.

Juliet said grace and the twins practiced their best manners, passing a plate of crumpets and a small bowl of ripe summerhouse strawberries. Nurse, usually hovering, had been given a leave of absence to visit her ailing sister in Aberdeen, and Juliet wondered if she'd return, having been scandalized by the . . . well, Buchanan scandal. A young maidservant from the nearest village had taken her place, at least for the time being. Beatrice was as jolly as Nurse was dour.

Bella yawned and Cole followed suit, as if sleepiness could be as easily caught as a cold. They'd stopped asking "Where's Da?" to Juliet's mingled relief and dismay. Children had that rare ability to live solely in the present, and for the moment that consisted of mostly milk tea and sugared pastries.

Beatrice soon entered, smiling. She whisked away the dishes and then the twins shortly thereafter while Loveday and Juliet went downstairs.

"I suppose we should keep indoors. No walking about in the garden or riding out." Loveday went to a window. "Your new guard is certainly vigilant. And elusive. I didn't even notice him following us on the drive from Glasgow."

"He's a fine horseman." Juliet joined her at the glass. "And one of Edinburgh's best private investigators."

"Ah, those enigmatic men who court crime."

Juliet sighed. "You make it sound more romantic than nefarious."

Loveday turned away from the window. "What did Tennant do with your first guard?"

"Returned him to the investigation regarding Leo Tate."

"I pray Mr. Tate reappears unharmed. You lost quite an ally, and the court an expert witness. But we mustn't lose hope. I find meaning in the double rainbow today, a special significance."

Hope? Juliet had forgotten what it felt to be hopeful. "For some time now it seems I've been fighting the darkness . . . and the darkness is winning."

"What do you mean?"

"From the first I sensed something awry with Euan. Hard as marble, he reminded me of Leith in his darker moments. Niall is entirely different. I see Leith and Euan as similar, their many choices hardening or softening them, decision by decision, depending on which has the upper hand. A contest between good and evil, if you will."

"And Euan had chosen the darkness. A world of selfishness and greed and far more."

Juliet put a hand to her head unwittingly. How had it all come to this? When a brother turned against a brother—or, in this case, two brothers. It had all the makings of a Shakespearean tragedy. Or at least a sonnet.

For I have sworn thee fair and thought thee bright, who art as black as hell, as dark as night.

63

Fill your paper with the breathings of your heart.

William Wordsworth

The next day Juliet awoke in one of Lamb Hill's bed-chambers, her first thought always of Leith.

She slipped from the bed to her knees, praying till she heard the house waking around her. Forcing herself to have tea and toast, she began another letter to Aunt Damarus, trying to be optimistic and inviting her to visit them if there wasn't to be a war. *That* was truly a stretch. Since Leith's detention, war with the colonies had been the farthest thing from her mind, even if it was on everyone else's.

After donning a simple linen dress, she joined Loveday and the twins in the summerhouse to check the progress of the pineapples and melons, then her sister showed her the still-room. Of painted white brick, the chamber boasted enormous windows and more cupboards than one could count, a lovely hearth at one end large enough to stand inside of, and even an oven. Juliet was taken aback by the beauty of so simple a space.

Loveday looked right at home. "Niall has been calling me

his stillroom queen, and I plan to be quite happy here, filling the shelves with jams and jellies, vinegars, spices and herbs, perfumes and cosmetics, and the like."

"What's that?" Juliet asked, pointing to a contraption that the twins were examining in a corner.

"An ancient seventeenth-century device to distill cordial waters. I cannot wait to try it." Loveday began bustling about.

Juliet's focus narrowed to the medicinal cupboard that rivaled Williamsburg's apothecary. "I spy calomel, which returns me to our prior conversation and the ongoing investigation."

"I've done a little digging since then." Loveday stopped her bustling. "Alchemists say 'tis a form of mercury. A white powder."

A sick sensation formed in the pit of Juliet's stomach. What was calomel doing at Lamb Hill?

"'Tis used sparingly, as it's known to cause tremors and severe nervous symptoms, though it is often found in Scottish cupboards."

Their eyes met in mutual concern, then Loveday passed to a window. "Who can that be that I hear on the drive? Father? Why don't you go meet him, as he might bring news."

Leaving the stillroom, Juliet saw Father arrive without Zipporah, who was nursing a cold.

"I'm feeling my age today," he said. "I had the coachman deliver me to Ardraigh Hall instead of Lamb Hill, quite forgetting where you are."

"I'm sorry, Father." They moved into the house and the smallest drawing room. "This travesty is taking a toll on everyone."

"Don't be sorry, Daughter. None of it is your fault." He reached inside his weskit and withdrew a letter.

From Leith? Juliet almost seized it in her joy, then pressed it to her bodice as if it could steady her rolling emotions.

"Shall I give you a few moments alone?"

"No, I don't want you to tarry, as Zipporah might need you."

"Tarry I must, and gladly." He took a seat in a chair Leith preferred. "While you read privately, I'll just have a bit of quiet and peach brandy."

"'Tis there in the decanter on the end table." She sat in the twin chair beside him, reminded of the times she and Leith had done the same, and broke the seal with some surprise. Somehow he'd been given the tools to pen her a few words.

My beloved Juliet,

So unlike Leith. Yet she had never had a letter from him, so how was she to know his style? Her heart, so sore, was assuaged somewhat.

I ken not how much longer we are to be separated, though I pray continually for our reunion. If anything good can come from our situation, it is this—being removed from myself, as it were, and all the temporal routines and obligations that bound me, has caused me to regard any time left to me, to us, as altered. My former life with all its trappings seems naught but dross. Little glitters or has value but you, the children, a life dedicated to what matters eternally. I apologize for being insufferable and behaving badly ofttimes.

I miss you more than words can say. My heart is yours, has been yours since the moment we met. Nothing can alter that, not separation nor silence nor even death.

You are my first waking thought and my last, and in all the hours between. You alone are keeping hope alive in me. You and God Himself

The letter left off abruptly and she felt the wrench of it, held captive midsentence by what he'd been about to say. Someone had come in, likely, and told him to stop. Pondering what might have happened since he wrote it, she folded the paper and slipped it into her pocket to peruse again later.

The twins' laughter carried from the walled garden where they were walking about with Beatrice. The sound buoyed Juliet like a drowning soul thrown a rope. The double rainbow, the twins, Leith's letter. All good things that kept her from unraveling completely.

Father poured himself another brandy. "The trial has now begun, and though we know nothing of what's happening inside those legal chambers, we will hope for the best . . . while preparing for the worst."

The worst. Juliet laced her hands together in her lap. "What preparations do you have in mind?"

"Let's start with the trial. Tennant has informed me of how matters stand. I'm stunned by the family perfidy, but it seems increasingly clear Euan is complicit. If he and Cochrane somehow manage to have Leith convicted, then we need you to leave Glasgow, as his estate will be contested, including the custody of Bella and Cole."

"Oh, Father. I couldn't bear it if Euan took the twins. I hope Loveday and Niall fight for them if it comes to that, if Leith and I cannot have them—"

"They are prepared to fight, aye. But first they will fight for your rights, and that Leith's will, which named you their guardian on your shipboard journey here, be upheld."

"Go on."

"Leith's legal counsel believes they have enough evidence to expose Euan and Cochrane as accomplices guilty of murder, fraud, embezzlement, and whatnot. The list is long."

"At least Niall is innocent of all this."

"Thank heaven for that. The guilty parties will likely go to trial," Father continued grimly. "If convicted, they face death or transportation."

"Transportation?"

"To the Caribbean is my guess. But I'm here to talk about you primarily, not them."

Mind awhirl, she was trying to keep up with all the repercussions and possibilities. Leith could go free. Leith could be transported to somewhere other than the colonies, once the favored destination for convicts. Or Leith could hang. On the other hand, Euan and Cochrane faced all of the same. She still knew nothing of Lyrica's involvement or the lack of it.

Another headache beat at her temples. "'Tis terribly complex."

"Should the worst happen and Leith is convicted, I advocate your coming immediately to Bath. Niall and Loveday will remain here, of course, for the time being, depending on what happens next."

Bath. Without Leith, Bath was an empty shell of a place. Would she spend the rest of her life missing him? Grieving him? Mourning the life they would have had with the twins?

"The tolbooth chaplain is the one who conveyed Leith's letter to me to give to you. If you'd like to pen a response, I will carry it back to him in hopes Leith will have it."

"Of course." She went to a writing desk along one damask-clad wall. Her hands fairly shook, and she willed her headache away.

Just then, Loveday swept in with a medicinal toddy. "I know that look," she said, setting the hot beverage down atop the desk. "You've had few of your spells since coming to Scotland, so 'tis especially apparent to me here."

Juliet thanked her, then took out ink, sand, and a newly sharpened quill. For a moment she froze as she stared down at the pristine paper. She exchanged her pen for a bracing sip of the toddy as Loveday took her seat beside Father and they conversed quietly by the fire.

Dearest husband,

I did not think it possible that I could love you more in absence, but I do. Each day without you seems a life-time, though I continue to hope and pray the door of that cell will swing open and you will take me in your arms again. Not once have I ever doubted you. The grievous wrong done you will come to light. 'Tis only a matter of time. God Almighty will make a way. Do not worry for a moment about me or our children. They are a consolation and joy to me without you, though bittersweet. More and more I see you in their changing faces, their moods, even the tone of their voices. They do you proud, and I am beyond blessed to be their mam.

We shall all be reunited. Think not of any future other than beautiful, restorative Bath. We shall have the honeymoon till now denied us. See you soon, my heart.

Your ever loving
wife, J

She leaned closer, a tear spattering the paper where she'd signed her name. The drop gave an extra flourish to the *J*. After drying the ink with sand, she affixed the indigo seal with her intaglio ring and wax from a lit candle.

She had sold Royal Vale to Nathaniel Ravenal, who'd manumitted the Africans. She was no longer an indigo heiress. She was Leith Buchanan's wife, and her future had never been more uncertain.

64

They that know no evil will suspect none.

Ben Jonson

The verdict was imminent, Tennant's note read. Juliet should return to Glasgow.

So, the hour had come. Quickly, she made ready. She wanted to be near Leith no matter what. Done with teetering between hope and trepidation, she would behave with strength and honor, as Proverbs said, and rejoice in time to come.

"Let me fetch Miss Loveday from the stillroom to go with you," Rilla said in concern.

"Nay. She's needed here." Juliet stood in Lamb Hill's foyer as Minette brought her cape. "I want her to be near the twins when they awaken from their nap. They love her company, and I would fret otherwise, especially since Bella is recovering from a fever. I'll send word as soon as I can from Virginia Street as to what's transpired with Mr. Buchanan."

"Your guard goes with you, I reckon." Rilla looked toward the front door a footman was opening, revealing a closed carriage being brought round the circular forecourt. "My prayers go with you too."

After a hasty goodbye, Minette followed Juliet outside, the guard tipping his hat to them as he waited on horseback behind the coach. Today there was no rainbow above Lamb Hill. A downpour turned the dusty driveway a deep chocolate brown as they rattled down it, shutters closed against the damp spring air. Minette looked so tense, so downcast, that Juliet was tempted to tell her Édith had been found. But she herself knew better, and Tennant had said the details would be revealed at the trial and not before.

"I've been praying for a maiden assize, madame," Minette said quietly.

"A maiden assize? I've not heard that term before."

"Oui, it is when the sheriff presents the presiding judge with a pair of white gloves, a sign of purity, that announces there is no death sentence."

How symbolic, even beautiful, a gesture. For a moment dread fought its way forward again at the mention of death, but the image of the gloves, a flawless white, righted her. Darkness and light. She still felt in the midst of a battle between good and evil. Which would prevail?

Thankful they were not far from Glasgow, Juliet sat back and took out her watch on its coral chain, a gift from Zipporah, to check the time. Half past ten.

When the coach rolled to a lumbering halt just shy of the city, she heard a rapid exchange of voices. Lyrica?

Instantly wary, Juliet leaned forward to raise the window shade and saw her sister-in-law's coach pull alongside theirs. When their door opened and Lyrica stepped inside, drawing it shut behind her, Juliet was so startled she dropped her watch. Taking a seat beside Minette, Lyrica stared red-eyed at Juliet, her tearstained face sending a warning as the coach lurched forward.

"I've come to tell you the terrible news." She took a vial of smelling salts from her reticule with gloved hands and offered it to Juliet. "Half an hour ago the jury found Leith guilty of murder."

Minette gave a hoarse cry. *Guilty* hung in the pungent air. Juliet ignored the offered vial, her whole world shrinking to a blinding point of pain she'd never known. As she grappled for her bearings, Minette seemed to withdraw like a snail coiled into its shell.

"The penalty is death." Lyrica's voice sounded odd, almost relieved, like a false note in a piece of music. "His execution is on the morrow."

With a sudden move, Juliet knocked on the coach roof to halt the driver, but the vehicle swung toward the Broomielaw, not Virginia Street. Leaning forward, Lyrica brought the shutter down hard, then drew a penknife from her reticule. She opened it, the mother-of-pearl haft agleam in the low light.

"Be cooperative lest you suffer an unfortunate slashing and ruin your lovely brocaded silk." She waved the knife at Minette. "Over there by your mistress so I can keep a better eye on the both of you."

Minette all but lunged toward Juliet, coming down hard on the upholstered seat in a flurry of petticoats. Their shared fear filled the coach as matters became clear. Lyrica was in league with her husband and Cochrane. But to what extent— and how far was she willing to go?

"Where is my guard?" Juliet pushed the words past her breathlessness, certain that he, too, had been waylaid en route.

A triumphant smile surfaced. "He took a wee detour."

They were along the waterfront now, the tang of tar and fish and salt water potent. Another turn and they came to an abrupt stop. The coach door opened, and she and Minette found themselves in a darkened tobacco warehouse. Juliet knew that sweet, earthy scent anywhere, and with it came a wash of memories.

Several men surrounded them, all strangers, as Lyrica disappeared through a side door. To struggle was futile, but Juliet still had a voice. "We are being held against our will and must be taken to Virginia Street—"

"We've orders to do otherwise," a thickset man said as he hurried them toward the dock. His fellows, all sailors, formed a ring around them as if to keep them from running.

The gangplank stretching ahead of them led to the *Black Prince*, Euan's pride. The irony was not lost on Juliet. Minette linked arms with her as they were hustled up the wooden walkway to deck. Juliet took a last look at Glasgow over her shoulder before they were taken below, out of sight. The dock was empty. Lyrica had obviously played her part and abandoned them.

They were shoved into a small, shadowed cabin. Juliet pushed hard against the door in a final protest, but it thudded shut, catching her lace sleeve in the process, before the door was locked. She faced Minette, who was crying now, collapsed atop the floor in a small heap. Since there were no chairs, only twin hammocks, Juliet sank down beside her and put her arms around her, their bent heads pressed together.

Lord, what are we to do?

If only she'd not left Lamb Hill. It had seemed insignificant yet in hindsight proved disastrous. Had Tennant sent the note for her to come to Glasgow? Or had Euan and Lyrica been behind that too?

Minette raised her head. "What will become of us?"

Juliet took a handkerchief from her pocket and pressed it into Minette's trembling hand. Shock scattered her thoughts, and she took a breath, groping for sensibility instead of the hovering hysteria. "I don't know where this ship is bound, but it could be worse."

We might have been murdered like Havilah . . . Leo.

"I'm afraid." Minette dried her tears with the handkerchief. "But at least we are together, no?"

For now. Who knew what the coming hours would bring? "I'm so sorry, Minette. 'Tis me they're wanting to do away with. You're just caught in the crosshairs."

"From the moment I met her I never cared for Madame Buchanan or her husband." Minette shuddered and looked at Juliet. "Do you believe what was said about Mr. Buchanan being found guilty?"

Did she? The weight on Juliet's heart failed to ease. Might it have been a lie? A part of the ruse? "We shall find out in time. The truth will come to light."

Exhaustion pressed down on her as if she'd run clear from Lamb Hill to Glasgow. She got up with difficulty, passed to the porthole, and looked out over the shipping lanes, wishing she faced the labyrinth of piers and docks instead. Here her cries for help would bounce across the water like a skimmed pebble. Gulls careened overhead, their cries shrill.

She crossed to the door if only to confirm it was still locked. Throat parched, she looked to a hammock, reminded of Leith's on the *Glasgow Lass*. Oh, to return to that time, almost hallowed in hindsight, when their future was before them, unmarred and bright.

65

To die is landing on some distant shore.

John Dryden

The shudder of the ship as it left its moorings was but one small alarm in a series of them. Juliet had lost track of the hours. Addled, she missed her watch. Where had she mislaid it? Her only clue to the time was the ebbing light fading from the porthole and Minette's soft snores in a hammock. Had it been two days? Three?

Throat sore, Juliet drank deeply from the pitcher of water that had been provided for them alongside a platter of moldy cheese, dry bannocks, and wizened apples. At least their hunger and thirst were sated if nothing else. She'd told the cabin boy to summon the captain, with scant confidence her message would even be relayed. So far he'd not appeared. And now, upon open water, what did it matter?

As she thought it, the rattle of the lock alerted her, though it didn't awaken the exhausted Minette. Summoning every shred of her dwindling strength and dignity, Juliet faced the doorway, bracing herself for she knew not what.

A sailor gave a little bow, his pockmarked face a pit of scars. "Permission to come on deck is granted, ma'am."

She dreaded the encounter, though fresh air would do her good. She followed him, a gust of wind tearing at her skirts. She'd entirely forgotten her hat.

The captain was at the wheel, his lined face testament to a lifetime at sea. "Mrs. Buchanan" was his gruff greeting, slightly slurred by the rum she smelled.

"Captain, you are aware that by transporting me, this is naught but a convict ship."

"Since yer husband is nae longer at liberty to manage matters, I take my orders from Mr. Euan Buchanan and nae other, ma'am."

"Euan Buchanan is a murderer and a thief." She all but spat the words. "Best follow your conscience—"

"My conscience? Seared beyond recovery, some say. As for my orders, I'm to sail this vessel to the Caribbean. With colonial American ports closed, it's become the primary destination."

"Where in the Caribbean?" She would keep him talking if she could, if only to lessen this dire feeling of being in the dark.

"Saint-Domingue, barring pirates or privateers or heavy weather."

"Why?"

"The Buchanans have business there." He bellowed an order, clearly done with their conversation.

That terrible lightheadedness was overtaking her again. She leaned into the ship's rail, trying to stay atop the crushing panic that seemed like the ocean's depth and breadth. The Caribbean was unfathomably distant, at least from the North Atlantic. Vasanti Hall in Jamaica had been sold by Father not long ago. She wanted nothing to do with going there. But if she must, then what? She had no funds to secure passage on a ship to the colonies. She couldn't even make her way to Aunt Damarus in Philadelphia.

Out of the corner of her eye she spied a hunched figure seated below the main mast. On his ankles were irons. Leo Tate? His face was battered, a medley of purplish-black bruises. His usual pristine garments were filthy. But he was alive, at least.

"Mr. Tate." She approached him, aware of several sailors' scrutiny.

He raised his head. Had he been dozing? "Mrs. Buchanan."

"I-I don't know what to say."

"Aye, ma'am. A bloody bad business, to be blunt."

"I believed you to be dead."

"Death is just what I've been threatened with if I ever set foot on Scottish soil again."

They looked at each other, a dozen different emotions passing between them. She wanted to bathe his face, apply some of Loveday's remedies. Words failed her and apparently him too, for he lowered his head again as if too weary to hold it up.

Shaking with rage, she returned to the wheel. "For God's sake, Captain, relieve that man of his irons and have the ship's surgeon tend to his injuries, or let me do it myself."

"Tate? I've threatened to throw him overboard should he cause me any more trouble." He eyed her with an especially venomous look. "Now finish yer airing and go below lest I vow to do the same with ye."

She stood still in defiance half a minute longer before turning away from him. Scotland's shores were growing dimmer in the dying light.

What was happening with Leith? The twins? By now

Father might have realized her absence. But he could hardly come after her. And Loveday . . . her dear sister would take it the hardest, perhaps. They'd rarely been separated. Add to that the sudden mystery of her disappearance and the situation was nearly unendurable.

"Never have I been aboard a ship, and it is dreadful." Minette stared at Juliet, the light of the hanging lantern giving her pale face a ghostly aspect. "A floating gaol."

"Being sick makes it far worse," Juliet said softly, giving her a drink of mint water begged from the ship's surgeon. "Hold tight to the possibility of seeing your sister again. Édith wanted nothing more than to be reunited with you after the trial."

But even this reminder failed to cheer Minette. Though the hammocks relieved some of the ship's tossing, the combined odor of the chamber pot and last night's supper lent to their queasiness. The hours lengthened interminably, peppered with memories of deep feather beds, cozy coal fires, and fine porcelain teacups ready at a moment's notice. But it was the faces of those Juliet loved who haunted her most. Leith. Bella and Cole. Loveday and Father. Lost to her. All lost. And yet what had Mama said?

What we once loved can never be lost to us—it is ours forever.

When dawn limned the porthole, Juliet stood watch. Her whole world had flipped and become an open ocean, a vast misery of gray swells and sky. But anguished as she was, Leith stayed uppermost in her thoughts. She reached into her pocket and withdrew his letter. If she could not have him, she had his words, penned in his own hand from his heart.

*My heart is yours, has been yours since the moment
we met. Nothing can alter that, not separation nor silence nor even death.*

She had memorized every word, could recite it like a child
at prayer. It brought small solace as the unknown ate at her,
demanding answers. If Lyrica's news was true, Leith had by
now been executed.

Dear Lord, help me to bear it.

She'd had but a few months of him. Not nearly enough
when she'd taken her vows "till death do us part." She'd
envisioned them growing old together with children then
grandchildren at the knee. She'd wanted to have children
with him—that quiverful of arrows Scripture spoke of. To
celebrate their union and find fulfillment in each other and
the home they made.

Minette moaned and turned over in her hammock. Ready
to abandon the porthole, Juliet paused at a flash of movement. Riding the silvered horizon was a ship bearing straight
for them. Three-masted, it cut through the white-capped
waves with the authority of a British warship. An armed
merchantman? She guessed twenty guns. The cut of its jib
held her captive. Soon it would be within hailing distance.

Her heart began to race as she saw its colors. The British
union flag?

In response, the *Black Prince* attempted to outrun the
merchantman's approach, but being heavily laden, it lagged.
After maneuvering within range, the merchantman fired a
shot to leeward, signifying friendly intent.

"What is this fracas I hear?" Minette was beside her now,
sharing her cramped view, fright scoring her face as she surveyed the guns. "Do they not know we might explode with
all this French powder in the hold?"

"See their colors?" Juliet's gaze ran up the main masthead. "They are not the enemy."

A bone-jarring shot raked their bow and called her a liar.

"Mon Dieu!" Minette sank to the floor and clutched Juliet's skirts as if to bring her down too.

Were the British colors false? The ruse was common enough, enabling the enemy to board and rob vessels.

Rattled yet transfixed, Juliet saw the action play out through the porthole as if watching a stage play from a theater box. Orders were shouted and the merchantman's crew gained the *Black Prince*'s deck. Privateers? Was their aim the coveted gunpowder?

She tried to shout their plight through the porthole, but the rising wind flung her attempt away. In moments, hasty footsteps sounded in the companionway. Was someone breaking the lock? Juliet turned toward the clamor as the door flew open so hard it collided with the cabin wall.

There, filling the doorframe, stood Leith.

66

Or bid me love, and I will give
A loving heart to thee.
                    Robert Herrick

Juliet sagged against the wall when what she wanted was to run to Leith. All the breath went out of her at his appearance. She felt lightning struck, incapable of moving. Every emotion she'd locked inside since his arrest burst open like a storm cloud. He was beside her in an instant, his own relief palpable as his arms went round her.

"You're unhurt?" He looked down at her in alarm as she wept with relief. "Has anything been done to you?"

She shook her head. All she wanted was a long look at him. *Not guilty. Not executed.* Just a trifle wan and a stone or so lighter. But still her vital, remarkably braw husband.

"You're free?" The hopeful question nearly choked her.

His eyes held hers, once ice blue but now filled with a strange, warm light. "Aye, freer than I've ever been."

"Free to go home? To be with me—the children?"

"Aye, all of it. Who told you otherwise? Lyrica?"

She nodded. The coach ride to the docks seemed night-marish in hindsight. "She said you'd been found guilty and would be executed. Minette and I——" She looked over her shoulder and saw the maid had vanished. "We were taken to a tobacco warehouse and made to board this ship. Leo Tate is being held too." He held her tighter as the words spilled out. "But all that matters right now is that you're here—safe—and well."

"I'll tell you the rest once we're safely on my ship." His arm still around her, he led her out of the cramped cabin and up the stairs to the quarterdeck.

Grappling hooks and lines kept the two vessels side by side. The *Black Prince*'s irascible captain and crew were knotted together under guard in the stern. It took consider-able humility for Juliet not to send them a triumphant glance.

With Leith's help, she jumped from the *Black Prince*'s gunwale to the other deck, Minette following behind her on Leo Tate's arm. As they prepared to resume sailing, Leith led her below to another cabin where they had complete privacy.

She sat in the chair he pulled out for her, exhaustion min-gling with welling joy, as he poured her a glass of ratafia. He poured himself the same as the ship's sudden motion told her they would soon be underway.

He pulled up a chair beside her, and they faced the stern windows, his fingers encircling hers. For a few minutes they said nothing, just sat in stunned, joyous silence.

"Tell me everything," he finally said.

"You go first. I want to know without a doubt you're truly free." She reached out and smoothed a strand of his hair that had slipped from his silk queue. He was as wrinkled as she was, his fine garments suggesting they'd been worn for more than a day.

"Where do I begin?" He took another drink, grimacing.

396

"The witnesses on my behalf won the day, primarily the doctor giving evidence of calomel."

"Havilah was poisoned, then. There's no doubt?"

"The missing maid—Minette's sister—confirmed it. Havilah was given calomel powders to drink at bedtime. Édith fled soon after Havilah's death because Lyrica threatened her to say nothing. She feared she'd end up like the other maid, Mary, who died of mysterious causes."

"Meaning Lyrica and Euan might have killed her too." Juliet thought of the web of deceit and turmoil that had ensued. "I've not said it before, but I'm especially heartbroken about Havilah. She was truly the victim here. If not for the evil that came against her, she might have kept a sound mind and known the joys of family life."

"If I had been more present I could have helped her. Could have prevented it."

"You didn't realize what was happening till it was too late."

"And now I'll live with that regret for the rest of my life." He paused as emotion got the better of him. "I kept her bedchamber unchanged after her death because I didn't think the matter was finished. I suspected someone meant her ill. Now I can let go of the past, her belongings with it."

"At least the truth is now known, Leith, however harsh."

He looked at her, his expression clouded yet relieved. "The jury found me not guilty to a man. The sheriff even presented a pair of white gloves declaring my innocence. There was enough evidence to charge both Cochrane and Euan at the last. They're now in custody awaiting trial, along with Lyrica."

"So you were freed first, then found me gone."

"I was on my way to Virginia Street when I passed and then halted Lyrica's coach. She seemed agitated to see me, and when I boarded, I found she had your watch." He reached into his weskit and withdrew the coral chain and timepiece. "At that, I nearly lost all reason. She denied having been with you, then admitted you dropped your watch and your coach was at the waterfront. I forced the remaining truth from her by driving her straight to the tolbooth and handing her over to the magistrates. She confessed everything, or so she said."

"Intercepting our coach from Lamb Hill, you mean, and then all the rest."

"Aye, all the rest. An ill-scrappit affair if there ever was one. I felt murderous toward Euan and Cochrane then Lyrica. They thought my conviction was certain and so you were told the same."

The steady cadence of his voice reassured her as all the pieces of this macabre puzzle fell into place.

"Euan arranged for you to be put on board the *Black Prince* as he'd done with Leo Tate. Your guard was also put in the hold. Euan used Lyrica to lure you to Glasgow by sending a faux note supposedly written by Tennant. They wanted to declare that you had abandoned me and left the country. The war would have prevented your return, or so they thought. With the both of us out of the way, Euan had fuller rein of the Buchanan firm, with Cochrane behind the scenes embezzling for the both of them as before. They likely felt their plan so seamless not even Niall would be the wiser."

"Niall had investigators working night and day on your behalf. He suspected Euan from the first, though we remained unsure of Lyrica's involvement."

He started to speak but stopped, the anguish in his face so unlike his usual stoicism it struck her hard as a fist. To be betrayed by a brother. A brother's wife. She took his hand in silent support.

He continued with difficulty. "Since they have nae heirs,

Euan and Lyrica also wanted custody of Bella and Cole. My release turned their plans on end and gave me time to come after you. I sent word to your father of my pursuit and to simply stay put and pray."

Prayer. Had it been the most powerful part of it all? "I've lost count of how long we've been at sea. Long enough for me to despair of you ever overtaking us."

"If not for the fastest ship in our fleet—this armed merchantman normally bound for the colonies but lying at anchor in Port Glasgow—I may have missed you altogether."

"'Tis nothing short of miraculous."

"Navigation and weather were also in our favor. We're not far off the west coast of Ireland or it might have been a different tale."

"What will be done with the captain and crew?"

"For now, they're chained in the *Woodlark*'s hold. Half our crew will return the *Black Prince* to Glasgow while we sail south."

"South?"

The sudden light in his eyes lent to his smile. "To Bath."

"Oh, Leith . . ." Her disbelief doubled. She was in no frame of mind to return to Glasgow and its taint anytime soon. Nor was he, it seemed.

He reached for her, pulling her from the chair onto his knee. "Once there, we'll send word for your family to join us. That will give us plenty of time to be alone first."

"I promise not to miss the twins too much."

"They'll be safe and sound till our return."

"And when shall we return?"

"Mayhap never. 'We adore springs of hot water as divine.'"

"You quote Seneca."

"One of the few philosophers I admire." He held her

closer, her head resting upon his shoulder. "We should see England soon, given favorable winds and weather. Both of us are in need of a respite."

"And a long bath," she teased. She hated her disheveled state, but at least she was alive and well and in his arms again. "I feel as if we've run away—or are eloping—without a stitch of clothing except what we're wearing and scant else."

"We'll soon see Bristol Harbor and rectify that."

She sat up again, her hands clutching his wrinkled waistcoat. "It all seems like a dream. I'm half afraid to let go of you lest I return to the nightmare of before."

"I'm nae dream, Juliet. Let me assure you of that."

He kissed her, the touch of his lips unfamiliar after so much time apart. It recalled his first attempt, that sweet, almost holy moment when they'd taken a step toward each other instead of another step back.

EPILOGUE

I ask you to pass through life at my side—to be my second
self, and best earthly companion.

Charlotte Brontë

BATH, ENGLAND

In the wide, curving row of elegant Palladian architec-
ture, the Buchanan townhouse was number 2. Overhead the patter of servants' feet in the attic reminded
Juliet of Cole and Bella. She stood in the formal withdrawing
room with its blue damask walls and gilded mirrors, so new
that a drift of sawdust scented the air. Awed, she looked out
a tall window at the most spectacular Bath sunset yet as it
broke over the chamber in soft coral waves. A benediction
on another blessed day.

What *hadn't* she and Leith done here in England?

They'd gone to the Pump Rooms and taken the waters.
Promenaded in the blossoming parks. Stood with mouths
agape in the grand abbey with its rainbow-hued stained glass,
where the voices of a convent of medieval women once reached
the vaulted ceiling in worship. Juliet was especially taken with
the abbey's west front with its stone ladder of angels.

Leith's practicality amused her. "Since they're winged, why rely on a ladder?"

"Have you not read of Jacob's ladder in Genesis?" she'd teased. "Since they're very old angels, perhaps they're simply tired or their wings are tarnished."

She pondered it now as the sun sank lower, till it was nearly extinguished like candle flame. The closing of the door behind her made her smile. Leith approached, encircling her with his arms so they faced forward and admired the remaining view.

"We should probably walk to the river in the last of the light," he said.

"The river—at this hour?"

"Nothing like seeing Bath by moonlight from the Avon."

"Romantic. Will you navigate?"

"Aye, though I can't promise smooth sailing with you in my sights."

"You've given me the honeymoon of my dreams." *And made me nearly forget the disaster in Glasgow.* She sighed as he kissed the hollow of her shoulder. "Just when I think there's nothing left to delight in, you find a way."

"And I'll keep trying till the end of my days."

"So you've forgiven me for thinking you a mere merchant and trying to matchmake you with my sister."

"I forgive you everything."

"How blessed we are to have come to this. I still can't quite believe that I'm yours and you're mine." She turned round again to face him, struck by the undisguised emotion in his eyes. "And a moonlit ride on the Avon followed by more hot chocolate and reading by the fire with you is heaven on earth."

AUTHOR'S NOTE

Stories set in Scotland have great appeal to me for many reasons, one of them being my ancestry. When I visited Glasgow prior to writing this novel, I found that a few street names of the foremost Georgian-era merchants still exist, but few buildings. One exception is the Cunninghame Mansion, now an art museum. The statue of King William III, Prince of Orange (King Billy, as the Scots called him), where wealthy merchants used to gather, still stands tall but has been moved around the city. Reminders of the once powerful tobacco lords of Scotland have all but vanished. Their legacy is understandably tarnished today.

Researching these shrewd, ruthless businessmen led to some eye-opening discoveries. During the height of their trading prowess, some Glaswegian merchants were known to be among the wealthiest men in all Europe. Loveday Catesby's fictional dowry, financed by the Buchanans, is roughly the equivalent of half a million dollars today. The staggering bedding plant list referred to in the novel mirrors an actual garden order for a British estate during that time period. Likewise, the menu for the christening that Juliet is shown by the servants at the Virginia Street mansion also reflects the time period. Needless to say, there's much about these men and their families that make a compelling novel, given all their color and controversy.

Much inspiration came from the life of Eliza Lucas Pinckney, a very remarkable eighteenth-century woman. Because of her, South Carolina became the leader in indigo production during that time period. Virginia grew indigo but with limited success. It was *the* colonial color back then, though there were many shades of blue, including the divinely named celestial blue. Several excellent biographies of Eliza Lucas Pinckney exist and are highly recommended, including *Eliza Lucas Pinckney: An Independent Woman in the Age of Revolution*, *The Letterbook of Eliza Lucas Pinckney, 1739–1762*, and *Eliza Lucas Pinckney: Colonial Plantation Manager and the Mother of American Patriots*.

I had many other wonderful sources, among them the *Diary of Colonel Landon Carter of Sabine Hall* and *Glasgow and the Tobacco Lords* in the Then and There series by Norman Nichol. The *Journal of Nicholas Cresswell, 1774–1777* was also enlightening.

Viewing the American Revolution's beginnings from both the British and American perspective was quite eye-opening. I had studied the revolution closely while in school in England years ago but had forgotten how inflammatory it became for all involved.

Especially satisfying was writing about the great-great-granddaughters of the characters in a prior novel, *Tidewater Bride*. Selah Hopewell and Alexander Renick would have been proud of their female descendants, I think. Though it was hard for me even fictionally to have them part with their ancestral home of Royal Vale (formerly Rose-n-Vale), that was true to history too. Many colonists lost a great deal when they remained loyal to King George III or returned to Britain.

The abolitionist movement was very much in play before and during the American Revolution. Many Quakers (viewed as radicals by some) and free Blacks in the colonies worked tirelessly and courageously and at great personal risk to end slavery. Benjamin Franklin actually became the figurehead for the Pennsylvania Abolition Society, one of the first antislavery organizations. Women played an integral though often hidden role in assisting slaves to freedom. Charlotte Catesby, Aunt Damarus, Loveday, and Juliet are a fictional tribute to them.

Heartfelt thanks to reader friend Kati Mills for helping me come up with a place name for Leith Buchanan's country house. Originally I'd called it Lanark Walk but Ardraigh Hall won out, Ardraigh being a place name near Glasgow. My inspiration for the country residence is the very real and recently restored Georgian gem, Dumfries House.

Last but certainly not least, a shout-out to the real Hobbes who resides in North Carolina with his mistress, Laura Harkness. The feline inspiration behind Loveday's beloved cat is much appreciated!

I invite you to author T. Elizabeth Renich's and my private Facebook group, Gorgeous Georgians, to revisit the Georgian era on both sides of the Atlantic and celebrate the facts and the fiction that honor and help keep that fascinating history alive.

ACKNOWLEDGMENTS

The world of a book, after all, is a private conversation between author and reader. Acknowledgments pages break that spell by bringing in the outside world. When agents and managers start to appear in acknowledgments, things get even weirder: here comes the world of commerce and deal-making, crashing the story party.

That excerpt from *Publishers Weekly* has given me second thoughts about adding anything to the end of a novel, even an author note. "A private conversation between author and reader" is something magical that I want to honor. I'm doubly skittish because acknowledgments fail to recognize everyone involved in the making of a book. But I remain very grateful.

Janet Grant, my remarkable agent at Books & Such. I wouldn't have stayed the course without your guidance and expertise.

The entire Revell team, beginning with Andrea Doering who opened the door to publishing years ago, Rachel McRae who is so good at knowing what makes historical fiction tick,

Jessica English—the grammar queen, Karen Steele who puts books in the most extraordinary places, Brianne Dekker who is so savvy about all that she does, the sales and marketing team who go above and beyond, and Baker Book House, which is a magical literary place for so many.

My dear friend and proofreader, Shelli Littleton, for the extra shine she gives words.

Laura Klynstra, whose stunning designs grace the *New York Times* lists. Thank you for creating this cover. You captured the essence of this indigo novel right down to the eighteenth-century pearls and ring.

Randy, my patron of the arts, who didn't even know I wrote anything when I married him and didn't balk once he did.

To readers who happen to enjoy my books and the eternal God who gifts us with anything good and edifying to share. I never take that for granted.

Thank you.

Laura Frantz is a two-time Christy Award winner and the ECPA bestselling author of sixteen novels, including *An Uncommon Woman*, *Tidewater Bride*, *A Bound Heart*, *A Heart Adrift*, *The Rose and the Thistle*, and *The Seamstress of Acadie*. She is the proud mom of an American soldier and a career firefighter. Though Kentucky will always be home to her, she and her husband live in Washington State. Learn more at LauraFrantz.net.

"FRANTZ IS A WORDSMITH EXTRAORDINAIRE."

—*Library Journal*

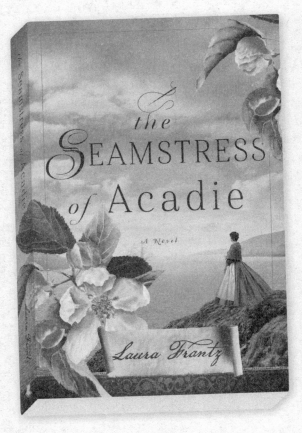

Caught between the warring French and English on Canada's rugged shores in 1755, Sylvie Galant is forced from her Acadian home and family and is alone in colonial Virginia. Now the enemy soldier who once tore her world apart might be the key to restoring her shattered past.

"A deeply atmospheric story of *faith, love, and sacrifice* that is as captivating as it is enthralling."

—Sarah E. Ladd, bestselling author of The Cornwall Novels

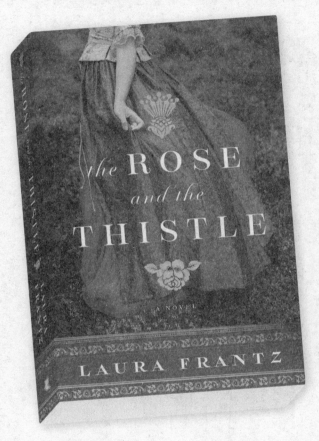

Amid the Jacobite uprising of 1715, an English heiress flees to the Scottish Lowlands to stay with allies of her powerful family. But while castle walls may protect her from the enemy outside, a whirlwind of intrigue, shifting allegiances, and temptations of the heart lie within.

Revell
a division of Baker Publishing Group
RevellBooks.com

"This tale of second chances and brave choices *swept me away.*"

—**Jocelyn Green,** Christy Award–winning author of *Shadows of the White City*

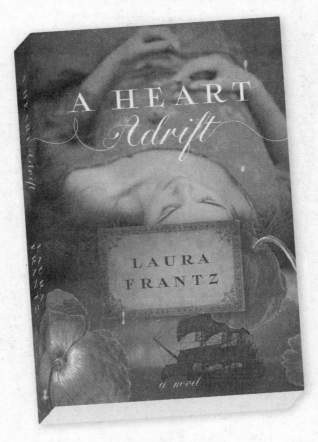

A colonial lady and a privateering sea captain
collide once more after a failed love affair a decade before.
Will a war and a cache of regrets keep them apart?
Or will a new shared vision reunite them?

MEET

LAURA FRANTZ

Visit LauraFrantz.net to learn more about
Laura and her books!

enter to win contests and learn about what
Laura is working on now

tweet with Laura

see what Laura is up to

see what inspired the characters and stories